"If you have ever delighted in Perry Mason's deviousness, you'll enjoy the exploits of Randolph and Quinncannon....Most readers will...simply luxuriate in the fascination of the story, the characters, the setting and the times."

Newsday

"A COMPULSIVE READ...
The crude brutality of the American scene, the euphoria of fanatical religion, the rough-and-ready management of justice—all are vividly realized."

The Village Voice

"A wonderfully entertaining twist to the traditional mystery."

Richmond Times Dispatch

"Lon Quinncannon is a terrifically charismatic and amusing character. Paul says the solution is based on historical evidence, but who cares? It's good reading no matter what you call it."

San Jose Mercury News

"A courtroom showdown worthy of Perry Mason ...An engaging enterprise and Paul handles the blend of fact and fancy with verve and a fine old melodramatic flourish."

San Diego Union

The Tragedy at Tiverton

Raymond Paul

An Historical Novel of Murder

BALLANTINE BOOKS • NEW YORK

Library of Congress Catalog Card Number: 83-47919
ISBN 0-345-32262-2
This edition published by arrangement with The Viking Press

Manufactured in the United States of America
First Ballantine Books Edition: July 1985

For, if once a man indulges himself in murder, very soon he comes to think little of robbing, and from robbing he comes next to drinking and Sabbath-breaking, and from that to incivility and procrastination. Once begin upon this downward path, you never know where you are to stop. Many a man dated his ruin from some murder or other that perhaps he thought little of at the time.
—THOMAS DE QUINCEY

The events portrayed in the pages which follow are drawn from and based on documented fact.
—THE AUTHOR

✿ CONTENTS

BOOK IV *The Final Witness*

If I should be missing enquire of the Rev Mr Avery of Bristol he will know where I am   Dec 20th

S M Cornell

Acknowledgments

Truth . . . loves to be centrally located.

HERMAN MELVILLE

It is rare for an author to find an editor who is both competent and symbiotic, and I am glad to announce that such creatures are neither mythical nor extinct. I have the good fortune to collaborate with two of them. For the unwavering support of Cork Smith and the exuberant shrewdness of Abby Luttinger, I am pleased that they are my partners and my friends.

Research for this enterprise took me to the far-flung reaches of Rhode Island, and I must acknowledge the generous assistance of the folks at Brown University Library, the Rhode Island Historical Society, and the Fall River Historical Society, as well as the New York Historical Society and the Newark Public Library.

Elizabeth S. Brown took infinite pains to explain the costumes of the period, complete, with beautifully detailed sketches. Patterson Smith, antiquarian of premeditated mayhem, graciously opened his matchless library to me.

And, Randy, old friend, once more I tip my calash to you. Dr. Gordon Randolph Kelly patiently guided his old college crony through the morass of medical evidence.

Troy Hills, New Jersey   RP

BOOK I

The
Amanuensis

1

The Skin Game

"*The prosecution offers, as Exhibit A, this advertisement* which appeared in the New York *Journal of Commerce* on January 17, 1832."

Robert Morris passed the newspaper to the court clerk, Mr. Bedell, who handed it up to the judge, and the stout, middle-aged gentleman whom Bedell had earlier announced as "The-Honorable-Abner-Aspinwall-Presiding," adjusted his bifocals, studied the exhibit, and nodded.

Morris began to read:

A bargain to immediate purchaser—a gentleman suddenly called away must sacrifice handsome roadster, 16 hands, warranted speedy, stylish and gentle; sound traveler; also elegant phaeton, sidebar, top buggy, harness, etc., in supurb order; sold separately; suit family, doctor or business. Deodat Peck, agent; Peck's Livery, 38 Bowery.

I was in court as Morris' clerk, stenographer, scrivener and general factotum to assist him in the prosecution of one of the city's more notorious "skin-stables" swindlers. The case should have been routine. The problem in convicting confidence men is that their victims, fearing public ridicule and ashamed of their own stupidity, are seldom willing to testify. Once the "mark" agrees to press charges, however, prosecution is generally a simple matter. It had been a long day—this was our last case of the afternoon—and normally my attention would have wandered, but on this occasion I remained alert, studying intently the figure seated at the defense table.

It was not the scruffy, wiry, slyly smirking little defendant who arrested me, but his attorney, a tall man with a long, sloping nose and a close-cropped, black moustache lining his upper lip, who relaxed in his chair, legs outstretched, elbows

3

propped on the chair's arms, chin resting on folded hands, eyes shut, looking for all the world as if he were sound asleep.

"Now, then, Dr. Willingboro—"

Morris approached our witness, a lanky, gangling man of about thirty, rather loosely constructed, with sharp eyes and a chicken-beak nose. He sat in the chair with his legs crossed at the knee and the dangling foot wrapped tightly around the opposite leg. I wondered absently if the position was as painful as the expression on his face suggested.

"You reside in Brooklyn and practice medicine in that city?"

"I do," said Dr. Willingboro.

"On January 17 of this year, did you read this notice in the *Journal of Commerce*, and, if so, what action, if any, did you then take?"

"I did, sir, and I came to this city by the ferry the next day to speak to Mr. Peck about buying the horse and carriage."

"Did you in fact arrange to purchase the roadster and phaeton?"

"Not the phaeton, no, sir. Mr. Peck informed me it had been sold before I arrived. But I did acquire the horse."

"Your honor—" Morris held up a small sheet of paper. "We offer in evidence People's Exhibit B, a bill of sale dated January 18, 1832, signed by Deodat Peck, transferring ownership of a horse named 'General' to Dr. Willingboro in return for the sum of thirty-five dollars."

I glanced up at the doctor. There wasn't a living thing in all of New York, on four legs or two, worth $35. Willingboro, I thought, was a dupe to bring tears to a swindler's eyes. To confirm that, I searched the pinched features of the aging accused. Old Deodat looked over at me through a few wisps of white hair and wiped away a tear.

"After your transaction was completed, Doctor," Morris went on, "what did you then do?"

"Well, sir, I intended to return to Brooklyn that afternoon by the ferry. I obtained a rope from Mr. Peck and led the horse away. We walked, as I recollect, about five blocks, until we had nearly reached the wharf, and then . . ."

The witness stopped in evident, red-faced confusion.

"And then . . . ?" Morris prompted. Abruptly he roared, "Tell the court *what happened then!*"

"Why," replied the doctor, "the horse dropped dead."

"The . . . horse . . . dropped . . . *dead!*" Morris echoed solemnly. Then he spun on his heel and growled, "Your witness, Mr. Quinncannon."

4

For a full minute the Irishman did not respond. In fact he did not alter his position or open his eyes during almost his entire cross-examination. I had begun to suspect he really was asleep when I heard him whisper, "Jimmy Perth?"

His client answered sheepishly, "Yessir," and the Irishman and I nodded simultaneously. Jimmy Perth was the usual confederate.

"Dr. Willingboro," Quinncannon said, in a tone that implied disinterest if not downright boredom, "did you purchase this horse for your own use?"

The physician shifted his eyes. "I . . . I don't quite understand, sir."

"Come, Doctor, the question is clear enough. Did you buy the animal for yourself or as an agent for someone else?"

"For myself, of course." He looked unhappy. "There was no one else about."

"Wasn't there, sir? Wasn't there a gentleman who came rushing into the stables soon after your arrival and attempted to bid for the horse against you?"

Willingboro hung fire. "Not," he replied at last, "to my recollection."

"I put it to you that there was, Doctor," said a soft brogue. "I put it to you that when this man appeared, Mr. Peck identified him as a horse-broker and refused to deal with him, insisting that his principal had authorized him to sell only to the prospective owner out of concern for the animal's welfare."

The witness uncrossed and recrossed his long legs. His other foot now writhed its way around the grounded leg and his expression became even more pained.

"Perhaps," Quinncannon suggested, "it would refresh your memory, Doctor, if I described this horse-broker for you. Might he have stood about five foot six, approximately 165 pounds, around fifty years of age, with a gray moustache overhanging his lip, exuding the gentle aroma of manure and gin?"

No answer.

"Do you now recall such a man, Doctor?"

Morris objected. "The witness has already answered that question, Your Honor."

The Irishman sighed. "Your Honor, the witness has said he cannot recall this man. I am merely attempting to aid his recollection."

Judge Aspinwall looked at Morris, grimaced and shrugged. "Objection overruled," he said with helpless regret. Every man

5

in the room knew perfectly well that Deodat Peck was as guilty as hell.

"I ask again," Quinncannon said, "do you now remember the broker?"

Willingboro resembled a cornered rat. "I have," he stammered, "a vague memory of a man like that. I forgot him because he was in the stables only a minute or two. Mr. Peck sent him away."

"And when was it that you next met with this broker, Doctor?"

The question clearly startled the witness. "I never saw him again, sir. I am not at all certain I saw him the first time."

Beside me Bob Morris was smiling and nodding vigorously.

Quinncannon appeared genuinely surprised. "Do you mean, Doctor, that he did not find occasion to draw you aside? That he did not say that he had a firm offer from another buyer for that horse which meant a great deal of money to him? That he did not ask you to buy the animal from Peck for thirty-five dollars and promise to meet you later that day and purchase the horse back from you at a profit of twenty dollars to yourself?"

It was an intriguing chess game. By his questions the Irishman had exposed every nasty nuance of his client's shabby swindle, yet in such a way that nothing could be proven against Peck. If Willingboro had entered into the arrangement described—as obviously he had—there was no hard evidence that Peck had been party to the deal, or even that the anonymous broker had intended to cheat the witness. Said broker might have done nothing more sinister than forget an appointment. Somehow, without consulting a note or moving a muscle or even opening his eyes, Quinncannon had swept the board. If Willingboro admitted to his agreement with the "broker," he convicted himself of stupidity and greed. If he denied it, he perjured himself. Either way he would completely discredit himself as a witness in the eyes of a judge who knew Peck's guilt for a certainty and was powerless to impose sentence.

My gaze shifted from one to another of the players. Aspinwall fingered his gavel and watched the witness. Willingboro folded his arms into a position quite as contorted as that of his legs and glared at the Irishman with ill-concealed fury. Morris strained forward, his whole body tense, his intertwined hands white-knuckled. Quinncannon remained motionless, yet, to my imagination, aces were tumbling out of his sleeves.

Then the witness committed perjury.

Morris relaxed, or rather collapsed, back in his chair. I heard him breathe, "Good boy, Doctor. Good boy."

For the first time Quinncannon moved. It was no more, however, than a thin smile and a slight elevation of one eyebrow.

"Do I understand, Dr. Willingboro, that it is your testimony that you did not enter into such an arrangement?"

"Objection!" Morris shouted. "Mr. Quinncannon is bullying the witness! The doctor has answered that question. If Mr. Quinncannon wishes to substantiate this fantastic accusation against a respected citizen, let him produce this phantom horse-broker on the stand!"

Morris was on his feet and crimson. I stared at him, astonished at his vehemence.

"The objection is sustained," said the judge, with obvious relief at being, at last, able to rule in favor of the prosecution.

Quinncannon's smile broadened. Finally he opened his eyes and fixed on the witness. "Very well, Doctor," he said. "No further questions."

"The People rest, Your Honor," Bob Morris said.

I expected the Irishman to move for acquittal immediately. When he did not, I wondered what he could do to top his performance on cross-examination. Then I found out.

"Defense waives opening statement," he said, "and calls to the stand one, uh, General I believe is the name."

Aspinwall gaped at him. "Are you referring, Mr. Quinncannon, to the *horse*?"

"To the horse, Your Honor."

"It is the understanding of the court, Mr. Quinncannon, that the horse in question is dead."

"In that event, Your Honor, defense will settle for the production of the carcass, or, alternatively, the report of the autopsy."

Morris yelped, "Oh, Your Honor, this is ridiculous! If Mr. Quinncannon questions that the beast is dead, we can produce a dozen witnesses."

"It is not the fact but the manner of death into which we are inquiring," the Irishman said. "It is on the record that the horse was purchased from Mr. Peck by Dr. Willingboro and led from the stable in a condition both sound and ambulatory. Surely, had the animal exhibited any sign of ill health or weakness, Dr. Willingboro would never have paid so exhorbitant a price as thirty-five dollars, and yet— And yet, Your Honor, within half an hour the beast falls dead! I suggest the defense has a right to question the cause of death, to inquire whether it be the result of mistreatment by Dr. Willingboro."

"Your Honor," Morris almost whimpered, "the horse was

7

sold immediately to the butcher. It was the only chance Dr. Willingboro had of regaining even a small part of his loss."

"Setting aside the question of the cause of death," Quinn-cannon continued, "the prosecution has alleged that Mr. Peck knowingly sold Dr. Willingboro a defective horse. I submit that this is unproven, given the absence of either the remains or an autopsy report."

"But, Your Honor," Morris wailed, "*nobody* does an autopsy on a *horse*!"

"The court surely appreciates the defense's predicament," the Irishman said. "We are presented with neither *corpus delicti* nor corpse—neither the body of the crime nor the body of the horse. Under the circumstances I have no choice but to move for dismissal of all charges."

Judge Aspinwall sat for a while contemplating the ceiling. Then he rapped his gavel once, sharply, and sighed with resignation, "Motion granted."

So that, I thought, while the judge wearily left the bench and Deodat Peck grinned broadly and Dr. Willingboro moodily stalked from the courtroom and Bob Morris muttered inarticulately into his handkerchief— So *that* is Lon Quinncannon.

2

The Enemy of Society

When I found Morris that evening at the Whistling Pig tavern he was working on his fourth Scotch and in a fouler mood than I had ever seen him. I brought a tankard of ale from the bar to his table and took a seat. Without raising his eyes he said, "The man is a venal leper, you know, Christy."

"I've never seen him work before, Bob," I said. "He *is* formidable."

"He is a pestilential scoundrel," Morris snarled into his glass. "He has the morals of a wharf rat and the ethics of a crocodile."

The truth was I had been rather impressed by Quinncannon's performance in court. That his client was so miserably disreputable and so clearly guilty only increased my admiration for the Irishman's wily yet dignified and even graceful defense. I had watched him with fascination, at times even imagining myself in his place, hearing, in my mind, my own voice biting off the clever question with a slight, sardonic smile.

Of course I knew better than to express any of this to Morris. In the end I restricted myself to suggesting he was overindulging in hyperbole and even there I went too far.

"Am I?" he growled. "Well, then, consider, my very young friend, that this afternoon Mr. Quinncannon applied his admittedly masterful talents to obtaining the acquittal of one of our slimier citizens, thus freeing the little reptile to continue practicing his insidious tricks on honest, decent members of the community."

He flung a wadded copy of the last edition of the *Evening Star* at me across the table. "Page four," he said, "last column."

I scanned the advertisements until I came to it: "A bargain to immediate purchaser—a gentleman called away must sacrifice handsome roadster, 16 hands. . . ."

"Don't bother to read it all," Morris said grimly. "It's the same advertisement, word for word. Peck must have placed it before the verdict." He leaned forward, massaging the bridge

9

of his nose between his thumb and middle finger. "Quinncannon knew Peck would go right back to the game, Christy. He *knew* Peck was guilty! And he *deliberately* connived to set him free!"

I watched him and it crossed my mind that, despite his assertion of ethical outrage, the real source of his anger lay in his sense of public humiliation by the Irishman. I ventured the notion that, in our enlightened nation, all men were entitled to the best possible defense.

His eyes narrowed. "The guilty man equally with the innocent?"

"It's not always so clear-cut, is it?"

"It was in Peck's case."

"I could," I said, "argue that Willingboro was as guilty as Peck. Each tried to cheat the other."

"Peck was more clever."

"Meaning, I suppose, that Willingboro remains inside the law only because he's too stupid to commit a successful crime."

"Damn it, Christy," he muttered. "Don't be any more obtuse than is absolutely necessary. As an attorney Quinncannon is an officer of the court, sworn to uphold the law. When he consciously aids a criminal to escape the law he breaks that oath— he becomes as much an enemy of society as the criminal he protects."

I reached for my pipe. "What would you have him do, Bob? Accept his client's money and trust, and then throw him to the wolves?"

"I would have him defend only innocent men."

"I would have us prosecute only guilty men," I replied aridly.

He dropped his eyes and I instantly regretted my sarcasm. "For God's sake, Bob, keep this case in perspective. It's not as though Deodat Peck was a rapist or a murderer."

Morris stared at me for a long moment. "Damnation, Christy, why *must* you insist on missing the point? Can't you see that the principle is the same regardless of the nature of the crime committed? Today Quinncannon defended a confidence man, successfully and without a twinge of conscience. Tomorrow, or next week, or next year, Quinncannon will defend a rapist or a murderer with equal success and equal moral irresponsibility."

He tossed off his whiskey and reached for his coat. "*And*, lad," he added darkly, "unless you outgrow your idolatry for the Irishman, when he frees that murderer you may well be standing beside him."

10

"Quinncannon?" Ogden Hoffman echoed. The district attorney regarded me across the table, stroking his beard and sucking on his pipe. Then his eyes wrinkled at the corners. "Ah! I see. The Peck case, a week ago. You assisted Bob Morris, if I remember." He threw back his great head and laughed heartily so that several other diners at Delmonico's turned in our direction.

It was Hoffman's practice to entertain each member of his staff, even the lowly law clerks, periodically at supper. "Good for morale," he liked to say, though the more suspicious of our number believed it was his way of monitoring intramural feuds and heading off bureaucratic espionage.

"I seem to recall the Peck trial," Hoffman said. "Our side accepted a Carthaginian peace, I believe." He became serious. "I'm afraid young Morris took the fall rather hard." He brightened again. "And you, lad? You find yourself intrigued by the Irishman?"

I nodded while the waiter cleared away the dishes. It had required most of the evening to work up the courage to raise the question.

Hoffman ordered two brandies and grinned at me. "Well, let me see if I can enlighten you on the subject of Mr. Lon Quinncannon. He is the most sinister character I know—a fox in fox's clothing—easily the most subtle legal mind in the profession. He moves with a singular grace between the highest levels of society and the dankest sewers of the underworld. Three of the most powerful men in this city have put prices on his head, and the name of at least one of them would astound you."

He paused while the waiter delivered our drinks, then leaned forward in a conspiratorial manner. "I'll tell you something else, lad, but if you ever repeat it I'll deny it. Quinncannon is the only attorney I've ever known that I'm afraid to face in court."

"Then what I've heard about him is true, sir," I said. "He *is* a dangerous, perhaps an evil man."

Hoffman's expression became quizzical. "Great God, Christy, what in hell did I say to give you that idea? Lon Quinncannon is one of my dearest friends."

3

South Street

I have heard the legends of the waterfronts at Marseilles, Shanghai and Stamboul, but no seaport on the globe can possibly rival South Street in New York City for picturesqueness or romance, or for debauchery and crime. It is the center of the nation's oceangoing trade and the busiest of her shipbuilders. From Coenties Slip to South Ferry are to be seen the steamships that make the runs to Boston, Baltimore, Norfolk and Washington City, and the great square-riggers bound for Europe, New Orleans, or round the Horn for California. Their prows, adorned with carvings of mythological and historical figures, point across the bustling street toward the rows of four-story, red-brick buildings wherein are found the offices and shops that provide every service and commodity required by the commerce. Merchants and money-changers nestle beside the purveyors of hardtack and jerked beef. Huge storage areas rise above tiny shops selling slickers, sou'westers, palms, marlinspikes, everything from a ball of yarn to an anchor chain.

South Street itself is thronged with a motley mob of humanity. No known tongue is unspoken there. Malay and Briton walk beside Portuguese and Scandinavian. The East Indian mixes with the Japanese—the Lascar with the Yankee. Some wear thick coarse red or gray flannel—some blue dungaree jumpers or yellow cotton. Their mixed drab pantaloons held up by braces or leather belts—on their heads woolen caps or stiff or soft felt hats.

They swagger, or stagger, swinging sunbaked, fantastically tattooed arms, through a crowd of grizzled, beefy longshoremen and itinerant hawkers pushing their wares on two-wheeled carts or spread out on oilcloths on the ground. Draymen maneuver their teams along the wharfs, dismount with an oath, and detach the sides of their carts to unload their cargo. Phaetons and hansoms clop and clatter on the cobblestones, preparing to dislodge finely dressed passengers with gladstones or heavy

12

trunks. On the wooden sidewalks, planks are laid over two or three barrels across which gin is peddled, with or without water.

The din is terrific.

From South Ferry north to the Dry Dock at Twelfth Street are the shipbuilding yards where lie magnificent packets and clippers in every stage of construction. Here are the great lumberyards, the block makers, ship-chandlery stores, the shops of workers in iron, brass, copper. The odors of fresh shavings and Carolina pitch drift south on a salty breeze and mingle with the smell of fresh fish being delivered to the Fulton Street markets.

Two blocks north of the seaport lies Water Street, and seldom do the tars wander beyond it. It is the most dangerous and degraded section of the city, a hellhole of bordellos and drug dens. Opium is cheap, gin cheaper still, and debauchery cheapest of all. Though the activity on South Street hardly diminishes after dark and is brightly illuminated by blazing torches, whale-oil flares and charcoal fires, Water Street is lit only by a succession of red lanterns that hang beside its brothel doors and screech eerily in gusts of wind off the East River.

Even by daylight Water Street is reminiscent of something out of Dante. Each house of call flies the ensign of the nautical nationality it seeks to attract—the tricolor, the Union Jack, and so on. The denizens of these resorts, a pitiful and hideous lot, squat on improvised settles built within the stoop line, and stare glassy-eyed at the passing parade of potential victims. Their practices extend from robbery to shanghaiing and even to burking, for seamen are sometimes smothered in the midst of their drug-induced dreams and their bodies sold to teaching hospitals for the purpose of dissection.

It has occurred to me that Water Street women, having been dragged as deep into the pit by men as is possible, avenge themselves in the most horrible ways they can conceive, and this within two blocks of the clipper ships that stand as a monument to man's technical skill, ingenuity and courage.

But I digress.

And I have since been forced to venture into worse hells than are dreamt of on Water Street.

On a bright, brisk morning in February, I hired a dray and went to South Street to meet the steamship *Pawtucket*, bound out of Providence and carrying my entire inheritance from my father: his law books, which I'd had shipped from Newport in antic-

13

ipation of soon passing the bar, and a splendid chestnut stallion that I had named "The Traveler."

It was a "sailing day." A California clipper was putting to sea for the savage voyage 'round Cape Horn. The scene was pomp and bustle—the Battery oarsmen loading the crew and dunnage aboard, two lots at a time, accompanied by a boarding-house runner—the seamen, as always, in varying stages of hilarious spiffiness. The more prudent mariners carried well-stocked sea chests. Others slung canvas bags over their shoulders and, here and there, a sailor could be seen with his outfit done up in a scarlet bandanna, the parting gift of a Cherry Street damsel. The most jovial of the tars were hauled over the side in bowlines and stowed, inert, in their bunks.

The mate was lucky to find a third of his men ambulatory, much less capable of pulling a rope or heaving on a capstan bar. Such of the crew as could be mustered on the forecastle were a motley gang, British, Portuguese, Italians, with a few "Down-Easters" scattered among them. They stood, more or less, in flannel and dungaree, for they could no more be induced to wear the uniform of a man-of-war's man than they could to eat food with a knife and fork. Their bronzed arms were evidence of the great profits to be made in the tattoo parlor.

A crisp breeze was blowing from the northeast. The blue waters of the bay danced and shimmered in the sunlight. On the quarterdeck the bearded captain consulted with the craggy-faced harbor pilot. It was nearly high water and the tide would soon run ebb.

There were no tow-boats to take her to sea. Soon she would drop down the East River and set her prow for Sandy Hook, the wind billowing her canvas, her departure loudly cheered by the fashionable crowds who had gathered at Castle Garden, her crew heaving away on the windlass breaks, her chantyman striking up in an intoxicated baritone:

> In eighteen hundred and twenty-six
> I found myself in a hell of a fix
> A-working on the railway, the railway, the railway
> Oh! poor Paddy works on the railway.

It was an incredible sight in an incredible era. There were vast fortunes to be made and uncountable opportunities to be pursued. Life spread before me like an endless, unfathomed sea, and, if there were Cape Horns to be weathered, there was a sun-warmed, pleasant port at the voyage's end. In a young

14

country I was a young man, twenty-two, lacking two months. What could I not accomplish?

I watched the clipper while the sound of the chanty died on the wind and, in my mind, I stood on her deck with the sea breeze whipping my hair and the pitch and roll of the ocean under my feet. When the great ship had vanished I nodded to the drayman and we trundled on, over the cobblestones of South Street toward the foot of Depeyster, to collect my inheritance from the Providence steamer.

I cannot remember ever feeling so exhilarated.

4

The Masked Ball

On the day I was examined by the New York Court of Appeals and admitted to practice, Bob Morris and I celebrated at the Whistling Pig. He raised his glass and proposed a toast. "To Christopher Randolph, Esquire—attorney-at-law! Gifted, though green. Clever, if callow. The best damn amanuensis I ever had!"

I grinned. "The only damn amanuensis you ever had."

He tossed off his gin-and-water and pounded his fist on the table. "Another round, landlord! God damn it! We've got something else to celebrate. Come, you grubby barkeep! You greasy publican! A little respect and a little service! It's not every day a man is offered a position in the district attorney's office within an hour of passing the bar."

I looked at him sharply.

He leaned across the table. "Hoffman told me a week ago, Christy. I knew before you did." He clutched my arm. "I'm so happy for you, lad. It's a great honor. Hoffman is a splendid patron—a man with powerful political connections. And of course it's a feather in my cap too."

"Bob," I said evenly, "I turned Hoffman down."

He released my arm. "Oh," he said coldly, leaning back in his chair. "I see."

We were silent while the waiter brought the drinks.

"I've moved into a small office on Reade Street and had my father's law books shipped down from Newport." I paused to light my pipe. "I'm going in for criminal law—defense work."

"I see," he repeated. He sucked at his gin and then stared at me. "Christy, how old are you?"

"Twenty-two, lacking one month."

"Do you realize you're probably the youngest man ever to be offered such an opportunity? Not Hoffman, not Daniel Webster, not Henry Clay, not even I—" He was deadly serious. "I

16

suppose this impulsive abandonment of self-interest is connected with your fascination with Lon Quinncannon."

"No, Bob, it's not." I really wanted to make him understand. "It's my father. He labored like a steer to send me to Dartmouth. His one dream was that I follow in his footsteps."

"If I remember what you told me, your father spent a lifetime in Newport defending wife-beaters and pickpockets and died prematurely of terminal poverty." He shook his head. "Damn it, Christy, do you know where this appointment could lead? You could become district attorney, mayor, congressman— there's no limit! Don't throw it away for some—some misguided sense of obligation to a man who's dead!"

"He's not a man who's dead, Bob," I answered softly. "He's my father. It's because he's dead that I can't let him down."

Morris watched me for a long moment. Then he threw up his hands. "Well, well, never mind. We're not going to spoil the evening with an argument. We're going to do something special in keeping with the occasion. The problem with this party is that there are too few guests. What we need, my boy, is—"

I returned his grin and we said in unison, "Women!"

"But not another night at Mother Gallagher's," I insisted.

"We shall not set foot on Duane Street tonight, Christy. Tonight—" He raised his tumbler and drained his drink. "Tonight there is a masked ball to be given at the theater, in your honor, I believe, or so I shall presume, and hither, or thither, we shall shortly wend, so soon as this scurvy landlord, this wretched, bar-sinister barkeeper condescends to provide some service to his custom. Yo! Tapster!" He thumped on the table, then winked at me.

"This evening, I understand, the ladies must come in character."

"And the gentlemen?"

"The gentlemen," he said, "must come in condition."

Attendance at a fancy masked ball, particularly one held at the Park Theater, requires considerable preparation and is not an affair to be entered into lightly. The ball began at eight p.m. but only an unpolished boor would arrive before eight-thirty and a true Gentleman of Fashion would never appear before nine. Bob Morris and I were both Gentlemen of Fashion, young men on the rise, and to rise in society a young man must dress the fashion and study his manners. Spend all you have on

17

fashion, my friend, though you must eat from a trough and sleep in a sty. At table do not rinse your mouth with your drinking water and then spit it back into the glass. Remember that soup must be eaten with a spoon, not lapped from the bowl, or, if you insist on lapping, always lift the bowl to your mouth, never lower your mouth to the bowl. Learn not to wipe your nose with your sleeve or clean your ears with a pen knife. Learn that the Lord created a carpet for one purpose and a spittoon for another. Back discreetly into a corner before pulling out the seat of your trousers, and there may yet be hope for you.

Near nine o'clock Morris and I strolled up Broadway looking as if we had just come from the hands of our barbers. We were freshly shaved, our side-whiskers neatly trimmed, our hair vigorously brushed into careless swirls as if recently windblown and swept down across our foreheads in a jaunty, devil-may-care manner. A cinnamon solution had removed the last traces, though not necessarily the last effects, of gin-and-waters. Every stitch we wore, save our boots and undergarments, was rented. Resplendent in our evening clothes and flowing capes, whistling casually, masks in place, we linked arms and sauntered down the center aisle, the perfect picture of two dapper, dashing tomcats on the prowl.

The interior of the theater was brilliantly illuminated and magnificently ornate. A great orchestra filled the hall with beautiful, lilting Austrian melodies. The three tiers of boxes that rose up at our backs were packed with spectators come to enjoy the dazzling, impromptu spectacle performed by their neighbors. But what gave the balls their charm and color, their intense, romantic excitement, was the women.

The women. I can close my eyes and see them—the deep blues, pastel greens, bright yellows of their costumes as they glided about the stage in the arms of their partners. Their waists were tiny when you put your arm around them—their bosoms full when they pressed against you—their little hands were moist when you held them. Some of them were the pampered daughters of aristocrats, some were shop girls, some were prostitutes, but on that wonderful night, as the flambeaux burned low and the hour of unmasking drew near and you flew across the floor to the magic rhythms of the waltz, every girl was a princess and every man, to his own mind at least, was a swashbuckling hero. We lived, for a few hours, in a dream.

There was not only romance but danger. Gamblers and confidence men mingled with the revellers. Married, respectable

18

gentlemen from Wall Street and Exchange Place danced openly with their mistresses, their features hidden behind ebony masks. Whores and pickpockets worked the crowds.

The balls were an innovation of Simpson, the Park Theater manager, to keep his building open during the unprofitable, late-winter season. They were well attended, especially by the young, but a general outcry was soon let loose in the press against them. The *Courier and Enquirer* said, "It will never answer to allow licentiousness to go abroad in public places with its face concealed." Application was made by the Common Council to the legislature for a law prohibiting masquerades, making them punishable by a fine of one thousand dollars, half of which went to the informer. Though the matter had not yet cleared committee in Albany, official feeling in New York was running high against the masked balls—higher, as it developed, than I realized.

By the time Morris and I reached the stage I had seen her. What struck me first was that, while all the other women had come as characters, she had not. In a small army of Du Barrys and Marie Antoinettes she stood alone and apart in a white linen ball gown beside a pudgy fellow at whom I barely glanced.

I said to Morris, "I'll see you later, Bob."

"How much later?"

"When I know I'll write."

I took the stairs to the stage three at a time.

The rules to this sort of game may be learned even at Dartmouth. Every action of the gentleman must be casual. He strolls casually, circles casually, tilts his head casually, smiles casually. The lady, of course, turns away abruptly and haughtily. It is the degree of abruptness and haughtiness that must be gauged. Does the lady, perhaps, glance back over her lovely shoulder? Does a brief smile, perhaps, flicker on her lips? The gentleman determines to hazard rejection.

I write for the edification of my younger, less experienced male readers. In the present age much is written to instruct young ladies in the means of protecting themselves from danger, but little to instruct young gentlemen in the means of creating the danger that young ladies must protect themselves from.

The gentleman, I reiterate, decides to risk rebuke. He then makes his approach, and here he may choose from three basic techniques. The insecure neophyte shuffles forward and shyly comments on the weather or, worse yet, offers to get the lady a glass of punch or an ice. This is called "the lap-dog maneuver."

Although some ladies are partial to stammering and blushing, this device is normally rewarded with disdain and is not recommended.

In the second, or "sly-dog maneuver," the gentleman sidles up and inquires, "Did we not meet at Mrs. Wilson's cotillion last spring?"

Now, it matters not a farthing whether there was such a cotillion, or even if there is a Mrs. Wilson. The significant thing is the lady's response, which, if affirmative, assures the gentleman of an evening's entertainment. The entertainment, however, seldom outlives the evening, and this strategy is generally employed only by voluptuaries or men who have been long at sea.

By contrast, a young man on the rise in society, with brilliant prospects, filled with confidence and self-reliance, prefers the direct, or "gay-dog maneuver."

I stepped boldly up to the lady in white. "You are even more lovely than the melody of the dance," I said. "May I have the honor of sharing it with you?"

She and I both looked at her pudgy escort.

"You don't mind," I said, "do you, old fellow?"

He responded, "Uh—" Unquestionably the lap-dog type.

In a moment she was in my arms and we were sweeping across the stage to the strains of the waltz.

"You dance beautifully, dear lady," I said, "as though your feet never touch the floor."

"Indeed, sir," she replied, "I don't believe they have. You quite take my breath away."

God knows I was trying.

She was small and delicately formed with rich brown hair that fell in long curls to her shoulders. Her face was round, her skin fair, her nose tiny and slightly upturned, and her brown eyes sparkled behind a white silk mask. The dimples in her cheeks deepened when she smiled.

Let other young men boast of their sweethearts' lineaments, ruby lips, full busts. I am a man who falls in love with a smile.

"May I ask your name?" I said.

She seemed startled. "I thought, sir, on occasions like this anonymity was respected."

"I see you have not before attended the balls," I said. "It is the custom, at the masquerades, to exchange Christian names. Mine is Christopher."

I whirled her about, sensing the dance about to end, deliberately leading her away from the youth who had brought her, and, when the music stopped, I drew her to a table of refreshments. When she tasted the punch I'd handed her, her nose wrinkled.

"Oh! What's in it?"

"Only fruit juices," I answered, "and perhaps a little gin."

"Really?" She took another sip. "I've never had gin before." She tried it again. "It *does* taste funny. A bit like medicine, but not really. I've often fancied what spirits tasted like. It stings my tongue."

I raised my own cup and watched her.

"Oh, my!" she exclaimed. "This *is* an adventure! I've never had gin before. I've never been to a ball before. I've never danced with a man before, except Roger, and *that* was always the cotillion or the allemande." Her voice became a whisper. "At school we were taught that the waltz is—" She hissed the word: "—*sinful*!" She finished her punch. "What would Grandmother say? Grandmother thinks the *minuet* is sinful. What would Cousin *Charlotte* say?"

She laughed brightly.

I gave her another cup.

She laughed again. "Do you know, I've never even *known* anyone who drank spirits, except, of course, Miss Heath at school. At least everyone thought she did. And Uncle Charles, but no one in the family ever talks about him." She smiled. "Not even Roger ever drank gin. His father would kill him!"

Suddenly she looked around. "Oh, dear! Poor Roger. We've quite abandoned him. I forced him to bring me here. It really isn't fair."

"Don't worry about Roger," I said quickly. "I saw him dancing with someone else."

It was a lie, but it produced the desired effect.

"*Was* he?" she said coldly.

The workings of the female mind never fail to confound me.

She took another sip of punch.

"Would you care to know something about me?" I asked as nonchalantly as I could.

Immediately her face lit up. "Oh, yes, you must tell me all about yourself. What do you do? To earn your living, I mean."

"I'm an attorney. I've been involved in some important criminal cases. Do you remember the trial of Pederson for the murder of Rice?"

"I don't think so. Was it in the Boston papers?"

"It may have been."

21

My principle was never to lie to a lady when it could be avoided. I had been amanuensis to Bob Morris when he was one of two assistants to Frank Greer who was junior to Ogden Hoffman in the prosecution of Pederson.

She looked at me with admiration. "Did you get him convicted?"

"He did not escape the gallows," I said solemnly.

When I brought her third punch she said quietly, "Amelia."

"What?"

"My Christian name. You said it was the custom at the balls to tell. It's Amelia, but I hate it. Everyone calls me Amy."

"Most people call me Christy," I said.

"That's a lovely name." She took another sip. "It sounds almost biblical. You're very tall, you know. Much taller than Roger. Roger's very short. He inherited it from his father who is *extremely* short. I have a theory." She giggled. "I think Roger planned to be taller than his father, but his father found out and ordered him to stop growing."

I guessed her age at about seventeen. I had already deduced that she attended a female academy in Boston. She was pretty, unspoiled, completely natural and unsophisticated. I couldn't believe my luck.

There was an oyster cellar on Broadway that was open all night and served champagne. It was only a block from the Clinton Hotel.

I asked her if she liked oysters.

Before she could answer I felt a hand on my shoulder.

Bob Morris said, "Christy, I've got to talk to you."

"Now?" I growled.

"Immediately!" His tone was urgent. "Tommy Boyle is here. He just warned me Old Hays is going to raid the ball tonight. Orders of the Common Council."

Old Hays was Jacob Hays, the city's chief constable, and Tommy Boyle was a roundsman assigned to the district attorney's office.

"Boyle's instructed to start a fight as a pretext," Morris continued. "There are police crawling all over this building, inside and out."

He hadn't finished the sentence before I heard loud, angry shouting from the opposite end of the stage. A scuffle broke out. Men bellowed and women screamed. The orchestra stopped playing. Chairs were overturned in the pit. A cymbal crashed against the floor. The doors from the lobby flew open and mobs of police and the watch swarmed down the aisles.

Morris grabbed my arm. "Come on! Out the stage door!"

My only thought was for the girl.

The screams had spread to the balconies. The revellers scattered or huddled together. The musicians fled, some abandoning their instruments. Near us a burly man lurched against the refreshment table and it collapsed. Glass bowls and cups shattered. A woman, dressed as Catherine the Great, toppled into the pit. The police had almost reached the stage.

"Damn it, Christy!" Morris thundered. "Do you know what an arrest will do to our prospects?"

I seized Amy's wrist. "We've got to get out of here!"

"But Roger . . ."

"To hell with Roger!"

I dragged her behind me, following Morris toward the rear exit. In the alley behind the theater we were confronted by two of the watch.

"Here now," one of them began.

Morris bowled his man over as he ran. I released Amy long enough to clip my man on the jaw. He was over fifty and he went down easily. When I turned she was staring at me.

"That was *marvelous*!" she exclaimed.

"Oh, for God's sake, *run*, girl!"

We sped after Morris, through alleys and fence gates, until, at last, we stood breathlessly on Chappel Street. While he hailed a hansom I stood beside her, heaving for breath, still clasping her dainty hand in mine. "Are you all right?" I asked at last.

"Miss Heath was right." She looked up at me. "That's my schoolmistress—the one who drinks? She said New York was an exciting city."

She made no effort to extricate her hand from mine. I tightened my fingers. A cool breeze blew east from the North River. It was surprisingly warm for the last week in February, offering the tantalizing but always unkept promise of an early spring. Morris was having trouble engaging a cab.

She said, "I do, you know."

"Do what?"

"Like oysters."

"Oh." I smiled. "No oysters tonight. I'll see you home."

"No you won't, Christy." She returned my smile. All the earlier school-girl silliness had vanished. I found myself not exactly fascinated, but curious.

"I've made a wager with myself," I said, "that tonight was not your first taste of gin."

Her eyes widened. "I really can't settle your wager. Miss

23

Heath does tutor me in French in her rooms after classes, and she has offered me a libation from time to time, but she's never told me the recipe." She paused. "Of course, there are rumors."

"Amy," I blurted, "won't you let me take you home? Or, at least, may I know your full name?"

"That, sir, is not the custom of the masked balls." The gas light of the street lamp flickered on her face. She was even more attractive and bewitching than I had first thought.

"Why," she asked, "should you wish to know my name?"

"Because I promised to buy you oysters."

She laughed. "In Boston, when a lady allows a gentleman to buy her oysters, her reputation is ruined unless they immediately marry."

Morris had stopped a hansom. Amy pulled me toward the curb. I assisted her up to the cab. "I will find you, you know," I said.

"Think you so, Christy?"

"I do," I responded. "I'm not only handsome and gallant. I'm also ingenious and resourceful."

The hackman cracked his whip. I watched her cab disappear north on Chappel Street. Behind me Bob Morris said, "Is the boy attorney in love?"

"Hardly," I scoffed.

"Infatuated?"

"Challenged," I said firmly. "I think it's a game, Bob. Something they play in Boston. I'm just learning the rules."

"Uh-huh." He studied me for a minute. "I hear there's some talent recently arrived from Paris at Mother Gallagher's."

For the first time in two hours I removed my mask. "No matter where we start out," I said, "we always end up at Mother Gallagher's."

"It's *déjà vu*." He grinned. "See? I'm already practicing my French."

In the cab on the way to Duane Street I said, "Bob, how many boys do you suppose were swept up and booked in that raid tonight who are short and pudgy, and escorted girls named Amy, and answer to the name of Roger?"

"As a rough estimate? One."

"Funny. I hit on the same number."

I thumped on the cab's roof and we stopped at the corner of Chambers Street.

"Where are you going?" Morris demanded.

"To the bridewell. I have my first client there, though little

Roger doesn't know it yet. Lend me twenty dollars for bail money, will you?"

Morris handed me the banknote and shrugged. "I was right the first time. The boy attorney is in love."

"You're wrong, Bob," I insisted. "The lady merely . . . interests me."

I found Roger that evening, whimpering in a detention cell, and through him, in time, I traced the lady in white. But the tale of what, for lack of a better term, I shall call our courtship, must be suspended while I recount a most remarkable event— one with which the reader is doubtless familiar but of which the true history has never been revealed to the public.

5

The Magnificent Hoax

The following evening, after a late drink in the Whistling Pig, Morris and I strolled back to Reade Street. My living quarters were in the back room of my office and he accepted my offer of a nightcap. Near midnight he rose to leave, pleading fatigue, and I accompanied him to the street door. When he opened it he stopped short.

There, on the threshold, in full evening dress, with a pipe in one hand and a walking stick in the other, stood Lon Quinncannon.

"Good evening, gentlemen," he said in his soft Irish brogue. "I'm gratified to learn you keep the same ridiculous hours I do."

I watched Morris' shoulders stiffen. He stood in the doorway, face to face with Quinncannon.

"Kindly stand aside, sir. I never make way for a scoundrel."

"On the other hand," replied the Irishman, smiling easily and stepping back, "I always do."

Morris stalked out and Quinncannon closed the door behind him, put his pipe in his teeth and extended his hand. "Your servant, Mr. Randolph," he said cordially.

"And yours, Mr. Quinncannon."

The Clinton Hall clock tolled midnight. I wondered what the devil had brought him to my chambers at that ungodly hour.

"I wish to discuss, Mr. Randolph, a matter of business."

"It is a strange time for it, sir," I said.

"Oh," he answered, "I often find it convenient to conduct business after dark." He settled into the chair beside my desk, withdrawing his wallet. "I trust a retainer of two hundred dollars would be satisfactory. The fee will eventually total five hundred dollars."

I was stunned. He glanced up and read the question in my face. "I assure you," he smiled, "it's all perfectly legal."

I groped for my chair and the bottle of Scotch. "May I offer you a drink, sir?"

26

"If you will join me, my friend."

I poured out two Scotches and reached for the pitcher, and the Irishman held up his hand. "Never water the whiskey, lad," he said. "Whiskey is not a rhododendron."

I gulped at my drink and studied him while he sipped his. I had already noted his features, the sharp brown eyes, sloping nose, dark, close-cropped moustache, firm chin. One eyebrow appeared to be perpetually raised, giving his face an expression of constant skepticism. His smile, though pleasant enough, was wryly twisted. He rested his elbows on the chair arms, holding the glass between his palms, and I noticed particularly his hands. The fingers were long and deft, suggestive of a professional gambler, yet his hands, like his face, were tanned and they bore the unmistakable callouses of a practiced horseman.

I was struck with the way the man moved. Every motion was smooth, effortless, relaxed. I suspected he never spoke or acted without calculation. Genial as his manner was, I still sensed a sinister air about him, perhaps a residue of the dark tales I had heard of him from Morris and others. It only served to make him more interesting to me. Altogether, I concluded, he was a man worth knowing.

"Forgive my curiosity, sir," I said, "but what brought you to me?"

Again Quinncannon smiled. "You come," he answered, "highly recommended." He took from his pocket two greenbacks and placed them on the desk. To my amazement they were new, thousand-dollar notes.

"Are you acquainted with the intersection of Spring Street and the Bowery?" he asked, and I nodded.

"With this money," he went on, "you are to rent every tavern, restaurant and oyster cellar in that area. Cover Spring, Rivington, Delancy, Broome and Prince—from Mulberry to Eldridge. Inform the landlords that you will underwrite all their expenses for one day only, May 21, in return for sixty percent of their profits. Then contact every cart-pusher and vendor of chestnuts you can find and offer them the same arrangement. When that's done send to me for further instructions."

He observed that I was puzzled. "Is that unclear, lad?"

"Not the orders, sir, but the purpose."

"Well, now," he said, "I'm something of a gambler, Mr. Randolph, and I have a strange premonition that business in food and drink will be rather brisk in that part of town on the 21st of May."

He gave me a wry smile and stood. "My sainted grandfather

27

used to say," he added, "that if you cast a whole loaf of bread upon the waters one little crust will come floating back."

He paused briefly at the door. "Contact me only by messenger. No offense, lad, but just at present I have no wish to be seen in your company."

Quinncannon touched the brim of his hat and vanished—a gust of wind from my door as he closed it extinguishing the candle and leaving me, literally and figuratively, in the dark.

But within a week a light began to dawn.

On May 6 the *Evening Post* carried this remarkable paragraph:

ASTOUNDING NEWS!
MANHATTAN ISLAND SINKING!

We have learned that, due to the excessive weight of the numerous buildings recently constructed in this city, especially the massive, bulging warehouses on Broad and Merchant Streets, the southern end of Manhattan Island is sinking into the bay. This alarming discovery was confirmed by a study undertaken by the engineering firm of Hoskins and Ventnor which was commissioned by Mr. Charles Lozier, formerly of the First National Bank, and Mr. John DeVoe, formerly of the Merchants' Bank. The danger was communicated today to the mayor and the Common Council. THERE IS NO NEED FOR ALARM AT THIS TIME. Mayor Bowne has urged all citizens to *remain calm. The danger is not imminent.* The mayor wishes us to state his confidence that *a solution to this perilous situation will be found!*

The following evening the *Post* reported new developments:

GOOD NEWS!
DISASTER AVERTED!
NEW YORK SAVED FROM THE SEA!

Mayor Bowne announced today that a means has been found to prevent lower Manhattan from sinking into the bay. The plan was developed by the firm of Hoskins and Ventnor and approved by the Common Council meeting with Mr. Lon Quinncannon, attorney for Charles Lozier and John DeVoe, in extraordinary session last night. The island is to be sawed off at its northern tip, at Kingsbridge, and floated down the North River past Ellis Island into the bay by means of two dozen longboats using tow ropes. In the bay, it will be turned around and towed back upriver and the Battery safely moored facing the north. This action is drastic but the current danger demands drastic measures. Mr. Quinncannon has declared that the tremendous costs of this venture are to be borne entirely by the private fortunes of Charles Lozier and John DeVoe, the gentlemen who first uncovered this near-tragedy, and to whom the citizenry owes a great debt of gratitude.

The news set the town on its collective ears. It was the talk of every salon, taproom and gentlemen's club. Some of the other newspapers scoffed and called it a hoax, but the early skepticism, what there was of it, quickly disappeared, and this for three reasons.

First, the stories were always reported initially in the *Evening Post*, and every respectable, literate soul in New York knew that, if Mr. William Cullen Bryant printed it, it *must* be true. Like all genuinely dull journals, the *Post* had an untarnished reputation for veracity.

Second, clearly Mayor William Bowne and the Common Council were convinced. With a re-election campaign looming, Bowne was strutting and preening, the savior of the city.

The third reason was the most compelling. Lavish amounts of money *were* being spent. The *Post* announced that dozens of saws had been purchased, each one hundred feet long with teeth three feet deep, to sever the island at Kingsbridge. Three hundred laborers were hired for the work. Thousands of yards of heavy tow-rope were brought up from South Street and deposited in the basement of City Hall. A small armada of longboats was obtained, each of a length of 250 feet, with two thousand oarsmen engaged to row them.

On May 18 the *Post* declared that the date had been fixed on which this grand enterprise would be launched. The entire city thrilled with excitement. But when I read the article I felt a cold shudder. The workmen, 2,300 strong, were to assemble in one place and, after a prayer of thanksgiving by the Reverend Dr. Spring, brief speeches from Lozier and DeVoe, and an oration from the mayor, they were to march north to Kingsbridge, there to commence the good work. The public was invited.

The place of assembly was the intersection of Spring Street and the Bowery. The date was May 21.

I smelled a rat—a rat with a brogue.

Every rotten thing Bob Morris had said about Quinncannon raced through my mind. I had accepted the Irishman's retainer—I had already spent it! I had completed all the arrangements he'd requested. It was far too late to back out. Damnation! I had trusted the man when he told me that what we were doing was legal—trusted him only for the inane reason that I liked him!

And the entire affair was a swindle—some sort of incredible, gigantic *swindle*! He had used me as a front, a shill, a setter. A stooge, I thought bitterly. Somehow a confidence game of historic proportions was in progress and, though I did not understand it, I was immersed in it up to my eyebrows.

At first I was furious at Quinncannon's duplicity—then at my own stupidity—and finally, when I had calmed down, my anger turned to stark terror. I visualized my career exploding before it had fairly begun. I had to talk to someone. Morris was out of the question. I recalled the Irishman saying I came "highly recommended." That could mean only one man. I scrawled a brief note and hired a messenger to deliver it to Ogden Hoffman.

The district attorney found me at six o'clock at a table in the darkest corner of the Whistling Pig, clutching a gin-and-water. I dispensed with the amenities.

"Sir, I believe I'm in trouble! How deep I don't know. I don't know the exact circumstances involved, but I'm in desperate need of information and advice. Please, sir, tell me what you know of the men named Hoskins, Ventnor, Lozier and DeVoe."

Hoffman kept his eyes on mine while he savored his Scotch. "So, Christy, you've gotten yourself involved in *that* scheme." He began to fill his pipe. "Well, lad, I'll tell you what I can. All four have two things in common. They're all mixed up in this nonsense about saving the city from the sea, and each of them has, at one time or another, been a client of Lon Quinncannon."

I drew in a deep breath. "I feared as much, sir."

"As to Hoskins and Ventnor," he said, "I first knew them under different names. Mr. Hoskins went by the moniker of 'English Charlie' Mason. His specialty was the gold-brick swindle. And Mr. Ventnor, let me see . . . He called himself 'Hungry Joe' Lewis. A man of talent and ambition, Christy.

30

He started as a lowly pickpocket and rose to the top of his profession by perfecting the horse-car game—an ingenious variation in which the satchels are switched *before* the dupe enters the car."

He finished his drink and ordered another. "A *most* original technique," he said with genuine admiration. "I prosecuted him twice and once won a conviction. Of course, at the second trial, Quinncannon defended." He looked up. "Either of them could sketch the floor plan of the Bellevue prison from memory."

My terrors were rapidly being confirmed. "And Lozier and DeVoe, sir. Are they also criminals?"

Hoffman laughed heartily. "My God, Christy, they're worse than the first two!"

He must have seen the dismay in my face because he became suddenly serious. "Lozier and DeVoe never operated outside the law, son. They're both retired from business now, both millionaires, both unhappy, friendless old men waiting to die. Each was a grasping usurer whose fortune was sucked from the veins of the poor. They've hated each other for fifty years—sued and counter-sued each other many times, the last occasion about seven months ago. Quinncannon represented one of them—I can't remember which. Do you know what the New Jail currently houses?"

I nodded. "Primarily debtors, sir."

"Well, Christy, more then half of those unfortunate souls are incarcerated through the courtesy of Lozier and DeVoe."

Hoffman stroked his beard and shook his shaggy head. "There's something I don't understand," he said thoughtfully. "Those old skinflints have been mortal enemies since they were boys. Either would steal the pennies off his dead mother's eyes. Yet here they are, apparently collaborating on this ridiculous hoax and throwing greenbacks around like confetti." He leaned forward and spoke in a hoarse whisper. "Do you know, Christy, two nights ago I sat with them and Quinncannon at the Irishman's table in the American Hotel taproom, and the old misers were laughing and joking together like fraternity brothers at a college reunion." He frowned. "I wonder what in hell Quinncannon is up to."

"Then," I said, "Quinncannon *is* behind this fraud?"

"Certainly, lad. Quinncannon is the mastermind. All the rest are puppets." He glanced at me quickly. "Sorry, son. I didn't mean that the way it sounded."

I felt my lips tighten into a terse smile. "No harm done,

sir. I'm aware that, in this Punch and Judy show, I play the role of Punch."

Hoffman puffed on his pipe. "Allow me to reassure you, Christy. I admit I can't fathom what the Irishman's motives are. I probably know him better than anyone and seldom can I anticipate the subtle intricacies of his thought process. But I can tell you this. Quinncannon is a decent man. Not a *good* man, mind you, but a decent man. If he has a failing it is that he will never deal directly with an injustice when he can slip up behind it and knife it in the back. He has an obsessive need to solve every problem with a Machiavellian strategy, and that, as I have often told him, can only be attributed to a serious flaw in his character."

He regarded me intently across the table on which the melted candle stump now barely flickered. "There's one other thing," he said. "I don't know how you're tied in to Quinncannon's scheme and I have no desire to know, but I can promise you that the Irishman would do nothing to enmesh you in an illegal act or to jeopardize you personally or professionally."

The district attorney finished his Scotch. "Quinncannon," he concluded, "would never do anything deliberately to harm you, Christy. And Quinncannon never does anything unless deliberately."

I left the tavern trying to feel reassured, though it was not easy. When I reached my office I found a letter shoved under my door:

Mr. Randolph:
  My premonition appears to have come true. On May 21 please attend the festivities scheduled for Spring and the Bowery. The following day kindly visit the establishments with which we have done business and collect the profits. I suggest requiring a strict accounting. Deposit all monies in the Merchants' Bank on Exchange Place. Further instructions will follow.

                                                                    Q

Enclosed with this note were three more hundred-dollar bills. I pocketed them and silently prayed that, in his evaluation of the Irishman, Ogden Hoffman was right.

* * *

For those who did not witness it, it may be impossible to imagine the incredible spectacle that occurred on the morning of May 21. Every carriage, gig, wagon and hack had been engaged by citizens come to cheer on the workers' army as it marched forth to rescue the city from a watery grave. The cream of New York society was there—along with more than a little of the dregs. The throng stretched north and south on the Bowery and west on Spring as far as the eye could see. It spilled over into the side streets, jammed the wooden sidewalks, lounged against the buildings, sat astride prancing horses, maneuvered and craned for a better view. The boys hung from gas-lamp posts and awning poles or sat on the edges of horse troughs, with their bare legs dangling in the water. The young studs and dandies slouched beside the stoops and barrels, leering and whistling at the prostitutes. The gentlemen and ladies relaxed in their carriages, many peering through opera glasses and already partaking of liquors and victuals from hampers generously supplied by the chefs and tapsters whom we were underwriting. There were thousands and thousands.

I arrived on horseback shortly after nine. A gigantic wooden platform had been erected in the center of the intersection facing Spring on which were seated the mayor, the aldermen, the justices, virtually every official of the corporation. Wedged before them in a place of honor stood the 2,300 oarsmen and laborers who were to accomplish the miracle, sleeves rolled up, tools in hand. A holiday had been declared. A glorious celebration was in progress.

I was struck with a terrifying thought. What would happen when this huge crowd discovered they had been diddled? When they realized the entire affair was merely an elaborate practical joke?

And discover it they must! For there was no way Quinncannon could cover it up much longer. The jovial crowd would become an ugly mob. A riot would surely break out when the workmen learned they were not to be paid. I shut my eyes and visualized the Irishman dangling from the end of a rope with a second man hanging next to him. With a shudder I realized the second man was me.

Then a voice said cheerfully, "It's a beautiful morning, Squire Randolph."

Quinncannon sat a splendid gray stallion beside me and scanned the sea of faces with casual satisfaction. "We have a fine turnout. When I host a party I never restrict the guest list."

33

I spoke my first thought. "They're going to lynch you, you know."

He laughed. "Ah, lad, if I thought so I doubt seriously I'd have come."

"Where," I asked "are Lozier and DeVoe?"

"At the moment? On a packet headed, I believe, for Savannah."

"So should we be," I said. "When these men find there's no work and no pay, things are going to get nasty. This is dangerous business."

He watched me. "Why don't you go home, lad? No one knows you're involved in this."

I found I had no need to think. "Oh, no! I'm staying with you. I took a hand and I'll play the cards I was dealt." I paused. "I don't suppose you brought a pistol."

"Never carry them."

"Well, I did. We'll take a few of them down at least."

Surprisingly my fear was gone. I felt only excitement.

Quinncannon put his hand on my shoulder and smiled. "You're a stout lad, Christy Randolph," he said. "There's no man I'd rather have with me in a fight."

He urged his horse through the gang of workmen toward the platform crammed with dignitaries and I followed him.

As the mob closed behind us I wondered just what in hell he was going to do.

6

Mr. Randolph Receives Instructions

The next day I *made my collections from the landlords* and vendors. It came to a huge sum and I didn't relax until I had deposited it in the Merchants' Bank. In the hansom, trotting out of Exchange Place north on Broadway toward Reade, I drew my first easy breath in five days, took the *Post* from my pocket, and again read the article:

ASTONISHING NEWS!
CITY SAVED BY UNEXPECTED MEANS!

Yesterday morning a great crowd of six thousand people gathered at Spring and the Bowery to attend the ceremonies marking the beginning of the grand project to prevent the southern tip of Manhattan from subsiding into the upper bay. The crowd was festive but the mood subdued as it was thought that the island must be towed into the bay and its position reversed to avert the calamity. A thunderous cheer was raised when Mayor Bowne announced that other means had been found to save the city. Mr. Lon Quinncannon, barrister, representing Messrs. Lozier and DeVoe, explained that the engineers, Hoskins and Ventnor, have determined that, by means of a huge pump of revolutionary design being constructed at Perth Amboy, it is possible to suck the bay waters through Kill Van Kull and Arthur Kill to the Raritan Bay. Thus the water level in the upper bay may be safely lowered as the city sinks and the need to detach Manhattan from its moorings is avoided. This speech was interrupted by hurrahs from the assemblage, the loudest of all when it was announced that the workmen hired for the original project would be paid their full salary. We are left to wonder at the marvels wrought by modern science.

35

I also was left to wonder at marvels, but not those of science.

When the cab halted I dismounted and removed my wallet before I realized we were not at my chambers but still on Broadway, at the American Hotel.

"This was not my destination."

"Beggin' your pardon, sir," replied the hackman, "this is where I was ordered to bring you."

"By whom?"

"By the Irish gentleman, sir. You can put away your purse, sir. The fare's been arranged for." He touched his whip to his hat brim.

An aproned waiter greeted me at the entrance to the hotel taproom. "Mr. Randolph?"

I confessed.

"I was told to look out for you, sir. Mr. Quinncannon is waiting at his table."

I trailed him to a round maple table near the bay window where the Irishman relaxed in a captain's chair, puffing on his pipe with a glass in his hand.

"Sit down, Christy," he said cordially. To the waiter he said, "Ralph, this is my friend, Squire Randolph. Give him anything he asks for except money or your daughter."

Ralph grinned and shuffled off with my order for Scotch.

"Have you the deposit receipt?" Quinncannon asked.

"Yes, sir," I said, handing it to him.

"Bury the 'sir,' lad. I believe we can address each other by our Christian names. We've been cronies, confederates, co-conspirators and"—he smiled—"as of yesterday morning, comrades in arms."

"I'm afraid I behaved rather foolishly," I said, feeling my face color. "I should have realized you had the situation in control."

His mouth tightened at the corners. "Listen, lad, never apologize for courage. You were convinced that my life was in danger and that your own was forfeited if you stood by me. I gave you a chance to turn up the white feather and instead you followed me into that mob and put your back to mine. Don't ever forget that, Christy, because I don't intend to."

He tossed off his drink and examined the bank slip. "Well, well," he said, "we did turn a decent profit, didn't we?"

"I still find it hard to believe."

He raised one eyebrow. "That we turned a profit?"

"That anyone credited the story at all!"

"We did tell a veritable whopper, didn't we?"

36

I grinned at him. "*Two* veritable whoppers! I never realized how credulous people can be."

"Oh," he replied, "when you've faced a few juries it will seem less surprising. Feed them a monstrous lie and they'll give you a testimonial."

"But how will people react when the truth comes out?"

"If it ever does they'll laugh at themselves and, when DeVoe and Lozier try to sneak back into town, they'll give them a parade. People love to be fooled if it affords them entertainment and isn't cruel or harmful. All we've really done is provide the rich with amusement and the poor with employment."

He picked up his pipe and relit it. "You need to know what action you must take tomorrow. You're aware, I'm sure, that the old New Jail behind the City Hall now almost exclusively houses debtors?"

"Yes."

Quinncannon leaned back and spoke through a cloud of tobacco smoke. "A ridiculous law, Christy. When a man can't pay his debts he is put in prison until he does, thus guaranteeing that he never will. The creditors go unsatisfied. The debtor languishes behind bars at public expense. His family, left shamed and destitute, either burdens their relations or must be supported, again at the public's expense, and all in the name of justice!"

The bitterness in his tone surprised me.

"Draw a draft on the funds you deposited," he continued. "Then go to the jail and settle the debts of every poor bastard incarcerated there. I want that hellhole cleaned out like the Augean stables!"

"I doubt that will exhaust the sum," I said.

"There is an orphanage on Vandam Street run by a decent couple named Kelly who take in Irish street boys convicted of petty crimes. Give the balance to them as a donation in the names of Lozier and DeVoe."

"Am I not to mention you at all?"

"Under no circumstances." He straightened up in his chair.

The man was an enigma. I stared at him, my mind racing through the conflicting reports I had heard of him. Countless criminals breathed free air because of his legal skills. I had myself observed his talent as a manipulator. Others swindled individuals—Quinncannon had swindled an entire city. Yet he was ready to give away the hugh profits of his confidence game to charity for reasons of principle. Was there any noble action to which he could not rise? Was there any duplicity to which he would not stoop?

Something Hoffman had told me came back. "Quinncannon has a law of his own."

Some minutes after Quinncannon left the table, the waiter delivered another drink. I tasted it. "Ralph, this isn't Scotch."

"No, sir, that's Irish, Mr. Quinncannon's brand."

"Mr. Quinncannon's left the hotel."

The waiter grinned. "No, sir, he's just gone upstairs. There's a lady waiting for him—that lady from the theater. He sent this over with his compliments. He thought it would do you good to swallow some *real* whiskey."

I said, "You like Mr. Quinncannon, don't you, Ralph?"

"Yes, sir, he kept my brother out of prison twice on forgery charges."

"Your brother was innocent?"

"No, sir!" he replied. "He was guilty as sin!"

The Quail Hunt

I must briefly return to events on the night of the Masked Ball as yet untold. When I left Morris in the hansom I headed for the Police Office on Centre Street. I had no difficulty tracking the boy named Roger, the escort of the lady named Amy whose escape from the raid on the Park Theater I had effected. He was a quivering, pasty-faced youth of about eighteen, a Harvard sophomore, whose abject terror of his father far exceeded his fear of the police. In return for a promise of bail and an assurance that all charges would be dropped without his parent's knowledge, he provided me with a complete profile of the lady.

Her full name was Amy Wrenn. She was seventeen and about to graduate, as I had surmised, from a female academy in Boston. Her parents had recently died and the girl had returned from Europe to complete her education. She was supported by a wealthy grandmother who owned a mansion on upper Broadway, and whom she was then visiting on school holiday. Her legal guardian, however, was her mother's cousin, a woman from my home city of Newport, Rhode Island—a spinster in her late twenties named Charlotte Prescott.

The coincidence of the connection startled me, for I knew Charlotte well and, I had long suspected, my late father had known her even better. When he died it was Charlotte who arranged the funeral even before word of his passing reached me at Dartmouth. She hired the undertaker, dictated the service, and restricted the guest list to exclude his more disreputable friends, which severely limited the number of mourners.

My father once said to me, "It's a man's world, Christy. We make all the important decisions, such as who will be President and how the grocer's bill is to be satisfied. We must leave to the women such minor matters as birth, marriage and death."

* * *

"The problem," I said to Bob Morris, "is to arrange a casual, apparently accidental meeting with the girl. Fortunately, her cousin Charlotte is in the city to supervise her activities."

"Why is that fortunate? I should think a chaperone would be the last thing you'd need, particularly from what you've told me about Miss Charlotte Prescott."

I touched a locofoco to my pipe. "I know Charlotte. She is something of a bluestocking, and a fiery disciple of the Mary Wollstonecraft Godwin stripe. She passionately believes that the pressures of society have forced women to be merely the playthings of men. She reads *Vindication of the Rights of Women* as if it were Scripture."

"I fail," he said, "to see your point."

I smiled. "Do you know who is delivering a lecture this evening at the Masonic Hall? Fanny Wright."

"The radical feminist?" Morris' eyes narrowed. "Ah, I understand. You think Miss Prescott will take the girl to the lecture."

I grinned at him.

"Assuming you do manage to meet them 'by chance'—how do you propose to dispose of the chaperone?"

"There are," I responded, "two wonderful qualities in Charlotte. First, she likes me—better yet, she *approves* of me. Second, getting around her will not be complicated. She is like Cerberus—easily tamed by throwing her a piece of raw meat."

Now his eyes became slits. I watched him with amusement. "Let me guess," he said finally, "whom you have in mind to be the raw meat."

There was a long, long silence.

Then he slowly shook his head. "Christy, I have loaned you money when it was my last dollar. I have diverted your landladies while you scrambled out of back windows with your gladstone. I have held your head in alleys behind saloons. But this—*this* I will not do!"

Thus it was that, on that evening, I journeyed to the Masonic Hall alone.

Though the furor over Fanny Wright has largely subsided since her recent return to Paris, the older reader will recall that in 1832 she was easily the most notorious woman in America and one of the most controversial characters of either sex. She was the darling of the feminists, the abolitionists, the champions and fomenters of "working class revolution" against what was called "capitalist oppression." Her inspirations were William Godwin, Thomas Paine and, especially, Mary Wollstonecraft. Her mentors were Jeremy Bentham and the Marquis de Lafayette. Every dissident, reformer and utopian flocked to her cause. To every liberal intellectual and radical lunatic she was the reincarnation of Joan of Arc.

To the conservative establishment she was anathema, a veritable Antichrist in skirts. The Whig press pilloried her as the "Priestess of Beelzebub" and "The Great Red Harlot of Infidelity." The clergy hated her. She advocated abolition of slavery, an end to capital punishment, and a national system of free state boarding schools, financed by a graduated property tax. Children were to be separated from their parents from ages two to sixteen and taught both traditional subjects and industrial skills in an atmosphere free of the influence of the "odious experiment in human credulity," as she termed organized religion. There was not a pulpit in the country from which she had not been castigated.

Nor, in the view of many, were these the most dangerous of her heresies. As a defender of "the rights of women" she promoted equal educational opportunities, legal rights for married women, liberal divorce laws, birth control, legalized abortion and free love. Her ultimate solution to the "cancer" of slavery was not limited to abolition but extended to racial miscegenation—then called amalgamation—the "gradual blending of white and black until their children become one in blood, in hue."

Her very name, mentioned in a group of any size, could not fail to provoke an argument, if not a fist fight.

What amazed me then, and has confounded me ever since, was that not only her most ardent admirers but her most heated detractors were invariably members of her own sex. She attracted, as such women always do, the support of many men—some from a sense of justice, some from guilt, some from a conviction of their own sexual inferiority—many, I suppose, from a complication of all three motives. But, generally, men remained indifferent to, at least, her feminist doctrines.

Not so the ladies. Among them Fanny Wright's ideas, especially those dealing with divorce, birth control, abortion and free love, unfailingly inspired either fanatical devotion or militant resistance.

* * *

41

I entered the crowded Masonic Hall shortly after the lecture began and, there being not one empty seat, I took a place along the rear wall among the numerous standees.

Fanny Wright made an impressive appearance on the platform. She was a tall, stately woman in her thirties, garbed in simple white muslin that hung to the floor in folds. Her features were either noble or masculine, depending on your prejudice, but they were certainly striking. Her blue eyes alternately flashed and became sadly solemn, depending on her topic, as her voice sometimes rose sharply only to modulate in a throaty, almost melancholy tone. She had a massive forehead beneath curly chestnut hair, worn short. She employed no podium, nor any prop save a leather-bound copy of the Declaration of Independence that she flourished but never consulted. The effect at which she evidently aimed was that of a Grecian statue, or perhaps a martyred saint.

"The existing marriage laws," Fanny Wright was saying, "may have a legal force but they have no moral force. No woman can forfeit her individual rights or independent existence, and no man assert over her any rights or power whatsoever beyond what he may assert over her free and voluntary affection.

"Nor, on the other hand, may any woman assert claims to the society or peculiar protection of any individual of the other sex, beyond what mutual inclination dictates and sanctions— while to every individual member of either sex is secured the protection and friendly aid of all."

I listened with but half an ear, searching the assembly for a glimpse of Amy or of Charlotte Prescott. The backs of scores of unidentifiable bonnets greeted my gaze. The only woman in the room with an uncovered head was Fanny Wright.

The lecturer warmed to one of her favorite subjects: the evil influence of the current wave of religious revivals on the female gender.

"The victims of this odious experiment on human credulity and nervous weakness are invariably women," she cried. "Helpless age is made a public spectacle! Youth is driven to raving insanity! Mothers and daughters are carried lifeless from the presence of the ghostly expounders of damnation! All ranks share the contagion, while the despair of Calvin's hell itself seems to have fallen upon every heart and discord to have taken possession of every mind."

I had sighted the lady. It was nothing more than a pert tilting of her head—I could not see her face—yet I was certain it was Amy. I sensed my heart begin to pound and held my hand over it as though that would slow its pace. I felt a strange excitement. It was damned annoying. A Gentleman of Fashion stirs excitement in his lady. He does not himself feel excitement. It is not—well, damn it, it's not *fashionable*!

The woman seated on Amy's right was Charlotte Prescott. Her face was also hidden, but the back of her neck betrayed her. It was long and thin and pale, and had always reminded me of a goose's neck. The truth was, in general appearance Charlotte resembled nothing so much as a goose. She was taller than average with narrow shoulders and small breasts, but her contours rather broadened from the waist down. Years of expensive dancing lessons had cured her of gangling but she still moved with what I can only describe as an awkward grace. Her small head, made even smaller by the tightness with which she bound her hair behind it, perched uncertainly on her long neck. Her nose protruded above thin, bloodless lips and a receding chin. Remarkably, her eyes were beautiful—deep and large and warmly brown—a doe's eyes. It was as if her Maker had had a last-minute pang of conscience.

Charlotte was a woman of decided opinions, most of which precisely coincided with those of Fanny Wright, and she believed in expressing them openly, not to say stridently. Her manner was often both fussy and officious—she enjoyed arranging things such as flowers and other people's lives. For all that, I had always liked her. She was basically kindhearted and well-meaning and, when she put her mind to it, she could even be tender.

The lecture was winding down. Miss Wright closed with a violent denunciation of slavery, poverty, ignorance, male supremacy, the Congregationalists, the Presbyterians, the Methodists, and several other things which just now escape my memory—and concluded with a call to arms of "all right-minded persons regardless of sex" to "carve out the cancers and extinguish the flames which threaten to destroy this great republic!"

To judge from the thunderous applause it must have been a masterful oration. I had barely heard it. My attention was riveted on Miss Amy. It was part of my strategy not to approach the ladies but to allow Charlotte to notice me. Accordingly I stationed myself near the exit. It worked like the proverbial charm.

"Christy!"

Charlotte waded through the crowd toward me, pulling Amy

43

with her. "How happily met! How pleasant to find a familiar face from home in such a great city!"

Even her voice, despite the costly singing lessons, retained a suggestion of a goose's honk.

"You must meet my cousin. Mr. Christopher Randolph, this is Miss Amelia Wrenn."

I accepted her hand and bowed. "Your servant, Miss Amelia Wrenn." I smiled. "Amelia," I repeated, remembering how she loathed the name. "May I remark, that is a lovely name. It sounds almost biblical."

I was enjoying her reaction. She regarded me with surprise and not a little suspicion, though perhaps with a hint of pleasure. She curtsyed prettily.

"I once knew," I said, "a lady named Amelia. She was quite beautiful, a wonderful dancer, and very fond, as I recall, of oysters."

Miss Wrenn looked at me sharply. "How interesting, Mr. Randolph. Whatever, I wonder, became of her?"

"Ah, Miss Wrenn, I have no notion. She vanished from my life in a hansom cab. She had, I fear, a bit of a taste for gin."

"How sad. I do have a preference for stories with happy endings."

"As do I, Miss Wrenn," I responded. "As do I."

Abruptly, as the crowds jostled past us, I realized I was still holding her hand.

"Come, come," said Charlotte, taking charge. "We must find our carriage. It is dreadfully late. Christy, you must come and dine with us next week and shock us all with terrible tales of life in the wicked metropolis."

"Nonsense," I replied. "It's barely nine o'clock. Why not allow me to show you life in the wicked metropolis? I insist you have supper with me at Delmonico's."

"No, no," Charlotte said with authority. "It is already time Amelia should be abed."

I recognized the determination in her tone. Miss Amy made no effort to challenge her guardian's will, but I noted with delight her obvious disappointment.

Then, as we emerged from the hall, Charlotte halted and tugged my sleeve. "My word!" she whispered. "What an interesting looking gentleman!"

She was staring at a tall, caped figure who stood at the base of the stairs, a man with a thin moustache. "Such a sensitive face," she continued. "I'm sure he must be a poet."

44

"Hardly," I answered. "He's an attorney, specializing in criminal law. His name is Quinncannon."

"Lon Quinncannon?"

"You've heard of him?"

"Oh, my dear," she said, "*everyone* has heard of him. Do you know him?"

"We've worked together," I said, with studied nonchalance.

"Come, Christy," she said, "you simply *must* introduce us."

All at once I had the feeling we'd be having supper at Delmonico's after all.

8

Supper at Delmonico's

Quinncannon ordered for all four of us—asparagus, cold pheasant and champagne—but Charlotte held up her hand.

"Amelia and I do not consume spiritous drink, thank you, sir. We will have lemonade."

One Irish eyebrow lifted slightly. "Cancel the champagne, Frank," he said. "Lemonade for the ladies and bring me an Irish."

The others looked at me expectantly. It was crucial to my plan to remain in Charlotte's good graces. Reluctantly I said, "I will also have a lemonade."

Quinncannon relaxed in his chair and addressed the waiter. "Frank, as we are awash with lemonade I'm reminded of a story. Did I ever tell you about the Irishman on the wagon who went into the pub and ordered lemonade?"

Frank grinned in anticipation. "No, sir," he said.

"Well, the barkeep gaped at him in astonishment." The brogue was getting thicker with every word. "'Are ye certain, Paddy,' says he, 'that ye don't want a wee splash of gin in it?' 'Be gorra,' says Paddy, 'and I'd be after havin' no objection, so long as it was unbeknownst to me.'"

The waiter threw back his head and laughed.

When the drinks arrived my lemonade was half gin. I caught Quinncannon's eye and smiled gratefully.

". . . divorced," Charlotte was saying. "That is the only reason, Mr. Quinncannon, that Hannah Kinney ever stood accused of murder. She *divorced* her first husband." She shook her head. "If a woman is capable of divorce, she is thought capable of murder. The intolerable *prejudice* of this male-dominated society!"

He smiled. "It was my impression when I defended her, Miss Prescott, that the majority of her detractors and accusers were women."

"*Bourgeois* women, sir!" Charlotte responded. "Not that I condemn them for their narrowness. They are the victims of their upbringing and environment. It is not their fault that their conversation is confined to the latest new publication, new bonnet and *pas seul*. They are not trained to be thinking, reasoning beings—indeed, they are taught quite the opposite. Women, Mr. Quinncannon, will not assume their rightful, equal place in society until they are encouraged to spend more time in being educated and far less time in church. That is why, when Amelia's parents died and she became my ward, I sent her to Mrs. Rowson's school in Boston. As you can see, she has turned out a most proper, independent young woman, quite capable of conversing on many subjects."

It irritated me that Charlotte spoke of Amy before her as if she were not present.

"As I *am* competent to discuss many subjects," Amy interjected, "let us talk about something other than me." She turned to Quinncannon. "Please tell me about Hannah Kinney, sir. All Cousin Charlotte ever says is that she was innocent."

The Irishman sipped his whiskey. "She was born Hannah Hanson, something over thirty years ago, in Lisbon, Maine, the only child of a publican. She first married a man named Ward Witham, by whom she had a daughter. After failing as a farmer and a tanner, Witham abandoned her and the child, and went to Boston where he—I'll phrase this as delicately as possible, Miss Wrenn. He allowed several ladies to believe he was unmarried."

Amy's eyes were sparkling with interest. I watched her, fascinated. "I understand," she said. "And Hannah learned the truth?"

"That she did," he replied. "She followed him to Boston and there obtained a decree of divorce on the charge of adultery. She then set up as a seamstress and married her cousin, Edward Freeman, a Baptist minister, whom she had known, and perhaps loved, since they were children. Because she was a divorced woman, she was not accepted by the ladies of her husband's congregation. When Freeman died and Hannah almost immediately married George Kinney, a man who had courted her before her second marriage, she was virtually driven from the church."

"Was there much gossip?" Amy asked.

"Not as much as after Kinney's death. You see, Miss Wrenn, Kinney died of a mysterious stomach ailment. The doctors discovered evidence of a lethal dose of arsenic. Witnesses testified that the last food he consumed was a bowl of tea prepared by his wife. Then it was recalled that Kinney's symptoms were similar to those exhibited by Freeman just before he expired. That is when Hannah was arrested."

Amy clapped her hands. "How intriguing!" she exclaimed. Then she caught Charlotte's disapproving glare. "I mean," she said, "it *is* awfully sad, but—" She suddenly brightened. "Wasn't it *exciting*? And *you* saved her from the gallows!"

She was again the schoolgirl, thrilled to be up past bedtime and out with the grownups. She was aware of the agony of Hannah Kinney but it didn't really touch her. I recognize now that it then hardly touched me. We were both, though the word would then have offended me, merely children, and like children, we were callous—not unfeeling, but lacking the experience of pain that teaches both tolerance and empathy.

It would come soon enough.

But, that evening in Delmonico's, I remember only her radiant smile and my emotions when she slipped her tiny hand into mine under the table.

I flushed scarlet. Quinncannon noticed—Quinncannon noticed everything. But Charlotte forged ahead, oblivious to all but her own thoughts.

"You *do* believe Mrs. Kinney was innocent, Mr. Quinncannon."

"In my profession, Miss Prescott, I deal with facts, theories and arguments. Opinions are a luxury I cannot afford."

Charlotte looked up. "Do you know, sir, the single most important cause of divorce?"

He smiled. "I should guess it to be marriage."

"Precisely!" she cried. "Marriage enslaves a woman. If she is poor she becomes a drudge—if she is rich, she becomes merely a decorative appendage. The relationship between a woman and a man should be free of social controls, and they should remain together only so long as they are bound by love and not a moment longer."

"I see, Miss Prescott, you are a follower of Mary Wollstonecraft."

"You have read the *Vindication of the Rights of Women*?" she asked with surprise.

"I am familiar with the work," Quinncannon replied, stretching his legs under the table. "As I recall, during the Reign of Terror in Paris, Wollstonecraft formed what she termed a 'free-love liaison' with an American adventurer named Gilbert Imlay and bore him an unlicensed child. When he offered to do—I believe the phrase is 'the decent thing'—she rejected his proposal on the same grounds you have just cited. Some months

48

later, in London, Imlay found a new mistress and abandoned Wollstonecraft, telling her he no longer loved her and quoting to her, at length no doubt, from her own book." The brogue was again growing thick. "The lady was so distracted that she attempted suicide by leaping from the Putney Bridge into the Thames. Fortunately her voluminous skirts kept her afloat and she bobbed about like a distraught cork until fished out by a passing boatman."

"But," Charlotte persisted, "consider the noble experiment that flourished at Nashoba."

Nashoba, a utopian commune thirteen miles east of Chickasaw Bluffs, Tennessee, had been founded by Fanny Wright in 1825, and dedicated to the cause of gradual emancipation by assisting slaves to buy their freedom through their own surplus labor.

"All that ever flourished at Nashoba," Quinncannon said, "were free-love, stupidity and malaria."

"May I assume," she asked curtly, "that you have an objection to free-love?"

He reached for his glass. "I have never experienced it, dear lady. It is sufficient to my purposes that it not be exorbitant."

Charlotte frowned. "Is it then your opinion, sir, that efforts to abolish the enslavement of other human beings are . . . 'stupidity'?"

"It is my opinion, Miss Prescott, that purchasing a dozen Negroes, handing them hoes, and depositing them in a primeval swamp with a million mosquitoes and a sex-crazed overseer is likely to prove counterproductive to the noble cause."

"You will at least concede that Fanny Wright is a woman of great charisma, ability and vision?"

"As readily," he responded, "as I will acknowledge that she is a demagogue and a hypocrite."

Now Charlotte stiffened and reddened. She controlled her temper only with great effort. "Excuse me, sir," she said through clenched teeth. "I must request that you explain your remark."

Quinncannon poured himself another whiskey. "Miss Wright established the commune at Nashoba and then abandoned it. It was principally the lack of her guiding hand that caused the project's collapse and the dismal suffering of its inmates. Miss Wright decries marriage, advocates free-love, yet, when her own sister became pregnant, she demanded, and got, a shotgun wedding. Miss Wright argues that women should be totally independent of men and claims that condition for herself. But I seem to recall that her abject fawning over the aging Marquis

49

de Lafayette and their unorthodox living arrangements at La Grange created a scandal even in Paris. When the Marquis made his last triumphal tour of America, she proposed to accompany him as his adopted daughter, which naturally he refused, given the inevitable overtones of incest. Nevertheless, she fled after him on the next packet out of Le Havre and pantingly tracked him like a bloodhound from Boston to New Orleans."

The Irishman paused and raised an eyebrow. "Shall I go on, madam?"

Charlotte merely sat and simmered.

The supper at last arrived and while it was being served, Quinncannon gently shifted the conversation into a more pleasant channel.

"Tell me, Miss Wrenn, have you been to the races in Harlem? Mr. Randolph is quite an accomplished horseman. My spies inform me he never loses . . ."

When I'd seen the ladies to their carriage I returned for a final drink with Quinncannon. Over my Scotch I grinned at him. "You've made quite an impression on Charlotte," I said. "She's convinced you are a misogynist and a male-supremacist."

"Well . . ." A smile slowly creased his face. "Not a misogynist."

🎔 9

Madame Killer

When Morris and I emerged from City Hall, the Clinton Hall clock had just struck six times. The warm May evening had attracted a number of New Yorkers to the park. Children rolled hoops or tossed balls under the watchful eyes of doting parents. Young couples sauntered, arms linked, along the gravel paths beside the beds of budding flowers, or stood admiring the fountain. Older folks lounged on the benches, talking or reading the newspapers. A watchman was posted to keep strollers off the new lawns and chase away stray dogs.

The din and jumble of commercial traffic were gone from the streets. Hansom cabs trotted quietly down Broadway and up Park Row. As Morris and I walked toward Broadway a huge carriage, drawn by four black horses, stopped at the curb. The footman leaped down, opened the door with a bow, and assisted to the sidewalk, with some difficulty, the most elephantine, grotesque woman I had ever seen.

She was richly dressed in maroon velvet trimmed with lace. Three strands of pearls encircled her fat throat and two more large pearls dangled from thick earlobes. She carried a small parasol that appeared ludicrous in contrast to her massive bulk. Opened, its spread could not have exceeded that of her flowered bonnet. Her bovine face was scarred with the evidence of a bout with smallpox. Her lips were rouged and heavy, and hung slack above several chins.

"Good God," I exclaimed to Morris. "Who or what is that?"

"That," he said, "is 'Madame Killer.'"

"The abortionist?"

He nodded grimly.

I had heard of her, of course, but this was my first glimpse of the monster. Mrs. Ann Lohman, alias Madame Restell, known to the newspapers as "Madame Killer," operated her home for unwed mothers in a mansion on Greenwich Street. She called it a "lying-in hospital." The press called it "The House Built on Baby Skulls."

51

Restell had been heard to suggest that the best way to relieve the problem of surplus population was to arrange that "all the children of the working people after the third be disposed of by painless extinction." This charming lady had practiced her peculiar form of birth control on the mistresses of many of the city's most prominent figures, and it was widely whispered, and doubtless true, that she owed her amazing immunity to the law to the protection afforded her by her highly placed and grateful clients.

Periodically the press would launch an outraged but fruitless campaign against her. A torrid editorial had recently appeared in the *Evening Star*, accompanied by a woodcut of a grim-faced Restell attended by a winged griffin gnawing on the corpse of a naked infant:

> Females are daily, nay, hourly, missing from our midst who never return. Where do they go? What becomes of them? Does funeral bell ever peal a note for their passage? Does funeral train ever leave her door? Do friends ever gather round the melancholy grave? No! An obscure hole in the earth; a consignment to the savage skill of the dissecting knife, or a splash in the cold wave, with the scream of the night blast for a requiem, is the only death service bestowed upon Madame Killer's victims!

Abortion, some said, was the least of Restell's crimes. She ran a black market in babies. There were rumors of burking and other forms of murder. I studied her gargoyle features, hideous yet unpleasantly sensual—the little red-rimmed rat's eyes, the bulbous nose, the powdered jowls, one carrying a penciled beauty mark in an absurd show of vanity—and I concluded there was no evil of which Madame Killer was not capable.

🌀 10 —————————————————————————

The Shoplifter

Having business for Quinncannon in Boston, I took the steamer *Pawtucket* the next day and, while she lay over in Providence to discharge some passengers and take on others for Boston, I left the ship and strolled toward Westminster Street with the intent of purchasing gifts for Amy, Charlotte and the dowager grandmother.

I crossed the channel at the Weybossett Bridge. A chill northeast wind whipped across the cove from the direction of the bleak state prison to the whitecapped waters of Providence Harbor, agitating the barges and fishing boats, and even driving the great steamers to groan against their moorings. I stood briefly in the middle of the bridge, listening to the shrill cries of the gulls mix with those of the hawkers from the Fish Market and the earthy, guttural oaths of the stevedores unloading cargo for the huge, weather-beaten warehouses.

The sky was overcast, slate-gray—promising nasty weather. With a shiver I wrapped my cloak more tightly around me and hurried toward Westminster, walking in the direction of Carpenter's Dry Goods shop and, as I turned to enter, a girl emerged suddenly and we collided.

She was short of stature, full-bosomed—under the circumstances I could hardly forbear to notice—rather plump but not unpleasantly so. She appeared to be in her mid- to late twenties and was dressed in a threadbare cloak fastened by clips over a somewhat dowdy dress of homespun. She wore a plain bonnet fastened under her chin by a black ribbon, and I judged her to be one of the girls who labored in the local factories.

She abruptly backed away from me and looked up. To my taste she was not pretty, though conceivably some farm boy or smith's apprentice had once thought her so. Her cheeks were too full, almost, but not quite, jowls. Her nose was small but perhaps the nostrils flared a bit too much. There was something about her face, asymmetrical, incongruous, a contradiction of her mouth and eyes. The latter, large, deep blue, peered up at me beneath brows mutually arched in pathos, begging for aid and understanding, filling with tears. But her lips, hardened into a terse, half-smirking grin, seemed about to snap open in uncontrollable laughter. Then she did begin to laugh, or rather she burst into a hysterical, self-mocking giggle that continued—though the piteous expression in her eyes never changed—until she felt a man's rough hand seize her shoulder.

The hand belonged to Charlie Hodges, who clerked for Carpenter in the shop. He handled her roughly, spinning her around and attempting to grab for her purse to which, however, she clung with a death grip.

"Here, now, missy, let's see if you've got a receipt to justify them lace goods you just appropriated!"

He pulled her back into the store and I followed while she tearfully protested her innocence, not to Hodges but to me.

"I didn't steal nothing, sir! I never took what didn't belong to me! I'm a respectable girl, sir, from a decent, God-fearing family!" She broke away from Hodges and whirled toward me. "Please, sir," she whimpered, "you look like a gentleman. Please don't let this lout of a counter-jumper maul at me. How do I know he didn't stuff some bits of lace into my purse unbeknownst to me just to get me in trouble?"

This theory of the case struck me as unlikely. Hodges scowled and moved to block the door. Two or three matronly customers ceased browsing through the thread and thimbles and stared in shocked confusion. John Carpenter, the elderly proprietor, left his cash drawer and approached us. The girl yanked a piece of paper from her purse and waved it at me, her pleading eyes fixed on mine, her voice growing more and more piercing.

"This will prove my good character, sir," she cried, thrusting the paper toward me though it remained just beyond my reach. "This is a certificate of my membership in the Methodist Society *in good standing*, signed by a minister up in Massachusetts, Mr. Avery!"

She glared around in a frenzy of anger and terror like a hunted wild thing and, catching sight of Carpenter, she spun again, shoving the paper back into her purse and backing up against me. I could feel her whole body shaking. Behind me Hodges said, "She stole some lace, John—tried to leave without paying."

"Did you follow her out of the shop!"

Apparently Hodges nodded, for Carpenter said, "All right, Charlie, attend to the custom."

I watched the old man's watery eyes while he focused them

on the girl's. He said nothing but gradually her head drooped forward and her shoulders began to heave with inaudible sobs. "I can't say what impulse come over me," she said softly. "I couldn't seem to control it. I saw the goods and— I *am* a respectable girl, mister. My sister—my poor widowed mother— they'd disown me if 'twas known about."

He reached out to take her purse but she only clutched it the more tightly. "My child," he said, "you have committed a—"

"*No!*" she screamed. She continued to face him, backing away, forcing me to retreat behind her, now again addressing me. "Don't let me be arrested, sir! The Methodists would drive me out, away from my salvation." She turned a ghastly face to me. "Don't you understand? I'll lose my *soul!*"

There was something piteous, desperate about her. I scarcely believed that her immortal fate hung on the outcome of her foolish little crime but I could not, at that moment, doubt the sincerity of her contrition or of her fear. "I hardly think, sir," I said to Carpenter, "that summoning the constable will afford you much satisfaction from the court."

The merchant eyed me. "Are you an attorney, young man?"

"I am, sir," I said, and then added, "recently admitted to practice."

"Well," he responded, "permit me to augment your education. Had this girl been apprehended in my shop she might have evaded charges by paying for the merchandise, but once out on the street, and lacking a receipt, she is clearly guilty of theft." He gave me a patronizing smile. "I have been in business somewhat longer than you have been on this planet, young sir, and I assure you I shall have my satisfaction of the courts."

"But not your money, sir," I countered. "Suppose I were to tell you that, planning to gift a lady with some lace, I sent this woman ahead to make the selection, and seeing me pass your window, in her excitement to show me her choice, she ran out of your door to meet me?"

Mr. Carpenter frowned. "Supposing you were to tell me that ridiculous fable, I would probably reply that you were a damn fool who owed me a shilling."

He bit down on the coin I gave him.

"Then we are free to go, proprietor?" I asked.

"As far as I'm concerned, youngster, you're free to go to the devil," he answered.

* * *

I followed the girl out of the shop and stood behind her on the sidewalk, feeling, I suppose, rather good about myself as her deliverer. Though I had saved her from legal prosecution, it now occurred to me that she *was* clearly guilty and that, in extricating her, I might have actually encouraged her in future criminal behavior. Then, too, there was the matter of the lace, which I had, in effect, purchased, and for which I had spent twice as much as anticipated. I carefully formulated a brief, pithy, moral lecture in my mind and, moved by tender concern, I reached forward and touched her arm. Before I could speak she wheeled on me in a perfect fury.

"Look out, young man, watch where you put your hands! Don't you think for a minute you can take advantage of a respectable girl!"

I gaped into her sizzling eyes, totally dumbfounded. Pedestrians froze and glared at me. Carriages slowed, then stopped, the Rhode Island gentry rolling up their curtains and peering out. My whole, well-intentioned speech dissolved into two stammered words: "My . . . lace . . ."

"You boys from the college are all the same—brutes! Animals!" Her shrill shouts were beginning to draw a crowd. "What makes you think you can paw decent girls on the public street and seduce them into God-knows-what sort of carnal depravity?"

A policeman was elbowing his way toward us. "All right, miss, is this young man bothering you?"

She stiffened regally. "I have no need of the protection of the law, constable," she proclaimed grandly. "A girl's chaste virtue is always proof against the lecherous advances of lusty youths! I am, constable, I will have you know, a girl who's been raised up proper, *and* a member in good standing of the Methodist Society!"

She spun on her heel and marched away up Westminster Street, leaving me to stare at her retreating back in utter stupefaction.

I was to set eyes on her again only three times. The last occasion was when I found her hanging by a rope from a fence-pole in the stack yard of a Rhode Island farmer, strangled to death.

🏵 11 ─────────────

Bristol

I passed that night, not in Boston as planned—where I should have supped on lobster and scrod at the Union Oyster House, and slept in a canopied bed in the Adams Hotel facing the Common, and awakened to the aroma of steaming coffee and the pleasant sounds of the daybreak traffic on Tremont Street—not, I repeat, in Boston, but in Bristol, Rhode Island— in a dismal flophouse near the waterfront where I went to my wretched cot like a chastised child, without supper, in a grimy chamber in which I shared tenancy with innumerable vermin and one drunken, bloated longshoreman who lay through that endless night on his broad back, comatose, rhythmically exhaling agonized snorts that would have done credit to a hog at the slaughter, and absolutely impervious to all endeavors to render him either conscious or keel-upwards.

In short, I never closed an eye.

Free will, fate, chance—all three have their roles in the shaping of a man's destiny. For myself, I maintain a firm conviction that the course of one's life, however convoluted, however tangled, is primarily in one's own hands. This notion has done me good service.

Nevertheless, there are times when a man senses the influence of fate, or chance—I confess my inability to distinguish between them. Chance implies luck, accident, a lack of design. Fate, that wondrous word of the ancient, advanced polytheists, which the modern Christians have degraded into their mean, plodding, piddling Providence—fate, I say, suggests form, intent, purpose—though whether beneficent or malevolent is not always at once apparent.

It was a small thing. I tarried too long at the Fancy Store over the matter of the pilfered lace, and the captain of the *Pawtucket* had the bad grace to sail for Boston without me, carrying with him my luggage, my horse, and the bulk of my funds in the charge of his purser. I was forced to obtain passage on a small steamer to Bristol, where I hoped to contact an old friend of my father's who might lend me the money to continue my journey.

Now, perhaps I was fated to meet him, or perhaps it was the merest chance. But, had I not been delayed by the affair of the shoplifting factory girl, I might never have encountered the Methodist minister whose destiny was to be so tragically entwined with her own—and so strangely involved with mine. It occurs to me as I write, that, with the exceptions of, of course my father, and of Amy Wrenn and Quinncannon, no other person was to exert as great an influence on my history as the Reverend Ephraim K. Avery.

Let those of my contemporaries who doubt—smugly secure as they may be in their Puritan notions of moral absolutism— who doubt, I say, that good and evil may inscrutably mingle and arise from the same causes and events—

Let them but read on.

Shortly after eight that morning I walked south on High Street, headed toward the Court House where I hoped to find my father's friend, a gentleman farmer and sometime lawyer named John Haile who had long served Bristol as one of her two justices of the peace. Exhausted by a sleepless night, I was further discomfited by a steady, soaking drizzle that slyly drenched me and chilled me to the bone. The weather seemed appropriate to the occasion. It suited my mood.

To my left lay the Bristol Common, stretching dismal and uninviting beyond the five buildings that fronted the avenue. The Masonic Lodge, a gray structure of quasi-classical façade, stood at the northwest corner of the Common. Beside it was the little First Baptist Church (there was no Second Baptist Church) and then the Court House, a brick colonial building of two full stories and a smaller third from which three shuttered windows peeped beneath a single gable. The requisite steeple loomed above, surrounded by the requisite narrow observation platform (from which nothing ever was observed) and crowned by the requisite weather vane. Beyond stood the tiny Bristol Academy, attended by the sons of the town's few wealthy merchants, shipbuilders and plantation owners.

At the end of the street squatted the unadorned, unpainted,

58

frankly and intentionally ugly Methodist Meeting House. At this time I had only the most general comprehension of these people and their delusions. In their theory that poverty was morally uplifting they were surely mistaken, though that hallucination was, and largely still is, cherished by this society, and especially by those who have been spared all direct experience with want.

The Methodists were despised by their more respectable, Calvinist neighbors, not only because they were perceived as disreputable, but because they seemed to be deliberately so. They drew their parishioners from the lowest classes and elements. Women, notably the youngest, poorest and most abandoned, were particularly susceptible to their blandishments. There were whispers of outrageous and immoral practices at their camp-meetings.

Of all this I was, as yet, only vaguely aware. Since then I have had the dubious honor of observing the Methodists, so to speak, in their native habitat, and I imagine I will eventually be put to the task of commenting further on the subject.

🐚 12 ─────────────

The Clergyman

John Haile greeted me warmly and, I like to think, for more than the sake of my father's ancient friendship. "Naturally, you are welcome to whatever amount you require, Christy, but mayhap there is a better solution to your problem. Would you wish to earn a fee that would more than cover your passage, and do me a boon into the bargain?"

"I should be glad to be of service, sir," I answered.

The old man's brow furrowed. "It is a devilishly tricky problem, lad. There is currently, in my chambers, a young woman desirous of charging her husband with assault. When you see her you may judge for yourself the justice of her cause. The difficulty lies in this—the man is the Methodist preacher in this town and a member of my own Masonic Lodge. I am placed in an awkward position."

"Am I to present her case?"

"No, no, Christy," he said quickly. "You are to defend the clergyman. If you have inherited your father's skills, as by the fine look of you you have, you will find some crafty stratagem by which I can justify an acquittal. To order a fellow Mason and a minister—even a Methodist—to gaol would never do!" He shook his snowy, venerable head. "Never do at all."

With this rather dubious compliment to my abilities, and this even more dubious charge, I went in search of his chambers, musing on how it might feel, just once, to defend a client who was innocent.

Within Haile's rooms sat two women, one on a chair beside his desk, the other on the carpet with her head in the first's ample lap.

"Your pardon for this intrusion, ladies," I said. "My name is Christopher Randolph. I am an attorney. Justice Haile has asked me to look in on you."

I saw no immediate need to disclose that I was to represent the accused. In some manner the women formed the impression that I was to speak for them.

60

The elder, a sturdy matron tastefully but simply dressed, regarded me from her chair. She was what Charlotte Prescott would have disdained as "bourgeois," a plain-spoken, no-nonsense woman who, I fancied, had spent her fifty-odd years in the kitchen and the laundry and the sick-room, never once doubting either the fitness or the nobility of her work. She had probably birthed seven children, of whom two died of fever or pox or whooping cough, and bullied them all with the same gentle affection with which she now doubtless pampered her grandchildren. I imagined she never spoke of a woman's "rights" or "place," but of a woman's "duty." She loathed idleness and kept busy every minute she was not in church or asleep—making work on those rare occasions when it did not readily present itself—and if she chafed at all it was not from railing against the injustice of her state, but from the harsh soap in her dishwater.

I make no moral judgments—I have learned at least that much from Quinncannon. Many women are ill-suited to such a life, and many have shone brilliantly in other spheres. I merely observe that where I have encountered such matrons I have generally found them the happiest, or perhaps the least unhappy, of all their sex.

But the great majority of men are poorly fitted to evaluate such things, and I count myself among them.

"Sir, I am Mrs. Rowena Bloss, and this unfortunate—" in dicating the woman whose face remained buried in her apron— "this is Mrs. Catherine Avery."

The latter now first cast her tear-filled eyes up at mine. She was slender—flimsy, I would say, without substance, not cor-poreal. She had a deathly pallor which but served the better to accent the purple bruises and ugly red welts that scarred her face, particularly on the left side. I noticed, with a shudder, that most of these marks had not been recently acquired. She lay before me like a battered doll flung aside by a willful and vicious child.

"Oh, my God!" exclaimed I involuntarily.

"Her back," said Mrs. Bloss in a steady, angry alto. "You may have my oath for it, sir—her back is worse hurt."

Though I later learned she was only twenty-seven, I then calculated her near to forty. Her black hair was unloosed and disheveled, already streaked with white. Her fingers, always tightly clasped when I observed them, were pale and even gnarled. She had once been pretty, possibly even spirited, but

61

it had all been beaten out of her by the brute who so undervalued and degraded her.

"She fled to me in terror last evening," said Mrs. Bloss, "and not for the first time. The children are as miserably harmed. I gave her refuge only on condition that she bring that *beast*—" she fought to control her growing rage "—that she bring that man before the court."

I lack words to describe the abject shame I felt at the treacherous part I was about to play in the betrayal of this helpless creature. What mattered Haile's mild, temporary embarrassment? What mattered my momentary financial troubles?

"I will pay you what I can, Squire," said the matron. "I am a widow of limited means with many claims upon me and this poor child has no resources, nor any possessions," she added bitterly, "but the rags in which she flew from her tyrant!"

I sank into a chair and drew a deep breath. Then I replied as I thought Quinncannon, had he been positioned as I was, would have replied.

"Keep your money, madam. I am content to take up your cause for a jar of your preserves and a bottle of homemade wine."

And to hell with Avery, and to hell with Haile. If need be I would work my way to Boston on a coal barge!

But, as I spoke these words, I watched the marked change in the expression of their eyes as they turned toward something, or someone, at my back. Rowena Bloss' expression went from relieved gratitude to smouldering resentment and defiance. But it was the alteration of countenance in Catherine Avery that was truly remarkable.

As her eyes moved upward to stare at something past my shoulder they shifted from a blank, listless stare into a shining glitter that was at once burning with stark fear and yet glowing with adoration. With a reasonably fair idea of whom I would confront, I looked around at the door.

There stood Ephraim K. Avery (for of a certainty it was he). He was tall, somewhat over six feet; broad-shouldered and well-favored. He was not much more than thirty and remarkably handsome. His hair was black and of a curly thickness, receding only slightly at the temples, without a tinge of gray. A high forehead rose above heavy brows that curved down around blue eyes no less piercing for their paleness. He was clean-shaven—even his side-whiskers were trimmed just above the lobes of his small ears. His complexion was olive, his nose long and straight, terminating in wide, flaring nostrils. His egg-shaped head sloped jowllessly down to a strong, clefted chin.

Only his mouth suggested want of character. The lips were wide and full—too full. They implied in some vague manner an unpleasant sensuality, almost a bestiality. And they drew down too much at the corners, conveying, to my mind at least, a hint of habitual surliness.

Altogether it was not difficult to understand why the battered woman at his feet had found him attractive—nor why, perhaps, the young women of his flock still eagerly sought his company and spiritual solace.

The clergyman never glanced at me. It may be he was oblivious to my presence. His stare burned straight into his wife's eerily illuminated eyes. Her skin, so ghastly a moment before, appeared suddenly rosy, almost robust. I noted that her bruises no longer stood out in clear relief. She never took her eyes from his. He strode across the floor until he loomed directly over her, placing himself between the woman and the whale-oil lamp in such a way that he cast a great shadow over her.

When at last he spoke it was in a deep, resonant voice well suited to his holy calling. "Enough of this folly, Kitty. Come home."

The final two words were more an invitation than a command, yet they seemed to me to contain an unexpressed but unmistakable threat.

He stretched out his hand to her. "Kitty, come home."

The Widow Bloss found her tongue. "She will not go with you, Ephraim. Not *this* time! *Not ever again!*"

But the man merely repeated, "Kitty, come home."

To my amazement, the woman took his hand and allowed him to raise her from the floor. He turned and slowly walked to the door, and meekly, worshipfully, she followed him.

"Catherine!" the matron cried. "Be warned! If you go with him now my door is forever closed to you. You shall not again presume upon my affections."

At the door Catherine Avery paused but did not turn back. "Forgive me, Rowena," she said softly. "The hand of God is heavy upon me."

So saying she left the room in her husband's wake, shutting the door behind her.

13

The Great Hoboken Buffalo Hunt

Early in August advertisements began to appear in the newspapers announcing that a buffalo hunt would be staged in Hoboken, across the North River, on the fifteenth of the month. A powwow, an Indian medicine man, was to preside at the festivities. New Yorkers had never seen either a redskin or a buffalo, much less a herd of the beasts, and there was terrific excitement.

Hoboken was a sleepy little village of less than a thousand, and then, as now, was a rustic playground for the inhabitants of the neighboring metropolis. Ferries ran regularly from Barclay Street to the docks at the foot of Hoboken's William Street. The town could boast of several pleasant public houses and two fine hotels, the Phoenix and the Vauxhall. A short walk north from the ferry slip brought you to a large, sylvan park, the Elysian Fields, which stretched from Tenth Street to the foot of Weehawken Hill. The park's shaded arbors, picnic groves and picturesque taverns attracted thousands of visitors each year.

The pleasures offered by the Fields were numerous. A quiet stroll along the paths beneath the famous poplars, a relaxing day of fishing or sailing on the North River, an ale in the Mansion House—all these enticed. At the foot of Seventh Street, below Castle Point, stood the Grotto, or Sybil's Cave, a natural spring formed by an excavation in the rock from which cool water flowed and was sold for a penny a glass. Near the Grotto wooden tables encircled the trunks of the poplars, attended by benches. A small tavern offered stronger refreshment than the spring could provide.

Just west of the Fields, across Washington Street, was the Trotting Course, an oval track where races were held and occasional bare-knuckle fights staged in defiance of the law. It was there that the "Great Buffalo Hunt" was to take place.

Few in New York knew who was promoting the hunt. P. T. Barnum, the exhibitor of "George Washington's nurse," had recently bought Scudder's Museum on Broadway, and I learned—from Quinncannon—that Barnum was behind the scheme as a means of publicizing his new venture.

"Because of the reputation as a charlatan young Barnum has already acquired," the Irishman explained, "he prefers to conceal his sponsorship of this dubious enterprise until it is over. Consider yourself sworn to secrecy."

"Shall I expect," I said drily, "that it will soon be announced that Hoboken must be sawed off at the Weehawken line and towed into the upper bay?"

"Oh, I doubt the joke will achieve that proportion."

"What, then," I inquired, "*am* I to expect?"

Quinncannon smiled. "I suggest you take your lady to Hoboken and see for yourself."

On the day of the buffalo hunt Charlotte was suffering from one of her numerous migraines. For the first time, I was permitted to escort Amy unchaperoned.

She had packed a hamper with cold chicken, hard-cooked eggs, a small cherry pie, and a bottle of champagne smuggled from her grandmother's wine cellar. I called for her in a hansom and we crossed the river at eight in the morning on an already mobbed ferry.

We walked north along the river. At the foot of Fourth Street we left the pavement and entered a wooded path. Steep cliffs loomed on our left, bare in most places, overhung with the deep green of the groves of trees that lined the top of the Palisades. A few feet to our right the waters of the river lapped against the shore. The North River was dotted with multicolored sails, reds, whites, yellows. Men and boys squatted in rented rowboats, their oars resting on the gunwales, their eyes fixed dreamily on the fishing lines that trailed behind them as they drifted in the light breeze.

At Sixth Street we turned west toward the Trotting Course. Long before we reached the oval we heard the sounds of the crowd.

Eventually there amassed a throng later estimated by Barnum himself at almost five thousand. Perhaps half that number had gathered around the oval when Amy and I arrived. A pineboard corral fence had been constructed in the track's infield within which there milled about a dozen or so scrawny, yearling buffalo calves, alternately whining and bellowing in sheer terror. On a hastily erected platform at the oval's southern end a string band, predominantly banjos, performed with feverish enthusiasm.

Near ten o'clock the powwow made his entrance. Even had I no foreknowledge of the truth, I would have recognized that he was a white man outlandishly done up in feathers and warpaint. He rode into the flimsy enclosure on an equine derelict, swinging a lasso over his head and yelling an easterner's notion of a war whoop, and, after several failures, each jeered by the crowd, he succeeded in tossing a loop over the head of the most skittish of the beasts, celebrating his accomplishment with a horrific yelp while the calf howled in astonished fear. The crowd let loose a thunderous cheer. The string band struck up a lively tune. The herd, already in a state of advanced excitement, panicked and stampeded, not all in one direction, as is the habit of their breed, but independently, toward all compass points at once, as if, being young and willful and early deprived of parental guidance, they had never learned stampeding etiquette.

The assembly was somewhat inconvenienced. The spindly corral fence shattered on impact. Horses reared, throwing their riders. Carriages overturned, spilling their finely dressed occupants into the mud. The crowd scattered, sprinting for cover, crouching behind rocks or scrambling up trees. The string band continued to play even as their makeshift bandstand collapsed, many of them striking the last note of their sprightly melody just before they struck the ground.

One of the animals appeared to bear a particular grudge against Amy and me. Wherever we fled, it pursued us like a Fury, dogging our trail with a grunting, vengeful singlemindedness until at last, well north of the Trotting Oval, we eluded it in a grove of elms in the center of which we flung ourselves down on the grass and further exhausted ourselves by laughing hysterically.

It was several minutes before I recovered. I rolled over on my side, supporting my chin with the heel of my hand. Amy lay on her back, her dress in disarray, still gasping for breath and sporadically giggling. She caught my eye and again burst into happy laughter.

"Oh, Christy! What glorious fun!"

I laughed with her.

"It's always fun to be with you," she said. "You know such fascinating people and we always do such interesting things." She closed her eyes. "It's so pleasant not to be bored."

The elms towered over us and, beyond their rich foliage, the placid blue of a cloudless sky, the color of a robin's egg, illuminated by the golden eye of heaven, not quite at meridian. We lay beside each other on a lush, green carpet, more a lawn

66

than grass growing wild. The sunlight broke in shafts through the leafy shade of the arbor. Though we had stood, not a quarter hour before, in the midst of a teeming throng of five thousand, I had the sense that we were the only two people on earth.

While her eyes remained closed I studied her face. Though I thought I had it memorized, there were always new discoveries to make. A tiny freckle just beside her nose. The slenderest of gaps between her two front teeth.

She looked up at me and smiled. "Did we save the lunch from the horned beast?"

I nodded toward the hamper. "It seems to be intact. Are you hungry?"

"Not unless you are."

"I can wait."

She drew a deep sigh. "What a lovely place. There is such quietness here. I wish—" She paused. "I almost wish we could freeze this moment in time and remain here forever, never growing old or unhappy. Like in the poem—

> Fair youth, beneath the trees, thou canst not leave
> Thy song, nor ever can those trees be bare;
> Bold Lover, never, never canst thou kiss,
> Though winning near the goal—yet, do not grieve;
> She cannot fade, though thou hast not thy bliss,
> For ever wilt thou love, and she be fair!"

Again she smiled. "Isn't that a beautiful thought, my 'fair youth'?"

I shook my head slowly. "You are mistaken, Amy. I am not the fair youth. As I remember he is doomed to an eternity of piping songs no one can hear. I have no wish for time to stand still. I'm impatient to get on with my life. When I pipe I don't want people merely to hear—I want them to listen. Maybe I want them to dance."

I sat up, folding up my legs and wrapping my arms around them. "I have such great dreams, Amy," I said with an earnest intensity which surprised me. "I want so much. I can't even put it into words. There's just such a *hunger* in me."

Behind me she said softly, "I know."

That was all she said. Two words.

When I looked around she was sitting with her back against an elm trunk. Without thinking I swung about and stretched out on my back with my head in her lap and closed my eyes and felt her fingers gently tousling my hair and I began to babble—I had almost said, to pour out my soul, but the proper word is babble.

My hopes, my prospects, my ambitions—I spoke of things, of past experiences and private thoughts and feelings and secret dreams which I had hoarded up unshared for twenty years. And she understood—she *knew*. My God! I cannot express the utter relief.

She knew and she cared. The realization crept upon me unawares even as, self-enthralled, I jabbered away. This child, this schoolgirl, this naive and sheltered infant knew and she cared.

Not only does a woman know she is in love before her man does—she knows *he's* in love before he does. A woman's wiles are overestimated. She operates not on guile but on instinct. She seldom traps a man as if he were a beaver. She simply waits for him to discover what she already has discerned.

Thus it was that, in the midst of my tedious recitation of my autobiography, when I had reached, perhaps, my twenty-first year, I opened my eyes abruptly and said, "Amy, I love you and I want to marry you."

She looked down at me, tracing the contours of my features with her fingers, her lips forming into a soft smile.

The foolish words of the poet crossed my mind: "Bold Lover, never, never canst thou . . ."

I reached up and took her face gently between my hands and bent it down until her lips pressed against mine. As we kissed my arms slipped gradually down until they encircled her waist. She slid away from the tree against which she had been leaning and lay on the grass. I lay beside her, my weight partially resting on her, feeling the rhythmic pounding of both our hearts. I held her tightly.

"You have not," I said, "answered my question."

"Which question?" she breathed.

"Will you marry me, Amy?"

Her eyes wrinkled slightly at the corners. "I must ask, Squire Randolph, is this another invitation to a supper of oysters?"

The question stung me. "No, no, Amy," I said fervently. "I *am* in love with you. Truly! You must believe me. You are the moon and stars to me. I would sooner cut off my right arm than hurt you."

She averted her glance. "Oh, Christy, please don't do that."

"Do what?"

I hadn't *done* anything yet.

"Don't try to talk like a character in a cheap novel. I don't

68

want to hear about the moon or the stars. I don't even care about your indifference to your right arm." She turned her face back to mine and smiled. "Besides, you're left-handed." She grew suddenly serious. "I think there is more of the 'fair youth' about you than you realize, Christy. It is that fair youth I fell in love with when he punched a watchman at a masked ball. That's probably a silly reason for marriage, but my answer is yes."

"Oh, Amy, you've made me the happiest—" I stopped short in mid-cliché, and responded instead with a kiss that evolved into a lingering, passionate embrace.

I attempt, in retrospect, to sort out and explain my emotions at that moment. That Amy Wrenn was not the first girl I had professed to love, or proposed marriage to, I freely confess, but I insist she was the first with whom, at the time, I believed myself sincere. It is true that my pronunciation of the word "wedlock" had always, in contradiction to Mr. Webster's rules, stressed the second syllable, but it was my conviction that, *should* I ever marry, it would certainly be Amy before all the rest.

"We have to wait, Christy," she said. "I'll need Cousin Charlotte's permission, you know."

"Yes, yes, of course." I unbuttoned my coat.

"She and Grandmother will insist on a big formal wedding and an absolutely *gigantic* party afterwards. And you know Cousin Charlotte. She always manages to get her way."

"Amy," I said huskily, "I can't wait."

She understood I wasn't speaking of the wedding.

"I know," she said softly.

She reclined on the grass with submissive trust. "Christy . . . ," she said, "you *do* love me?"

I was fumbling with a button-hook. "With all my heart," I said.

I will never comprehend the complexities of the female costume. I verily believe it would be easier to dismantle and reassemble a steam engine than it is to undress and redress a woman. The dresses, with their puffed sleeves and voluminous skirts, are fastened with uncountable button-hooks, and even when their mystery is solved a gentleman must deal with six or seven underskirts. Whoever invented the whale-bone corset may go to the devil with my blessing. I would have given a week's pay for a pair of pliers.

Contrast the simplicity of a man's garments. Frock coat, vest and blouse are quickly removed and, if a button or three is lost, the sacrifice is well rewarded.

Though agitated almost to distraction, I was gentle with her.

My voice was soothing, my words reassuring, my caresses tender. I could sense both her exhilaration and her terror. With a monumental effort of will I fought back my intense excitement and acted with cool deliberateness, doing nothing that would surprise or alarm her, and gradually I won her confidence and she yielded to me completely.

And God! She was beautiful. Unhooked, unbuttoned, unlaced, unstrapped—freed of the cumbersome camouflage imposed on her sex by puritan priggishness, garbed as her Creator intended her before His plan was sabotaged by a conspiracy between Geneva and Paris—she *was* beautiful.

We lay together for more than three hours, alone in a world of silence and slow time, now making love, now talking in low tones, now quiescent and lost in our own thoughts—and at last she sat up and playfully pulled my face toward hers, and twirled a lock of my hair around her tiny finger.

"Your hair is so marvelously curly," she said. "I would *kill* to have your hair." She smiled warmly. "My bold lover, my fair youth. You were right, Christy. We cannot freeze time. Why should we wish to, when we can love each other over and over again? This is no cold pastoral. I feel so wonderfully alive!"

She threw her arms around me and I held her warm, supple body against my breast. "Oh, Christy," she breathed, "I never imagined life was so wondrous and fine. I love you. My beautiful, beautiful man. I love you—I love you."

"I love you, Amy," I whispered.

And I meant it. Damn it! I meant it!

We strolled back to the ferry docks while a vermillion sun slipped gradually behind the cliffs of the Palisades, and she held my hand, squeezing it often, and laughed, and made plans. There is absolutely nothing a woman loves more to do than make plans. She exuded, she overflowed, she fairly exploded with plans. Before we reached the Trotting Oval the church had been determined and the wedding party chosen. We had not attained the Grotto when the guest list was complete. From Seventh to Sixth Street the china pattern was selected—from Sixth to Fifth the crystal. The silver was a two-block problem but then the pace picked up briskly and the entire house was furnished before we set foot on the boat. Upon my word, I was fairly reeling.

"Oh, Christy, I simply can't *wait* to tell Grandmother and Cousin Charlotte!"

"Perhaps," I said, keeping my eyes on the river, "you should wait, just a little while."

I felt her grip on my arm tighten. "But why?"

"It's only that it's such a big step and you want to be sure that—"

"But, darling, I *am* sure." A frightened edge crept into her voice. "Christy, you still want to, don't you? You haven't changed your mind?"

"No, no, of course I want to." I was thinking as rapidly as I could. My tongue moved with the speed of a serpent's. "I just mean that there are so many arrangements that have to be made. I have to settle my affairs here—there are a lot of loose ends—and I have business for Quinncannon that will take me out of town. I want to be certain I can support you properly."

"Oh, Christy, I have some money of my own."

"No," I said firmly. "I won't take your money. Besides there's Charlotte to consider. You said yourself that, once she knows we're to be married, she'll seize control of the whole affair and run it to suit herself regardless of our wishes. You know her capacity for generalship. Isn't it better to lay our plans in secret and spring them on her all at once?"

For the first time I risked looking at her. "Well...," she said slowly.

"Don't you see, Amy? We'll take her by surprise, catch her off guard. Until then it will be our special secret, something for just the two of us to share together, like," I added, "our love."

There was a long pause. "It *would* be fun to plan things without Cousin Charlotte's interference. To visit little shops and browse and pick things out, just the two of us." She frowned slightly and her small nose wrinkled. "How long must we wait?"

"Only a couple of months," I answered. "Six at the most."

Her frown deepened. "It will be winter. I did so not want to be married in a blizzard."

"Then," I said quickly, "we'll wait until spring. That would be the perfect time. You'll have graduated from school and I'll have my practice established and we'll be able to arrange our future without Charlotte's meddling."

I waited. At last she said, "I know you must be right. You're so much cleverer than I... But it seems so strange to decide without Cousin Charlotte's... without *someone's* advice."

I took her hand. "You have my advice."

She smiled up at me. "And you are to be my husband. You *are* my dear husband."

I drew a deep breath.

"But am I to tell *no* one?" she whispered. "Oh, Christy, I'm so happy! I'm absolutely bursting! I must tell *someone*!"

Abruptly she spun about and pulled me by the hand toward a stout man lounging against the ferry rail with a newspaper. "Sir," she cried, "we are to be married! You must pardon me for addressing you so boldly but you have such a kind face that we wanted you to be the first to hear."

He put down his paper and beamed at us both. "Please accept my best wishes," he said. "May you be very happy together."

"Oh, we will," Amy laughed. "We will. I know it." She tugged me toward two other passengers, plump, aging, obviously married. "Did you know, this young man and I are pledged to each other. I'm sorry you are not the first to hear but you were not standing so near as the other gentleman."

The woman smiled. "Alfred and I hope you will be as happy as we have been, my dear." Her voice lowered. "*Don't* we, Alfred?"

Alfred nodded. He didn't look very happy to me.

I told myself it was the furniture. I could have managed the china and the crystal and the silver pattern, but four rooms full of furniture had done for me.

Amy was sitting beside a sour matron whose features thawed in the warmth of the girl's joyous excitement. ". . . only we've agreed not to tell my family just at present. Just until he's gotten himself established. It's to be our secret, just we two."

The dowager's face instantly refroze. Her eyes shot to mine and held them with a glare electric with suspicion.

"Give us your blessing, madam," Amy said.

"You have it, my child," the matron croaked, "but heed an old woman's wisdom. Marriage is the ultimate fulfillment of a woman. It brings her purpose, satisfaction and the opportunity to give and to love. It has only one serious flaw." Again her eyes were on me.

"It requires," she said, "a man."

🐾 14 ──────────────────────

The Factory

On the 22nd of August I traveled to Fall River, Mas-
sachusetts, by steamer, in connection with one of Quinncannon's cases, to obtain a deposition from an overseer in one of
the manufactories. The boat was behind time and when I had
arranged for my horse and secured accommodations it was past
seven-thirty and the mills were shut down.

Fall River is a bleak, dingy factory town—a world devoid
of color. Great clouds of greasy smoke hang forever over it.
Its buildings, its streets, even its dour residents seem perma-
nently encrusted with wet soot.

There are no decent hotels or restaurants, or even a congenial
saloon. I ate such supper as I could swallow and amused myself
by attending a meeting of the local Temperance Society where
a raucous debate broke out over whether wine and beer were
properly to be considered "spiritous fluids," and therefore proscribed. In the end a vote was taken and the nays carried the
question although the ayes loudly protested the result on the
ground that many of the nays were drunk.

In the morning I rode up Annawan Street past the Pewter
Works, the Gas Works, the Print Works, the Oil Works and the
Iron Works until, near an odious tarn called the Print Works
Pond, I located the Cotton Works. All these mills, the Cotton
Works no less than the rest, resemble nothing so much as
penitentiaries. Built of brick and rising four to six stories, they
constantly belch murky smoke from square, towering chim-
neys. Each story is marked by a long row of approximately
twenty high, narrow windows that are cracked in summer but
kept shut during the colder months and closed at night the year
around. There is little or no ventilation—the air may go
unchanged for months—and at least fifty solar lamps are always
kept burning in each room, so that not only does the atmosphere
become putrid, but the temperature may rise, even in January,
above one hundred degrees.

I entered the mill in search of my witness, a Mr. Whisker,

and was ushered to a huge, long room whose walls were lined with power looms. The noise was crashing, shattering. The air was close and the heat terrific. The looms were operated by women, most young, some still children, and they worked mechanically, like automatons, with glazed eyes, disheveled hair and gray, blank faces, tending two or even three machines.

The work of weaving, whether cotton, wool, silk or lace, is done almost entirely by women under the supervision of male overseers, and the system has changed for the worse in recent years. No longer are the workers farm girls thrilled with the notion of independence in the big city. No longer may they relieve the monotony of their labor by spelling each other to snatch a rest or propping a book on the frame. The work-day runs from five a.m. to seven in the evening with thirty minutes granted each for breakfast and dinner. The salary averages $2.50 per week from which $1.25 must be paid for room and board, and absence is allowed only for illness, the haunting fear of these women since earnings are based on piece-work and the rule is, no production, no pay.

In Waltham and Lowell the companies exercise a puritan paternalism by which the girls live in company-owned boarding houses where their moral activities are monitored and church attendance mandated, but in Fall River they must find their own accommodations and supervise their own conduct—and many of them fall prey to the temptations of the town. In most manufacturing communities associations of young men called "Old Liners" form understandings with the mill girls, often after seducing them, and then introduce them to other young men, visitors to the place, for immoral purposes.

I record this without pretense of moral indignation. Such a posture would be rank hypocrisy. Had I lived in a mill town when I was twenty-two, I should doubtless have been an "Old Liner," though, in justice to myself, I would have played the rake but not the pander.

Mr. Whisker, when I found him, proved a sallow, pinched little martinet who ruled his tiny fiefdom with a mixture of fastidiousness and fury. He was what I expected. The mills have strict rules against romantic entanglements between employees and, to assure compliance, they often hire men whose immunity to such temptation is obvious.

As Whisker was forbidden to leave his post I conducted the interview in the slamming din of the weaving room. At last, as I was about to make my escape, I saw his lips form the word "Aha!" Atremble with excitement, he scampered past me

74

toward a young woman seated at one of the looms. Without any idea of what he was about to do, I concluded that it would be the high point of his day and the subject of his supper conversation that evening with his mother.

He commanded the girl to rise, reached down to her stool, and seized—a book! Horror of horrors! A flagrant violation of manufactory policy! Expressly disallowed by company rules!

Our hero held the book aloft in triumph and I realized it was a copy of the Bible. In the next moment I had recognized the girl. It was the same young woman who had been caught shoplifting lace goods in Providence.

She didn't see me. Her eyes were riveted on the confiscated Scripture. I think I shall never forget the look of utter despair on her face.

🌸 15 ———————————
The Camp-Meeting

Quinncannon required another deposition, this one from a Methodist minister in Providence, a Reverend Mr. Clapp. Inquiries in that city told me that Reverend Clapp was away attending a camp-meeting in Thompson, Connecticut, and was not to return until August 30. It was then Monday, August 25—the meeting was to run from the 26th to the 29th. Though I longed to see Amy she was sure to ask questions with which I was not prepared to deal. As my expenses were not being paid from my own purse, I determined to remain in Providence until Wednesday. I took a room in the finest hotel and sampled all the pleasures and delights of the town so lavishly that, when I at last saddled my horse and rode for Thompson it was with the thought that my soul could use all the glory and redemption the Methodists might provide.

I secured two nights' lodging at a small inn and, as the hour was late, I delayed my visit to the camp until Thursday. Though exhausted I slept little, in part because of the oppressive heat. There had been no rain for days—not the slightest breeze stirred the heavy, humid air—the temperature could not have dropped below eighty degrees. Worse than this, the inn was filled to its rafters with the Methodist faithful who never ceased shouting hosannahs and singing their Glories! and Hallelujahs! and Amens! at the top of their lusty lungs. The effect was less that of a religious exercise than a drunken brawl. I concluded that these people's Deity is offended by silent worship.

No physical exertion is more fatiguing than an unsuccessful effort to sleep. By sunrise I was drained. I dressed and went down to breakfast feeling as though I was kicking my eyelids before me as I walked. Then, with directions from the landlord, I set out for the camp on horseback.

An avenue had been cleared through the wood from the road to the camp about a quarter mile in length. It was very early in the day but already the path (I can hardly call it a road) was mobbed with traffic—many traveling in carts and lumbering farm wagons, but most on foot, men and matrons, often dragging children at their skirts or toting infants in their arms. By far the majority of the Methodist infantry were young women who giggled and tripped gaily along in small sisterly knots toward the holy bivouac.

The going was treacherous, particularly for the foot soldiers. One girl lost her balance and fell beneath the wheels of a wagon, saved only by the quick reaction of the grizzled teamster who pulled up his horses sharply with a pungent, un-Christian oath. At that moment a company of young men in boisterous high frolic rode their horses through the crowd, Jehu-like, unmindful of the stumps and stones, shouting war whoops. I urged my mount up beside the wagon and asked the meaning of the outburst.

The driver shrugged. "They're professional gamblers and horse jockies. They follow these religious shindigs regular as crows and vultures follow an army."

I could not help smiling. "So the Christian soldiers also have their camp followers."

"Camp followers?" he echoed grimly. "Aye, you'll find them here too aplenty, son, if your taste runs to that. Look there." He pointed to the woods with his whip at a row of makeshift stalls. "Do ye know what they be?"

I shook my head.

"Sheds for selling liquor, son. New rum! Rotgut that'll send a strong man to his Maker aforetimes. And these young females swill it like water. That child that almost got herself squashed under my wheels—she's already out of her senses and the sun ain't half high." With another, fouler oath, he cracked his whip over his team and trundled on.

The area of the camp ground was extensive and circular. Many trees had been felled but sufficient remained to provide shade from the already blistering sun. Large white tents stretched far and wide from whose flaps the denizens had emerged to stroll, or rather mill about the place, some arm in arm. The women outnumbered the men and the majority of both sexes were young. Their faces were scrubbed and happy—their dress simple homespun. This rustic place of worship had literally been carved out of the forest and gave the appearance of a pleasant grove within an impenetrable wood. From fires before the tents arose the hospitable aroma of brewing coffee which mingled with the refreshingly cool scent of the pines. But in a few seconds I became aware of another odor, a reeking stench which suggested that the latrines had not been properly dug.

77

The ground was an inclined plane that descended gradually toward a small platform familiarly termed "the preacher's stand." Upon this structure stood an ancient, hoary patriarch of few hairs, stooped by age but still powerful of arm and, especially, of voice, loudly calling upon this yet unpurified remnant of the people to repent. There was little sense or connection in what he said but he seemed to be vigorously earnest and sincere.

The Elijah of the place, thought I, preaching a faith of reason and morality rather than sensual frenzy and ecstasy—warning the faithful against the corruption of the nature-worship of Baal.

Though he howled his heart out, his exertions seemed thrown away. Except for a strolling party that occasionally, briefly, halted near him, he had no auditors. The vast assembly wandered beneath the pines or squatted before their tents cooking and eating, or lounged on the grass chatting and laughing, oblivious to the thunderous cries of the venerable prophet.

Alas, poor Elijah, I fear your day is past, your day being, if I recall the Christian calendar aright, July 20.

A group of older matrons stood aside not far from the edge of the clearing where horses were hitched to stakes driven into the ground. I was surprised to recognize one of them as Rowena Bloss. Dismounting, I approached her and found that she remembered me.

"And are you then a Methodist, Squire Randolph?"

I assured her I was worse than that. "I am an attorney, ma'am, and I am here on legal business. Do you know a clergyman named Clapp from Providence?"

She shook her head and frowned. "You might inquire of the Reverend Avery," she said aridly.

"Ah, so *he's* here," I said, thinking that might explain her presence. "And his wife also?"

Her eyes narrowed at the mention of the woman.

"Mrs. Avery is never permitted to accompany him to the camps," she replied. "He fears it might distract him."

"From his preaching?" I ventured.

"*That,* too," she said darkly.

All attempts to locate my elusive, ordained quarry that morning proved fruitless. I moved methodically through that canvas city but the few persons who knew him were ignorant of his whereabouts. Speaker followed speaker to the stand, many of them females, which surprised me as I had understood that the Methodists did not allow women to preach. I was at last informed by one of the "good people" (for such they term themselves) that while females could not *preach*, they could *exhort*. When a man addressed the crowd he was preaching—when a woman spoke she was *exhorting*. This was explained to me with such infinite patience that I felt compelled to thank my informant profusely for his instruction. Thereafter I listened carefully to several vehement tirades in succession by both sexes but, being of the uninitiated, for the life of me I could not tell the difference.

This effort at self-education caused me to be near the stand at noon when a bold young woman mounted the platform and began vigorously to urge the mob to "repent your sins and sink into Jesus!" Her voice was shrill and harsh, her manner coarse and her language vulgar. She stomped about the stand, gesturing crazily, and so contorting her features that, though positive I knew her, it was not until I had maneuvered through the crowd, until I was positioned just below her, that I could verify her identity.

I had witnessed the plaintive thief, the saucy street girl, the forlorn and bullied mill worker, and here was yet another side of this enigmatic young woman's personality—the fiery religious fanatic.

Though she harangued the multitude with more violence than any previous orator, she did not elicit the usual choruses of Amens! and Hallelujahs! Her congregation received her teachings with derision, hooting and jeering until at length she spread her feet and squared her shoulders and, fists on hips, she faced them in furious defiance.

"Go on then, laugh at me, you evil sinners! You vile backsliders!" Her face was a vivid purple. The veins in her temples and neck stood out like cords. "Revile me," she cried, "as our Savior was reviled, you Philistines! I don't care nothing for your laughter! I don't care for nobody—not a snap of my finger!" She snapped her fingers several times, noisily and with great style. A lock of unkempt hair fell across her face. She didn't bother to push it back. "I'll have my chance at you!" she shouted. "There's a day coming I'll laugh at you when I watch you dragged screaming to torment by the serpent of hell!"

Again the mob broke into raucous laughter. She continued to shout, holding her ground. I felt an inexplicable sympathy for her—a deep sadness that I did not understand. This poor, luckless child, abandoned by the Divinity to whom she clung for protection. For some insane reason the image of Catherine Avery flashed into my mind and I saw her again at the door of Haile's chambers and heard her whisper: "The hand of God is heavy upon me."

For a moment I was seized with the ridiculous notion of springing to the platform and interceding on her behalf, but common sense prevailed and, unwilling any longer to watch the painful scene, I turned away from her and worked my way slowly toward the rear of the crowd. There on its edge I came face to face with Rowena Bloss.

"So, Squire, you feel pity for the girl."

Her gray eyes looked straight into mine.

"I regret her humiliation, ma'am, yes."

"Humph!" the widow snorted. "These people thrive on humiliation. Offer me your arm, young man, and I will show you things worthy of your pity."

She led me toward the high ground of the camp. We passed within several rods of the African tents that were isolated from the rest at a remote part of the clearing, and I observed a tall, thick-set black man perched on a stump, surrounded by a huge sable congregation who attended with wide eyes and gaping mouths to the Word. Some wiped their eyes, many shouted, others grinned. I could hear snatches of the sermon:

"Deble fadder ob lies—he be liar from beginning. . . . Some say poor nigger hab no shoule. Vel dat I don't know, but dis I know. I got somethin' in my body make me feel tumfortable." Here he clapped his hands vehemently against his great chest. The others began to clap their hands and yell, drowning out the big man's voice and we pressed on, but I was left with the impression that I had just heard the only preaching in that place which contained even a modicum of sense.

Our destination was the "preachers' tent" under a mammoth pine where another "pulpit" had been erected by placing planks across four small kegs. From this stage one of the ministers was asking a large group of worshipers gathered before him to kneel in prayer. The configuration of trees and boulders around the tent had forced these people to wedge themselves into a space too small for their number, and they knelt with great difficulty, particularly the young women of whom there were many. The prayer commenced and I began to notice that several of the men took advantage of the cramped quarters by pressing up against the women or jostling them. In time they grew bolder, pinching the girls or grabbing their arms, though these attentions were clearly uninvited and unwanted.

The actions of one impudent young buck near us particularly arrested my notice. While the preacher droned on beseeching this and beseeching that, this fellow increasingly forced himself on a pretty girl kneeling next to him. He progressed from pressing to joggling to pinching and grabbing, and finally he put his arm around her waist and with his free hand performed an act that any male worth a damn has outgrown before his twelfth year—he lifted the rim of her bonnet and peeked under it.

I gripped the collar of his coat and dragged him back, looming over him with my fists clenched. The girl gave me a look of grateful relief. The puppy remained on his knees throughout the interminable beseeching, staring up at me less in fear than in startled amazement. At the prayer's conclusion he scrambled to his feet.

"Sorry, friend," he said. "If I'd known you wanted her I'd have cleared a path. Go on and take her. She's all yours."

That's when I knocked him down.

Widow Bloss steered me toward one of the larger tents in the middle of the compound from which emitted low groans as if someone were in great distress. I threw back the flap and discovered a young woman reclining on the straw in a languishing attitude and apparently quite helpless. I recognized her as the girl who had almost been crushed under the wagon wheels that morning, but her aspect had altered radically. Then I had thought her pretty, but her bloom had vanished, and her haggard look and tangled hair gave her the appearance of an escapee from a madhouse. Three young men sat beside her chafing her arms and rubbing her belly in a show of attempting to revive her. The widow rushed forward with a compassionate cry, saying, "My poor child, how do you fare? Have you no mother at home to care for you?"

She knelt beside the girl, feeling her forehead and grasping her wrist to determine her pulse, and the girl, slowly opening her eyes, turned a look of such scorn and rage upon the matron that the poor woman recoiled. The girl then exchanged a leer with the young men and all four burst out in mocking laughter.

I stepped forward quickly, assisted Mrs. Bloss to her feet, and led her from the tent. The canvas flap snapped shut behind us. I continued to support her until we were out of earshot of the laughter.

She was still shaking, a fact which she herself remarked. "One would think I was a New Lebanon Quaker." She smiled. "Oh, Squire, I'm afraid I'm growing senile. For a moment I imagined that unfortunate child was my poor Alice, and how could she be with Alice gone these seven years?"

"You must let me see you to your inn," I said.

"No, no, my friends and I have engaged a wagon. I came here to learn if the rumors of these meetings are true and I have seen quite enough. I shall not come back, but you—" She took my arm. "*You* must return, at least for one evening. There are evils here you have yet to discover." She paused. "You are a good man, Squire Randolph, better, I think, than you yet realize. A young woman senses such things; an old woman knows them. And there *is* a young woman." It was an assertion, not a question.

We began to walk toward the entrance to the grounds. It was a while before she spoke again. "Love and cherish her, Squire, and you will have happiness in this life and a place in the heaven in which you do not believe. That is sixty years worth of wisdom and the only payment I can give you for your kindness to us at Bristol."

We had reached the wagons. The Widow Bloss took my hands between her own. "There is an old superstition that the devil appears only in darkness." Her voice suddenly lowered. "It is said," she whispered, "that Avery preaches tonight."

🍃 16

The Slain

I found the Reverend Clapp at the Inn and, over supper,
I obtained the affidavit that had brought me to Thompson. I
might have retired early, slept while the rioters were at their
sacred revels in the forest, risen when the cock crowed, and
ridden to catch the steamer from New Haven. That would have
been a rational plan, but some irresistible force drew me back
to the camp-meeting.

The path through the wood was even more congested and
treacherous than before. Were it not for the lanterns that hung
from the liquor stalls and the wagons, and were carried by
some of the pilgrims, the increasing darkness would have made
passage impossible. As I rode I had the strange sense that I
was on my way, not to a Christian service, but to one of those
witches' Sabbats so vividly described in the trial records of the
Salem delusion of 1692 when worship of Lucifer was thought
to have occurred in the minister's own pasture and the devil
himself was said to deliver the sermon.

But I was mistaken. The Puritans' Satan conducted his rites
in a sound, orderly fashion. What I was about to experience
was Bedlam and Babel—a religious exercise for which the
only parallel in nature is spontaneous combustion.

I reined in at the barriers and gazed over the vast area of
the compound in wonder. The sun had all but set and fires
blazed before the tents of God's legions. Torches soaked in
whale oil burned everywhere, propped up in barrels or thrust
into the ground. The city of white tents gleamed in the reflected
glow of the artificial light. The mass had swelled to at least
thrice the number of daytime faithful. They moved about in
front of the fires, fantastic dark shadows against the red flames,
many of them in various stages of intoxication. Such must have
appeared the armies of Joshua on the night before Jericho's
walls fell. But the walls that encompassed us, or rather the
thick, lofty pines that towered around the clearing, still per-

ceptible in silhouette against the deep blue of the late evening sky—these walls seemed sturdy enough to me.

It was evident that the Methodists were solidly determined to battle the forces of evil to the last drop of whale oil and new rum.

I determined not to separate myself from my horse for reasons of personal safety and led him around the circumference of the camp until we attained high ground from which I could observe the plain and its throng. Everywhere was hubbub and confusion, which only increased with each new preacher who mounted the stand. The platform was illuminated by flambeaux, and the speakers, though inaudible to me at the rear of the compound, were clearly visible, ranting, to my ear, dumbly and wildly, grotesquely gesticulating.

It is a strange, haunting experience to watch a scene being played in such deafening clamor that the tumult begins to seem as silence and the actors to move in pantomime. So the Methodist meeting presented itself to me. Hearing everything, I heard nothing. I concentrated all my energy on my optical perceptions. I saw the ministers strutting and flinging their arms about. I saw the faithful leap up as if shot and then tumble to the earth and grovel in the dust. I saw the gamblers at the outskirts of the crowd raise crooked arms and shake their hands. In my mind's ear I could hear the dice rattle in the cup.

Then—it must have been very late—as I stretched out on the grass near sleep, the racket abruptly stopped. I wakened from semiconsciousness unsure whether I had just been dreaming or was dreaming now. Raising myself on one elbow, I peered down at the preacher's stand. There on the podium, garbed in black, erect and awesome, with a Bible in his right hand and an unsheathed sword in his left, stood the unmistakable figure of Ephraim K. Avery.

His mere appearance had stunned the great mob into silence. I sat up, crossing my ankles and wrapping my arms around my knees, and strained to hear him. But I had no need to strain. His magnificent voice reached every remote area of the camp, reverberating off the rocks and the pines. He spoke of the glories of heaven and the horrors of hell. He spoke of "taking the Kingdom of God by force!" He warned them that the fate of their immortal souls was in their hands alone.

"The Calvinists would have you believe that your doom is preordained by God—that God has determined whether you are to be saved or damned *before you are even born!* But I tell you—nay Scripture tells you—*it is not thus!* God has given

84

to you the greatest and the most terrifying gift of all, the gift of freedom of will!

"The Calvinists would have you believe you are born in a state of Natural Depravity!—that your soul is bent unto sin, *only* unto sin, *and that continually*! But I tell you—nay *Scripture* tells you—*it is not thus*!

"Did Adam sin and fall because *God* willed that he do so? The idea is monstrous, brothers and sisters. It is *blasphemous*! Is *God* to be held responsible for the evil which men do?

"Again I say, it is not thus! It was in Adam's power to choose between good and evil and he *chose* to do evil! In his abject fall from grace Adam involved all his progeny. We are *all* liable, vulnerable, susceptible to sin and damnation—myself no less than you, brothers and sisters. But—heed my words unto you—God is not arbitrary! God is merciful! He hath sent His only begotten Son to suffer and be crucified for *our* sins! The Truth and the Light are opened unto you. It is given to you this night to save your souls. Repent your sins! Cast out the demons within you by the power of Jesus! Repent! Repent!"

The mob was spellbound. That Avery was not interrupted by choruses of Amens! was not a sign of indifference but a tribute to the respect, the awe in which they held him. I drew my knees up to my chin and observed him with fascination. I had heard terror preaching many times but this was terror preaching with a unique twist—first he gave them hell and then he gave them hope. With the studied cynicism that youth invariably substitutes for sophistication and wisdom, I easily dismissed him as a faker and a charlatan, but I was curious as to what effect his impassioned sermon would have on the multitude.

He began to enumerate, one by one, the sins that they were required to repent. He spewed out a litany of crimes and, at each one, twenty or more of his gigantic audience began to bellow their guilt and fall down, rolling about like hogs in the mud and pleading for mercy. When he came to the subject of lechery, I thought that half the female population of the place would never let off screaming.

In the next moment a young woman—the same who had been caught shoplifting—flew through the crowd, flailing her arms and shouting, "There are grapes here and they are good! Heavenly times! Heavenly times!" She halted within a few feet of me and commenced to rotate her torso, slowly at first and then faster and faster, bending at the waist, until she was whirling like a dervish, her long hair streaming at right angles from her head while she cried in anguish, "God, I'm willing! I will own my Savior! I will! I will!"

The torches cast a ghastly light on her tormented features and the lunatics near us began to howl and clap their hands or slap open palms against their breasts and thighs. I stared at her gyrations in a state bordering on hypnogenesis. She screamed, "Lord, I want to die! I'm ready to die and fit to die! Lord! I want to die this night!" Of a sudden she stopped twisting and froze in a silent trance, her head thrown back, her eyes rolled up so that only the whites were visible, while the chanted chorus of the faithful rose to a crescendo—and then from her ashen lips there issued a guttural moan that increased in volume as it altered into a piercing shriek of horror and despair, such a sound as may be duplicated only in the surgery when the cruel blade of the healer slices into the living flesh—and then she collapsed in a torpid stupor and lay insensible, wriggling worm-like on the ground.

I leaped up, fearing she might be near death, but others reached her before me. They raised her and bore her into a large tent, one of them assuring me that she was "slain" and a great many were slain there every night. I followed them into the tent and found myself in the innermost ring of the circle that formed around the straw on which they placed her. An old woman informed me that the girl had just "come to," by which I gathered she had passed through some process of sanctification and was now in ecstasy, her soul "united with Jesus."

The meeting people were singing a hymn that came near to drowning out the renewed screams of the slain. As the hymn ended several of the women moved forward to pray over the girl. "Come, Lord Jesus, come quickly!" Their cries were echoed from every corner of the tent. "God, come down here! Jesus, come this minute! We want you tonight! We want you *now*!"

These unseemly demands having been urged upon the multiple personalities of their Deity, the remnant of "good people" paused to catch their breath while one young girl pleaded for "the crumbs which fall from our Master's table." Another immediately responded, "Give us not only crumbs but loaves, good God!" This sentiment delighted the inmates of the tent, and soon it was filled with boisterous clapping and deafening Amens! The dust being kicked up from the straw was suffocating. Many, particularly the young men, now tumbled about, violently proclaiming their willingness to accept the Holy Ghost and die on the spot. "I'm full!" they bellowed. "I'm running over! I'm eating heavenly manna! Glory, hallelujah!"

86

It was nothing short of Pandemonium. I felt a desperate need to escape. The entrance was completely wedged with faces, one above the other. The clamor had reached a hysterical pitch, which I could compare only with the thunderous rattle of the power looms in the cotton mill, when the red sea of faces at the entrance parted and the figure of Ephraim Avery loomed against the flames of the torches.

Within moments the faithful fell silent, with the exception of the afflicted girl on the straw who continued to writhe and call aloud for all three persons of her trinity at once. Avery moved solemnly, majestically through the horde of true believers until he stood above her prostrate form. He frowned darkly while she cringed submissively at his feet. Then he stretched out long, pale fingers to her without bending his body.

"Arise, Maria, and leave this place," he intoned.

She gaped up at him, her expression a mixture of terror and sneering mockery. "I would sooner take the devil's hand than yours, Ephraim."

But he only repeated, "Arise, Maria. You have defiled this holy ground and debased yourself. Our Lord is not impressed by your fell antics, my child. Arise and be instructed. 'Let the woman learn in silence with all subjection.'"

"You dare—" Her eyes blazed. She spat out the words. "You *dare* to quote Scripture to me! You hypocrite! 'Thou shalt not commit adultery.' *There* is Scripture enough for the likes of you to chew on!"

She sprang to her feet and fled from the tent while he gazed after her with inexpressible sadness.

17

The Ordeal of Amy Wrenn

Though I deeply regret the necessity of doing so, I must now relate an episode which was at once the most shameful and the most terrifying of my then young life.

Amy and I had kept the secret of our engagement for three months, and our few meetings when we were allowed to be alone had become increasingly painful for me. Though I felt a deeper affection for her than for any other girl I'd known, the notion of marriage and the wonderful zeal with which she pursued it quite unnerved me. I began to invent excuses for evading Charlotte's little suppers and theater parties, and fled for relief from my conflicting emotions to the posh, gaudy decadence of Mother Gallagher's "hotel," where a man could tell the most outrageous lies with the comforting knowledge that the girl never believed a word he said.

Was it love I felt or only infatuation? And even if love, was love an adequate excuse for marriage?

The winter of 1832 came early to New York. On an evening in early November a terrific storm was unleashed on the city, pelting her with hailstones the size of a man's fist before settling into a drenching downpour. Howling winds swirled madly and the deluge came at you from all directions at once—no precaution save remaining indoors was proof against being soaked through to the skin. Willingly would I have sat before my hearth with a toddy and my copy of Fielding's *Tom Jones*, but business had taken me out of the town for several weeks and I was strangely resolved to see Amy again. I braved the primeval elements and, unable to find a cab, I walked the many blocks to her grandmother's home on upper Broadway.

The housekeeper admitted me and immediately announced that Miss Amy was not at home but that Miss Charlotte was in the library and "perhaps" would consent to an audience. Her manner was chilly and distant, and she vanished immediately, leaving me to wonder at this odd reception in a house where I was always a welcome guest. I speculated uneasily on what errand could be so urgent as to call Amy away on such a miserable night and without her cousin's guardianship.

In the midst of these disturbing reflections the servant reappeared, ushered me to the library in silence, and closed the door behind me.

Charlotte stood at the mantel before the fire, her back to me, her shoulders squared rigidly. I remained at the door, dripping from the surtout which no one had offered to take from me, unsure whether or not to speak. The room's atmosphere was as forboding as the city air had been that afternoon just before the furious storm broke. Long moments passed in intolerable tension. It was as if an invisible but impenetrable wall had been erected between us. I felt a growing dread, and at last I blurted out, "Charlotte, where is Amy?"

She did not turn and when she answered her voice was low and her tone caustic.

"Do not speak her name."

"Is she in danger, Charlotte? I have the right to know."

"You have no rights, Mr. Randolph, where my cousin is concerned."

Something was terribly wrong. I was becoming desperate. "For God's sake, tell me what has happened!" I gave vent to my worst fear. "Is she dead?"

"She is dead," Charlotte returned, "to you. I have sent her away."

"Where? You *must* tell me. Damnation, Charlotte, I love her!"

"Love?" She spun to face me. "You *love* her?" she echoed mockingly. "Your love has debased her, shamed her, ruined her! You lecherous young fool! *She is carrying your child!*"

"Oh my God," I breathed, "no!"

"You have betrayed my trust and destroyed the girl," she said in a furious whisper. "I count myself to blame. I, no less than she, was deceived by your soft, handsome features and charmed by your boyish air of innocence. I thought you a harmless puppy but your faithless heart pumps the lascivious blood of the old goat who sired you."

She took a step toward me. "You seduced her as your father

89

sought to seduce me, with endearing lies and false pledges of devotion, and I——" She paused, then added bitterly, "I, who was so careful of my own honor, have failed totally to protect the honor of the child whose trusting parents placed her in my care."

I shook my head in disbelief. "My God, Charlotte, my father *loved* you! He told me so many times. He would have married you if you had not turned away from him. Now I understand . . ."

I stared at her livid face and cold, angry eyes. "Tell me where Amy has gone, Charlotte. It is not yet too late. I will make her my wife."

"That," she hissed, "you would never do! I told the girl so. You young rakes never marry your whores. She is damaged goods, Mr. Randolph. She is spoiled meat! Is a young gentleman such as yourself, on the brink of a brilliant career, likely to risk his prospects by tying himself to a fallen woman? I think not, sir. I have made up my mind that you shall never see her again."

"It is not your decision to make," I said. "It is a matter between Amy and myself. How dare you interfere!" I crossed the room and seized her by the shoulders. "Do you want Amy to become a frozen, bloodless spinster like you? Damn it, Charlotte, is this your revenge for rejecting my father's love and destroying your own happiness?"

She tore herself free and stood trembling with rage. "You insolent whelp! By what right do you lay violent hands on me in my own house? I demand you leave here at once! You shall never find the girl. Never!"

I had an overpowering urge to strike her. I had almost raised my hand when the door behind me burst open and Quinncannon entered. Rivulets of water ran down the folds of his cloak onto the carpet. He leaned on his walking stick and glanced quickly from Charlotte to me through narrowed eyes before addressing me. "So," he said grimly, "you know."

"That Amy has conceived my child, yes. But not where Charlotte has sent her. She refuses to tell me."

"You are wasting breath and time, lad," he answered. "This woman has no idea of the girl's whereabouts."

"That is a lie, sir," Charlotte snapped. "I gave my cousin money for passage to a remote village in New England where we have friends. There she can birth the child with a minimum of scandal and pass her days in the seclusion that her circumstances require."

The Irishman glared at her beneath knotted brows. "Hold your tongue, hypocrite! You drag the girl to hear Fanny Wright champion free love and bastardy, and when she turns to you for help you revert to squeamish respectability and cast her out on the streets in the teeth of a brutal storm."

Charlotte returned the glare. "I will not be insulted under my own roof," she said grandly. "I have provided for all the girl's needs. This evening she boarded a steamer for Boston."

"You will be insulted, madam, when and where I please. This evening Amy came to my rooms."

"To *your* rooms!" She was thunderstruck.

"Where was she to go, madam, after you failed her? She feared to go to Squire Randolph."

"But," I cried, "*why*, Lon? She knows that I would marry her."

"That, Christy, is what she feared. This woman told her you would not marry her because it would blast your prospects, but the lass is in terror that you *would* marry her and thereby, as she supposes, destroy your career."

"That is utter nonsense," I said.

"So I informed her, but she refused to believe me. Her mind has been poisoned by this woman's absurd prejudices." He put his hand on my shoulder. "She loves you deeply, Christy. So deeply that she is determined to sacrifice herself rather than hurt you."

"But it is I who have hurt *her*!" Something in his eyes alerted me to a horrible possibility that I lacked courage to contemplate.

"I was not at home when she came," he said. "She sat for almost an hour in sopping wet clothes before I returned. She was shivering violently and her mind was distracted. I immediately ordered my housekeeper to change the girl's dress and place her in my bed and I went for a doctor, leaving the houseboy to watch outside my door." He shook his head. "I should have stayed with her but I was reluctant to send the boy out in the storm. While I was gone she persuaded the lad to find her a hansom. He overheard her give her destination to the driver."

Charlotte asked the question I was powerless to ask. "Is she alive or dead?" Her voice quivered with alarm.

"Not dead yet, I think, madam," Quinncannon responded, "though she may be soon unless we act quickly. And if she dies you may count yourself her murderer."

"I?" She flared defensively. "In this entire, sordid affair I am the only one who has acted properly!"

91

"Think you so, Miss Prescott?" He raised one eyebrow and I watched his look of withering scorn soften into pity. "Yes," he said, "I see that you do. You mistake love for submission and loneliness for independence—you rail against injustice, but you forget, madam, that nature requires us to be either men or women and, resenting the former and denying the latter, you are self-neutered. I would sympathize, Miss Prescott, if I had the inclination and the leisure."

He turned to me. "Get hold of yourself, Christy. The address the girl gave the hackman was the hospital of Madame Restell."

18

The House Built on Baby Skulls

The hansom thundered down Broadway and careened into Rector toward Greenwich. The storm raged on, a harsh, gusting wind dashing stinging sheets of rain into my face. My mind whirled with terror for Amy's life and horror at what I had done to her. I formed a dozen plans of action, the most rational of which was to tear Restell's hospital to pieces with my bare hands.

The driver stopped so abruptly that the cab almost capsized. I threw open the swing-gate and grabbed the side-lamp in the act of leaping to the cobblestones and sprinting toward the infamous mansion, a turreted, bay-windowed monstrosity that loomed up, a grim black shadow against the bleak, moonless sky—but Quinncannon seized my shoulder and pulled me back into the hansom.

"Don't do anything stupid, lad." His manner was icy calm.

"My God, Lon!" I cried. "She may already be dead!"

"You've considered that, have you? And if she is, have you a wish to join her?" His voice became a savage whisper. "Listen to me, Christy. We are about to deal with the Queen of Hell on her own turf. The moment we cross her threshold our danger is as great as your lady's. These people fear nothing. They are professional killers. They murder for a living and with impunity—do you comprehend me, lad? They murder with the implicit consent and protection of the authorities. We are outnumbered five to one. If we fail to keep our heads clear, we will both be dead before the rain stops."

If he was trying to frighten me he succeeded. "What *do* we do?"

"We walk up to the door and knock as though we were delivering the milk. Once inside your task is to find the girl and remove her from the premises as speedily as convenient. My role is to hold Medusa and her minions at bay." He tapped

93

on the ceiling with his walking stick and the driver opened the trap.

"Gabriel," he said, "stop here until my friend's return. He will have a lady with him. Drive them at once to the American Hotel. Their accommodations have been arranged. Under no circumstances wait for me."

"Yes, sir," the hackman shouted over the wind.

"Have you your pistol?" Quinncannon asked, and I nodded rapidly.

"Keep it in your pocket but use it if you have to. And, Christy, be warned. You will see things in that house beyond all abomination and loathing."

And Amy was in that chamber of horrors! And *my* careless, selfish folly was responsible for her peril! I could gratefully have exchanged my life for hers.

"Do you grasp my meaning, Christy?"

Though I did not—how could I have anticipated?—I said I did, and in the eerie glow of the side-lamp through the driving, drenching streaks of rain I watched the incredible Irishman smile. I half-believed he was enjoying himself.

"Good," he said quietly. "Then let us cross the Styx that is currently roaring down this gutter and pay our respects to Persephone."

He swung down from the hansom and strode toward the house, and at the door he rapped loudly with the head of his cane until the portal swung back heavily on iron hinges.

The man who opened it was gargantuan, hulking and misshapen. He was nearly seven feet in height and weighed over 250 pounds. His waist, hips and legs, garbed in old-fashioned leather breeches, were remarkably slim and even graceful, but his chest and shoulders were bulky and broad and atop them sat a massive, ugly, shaggy head without a hint of a neck to connect him up. His right eye was covered with a bluish, glutinous film. His flat nose had been often broken and appeared squashed, not against but right into his face. His jaw jutted well out beyond his upper lip, and from it two or three blackened teeth arose. Though his left arm and hand were thick and powerful, his right arm was puny from a disuse explainable by the scarred stump of a wrist that terminated it.

"Good evening, Gorgan," Quinncannon said pleasantly. "I trust the lady of the house is at home."

With a snarl the gargoyle sought to slam the door but the Irishman wedged his cane against the jamb and put his shoulder to it, shoving it back and stepping inside. I quickly followed him, my hand in my pocket already closed around my gun.

Quinncannon performed the amenities. "Gorgan, this is Squire Randolph. Gorgan is an old acquaintance, Christy, for whom I have done a legal favor or two in the past as—" The brogue lowered. "—as I'm certain he remembers."

The giant grunted. I thought he must be a mute or an idiot.

"Gorgan is Portuguese by birth," Quinncannon continued, "and originally a whaler by profession, but he turned his hand, so to speak, to picking pockets, and had it lopped off in some Mediterranean capital for that offense. It was in Lima, I believe, that his tongue was cut out for some unspeakable crime." He smiled at the monster. "At least Gorgan never speaks of it."

I could hold my own tongue no longer. "For God's sake, Lon! We *must* find her!"

"Slowly, lad, slowly." He addressed the doorkeeper. "Gorgan, I will see your mistress at once." He withdrew a calling card and thrust it into the titan's huge hand, and, after some hesitation, Gorgan vanished into the darkness.

Several minutes passed. My fear for Amy grew beyond endurance—my patience was exhausted. My fingers tightened on the pistol.

"Take your hand, *gradually*, out of your pocket," Quinncannon said, under his breath. "We're being watched and there's a gun aimed at the base of your skull. The girl's alive."

My heart jumped and I extracted my hand with deliberate slowness. "How do you know she's alive?" I at last whispered.

"Were she not," he replied in a normal conversational tone, "you and I would now be dead. We must not underestimate Madame Restell, Christy. She knows which of her patients we have come to collect. I expect she has also calculated the annoyance that our untimely disappearance might cost her personally, not to mention the disruption of her business and resultant loss of revenue, or—" He glanced suddenly up into the shadowy dimness of a staircase at the left of the entry. "—or am I wrong, Madame?"

The voice which answered was throaty, almost masculine. "Your powers of logic I have always found unerring, Mr. Quinncannon."

I became suddenly aware of others—massive, chimerical, deformed shapes that shuffled heavy shoes and cocked pistol-hammers in the gloom around me. Every muscle in my body was as taut as a watch spring.

"There is," Quinncannon said, "a young woman under your

95

roof of whose charge we wish to relieve you. It is a simple matter. Merely direct my friend to her, madam, and, providing she is unharmed, we will leave your household to its slumbers, or whatever."

"The girl is here of her own free will," Restell replied, "and unless I'm much mistaken, that young buck beside you is the ardent stripling whose unbridled desire drove her to seek my aid. I'm obliged to you, Mr. Quinncannon, for bringing him to me. Now that I've seen what fine specimens they both are, I'm inclined to let her carry to term."

Quinncannon smiled. "How's Charlie, Annie?"

"My husband is dead," came the cold voice from the landing.

"Is he now?" The smile widened. "Well, I'm sorry to hear it, but not surprised. Just last week I remarked to my old friend Jacob Hays, the High Constable, that I feared Charlie Lohman wasn't long for this world. The fatal symptoms were obvious."

Ever so slowly she emerged from the shadows and began to descend the stairs. "What are you saying? There *were* no symptoms. Charlie died unexpectedly of food poisoning."

"No, darlin', Charlie died on cue of ratsbane. However, it's not his medical symptoms but his financial ones I'm speaking of." Quinncannon leaned casually against the street door and risked reaching for his pipe and pouch. "As I understand it, your husband used the profits from his patent medicines to purchase several lots on upper Broadway between Broome and Spring. On this property he erected an office building and warehouse by mortgaging the land with the Mutual Life Insurance Company for $27,000. Now, during one of your numerous separations you acquired the mortgage without his knowledge, and shortly thereafter you loaned him $100,000 in cash to build flats on an adjacent lot. Your two mortgages now totaled $127,000 on properties valued at nearly $500,000."

He touched a match to his pipe. "Obviously," he resumed between puffs, "only Charlie's life stood between you and a promising career in real estate. And *that*, Annie, is when I began to suspect that your husband's medical prognosis was dire."

I could see Restell plainly now, near the bottom of the staircase, her bulk wrapped tightly in a purple silk dressing gown, her little red eyes gleaming from a swinish face devoid of cosmetic pretensions. She was hideous.

"And you have, I suppose," she said in a mocking tone, "a

letter containing these allegations addressed to the district attorney to be mailed in the event of your disappearance."

"Better than that, darlin'. I have a letter for Charlie's relatives in Prussia. I shouldn't be at all surprised if they wanted the body exhumed." Again he smiled. "And all we ask in return for silence is Miss Amy Wrenn, alive and well." His eyes became slits and the brogue grew menacing. "*Alive and well*, dear heart, or there'll be hell to pay!"

There was a long pause.

Then Restell moved aside and I bolted up the stairs.

The second floor was a labyrinth of hidden rooms, concealed passages, trap doors, false walls and ceilings, rooms without doors. Rooms were not entered from a central corridor but off one another, unconnected by hallways or logic, like a maze in a nightmare. Each apartment contained six or seven beds with two, even three young women to a bed. Some were dimly illuminated by whale-oil lamps—others were not lit at all, and many seemed to have no windows. I stumbled over chamber pots and worse. Twice large rats scurried between my feet, almost tripping me. The stench of urine and vomit was overpowering.

At last I found a room from which there was no exit except by the door through which I had entered. Before I could spin around I felt a heavy blow across the back of my head. Then the floor opened under me and I was falling.

I was on some sort of chute, sliding rapidly, helplessly into pitch darkness. Then I found myself lying on a cold stone floor. Though there was no light, the air was dank and close, and muffled sounds of scurrying alerted me to the presence of rats. Evidently I was now in the cellar of the building.

I thought of Amy. Quinncannon had concluded she was alive because he and I had not been killed, but now it seemed certain that I was marked for death. She must have been alive when we arrived, for Restell had spoken of letting her carry the child.

The child! *My* child. For the first time I fully comprehended that I was trying to save, not one life, but two. No, three, for my own was surely in peril.

I thought of Quinncannon. I knew he'd had no time to prepare a letter for Charles Lohman's relations in Prussia, if there *were* any relations in Prussia. Had Restell penetrated his bluff? The attempt on my life suggested that she had. If I was to be killed, then obviously he was also. He might already be dead. The damn Irishman didn't even have a gun.

I groped for my own pistol and found it in my pocket. The

97

hopelessness of my situation pressed upon me. I had no clear notion of where I was in that convoluted jumble of apartments and dungeons. Nor did I know how to reach my friends. If Quinncannon still lived he must, by now, have realized Restell's lethal intentions. Could I look to him for aid, or was his position as desolate as my own? Circumstanced as I was, I could form no plan of escape—had it not been for my pistol I'd have been completely at the mercy of my captors—and in any case I could not leave the house until I had determined the fates of my friend and of Amy and my child.

The idea struck me with painful intensity. Restell had had no intention of murdering Amy. Had I, by my blundering attempt to rescue her, doomed us all?

I became aware of a noise, screeching, grating, as if a rasp were being drawn across a rock. It grew louder and more urgent, and simultaneously a shaft of bright light appeared from ceiling to floor in the wall before me. I sprang to my feet. The lighted area widened steadily. I discovered that the cell into which I had fallen was no larger than a closet. The grinding noise redoubled, accompanied now by the clank of chains and pullies. The stone wall was being moved aside by some huge mechanical device.

The chamber thus revealed was brilliantly illuminated by gas jets burning without glass lamps. It contained a pot-bellied stove, two or three chairs, and several wooden casks. Beyond that I could not yet see, my view being obstructed by the wall that suddenly arrested and then reversed its motion, threatening again to imprison me. I ran for the opening and slipped through just before it slammed thunderously.

The whole of the chamber's interior was now visible. I confine myself to describing it. Let the reader imagine my horror.

To my left stood a dissecting table and a massive oven-cremator beside which were placed at least a dozen full scuttles of coal and a cord of wood. From the wall near the table hung surgical tools, gleaming in the glow of the gas flames. Before me was a large double-sink of cast-iron adjoining a wooden platform on which a water-pump had been mounted. Next to the sink was a chest lined with teabark such as is used to preserve human organs in the teaching-hospitals.

Two underground, metal-lined vats or pits lay to my right, one containing quicklime, the other acid. The wall on my right was decorated, not with surgical instruments but with the knives and cleavers common to the butcher's trade. Directly beneath

98

this hardware stood a crude operating table furnished with the leather straps used to confine patients during the agony of surgery.

Strapped to this table and covered only by a sheet lay Amy Wrenn.

She cried out my name. I was already feverishly untangling the knots in the thongs. I remember asking if they had harmed her and my inexpressible relief at her answer. I managed to free her ankles. She was crying. I think I was crying too, but I'm not certain. I was trying to untie one of her wrists. She was saying something—I was vaguely aware of that—but I couldn't hear her—the knots were too tight—and then I realized I could cut her loose with one of the knives and I reached for it but I didn't take it because she screamed and I whirled around and there stood the gargoyle, Gorgan.

He seemed to have materialized through the wall. He swayed slowly, his knees slightly bent as though his legs contained coiled springs. He wore a butcher's apron that numerous launderings had failed to cleanse of blood stains. Saliva dripped from his lantern jaw onto his apron bib. In his hand he clutched a cleaver.

At my back Amy whispered, "Christy! *She* was here when you came. She laughed. She said this table was for me and the dissecting table for you. They mean to murder you."

One of her wrists was still tied to the table. I kept my eyes on the giant and took out my gun. I said, "Is there a way out of here?"

"There's a panel behind him. The catch is somewhere near the sink. I've watched her work it."

"I'm going to try to cut you free," I said, keeping the pistol aimed at Gorgan's chest. "When I do, get out as fast as you can. *Don't wait for me*." I was moving toward the knife rack. "Quinncannon is upstairs. He'll help you if he can, but don't search for him. There's a cab waiting in front of the house. The driver has his instructions. Do you understand, Amy?"

Before she could answer the monster lunged. I fired the gun and he staggered back a step. I seized a knife and severed the last strap that bound Amy, and then he lunged again and again I fired; still he kept coming and I pulled the trigger a third time but the gun misfired and he was almost on top of me when I spun away and dropped into a crouch.

Gorgan grinned at me, a contorted, ugly leer, and once more he lumbered toward me. Somehow I had lost the pistol. I grasped the knife and waited for him. There was fresh blood on his apron. My weapon was in my left hand and I anticipated he would attack me from my right. When he did I dodged him, slashing upward as I leaped so that my blade cut into his withered arm, and, with a bestial growl, the massive troll wheeled and, with upraised cleaver, hurled his bulk at me in maddened fury. I stepped aside to evade his charge and he fell headlong into the pit of acid.

I dropped the knife and stood heaving for breath. Amy rushed into my arms, and I held her, hardly daring to believe she was still alive.

"Christy, you're all right? You're not hurt?"

I threw off my surtout and wrapped it around her. "Hush, Amy, we're not safe yet."

I found my gun and retrieved the knife before searching for the catch that released the sliding panel. With her hand in mine we slipped into the passageway and up the staircase that terminated it. At the door above I motioned her behind me and slowly turned the knob.

We were standing in the vestibule fronting the street door. Scattered about on the carpet were the prostrate forms of three men trussed up, lying face down. A fourth sprawled nearby, his hands untied. It required only a brief glance to determine the reason why restraint was unnecessary.

Madame Restell stood erect in one corner of the lobby, scowling, her fat arms folded. Behind her in a posh, velvet-upholstered chair, sat Quinncannon.

The Irishman smiled at me. "Well, well, Christy, so you and your lady have finally arrived and here it is the shank of the evening and the party almost over."

I pocketed my weapons and took Amy's hand before stepping forward. I could see that Quinncannon was resting the tip of a long, slender steel blade against the small of Restell's back. For the first time I realized that he carried a sword-cane.

"We had," I said, "a small party of our own downstairs."

His voice was somber. "I cannot tell you, lad, how pleased I am to have my conviction of your resourcefulness and courage again confirmed." He met my eye for a long moment. Then he added in a light brogue, "Now, take Miss Wrenn and get the hell out of here."

"Is the hackman still waiting?" I asked.

"He's waiting. He's paid by the hour."

At the street door I paused. "Are you coming?"

He raised an eyebrow and shook his head. "No, no, little brother. Mrs. Lohman and I have much to discuss regarding

100

her interesting business practices and her Prussian in-laws . . ." Again he smiled at me. "I may have to audit the books. I might be here for a month. But I'm sure Mrs. Lohman could provide me with a bed, or at least a table, couldn't you, Annie, darlin'?"

Restell froze. I put my arm around Amy's shoulder and felt her trembling. All at once I sensed that there were others around us, unseen in the darkness, watching. I understood the risk Quinncannon was taking.

"Lon," I said, "take good care of yourself. The district attorney and the high constable will be concerned over your welfare."

"Christy," he replied, "I am deeply touched by your interest in my affairs, but—" He glared at me and his tone was harsh. "I strongly advise you to take the girl and *go!*"

I threw open the door. The side-lamps of the hansom glowed in the gloom of the rain-swept street. I grasped Amy's wrist and we fled together into the night.

BOOK II

Murder in Tiverton

The Lady Vanishes

"I know she's gone, damn it! Gone where is the question."
The desk clerk shot me a look of pettish annoyance. "I'm sure I have no notion, sir. I came on duty this morning just before she checked out of her room. Miss Wrenn did not seem altogether well. The lady who called for her said that the gentleman with them was a doctor and Miss Wrenn was in his care. Miss Wrenn appeared to be under sedation. The other lady insisted on paying for Miss Wrenn's room although I explained that Mr. Quinncannon had settled with the hotel in advance." He sighed deeply and wiped his upper lip with his handkerchief. "It was all really quite trying."

I read again the note from Quinncannon and strode into the dining room of the American. The Irishman sat alone at a corner table near a window. He put down his coffee cup and pushed a small envelope toward me.

"That is a ticket on the noon steamer to Providence, Christy, if you wish to follow her."

I stared at him. He buttered a piece of toast and answered my unphrased questions. "I anticipated Charlotte would spirit the girl away while you slept and set my hackman to stand watch, lad. He actually drove them to the pier this morning before dawn, learned their destination, and purchased that ticket. You have," he added, consulting his watch, "very little time to pack."

"Lon," I said, "at first it was just a challenge. I've told you how we met. I thought she was teasing me. I said . . . I said whatever she wanted to hear, whatever was needed to get her to—It was a *game* to me, Lon. Every time it's always a game, but last night when I saw her strapped to that table in that hell, I realized—"

He put his hand on my arm. "I know, lad, and I'm not the one you should be saying this to."

"But how can I find her now?" Suddenly I was angry with him. "You *knew* this could happen. Why didn't you stop it?"

"How?" he asked quietly. "The girl is a minor and Charlotte Prescott is her guardian. Are you suggesting I should have kidnapped her?"

I picked up the steamboat ticket. "I have to find her, Lon. I must marry her as soon as possible. I know Charlotte will do whatever she can to prevent it but she has no right. Amy's carrying my . . . our child, damn it, and I—"

I stopped abruptly and then surrendered the supreme confession. "Oh, damnation! Lon, I love the girl."

"The steamer," he replied, "sails for Providence at noon."

❦ 20 ─────────────────────

Pursuit

I may pass briefly over the events of the six or seven weeks that followed my interview with Quinncannon, as there were very few events to recount and those few were both painful and frustrating. I followed Amy and Charlotte to Providence and traced them to Newport, less by any detection of mine than from the obvious assumption that Charlotte would require papers and bank draughts that she could obtain only in our old home town. As they traveled by stage while I was on horseback, I gained some time and arrived at the Prescott house scant hours after their departure.

The housekeeper, Mrs. Brummell, regarded me soulfully. "Oh, Mr. Christy, Miss Charlotte *was* furious. She did say the most dreadful things against you. Indeed, I haven't seen her so taken up in anger since . . . well, since your father died, sir. My goodness, how that man could rile her!"

The old woman produced a folded sheet of foolscap. The note, in Amy's delicate hand, informed me that I had betrayed and ruined her and that she never again wished to so much as lay eyes on me.

"You see where the ink is smeared, sir," said Mrs. Brummell. "That's where the poor girl wept as she wrote it. Indeed, it was Miss Charlotte told her the words to write."

I nodded. "Mrs. Brummell, you must tell me where Miss Charlotte has taken her!"

"Indeed, sir, I cannot. Miss Charlotte made me swear not to tell, though it hardly matters."

"You will not tell me?"

She wrung her apron in her reddened hands. "Indeed, Mr. Christy, I don't know."

Charlotte was well known in Newport and I had little difficulty in learning she had hired a coach for Bristol. From Bristol she and Amy had sailed for Boston, to which city I followed them and lost three days before discovering they had doubled back to New York. When I debarked at South Street I was five days behind them and a return to the home of Amy's grandmother taught me only that Charlotte had ordered all their trunks packed and had disappeared. Though I checked every steamship line and every departing clipper, I could not pick up the trail and at last, in desperation, I went to see Quinncannon.

"Gone," said his landlady. "Gone this day a week, and where he is is known only to himself and his God, if the man has one. The man arrives and departs like a shadow on a partly cloudy day. I keep a fire laid and a bottle on the dry sink but no more a candle burning in the window. It's a waste of tallow." She peered at me. "You're Mr. Randolph?"

I nodded.

"Then he's left a letter for you."

I tore open the wax seal.

12 November, 1832

My dear Randolph,

If you are reading this you have lost all hope of locating Miss Wrenn. Give up the chase. Close down your New York office and reopen your father's practice in Newport. There, it may be, your lady may come to you.

A premonition is on me, little brother. My crystal ball begins to clear.

Q

And, strange as it seems to me even now, so great was my trust in the Irishman that I followed his instructions to the letter.

I shuttered my quarters in Reade Street and shipped my law books and meager possessions to Newport, where I used the last of my savings to rent my father's old law offices. The back room was furnished for sleeping and in the front room I received my few clients, the same petty thieves, drunkards and wife-beaters who had once been defended by my father. Among them I became known as Squire Chris. Their fees, when paid at all, were settled with poultry or vegetables or home-made pickles and preserves. My creditors, who at first tolerated my defaults for the sake of their old friendships with my father, began to grow restive.

There is nothing like poverty to cure a man of vice. I gave up liquor and then tobacco. I even thought seriously of selling my horse.

21

Lathrop Waterfield's Orders

On Tuesday, December 18, I got a case in Bristol. Charlie Woods, who kept a fancy store, was accused of receiving stolen goods. He was guilty, as usual, and, as usual, I got him acquitted, but the trial dragged on until well past sundown. It was too late and too cold, and I was too tired to ride back to Newport. When I finally left the court house I turned toward the Bristol Hotel, intent on a late supper and an early retirement. I had not walked a block when a huge black man, dressed in livery, stepped out of the shadows and confronted me.

Instinctively I probed my pocket for my pistol and found I had forgotten it.

"Are you Squire Randolph?" the black man asked in a voice part thunder, part gravel.

"I am."

He indicated a coupé at the curb. "You are," he said, "to ride with me, sir."

My eyes traveled slowly upward until they met the black man's own. He was at least a foot taller, and fifty pounds heavier, than I was. "Suppose I choose not to ride with you, my friend?" I said.

"That, sir," he rumbled, "would disappoint the lady."

He pulled open the door of the carriage. Inside Amy sat, looking at me and smiling. I ran to the coupé and jumped up. "Darling, have they hurt you?"

"Of course not, Christy," she answered.

The carriage door slammed shut behind me and seconds later we began to move.

She watched me with growing alarm. "Christy," she said, "didn't you send for this coach?"

I shook my head slowly.

"Oh my God," she breathed.

My first thought was that rumors of her pregnancy had gotten

109

abroad. It was not unheard of for ad hoc committees of vigilance, whipped into a frenzy of self-righteousness by their wives and sisters, to seize a woman suspected of immoral conduct and drag her to an isolated place where the rawhide was applied to flail the "devil" out of her. Usually the victim was a poor farm girl or a black, but not always. A year before, a gentlewoman from Warren had been kidnapped, stripped to the waist, and severely flogged while her lover was forced to watch. When he attempted to intervene, he had been strung up by his wrists and lashed almost to death.

My mind raced. I was not armed. I cast my eyes around the interior of the coach and found nothing that could be used as a weapon. Jumping from the coupé was impossible. Though I could have made it, Amy could not, especially in her condition. Even as I dismissed the idea the coach gathered speed rapidly. We had cleared the Bristol limits. Once in the countryside we might reach our destination in minutes. Then I would be facing a mob. For the moment I had only the black to deal with. Formidable as he was, he was only one man. If I could get outside the coach and swing myself up behind him, I stood a chance of knocking him off the box before he could set to defend himself. It was our only hope.

I wrenched the door open. It flew back against the wind. Grasping the roof with both hands, I threw one boot up and hooked it under the box. He began to turn his head. I yanked up the other leg, hooked that boot, dislodged the first and began to kick at him savagely. I caught him in the shoulder before he could raise his whip and he lurched over but did not fall out. His hands went limp and the horse began to run, free and in terror. I pulled myself up beside the huge African and grasped the reins at the same moment I saw something metallic flash in the glow of the side-lamp. I struck him across the face as hard as I could and grabbed the pistol as he slumped back. The horse was still running at top speed and the heavy carriage careened insanely down the narrow road.

Bracing both feet against the dash, I pulled on the reins using all of my weight. There was no point in shouting commands. The horse couldn't hear me and would not have obeyed if he could. It was a question of how long it would take before the pain in his mouth became more acute than his fear. When I sensed him slowing I shifted one foot to the brake and applied it gradually, and at last we stopped.

The African was stirring and I aimed the pistol squarely between his eyes. We were both gasping for breath. I cocked

110

the hammer. Then I motioned him to get down and called to Amy. She called back in a thin, frightened voice. I heard her descending from the coach.

"Amy, are you all right?"

"I'm not hurt," she answered, "but, oh, Christy, you're bleeding!"

"I am feeling splendid," I said, keeping the gun trained on the sable giant who now stood on the ground below me.

"Be easy with that pistol, Squire Randolph," he said. "I can see you are a dangerous man with or without a gun, but you do not want to shoot me. I am not a bad fellow, you know." He grinned in the gleam of the side-lamp. "The man did not tell me I would be risking my life tonight."

"What man?" I asked sharply.

"The man who hired my coach, sir. He gave orders to bring the lady and you out here."

I scanned the countryside. We were, I knew, somewhere north of Bristol, but I could see no sign of the torchlight of a vigilante mob. The only hint of human life was a tiny dot of light at least a mile distant, probably a lantern hung outside a farm house.

"Out where?" I demanded.

"Out there, Squire." He pointed a long finger toward the pinpoint of light. "That's where Judge Elkins lives."

I vaguely remembered Leopold Elkins from my childhood. He had been justice of the peace in Bristol fifteen years before. If he was alive he was nearly ninety. *If* he was alive.

The Negro was reaching into his pocket. I kept both my voice and my pistol level. "Slowly, my large friend. What is the object of your search?"

"I have a letter, sir, which the man told me to deliver to you outside the court house. Had I remembered to do so," and again he grinned, "we might now be better friends."

He extracted the note carefully and handed it up. I told him to step back five paces and passed the paper to Amy. She held it under the coach lantern, broke the wax seal and read it aloud.

Christy,

This will introduce Mr. Lathrop Waterfield whose services are at your disposal. He is engaged to drive you and Mistress Wrenn to the home of Justice Leopold Elkins where, should you desire to marry, you will find Mr. Elkins prepared and empowered to perform the ceremony, and hopefully sober.

111

Mr. Elkins has an upper room which is available this evening. Mr. Waterfield will transport you back to Bristol in the morning.

My respects to Mrs. Randolph.

Q

I gauged Justice Elkins' age, charitably, at ninety. He was a frail, stooped little man with a few wisps of white hair and baby-pink skin here and there blotched with brown. With a Bible in one hand and a pint bottle in the other, he greeted us unsteadily in his shirtsleeves with a toothless smile and squinted at us behind spectacles thicker than window glass. Lathrop Waterfield presented him with the necessary legal papers, which I noted had been signed by Quinncannon as an "attorney-at-law." This seemed to convince the justice that Amy was to marry the African. In fact he was quite vehement on the point and it required a quarter hour to dissuade him.

Even then he found several reasons to delay the ceremony. First he insisted he could not properly discharge his duty without his teeth. Their installation proved a complicated but fascinating operation. Next he, with some difficulty, managed to communicate his conviction that the marriage would somehow not be legal unless he was wearing his coat. Eventually the garment was located under the sofa cushions. Waterfield got one sleeve on while I struggled with the other and, at the instant I achieved success, the old gentleman twisted round in such a way that his arm came out of the first sleeve and yanked it inside out. After several minutes we were able to get the coat on the justice, though it was now completely inside out. He seemed satisfied, notwithstanding his concern that he could not find his pockets, and his vague suspicion that we had somehow absconded with them.

Now he busied himself in searching for his "readin' specs," rummaging among the fifteen or so pairs on his table, trying them each several times until he settled on one pair which, as far as I could determine, were merely empty frames. These he adjusted for a period, shoving them up and down his nose and peeping lenslessly at his scripture until he had them precariously but satisfactorily positioned, at which point he announced himself ready to proceed and then, discovering that we were short a witness, he declared his intention to summon "Mother."

I braced myself, trying to imagine what his mother would look like, but "Mother" turned out to be a term of endearment for his wife, an ancient lady at least a head taller than her

112

husband, with more hair on her upper lip and chin than he had on his scalp, if not his entire body. She toddled out from the kitchen, managing to appear simultaneously mammoth and fragile. Evidently she had been working on her own pint bottle, twin to the one that the justice had been steadily killing and from which he now took a final pull.

"Mother" swayed behind Amy. Lathrop Waterfield stepped up beside me. The justice endeavored to face us, though he was spinning in a manner reminiscent of a weathercock in a shifting wind. In the end, as I later reflected, he seemed to include all portions of the ceremony, though not necessarily in the prescribed order.

"Who giv—giveth this woman to be married to this man?"

As an answer was clearly required and no one else was disposed to speak, I said, "I do."

"Where's the ring, lad?"

Of course I had no ring. It struck me suddenly that, without one, the justice might refuse to continue. Then I felt a huge hand on my shoulder. The black extended a beautiful gold ring and grinned.

"I'm instructed to say, Squire, that this is a wedding gift to you and the lady."

I took it and placed it on Amy's finger. I wasn't even surprised when it fit perfectly.

"Kiss the bride!" the justice commanded.

I shrugged, took Amy in my arms, and kissed her, rather more passionately than I had planned.

The justice was squinting at his book through empty rims and obviously displeased. At last he muttered, "Damn things are filthy," and threw away the frames. Immediately he brightened. "Don't need 'em anyway," he told himself. "Still got the eyes of a boy."

He looked up, holding the book at arm's length. I observed it was upside down. Then the old gentleman cleared his throat and began.

"Bearly deloved..."

When we had closed the door of the Elkins' upper room behind us Amy broke into bright, uncontrollable laughter. She removed her bonnet and lay back on the bed, still laughing with happiness and relief, and looking up at me with shining eyes until, gradually, her laughter subsided into a warm smile. "Oh, Christy, don't look so sour."

"It was hardly the sort of wedding a boy and girl dream of, my dear."

"Oh, darling, it was priceless!" she cried. "Anybody can have a stuffy, formal wedding in a stuffy, formal church with a herd of stuffy, formal relatives who have to get drunk to forget how much they hate each other. Christy, every girl wants her wedding to be special, to be one she will never forget and ours . . ." She began to laugh again. ". . . ours was so . . . *unique*. That marvelous, funny, tipsy old man with his coat on inside out—do you know he ordered you to kiss me *five times* during the ceremony?"

Her laughter grew. "And that wonderful old lady, absolutely reeking of gin! She stood so close to me I thought I would faint away. She must weigh two hundred pounds, yet I believe she would have been felled by the breeze from a bird's wing. And, darling, the look on your face when Mr. Waterfield handed you the ring—!"

She stopped suddenly. "Oh, Christy, you didn't mind that I . . . ?"

I knew what she meant. After the interminable ceremony the African had momentarily considered giving me his hand and decided against it before I realized the cause of his embarrassment. He had then bowed to Amy and discreetly backed away, but she had smiled and said, "You have been a good and faithful friend, Mr. Waterfield." She'd extended her hand and, when he'd taken it, drawn him closer and offered him her cheek. It was a gentle, gracious gesture, and, as I looked at the concern in her eyes, the last of my bad temper melted. I sat on the bed and took her face between my hands. "Hush, Amy. Of course I didn't mind."

I bent down and kissed her softly, again and again and again, and then, as she sat up against the pillows, I rolled a half turn and rested my head on her lap. She kissed my eyelids and gently tousled my hair. "You were, you know, quite magnificent this evening," she said.

"I behaved like a fool."

"No, darling," she said. "We both thought of the same thing: the terrible flogging of that poor woman in Warren a year ago. I remember the report in the Boston papers. You really are a wild, ungovernable man. I'm afraid I'll never tame you." She kissed me again and whispered, "At least I hope not."

I smiled. She began to massage my temples.

"Christy, did you look closely at the marriage papers?"

"I saw that Quinncannon executed them."

"Did you see the date? It's September."

Suddenly she gave a little start. "Christy," she said softly, "I felt the baby kick."

"Dear heart, the baby is too small to kick."

"The baby definitely kicked," she responded with mock sternness. "A mother knows these things. Do you want to argue the point?"

I was trying to work one boot off with the other. "No, little mother. I'd rather lose immediately than eventually. I'll save my strength."

"He's going to be beautiful, just like his father."

"He?" I looked up at her. "It's going to be a boy, is it?"

"Don't you dare call your son an 'it,'" she scolded.

"And it's going to look just like me, is it?"

"Exactly like you."

"Not going to favor you at all, I understand."

"Not a bit," she said firmly.

"Unfortunate child."

I got one boot off and started on the second. She continued to rub my temples, occasionally running her hands back through my hair and then smoothing it forward over my forehead. I felt myself settling into a drowsy fog and tried to sit up but without success.

"Relax, Christy. You're exhausted."

"Hell," I growled. "I'm just getting my second wind, Mrs. Randolph. In a minute I'm going to spring to my feet and get ... this ... god ... damned ... boot ... off! Then I'm going to rip off all my clothes. Then I'm going to rip off all your clothes. And then, madam—tremble and thrill in anticipation!—we're going to make Antony and Cleopatra look like two school children playing behind the outhouse."

"Shhh, Squire Chris. Lie still and shut up."

"Damn it, Amy. On their wedding night a man and his wife are supposed to make love."

She leaned over and pressed her lips against mine. "My gallant husband," she whispered, "we *are* making love."

It was the last thing I remember until morning.

🦢 22 ———————————————

The Night Rider

The next morning, December 20, Amy and I returned
to Bristol in Lathrop Waterfield's coach. I recall many questions
preying on my mind. What had been Charlotte's and Amy's
movements since they left the hotel on the morning after the
ugly episode at Madame Restell's hospital? How had Quinncannon traced them? How had he managed to separate Amy
from Charlotte and where was Charlotte now? For that matter,
where was the Irishman?

With none of these questions could Amy help me. She slept
throughout the journey, her head resting on my shoulder, and
when we reached Bristol I directed Waterfield to the house of
Rowena Bloss.

"Are you married?" the widow asked sharply.

"Yes, ma'am," I responded, "but my wife is four months
pregnant and I have no decent place to take her nor anyone to
care for her while I'm away. If you will do for her I'll gladly
pay whatever is required, ma'am."

"Humf," said the widow, looking past my shoulder at Amy
in the carriage. "You cannot afford what I would charge you,
Squire."

"But ma'am," I began, and she interrupted me.

"Therefore, I shall take her in and you shall pay only for
the doctor and the medication, which will doubtless be suffi-
ciently extortionate." She glared at me. "Well, young man,
fetch the girl inside."

I had two cases in Bristol and another the following day in Fall
River. My intention was to spend the night at Lawton's Inn,
midway between the two towns, but the second Bristol case
ran late. I saddled my horse, the Traveler, rode hard for the
last run of the Bristol Ferry, and missed it.

Billy Pearce was unhitching the horses when I reined in at
his dock. He was a strapping, likable youth of eighteen who

116

ran the ferry when his father was on a binge, which is to say approximately seven days per week. Billy looked dolefully at me, dolefully at the bleak shale-gray sky, dolefully at the two elderly nags he was again hitching on the treadmill that powered the paddle wheel. "There's a wicked wind blowin' up off Hog Island, Squire Chris," he shouted. "Wouldn't cross again for nobody but you."

I led Traveler onto the deck and drew my surtout tighter against the biting wind. The angry waters slapped the ferry's sides with foamy curds. Billy cast off. "No sense puttin' up canvas in this weather. It's up to the horses and it'll be slow goin'." He brought a switch down lightly on the animals' rumps. I watched the beasts lumbering, patient, impassive, and thought that one day, not far off, they would drop in their traces and be found hanging by the halters round their necks. A treadmill is an unjust sentence for any of God's creatures.

I turned my eyes from those wretched bond-servants to my own horse. The Traveler had no large affection for ferries. Forced to stand still, he had, I suspect, no sense of making progress. Great gusts of steam exploded from his flaring nostrils. He stamped the rotting deck impatiently, and raised and shook his noble head in the salt spray. The east wind blew wildly through his thick mane.

I am an American, by birth and breeding a democrat and an egalitarian. Never would I incline my head before kings or emperors. But no man with a soul can fail to feel humbled in the presence of equine aristocracy.

"Pa'd want to be remembered to you, Squire Chris," Billy Pearce bellowed over the rising wind. "Him and Ma's still obliged to ye for getting him out of that assault charge."

"Really?" I shouted back. "It was your ma that brought the charge."

"Yeah, well, I figure she thought better of it when the swelling went down."

"How *is* your pa, Billy?"

"Oh," the youth hollered, "not so good, sir. He's off on another spree."

"Spree" was the word respectable New England country folk used for delirium tremens.

"It ain't like he don't try to change, Squire Chris. He joined up with the Temperance people. Went to all the meetings. When they got to fightin' over whether beer and wine was spiritous liquors, Pa was right in the thick of it. Made a great speech all about how Jesus turned water into wine." He paused. "Anyway it would've been a great speech if he hadn't passed out in the middle of it."

"I heard, Billy, he was going to join the Methodists."

"He tried that, Squire. Went up to the Meeting House in Bristol. Reverend Avery, he says to Pa, 'You got to confess all your sins. Make a clean breast, Brother, and your soul will be all washed white and Jesus will love you.'"

He fell silent. I waited for a reasonable interval. "What happened?"

Billy shrugged. "Pa confessed all his sins and Reverend Avery threw him out."

He tried to grin but it didn't work. I shouted, "Sorry, Billy."

"Well, sir, I figure Ma's happy over it. She says the only reason Pa went after gospel was so he could go to them Methodist camp-meetings." He addressed me as one man of the world to another. "You know what goes on in *them* places!"

I said, "I've heard rumors."

We landed at the Portsmouth wharf just after dark. There was now a heavy cloud cover, and a dense fog was rolling in ponderously off the choppy water. I did not envy Billy Pearce the return crossing and said so.

"We'll be all right, sir," he answered cheerfully. "Me and the girls..." he patted one of the old mares affectionately "...we could cross blindfolded."

Lights glowed from the windows of the four houses that huddled near the pier. From the closest, that of Jeremiah Gifford, who ran the ferry from the Portsmouth side, came the eerie screech of the whale-oil lamp that swung in the wind on a rusted hook above his door. It served as a beacon to guide Gifford home when he was caught on the water after dark. Tonight it was not lit. These industrious, enduring people were sparing with whale oil, as with everything. The cold lamp was a sign, a stubborn assertion, that Jeremiah Gifford would not cross to Bristol again until sunrise.

The lone light in the Gifford house flickered from the small kitchen at the rear. Though it could not have been much past six o'clock, the supper was finished, the dishes put away, the evening ritual of reading aloud from the Scripture almost over, and soon the family would be asleep in snug little beds in stuffy little rooms whose windows were tightly latched against the hundreds of dread diseases supposed to permeate the night air.

They slept but did they dream? Doubtless the younger ones

118

did. The older ones were too exhausted to dream. They merely slept, a state of existence a half-step closer to death than what they endured awake. Perhaps, at odd moments, while the plow horse was being rested, while the boiling of the pot was awaited, they tried to remember the dreams of their youth and could not, except for a dim recollection that they had not dreamed of Portsmouth. They were born in Portsmouth, raised in Portsmouth. They married, had children, labored, worshipped, died and were buried in Portsmouth. Surely they must once have dreamed of London or Paris or New York or Boston. . . .

The Traveler lifted his head and snorted. A fast, hard ride was the second greatest pleasure either of us could experience. I sprang up into the saddle. He wanted to run and I gave him his head. We tore across the island as if there were a fat purse waiting for us in Tiverton. Faster, and yet faster we flew. I yanked off my cap and let the wind whip through my hair and opened my mouth and gulped in the cool night air and several dozen dread diseases.

The night was pitch black and I could not even see the horse's nose, much less the treacherous road, and, yet, suddenly, my mind cleared and I had the sensation of rushing, deliberately, uncontrollably, fatally, toward some elusive something, wonderful, sinister, interesting—already prefigured—as yet undefined.

The flying horse crested the last hill. A mile ahead the lamp above the door of George Lawton's tavern glowed like a distant star. We raced down the hill and gradually I could make out the Stone Bridge spanning the watery gap between the island and the mainland. In an instant I debated stopping at the toll house on the Portsmouth side and rejected the notion. Old Peleg Cranston, the toll keeper, was probably in bed. My toll was paid by the month in any case, and there was no lamp visible at Cranston's door, as there had been none at Jeremiah Gifford's. The only light in my corner of the universe was burning in Tiverton.

The Traveler, running wildly and with no restraint from me, thundered toward the bridge at a speed which threatened both our lives. I dropped the reins and leaned forward, grasping the horse's mane in the way I had not done since I was a child. Now he was truly free, without rein or curb or bit. I was both in control and out of it. I clung to him and felt the power of his muscles, felt his strength and noble soul flow into mine.

We reached the bridge and I watched his hooves strike sparks from the cobblestones. At that moment there seemed to be nothing I could not achieve, nothing beyond my reach.

The feeling was magnificent.

🐚 23

Lawton's Tavern

George Lawton, a pot-bellied, balding man in his late forties, lighted me to my room with the genial, slightly patronizing air of the born innkeeper. The accommodations he offered, however, were not his best.

"There is another guest staying the night, Squire Randolph," he said by way of insincere apology, "who arrived anterior to you, sir. I believe he is also a member of the legal profession. He *is*," the host added with a bit of a Yankee sneer, "a Paddy. But, nonetheless, gentry. He paid in advance."

Even had I not seen his gray stallion in the stable, I would have known that Lawton was referring to Quinncannon.

Having bathed and dressed for supper, I descended the stairs and stood at the threshold of the vacant taproom. Though the tavern had thrice burned to the ground, the taproom had each time been spared and appeared much as it had in Revolutionary days. Oaken walls and beams still were scorched by flames that had burned on another cold, bitter night more than half a century ago. Three round tables, attended by comfortable captain's chairs of New England maple, sat before a roaring fire in the massive stone hearth.

The past and the present came together in that room. The huge grandfather's clock, looming in one corner, had stopped before my conscious memory. Someone had removed the hands and the clock's face, thus uncovered, gazed over that congenial room, presiding in benevolent, chimeless silence.

Gardiner Coit entered through the door behind the bar, fresh from currying my horse and still smelling of the stable. He was a good-natured fellow, just two years my junior, with an easy grin and an infectious laugh. He wore the leather apron that served him in his varied capacities as barkeeper, hostler and man-of-all-work.

121

"Evening again, Squire Chris. Can I offer you something to take off the chill?"

I nodded, smiling. The man was as warm and pleasant as the room. "Seem's like it's been a slow evening, Gardiner."

Coit produced a wipecloth and a grin. "Well, sir, there's the Irish gentleman."

I nodded. "Mr. Quinncannon."

"Yes, sir. A fine gentleman. He paid me handsomely to care for his horse. Then he ordered a hot bath and a bottle of Irish whiskey. And, 'Landlord,' he says to George, 'It's been a long dry day and I plan to get thoroughly wet inside and out.'"

He laughed and poured my Scotch. "I'm not finished in the kitchen, Squire Chris. Help yourself to what you want."

I remained at the bar, mulling the events of the previous evening and formulating a dozen questions for Quinncannon when he should come down for his dinner.

Then a voice at my back inquired, "And how is Mrs. Randolph, Squire?"

The man moved with the stealth of a cat. He was seated at the table nearest the fire. It struck me that he always sat with his back to the wall.

"Mrs. Randolph wishes to thank you for your wedding gift."

"Gift?"

"The gold ring," I explained.

"That," he said, "is a gift from Charlie Woods, a receiver of stolen goods whose acquittals you routinely obtain. A token of his esteem and affection." He regarded me with perfect seriousness. "Why should I give you a gift? You didn't even invite me to the wedding."

I took a chair. "How the devil did you trace them, Lon? I nearly went mad trying. The faster I pursued them, the more distance Charlotte put between us."

"That is because you were following them, lad. Charlotte knew where she was headed and you did not. Whereas I simply determined her destination and went straightway to await her."

He filled his glass and answered the question he read in my eyes. "Recall, Christy, the night we paid our respects to Restell, that Charlotte thought she had sent the girl to friends in a remote New England village. In this part of your country the word 'friends' invariably means—"

"Family," I finished.

"It was not difficult to learn that the only Prescotts fitting that description were two maiden aunts in a tiny Vermont town."

"But how did you get Charlotte to agree to our marriage?"

122

A wicked gleam in his eye made me say, "You didn't kidnap her?"

Quinncannon smiled. "Your nuptials occurred with Charlotte's blessing."

I shook my head. "I believe you can work miracles, Lon. The woman's heart is frigid enough to freeze gin. Imagine! That bitter, vengeful virgin!"

"She certainly was," he said quietly.

"Was?" I echoed, and the Irishman smiled again.

"Little brother," he said, "for you I have made the ultimate sacrifice."

Murder in Tiverton

*Quinncannon and I had supper together, and the fol-*lowing morning, as we both had business in Fall River, we rode north toward the Massachusetts line. Near nine o'clock, within half a mile of the line, we suddenly heard a loud cry of alarm. We reined in and listened, and again the cry came, the agitated shout of a man, echoing in the chilling wind that gusted east off Mount Hope Bay. Quinncannon turned his horse toward the east, urging the big gray up the hill, and I followed him and pulled up short beside him at the crest.

Before us neat, stone-fenced lots, white houses, red barns and out-buildings, immaculate brown fields divided by trim rows of birch and maple, all spread out and down to the slate-blue waters of the bay. The harvest was long over and great stacks of hay, some three stories high, dotted the landscape, gathered and stored against the approaching winter. The stacks sat beneath birch-branch awnings resting on lofty maple poles and surrounded by stout fences to insulate them from the cattle that lowed beside them, lingering over an occasional salt lick or grazing optimistically on the brown, matted grass.

The largest of these haystacks was directly before us, no more than thirty rods distant. Ten rods to the north of the stack a team of draft horses stood quietly before a wagon. Further north, perhaps fifty rods, lay the nearest farm house, partially hidden from view by a corn crib and small orchard. Two men were running toward a third who seemed almost to dance within the fenced circle of the stack yard, frantically waving his arms, still shouting. Beside him, dangling by a halter from one of the fence posts, hung the corpse of a woman.

We rode down the slope to the stack yard, dismounting seconds before the two runners reached the shouting man.

I knew all three. They were Durfees and we were on Durfee land. The eldest was Richard, the patriarch, a gnarled, sinewy old farmer of almost eighty, a man unenlightened by any education and so hardened by grinding labor that his physical strength had outlasted his mental capacity by twenty years. The second running man was the oldest son, Williams, a ruddy, bulging man of fifty-five who carried, and felt, the full weight of his years and his belly. He fell against the fence, gasping, glaring at his younger brother.

John Durfee, the offspring of his father's old age and fourth wife, was perhaps thirty-three, tall, strapping, vigorous—the bulwark of the Durfee Agricultural Enterprises and the pro-verbial apple of the old man's half-blind eye. Other Durfee boys had drifted away, or fled, to the West, to the sea. The daughters who survived the yellow or scarlet fever grew up to marry Bordens, invariably Bordens. Even Williams had run away to New Bedford at fifteen and spent the next two decades on whalers before turning up again on his parent's doorstep. Williams had since buried two wives, but no children, for there were none to bury.

But John had remained at home, overseeing the farm and the herds, marrying Serafin Dison against her family's will, presenting old Richard with five healthy grandsons in seven years. John Durfee was respected, even feared by his neighbors. He was normally a soft-spoken, almost menacing man. At the moment, he was still shouting.

And the dead woman still hung from the stack-yard fence.

Quinncannon had already eased between the rails and stooped beside the body. Springing over the fence, I knelt beside him.

"Will, give me your knife," John ordered his brother. "We must cut her down!"

Williams made no effort to comply.

The body was suspended by a short cord of marlin hemp. The cord was tied to the pole by a slip knot about six inches from its top. She was fully dressed for cold weather, in a cloak fastened nearly the full length, except for one open hook at the middle of her chest. Through the gap in the cloak her left hand partially protruded, fingers extended, palm facing front, as if trying to ward off a blow. The left elbow was close against her side. Both hands were gloved. Her head fell forward and on it she wore, not a plain bonnet, but a calash whose ribbed top was somewhat pushed back. From beneath it long, frowzed, matted black hair overhung her face and concealed it.

"Williams," John Durfee demanded, "your knife!"

"Oh, shut up, man, damn it," Quinncannon growled.

Surprisingly, John obeyed.

The Irishman gently parted the dead woman's hair.

With shuddering horror I recognized her as the shoplifting,

125

exhorting factory girl. Our paths had crossed again for a final, fatal time. I got to my feet and looked down at her, feeling once more the deep pity that had gripped me at the camp-meeting when the Methodists mocked her. She was utterly alone in her miserable death, as alone and friendless as she had been in life.

One of her lips was swollen, her tongue projected slightly, and frozen froth clung to her mouth. The twine, twice encircling her neck, terminated in a knot just hidden by her right ear. The distance between the knot at her ear and the knot on the stack pole was no more than six inches. I noticed that the ribbons of her calash were untied but hung down inside the cords around her throat.

Quinncannon lifted her head under the chin. Her eyes stared lifelessly into mine. Her face was calm, even resigned, and remarkably pale. I reached out to touch her and found her stiff and cold. I glanced at him. "Rigor mortis?"

He nodded, letting her head fall again into a grisly, aimless posture. I took in the area near the body. Her shoes were off her feet and sat, side by side, eighteen inches to her right. Eighteen inches to her left lay a red bandanna handkerchief, wadded and frozen. The hood of her calash was folded back on the right side, so that her cheek rested against the post from which she hung. The ground was hard and showed no sign of either footprints or struggle. The dead girl's knees were bent, her legs drawn straight back beneath her, her dress smoothed back under her legs, her stockinged toes touching the ground and her knees hanging within inches of it.

My first thought had been that she had hung herself. Now I tried to imagine how, and found I could not.

The Irishman was inspecting the knot behind her right ear. Williams Durfee had entered the stack yard and bent, fascinated, over his shoulder. Behind Williams his brother grumbled, "It is sacrilege to let her hang this way."

Quinncannon ignored John but looked up at Williams. "What do you make of it, my friend?"

"Damn me," the stout man breathed, "it's tied in a double hitch!" He paused and amended, "A clove hitch!" and Quinncannon smiled.

"Ah, a man who has followed the sea."

Williams nodded. "Ay, sir, 'tis a sailor's knot all right, and how would a girl like that learn to tie one?"

Quinncannon's deft fingers were busy at the twine. "Look here, Christy. The cord is embedded deeply into the flesh of

126

the neck, half an inch at least, and it is very nearly horizontal around."

He pulled the head away from the fence post and twisted it and I forced myself to look. I could see the twin, parallel, angry scars that ran searingly an inch or more below the right earlobe and even further beneath the clove hitch.

I became aware that other men were running toward the stack yard even as the Irishman eased the head back against the post, and once more parted the hair covering the corpse's face.

"Take a look, Christy. What would you guess her age and occupation?"

For the first time I informed him that I had seen the girl in life. "She was a factory girl in Fall River, Lon. Probably in her late twenties."

He nodded, watching me. "Are you all right?"

I said I was.

The men reached the yard and John Durfee barked out orders. "Allen, there's a dead girl here. Send for Elihu Hicks. Negurs, take my wagon up to Fall River and get word to Colonel Harnden!" His eyes flashed angrily back to Quinncannon. "As a duly elected Town Councilman and Overseer of the Poor, I'm taking charge!"

Quinncannon kept his eyes on me. "Can you estimate the height and weight?"

"Maybe 112 pounds." The post from which she hung was not much over five feet. "Four foot ten or eleven, Lon, at a guess."

He straightened, still apparently oblivious to the angry John Durfee, and addressed Williams. "On shore, my friend, to what use might a double, or clove, hitch be put?"

Williams pondered the question. "After slaughtering a beef creature, sir, we sometimes use such a knot to hang up the quarters."

Quinncannon glanced behind him at the dead girl. "It is easier to imagine her on board ship than slaughtering beef creatures," he said.

John Durfee attacked the knot on the fence post and tried to yank it up and free. The more strenuous his struggle, the more stubborn the slip knot became. The Irishman watched him with amusement for a time, and then handed him his own knife and the farmer angrily sliced through the twine an inch or two from the slip knot. The woman's body fell forward. Quinncannon caught her shoulders seconds before her face

127

would have struck the ground. He laid her on her side and remained kneeling for a moment while his hands probed her abdomen.

When he again stood he smiled slightly at the still bristling John Durfee. "Very well, duly elected Town Councilman and Overseer of the Poor, the unfortunate lady is yours." He swung up onto the gray while I mounted the Traveler and we rode to the base of the hill before stopping.

I said, "What do you think, Lon? Suicide or murder?"

"The girl was carrying a child, Christy."

"Then the husband should be notified." He raised an eyebrow and I realized the foolishness of the remark. "The *father*," I amended.

"Oh," he replied, "I expect there will be a vigorous search for the father."

"At all events, an unwanted, illicit child is an excellent motive for suicide, Lon."

"It is also," he said, "a pretty fair motive for murder."

"All right," I demanded, "which *was* it?"

Without answering he turned the big gray's head northward and galloped away. I rode after him, but more slowly, pondering the tragic fate of that sad and desperate woman.

Who was she? I speak not of her name—that hardly mattered, though I came to learn it was Sarah Maria Cornell—but which of the several personalities I had witnessed came closest to revealing her true self? And what chain of circumstances had led to the calamity in the stack yard?

🜨 25

The Magi

Christmas Eve was a Monday. All celebration of the Savior's birth, however, was banned in the New England of 1832. The holiday was considered a pagan ritual. Holly and ivy were Druidical obscenities. The Christmas fir was no less to be dreaded than the heathen May Pole. The mistletoe was outlawed—the wassail proscribed—the spirit of John Endicott rose up to drive, with scourges and Gospel Truth, the Lord of Misrule from the sacred land.

At sundown I entered my office in Newport and found three distinguished, elderly gentlemen waiting for me. All were dressed in funereal black and enfolded in greatcoats. All were silver-haired and clean-shaven except for great bushes of side-whiskers. At three throats gleamed the hint of white clerical collars. Two of them sat uncomfortably on a high-backed, narrow bench. The third rather lounged in what I called the "client's chair."

I went to the desk and lit the whale-oil lamp that stood beside a half-empty bottle of Scotch. I noticed that one of the gentlemen on the bench was tall and lean and wore bifocals. His companion was short and stout and rested his gloved hands on a brass-handled cane. The third man, in the client's chair, wore, I now saw, a thin, white, whiskery wisp that encircled his strong jaw and grew longest from a furrow separating his chins.

"He is only a boy, Brother Joseph," said the bifocals.

"He drinks spiritous fluids, Brother Samuel," said the brass-handled cane.

Having drawn the shades, I sat down behind the desk and withdrew my pipe and pouch.

"He indulges in the devil's weed, Brother Joseph," said the bifocals.

"He defends the thieves of pigs, Brother Samuel," said the brass-handled cane.

"And successfully, Brothers," said the chin-whiskers. The

corners of his thin lips drew down in an approximation of a smile and he extended his hand across the desk.

"Squire Randolph, allow us to introduce ourselves. This," indicating the bifocals, "is Elder Samuel Drake of Portsmouth. This," indicating the brass-handled cane, "is my brother, Reverend Joseph Merrill, Presiding Methodist Elder of Providence. I am Reverend Abraham Merrill of Lincoln, Massachusetts, empowered to speak and act for the Bishop of Boston."

I accepted chin-whiskers' hand and nodded at each of them in turn. They nodded back to me like three poppets on strings. Brother Abraham's hand, even through his glove, felt clammy.

"He is not of the chosen, Brother Joseph," said the bifocals.

"He is a mere stripling, Brother Samuel," said the brass-handled cane.

"Brethren!" Reverend Abraham spoke sharply and raised his hand with the unquestioned authority of the Bishop of Boston. "Squire Randolph, we are here to engage your services in a legal matter of the greatest delicacy. You have been highly recommended, sir."

I puffed on my pipe and waited.

"Possibly you are aware, sir, of the unfortunate death of a factory girl named Sarah Maria Cornell at Tiverton last Thursday night?"

"Possibly, Reverend."

"The coroner's jury found for suicide, Squire, but, alas, they were not legally constituted and a second jury has found for . . . for murder, I am saddened to say."

I kept my eyes on his and said nothing.

"It is regrettable, Squire, but the dead girl appears, on various occasions, to have managed to get herself admitted to membership in our church, although she was always expelled for actions of the vilest nature."

"Vile actions," muttered Elder Drake.

"Wicked, evil girl," muttered Reverend Joseph.

"The girl has been convicted, in a trial of our church, of falsehood and theft and . . ." he became barely audible " . . . of fornication. Though unwed, sir, it is apparent that, at the time of her death, she was . . . in trouble."

He seemed to expect a response so I nodded.

"The letters, Brother Abraham. We must not forget the letters."

This came from one of the elders on the bench. I didn't bother to notice which one.

130

Abraham Merrill said, "Three letters have been found among her pitiful belongings, one on white paper, one on pink, one on yellow. They appear to have been addressed to her by the man . . ." again he hunted for the delicate phrase ". . . responsible."

"The note, Brother Abraham," a cracking voice prompted from the bench.

"A note was also discovered, written in pencil, at the bottom of her bandbox. Tragically, it has cast suspicion for her death on . . . on one of our most respected and unimpeachable Brothers in the good work."

He slowly extracted a piece of paper from his pocket.

"This," he said, "is a transcription." He pushed it across the desk and I unfolded and read it:

If I should be missing enquire of the Rev Mr Avery of Bristol he will know where I am

> Dec 20th
> S M Cornell

I looked at Merrill. "Dated the day of her death," I observed.

"Most unfortunately, Squire."

"Can the girl's movements on Thursday night be accounted for?"

"We have some notion," Reverend Abraham responded. "She was employed in a Tiverton mill and boarded with a Fall River widow and her daughter. Her work day extended until seven-thirty, but, on the twentieth, she had permission to leave two hours earlier. At the mill she asked directions to a Joseph Durfee's. She took an early supper with her landlady whom she had informed, that morning, of her intention to return from the factory before her time. She changed her cloak and replaced her plain bonnet with a calash. She left the boarding house a little after six, telling the landlady she was going on an errand to Joseph Durfee's and might return at once, but in any case not later than nine."

"But she, in fact, never returned at all."

"She did not, Squire Randolph."

I leaned back and swiveled in my chair. "Well, Reverend Merrill, it should not be difficult. The dead girl was found in Tiverton. Mr. Avery resides in Bristol. The width of Rhode Island—that is, the island itself—yawns between them."

I heard the simultaneous intake of breath from all three of my ordained visitors and instinctively reached for the Scotch.

"Uh," said Elder Abraham, "I am in fear that it may not be that simple. Brother Avery *was* on the island that night. He did not return to Bristol until the next morning."

"On the island?"

"Yes."

"Did he cross the Stone Bridge to the mainland?" I asked in the tone I reserved for cross-examination.

"No. he did not. His purpose in going to Portsmouth was—"

I put up my hand. "I would prefer to hear his purpose from Mr. Avery, himself." I eyed all three of them. "May I assume Mr. Avery has witnesses to his sojourn?"

Elder Drake nodded. "Oh, yes, witnesses. Plenty of witnesses."

Drake's nodding seemed to set Reverend Joseph's head in motion. "Plenty of witnesses," he echoed. "Leave the witnesses to us."

"*And*, young man," Elder Drake added, "there are plenty of witnesses to the dead girl's *abominable* character."

"An army of witnesses," Reverend Joseph agreed. "Just leave the witnesses to us."

"The problem, Squire," Elder Abraham said, "is that a meeting of the Fall River Vigilance Committee was held on the evening of the twenty-second. As a result a warrant was sworn against Brother Avery before Justice Howe of Bristol on Sunday by a Colonel Harnden and a Town Councilman named John Durfee. There has been no arrest, but emotions in Fall River are running alarmingly high. There is to be a hearing in Bristol the day after tomorrow." The old man reached across the desk and put his hand on my wrist. "Brother Avery requires the best legal advice we can provide, despite his obvious innocence. He is both a Methodist minister and a Mason, sir. There are those to whom either one is intolerable, and those to whom both together are anathema."

He tightened his grip on my arm and his voice lowered to a hoarse rasp. "It is said, in Fall River, Brother Avery has already been measured for the noose!"

I waited until he released my arm, then relit my pipe. "You mentioned three letters, gentleman. Do you have copies?"

Elder Abraham appeared glum. "No, they are in the possession of Justice Howe."

"Squire," Joseph Merrill said, "we are prepared to offer you a fee of two hundred dollars."

It had never occurred to me that the entire Methodist estab-

132

lishment was worth two hundred dollars. I gulped hard and swallowed down all my distaste for Methodism and all my bleak, unformed suspicions of Brother Avery and while I was still choking on the whole, indigestible lump, Abraham Merrill said, "Three hundred dollars," and placed the bills on my desk.

They were payable by Mr. Biddle's National Bank.

With the expenses of my marriage and impending fatherhood I was in desperate need of a decent fee.

I slid my hand casually over the greenbacks and said, "Very well, gentlemen. I will ride tomorrow for Bristol and see what can be done."

26

The Physician

On Christmas morning before sunrise I rode north on the turnpike to Portsmouth and turned the Traveler's head in the direction of the Stone Bridge.

Peleg Cranston, the toll keeper, a middle-aged man with a drooping moustache, leaned over the bridge, his elbows resting on the rail. He was whittling lazily on a piece of driftwood. Four fishing lines hung idly down in the shallow water. They had been baited hours before and all four hooks had long since been stripped clean. The fish had moved on. Peleg never rebaited. He had fished off that bridge for years and never caught a thing. It didn't bother him. He never called it "fishin'." He called it "feedin' the fish."

"Mornin', Squire Chris. You hear about the murder?"

"Murder? I heard it was a suicide, Peleg."

He shook his head slowly. "Nope. 'Twas murder, Squire. Little mill girl got herself strangled by the Methodist preacher up at Bristol. There's a hearin' tomorrow and I'm to be a witness." He paused, and added with pride, "Colonel Harnden's sendin' a wagon to fetch me to the court."

"Now, Peleg. What evidence could you give that would be so important?"

"Oh," he answered, "I expect I saw the killer crossin' my bridge between two and half past three in the afternoon. Dressed in black, he was, like a preacher, and he pays his toll and remarks on the cold as he has to go to Fall River. And I says, 'That's a long trek, mister, when a man's on foot.'"

I said, "Did you recognize him?"

"Nooo, Squire Chris. I ain't no Methodist! The wife's a Baptist, but I don't hold it against her. Live and let, I say. But I never seen *him* before."

"Well, Peleg," I said, "it doesn't seem to me your testimony is worth much if they're trying to prove Avery crossed your bridge to Tiverton on the twentieth."

"No, sir," he agreed. "I suspect they want me more for the other I got to say."

"Oh?" I managed to sound casual. "What else do you have to say?"

"Well, Squire Chris, you know how I shut the gate on the bridge at nine o'clock just before I go to bed? Sometimes folks cheat on the toll by getting down on the beach and wadin' through the water to the other side. I always check for tracks the next morning. Now, the morning after the murder, there was a set of footprints comin' up out of the water and across the mud from the Tiverton side. I figure they was Avery's prints, made when he came back from the mainland headin' toward Jeremiah Gifford's place."

"Gifford's?" I repeated. "Do you mean Gifford ferried Avery over to Bristol Thursday night?"

Peleg Cranston pretended to be busy with his fishing lines. After a minute he said, "Not a chance, Squire. Gifford's lamp was out when Avery knocked him up. You know Jeremiah when his lamp is dark. He ain't goin' to cross if the devil were after him. The way Colonel Harnden tells it, Mr. Avery got to Gifford's about half after nine and demands passage to Bristol, and old Jeremiah flat refuses, but he lets the preacher stay the night. Then, come sun up, he ferries Avery over."

So the minister had spent the entire night of the twentieth on the island, and the opposition was preparing to offer evidence that he'd crossed to Tiverton on the afternoon of Cornell's death. Three hundred dollars matched the largest fee I had ever received, but I began to suspect I had sold too cheap.

A quarter mile north of John Durfee's stack yard, just south of the Massachusetts line, stood the cottage of Dr. Thomas Wilbur. The doctor was nearly eighty, but a spry step, a twinkling eye, and a razor-sharp mind were excellent advertisements for his physick. The very model of plain, old-fashioned republican simplicity, he greeted me in his parlor, accepted my card, and smiled. I noted with surprise that he still had his own teeth.

"Ah, Mr. Randolph. I knew your father well." He motioned me to a chair. "You appear to be in robust health."

"My complaint, sir, is not medical but legal," I said. "I am engaged to defend Avery at the Bristol hearing."

"I see." There was an edge on his voice. "Squire Staples

has summoned me to testify for the prosecution, you know. I do not envy you your task, young man."

"Perhaps, sir, you would tell me what you know of the unfortunate girl. I understand she consulted with you prior to her death."

He eased his thin frame into a swivel chair behind his desk and took up a tobacco pouch and a meerschaum pipe. "Unfortunate she was, Mr. Randolph, but no longer a girl. She first came to me on the evening of October 8, with symptoms which made me strongly suspect pregnancy, though at that time I was unsure of the diagnosis. She was in such distress that I ventured to question her, as delicately as possible. I ascertained that she was not married and was employed in one of the cotton mills. She said she had no connections in this area except religious connections—that she was a member of Mr. Bidwell's Methodist Society."

Dr. Wilbur touched a match to his pipe and sucked vigorously, his pale cheeks alternately full and hollowed.

"After my second examination I told her her condition, and I urged her to seek relief of the villain who had preyed upon her. She wept, Mr. Randolph—in fact I seldom saw her with dry cheeks. She said that the man was poor and could not aid her, that he was respected, a married man with children, that she had advised him of her circumstances and he had refused— mind you, he had *refused* to give her assistance."

His voice rose in bitter anger. It was a strong voice with none of the treble of age. "And *then*," he added, "she brought me the oil of tansy!"

I glanced up from my notes. "I'm sorry, Doctor. I am unfamiliar with the drug."

"Most laymen are. It is extracted from the *tanacetum vulgare*—" One eye closed in a wrinkled wink. "That's a plant, Mr. Randolph. It is an ancient tonic, once used as an antihelminthic and stomachic—that is, for deworming and aiding the appetite. Its use now is most rare and always under close supervision."

His brow darkened. "Miss Cornell told me she had met with the man briefly, in the evening at Fall River on the meetinghouse steps. He had given her the drug and advised her to take it to induce miscarriage. Fortunately she consulted with me before ingesting it."

"Fortunately?"

Wilbur's countenance was grim. "The dosage he recom-

136

mended to her was thirty drops. I informed her that five drops would have killed her."

It was not yet noon and, outside, the sun shown brightly, but in the small parlor a cold darkness seemed to have fallen. Though I sat beside the roaring grate, I felt a sudden chill.

"I now demanded of her the name of the man and, after much weeping and gnashing of teeth, and cries of 'I dare not!' she surrendered it. It was . . . Avery!" The old man spat out the name. "I told her she must threaten to publish his identity at once and force him to help her, but she absolutely refused. She appeared to regard him with a mixture of awe and dread and affection that I found incomprehensible. I said she must demand no less than three hundred dollars. 'Yes,' she replied, 'that is the figure which my people suggest.'"

The physician scratched his head. "Her mention of relations surprised me, Mr. Randolph, for I had understood she had no family to whom she could turn. Now I learned that her single intimacy with Avery had occurred at a Methodist camp meeting in Connecticut in August, at a time when she was living in that state with her sister and brother-in-law. She had suspected her condition in September and confided in her relatives. The brother-in-law consulted with his clergyman and an attorney, and advised Miss Cornell *to remove to Fall River* that she might be close to Bristol when she applied for Avery's support."

Something in his tone led me to the question. "Did you find that odd, sir?"

"Decidedly peculiar. I thought, given her circumstances, that her people would have insisted she remain with them. I could not understand why Avery could not as easily be reached from Connecticut, nor why it was necessary for the girl, herself, to deal with him." He leaned across his desk. "You are a lawyer, Mr. Randolph. Are there not, in such cases . . . negotiations? Is it not regular for a male relation, or his attorney, to conduct this sort of unfortunate business?"

"It would be preferable, sir," I responded, "but often the family is too ashamed to face the situation, and, perhaps, too concerned with what the neighbors will say."

"Yes, yes, yes," he nodded, "that explanation crossed my mind. Especially when I learned that her people are *Congregationalists*! All too frequently such people are more concerned with respectability than decency."

I could not forebear thinking of Charlotte Prescott.

He gave me a thin smile. "Forgive me, young man, if I offend you. I have never been a very religious man. I find it rather difficult to be at once a man of science and a man of faith. I suppose I am considered a Quaker—oh, we don't all say 'thee' and 'thou,' my friend. I joined the Society sixty years ago, largely out of the perversity of youth. I was struck by the fact that, when Roger Williams founded this colony waving the banner of religious liberty, he tolerated every lunatic sect . . . except the Quakers." His smile widened. "After all, Mr. Randolph, toleration is all right within reasonable bounds, but a prudent man has to draw the line *some*where."

I returned the old man's smile.

"What angers me, Mr. Randolph, is the advantage Avery took of that sad young woman."

His quiet rage stung me for reasons at which he could not have guessed. What I had done to Amy—was it so different from Avery's seduction of Maria Cornell? Had I been less dishonest?—less lustful?—less hell-bent on satisfying my own desires at her expense?—less careless of consequences? True, Maria was dead and Amy still lived. But she owed her life to Quinncannon's quick thinking, and her near brush with death to my hedonistic selfishness. Had she died under Restell's knife, I would as surely have been her murderer as I now thought Avery was Maria's. And the final irony was that it was I who was to defend Avery!

"Avery's profession is the care of the soul as mine has been the care of the body," Wilbur continued. "In both professions it is possible for men to assume an awesome, god-like power over those who seek their help . . . particularly over young women. These people put their lives into our trust. To violate that trust is past forgiveness."

"We cannot be certain, sir," I said, "that Reverend Avery is guilty of anything. You have only Miss Cornell's unsupported word."

"No, no, my young friend. She never lied to me. She sometimes withheld the truth, but she never lied. I blame myself, Mr. Randolph. When she brought me the oil of tansy I knew he had tried to murder her. I should have forced her to denounce Avery. I should have advised her family, contacted the authorities. Instead I allowed her to silence me with passionate tears and foolish vows of secrecy."

It now occurred to me then that there was at least one other explanation for the oil of tansy. Suppose she had obtained the drug herself. Suppose she had invented the story of Avery's giving it to her and suggesting a lethal dose. After all, she had not taken the poison, despite the power Avery was assumed to

138

have over her. Instead she had come directly to Wilbur. Was it part of a scheme to convince the old man that Avery was the father of her child—that Avery had deliberately attempted her murder?

The physician was a kindly and benevolent old man. Cornell was young enough to be his granddaughter. Had she consciously played on Wilbur's sympathies? I pitied the doctor's galling self-reproach. Like most of his neighbors, he had already cast Avery as the black-hearted villain and Cornell as the innocent—seduced and abandoned.

I ventured, "Possibly, sir, Avery did not understand the properties of oil of tansy. You, yourself, said they would not be known to a layman."

"To the layman, no," Wilbur replied. "But Mr. Avery is not a layman. He spent some years in the study of medicine." He paused. "It was cold-blooded murder, Mr. Randolph."

"Yet the coroner's jury found suicide, sir," I said.

"The *first* jury, on Friday. It wasn't even legal! Coroner Hicks has been a damn fool, man and boy, for eighty years. He would not even allow me to do an autopsy, Mr. Randolph. In fact the dead girl's privacies were kept covered by a napkin during the entire inquest, partially due to the old women's delicacy, but primarily out of Hicks' fear he would faint at the sight."

He spoke with a rising temper that was not directed at me but at Hicks and himself and, principally, at Avery. "It *was* murder, Mr. Randolph. The rope burns were one inch deep and horizontal—the depression was exactly one and one-eighth inch below the tip of each earlobe. All circulation to the head had stopped almost at the second of death. There were no signs of a struggle under her feet on the ground, yet her neck was not broken." He straightened his back and eyed me. "Let me give you a short lesson in medical fact, young man. If she had hung herself, the mark of the cord would have formed an arch, not a perfect circle. Circulation to the head would have somewhat continued at the right side after death, because that is the side at which she was suspended. For the same reason there would be no cord mark on the neck below the knot. When the neck is not broken there is a furious death-struggle, yet we find no such evidence. Her face would be livid and contorted, not pale and composed. *And*, there is the matter of the feces."

His expression became even grimmer. "In cases of sudden strangulation feces are invariably excreted. In this case they were mashed against her back and frozen there."

"Meaning . . . ?"

"Strongly suggesting, with the other factors, that she was murdered while lying on her back and allowed to lie there for some time before being moved. Moreover, there were bruises on her mouth, limbs, side, and abdomen, indicating she had been physically abused. Yesterday, when the body was disinterred and I was permitted to perform an autopsy, Dr. Hooper and I discovered evidence of internal bruises as well, most especially at the lower back and in the area of the privates. We also opened the uterus."

There was a long pause. "And found the child," I prompted.

"It was a female," he said quietly. "I disengaged it from the membrane, but not from the placenta, and held it up before the jury. Hooper and I estimated she was half through the period of gestation. We weighed and measured the foetus and found it to be five ounces and eight inches in length."

Dr. Wilbur glared into his hearth as though he were looking at the flames of hell. "Avery committed *two* murders in that stack yard, Mr. Randolph. Nothing will ever dissuade me from that conviction."

The horse stopped of his own accord before Jeremiah Gifford's ferry dock. Gifford, a sinewy, grizzled man of sixty, was in abnormally good humor. "That killing's sure been good for business, Squire," he shouted as we began the frigid crossing to Bristol. "Colonel Harnden went over about an hour ago with Squire Staples and John Durfee. Them Methodists been buzzing around like flies on a hog. Everybody's asking me questions about Avery's sundry and divers activities on the day the girl was killed."

"What did you tell them, Jeremiah?"

"Only what I know, Squire. I seen Avery get off Billy Pearce's boat on Thursday between two and two-thirty. I recollect 'cause I had a boat aground on Hog Island and I was going over there to dig round her at low water and float her off. Low water on Thursday was 'bout two o'clock."

"Which direction did Avery travel?" I yelled above the wind.

"Well, I don't rightly know. I was just shoving off and keeping busy with the horses. But he came back that night, Squire, 'bout nine-thirty. Got me out o' bed and wanted to cross right then—said there was sickness in his family. I says there are plenty o' doctors in Bristol. I says it's peculiar a man should go wandering when there's illness in his house. He says he's been up the island on business and he's got to get back to Bristol that night. The clock just lacked a quarter to ten. I didn't open the fire and I'm standing there on my bare feet with the wind whistling up my nightshirt and, no, brother, I says. My lamp is out and the weather's too tedious."

I hitched my horse to the rail near the pump and went into the Bristol Hotel. "You're already registered, Squire Chris," said Luther Pincus, the desk clerk. "They're expecting you in the smoking room."

"Who are 'they,' Luther?"

"I don't know, sir. I just came on duty and found the message."

With some curiosity I crossed the lobby and opened the door of the smoking room. To my right Reverend Abraham Merrill stood, his hands folded on his paunch, regarding me with sorrowful eyes of indeterminate color. "Squire Randolph," he said, "it is my sad duty to inform you that you have been dismissed from the defense of Ephraim K. Avery."

27

The Union of Sorry Men

"*All right, Reverend, what is your grievance?*"

He regarded me with exquisite sadness. "Believe me, Squire, I regret with all my soul this heavy burden that has been placed upon my stooping shoulders. I must reiterate, sir, that your services at the hearing of Reverend Ephraim K. Avery are no longer required. It is at the request of Mr. Avery, himself, Squire."

Merrill took a seat in a small chair beside the window, clasping and unclasping long white fingers. "Last evening, when Elder Drake, my brother and myself visited your office, we were taken back by your obvious youth and ... And, to speak openly, Squire, we were somewhat dismayed by your use of tobacco and strong drink. However, because of your professional reputation, we *were* willing to exercise charity toward these failings, serious though they are. My brother, Joseph, even remarked that Paul, in his youth, had been a great sinner and the glory had come to him." He cast his eyes briefly upward. I think he was waiting for someone to say "Amen."

I said, "Go on."

"This morning, Squire, we received some further intelligence concerning your conduct that led us powerfully, albeit reluctantly, to the conviction that you are not—forgive me, sir—you are not *morally* fit to represent our Brother in this sore hour of his trial. I fear a diabolical charge has been brought against you."

I sat down across from the old man, trying to decide whether to laugh or pull his nose. I was grimly determined to be amused. "By all means, Reverend, let us have the coup de grace!" I closed my eyes and tried to picture him in a cap and bells.

"Three sisters of our church," he intoned gravely, "after discussing the matter through the night, and praying long for guidance, were compelled to come to me and communicate that you, while residing in New York, formed an illicit connexion with a young female of the town who is at present carrying your child."

Before he had finished I was on my feet. I stood, almost blind, trembling and swaying in a vertigo of rage. The ugly phrase "female of the town" polluted the air like a rancid stench. "Whore," it whispered. "Whore—whore!"

I said, "For your own safety, sir, I advise you to leave the room at once."

"You cannot intimidate me, Mr. Randolph."

Intimidate, hell! I was ready to kill him.

"Naturally," he went on, "we consulted with Brother Avery. He heard this news with much distress. I can repeat to you his very words. 'I shall pray for the young man, brethren,' he said 'but, alas, I cannot permit a liar and fornicator to speak for me when I stand before the judgment seat.'"

It wasn't the words he was speaking but the fact that he was still talking at all that drove me to take a step toward him. The corners of my mouth tightened. My fists clenched. I took another step.

Then someone laughed. It was the deep, rich laugh of a man who had just found something genuinely, irresistibly funny. It broke my concentration on Merrill's throat, and I turned toward the hearth at the other end of the room. The laugh rose from the high back of a wing chair facing the fire. Rising with it was a thin, spiraling thread of tobacco smoke. When the laugh finally subsided there was a pause. Then a slight brogue said, "'Woe unto you, scribes and Pharisees, hypocrites!'"

Quinncannon stood and regarded Merrill. "Do you recall the text, Pastor? It is attributed, I believe, to one of your folk-heroes."

"It is Matthew, 23:23. You will allow me to remark, Mr. Quinncannon, that I find your evident allusion offensive."

"Brother, I will allow you to remark anything that pleases you." He came forward and relaxed comfortably in the chair I had just vacated, nodding genially to me. "Brother Abraham," he said, "I am saddened that you do not approve of my text for I had planned to preach upon it. However, fear not for behold I shall think of another." His brown eyes narrowed. "Did I understand you to say that Brother Avery disdains liars, Reverend?"

"You did, sir," Merrill replied stiffly.

"Well, that seems odd, Brother, because..." he extracted a notebok from his pocket "... because in 1830 in Saugus, Massachusetts, Mr. Avery conducted from his pulpit such a

143

vicious oral assassination of the character of a fellow clergy-man, one Thomas F. Norris, that Mr. Norris brought suit in civil court for slander and appears to have won. The jury found Avery's remarks 'wanton, malicious, false and unprovoked.' Avery accused Norris of theft, heresy, lying . . . fornication.''

Quinncannon raised an eyebrow. "It does seem Brother Avery has a preoccupation with fornication."

Merrill scowled. "As you are well aware, sir, Mr. Avery appealed that misguided verdict."

"Yes." The Irishman turned to me. "Avery's counsel made a motion in arrest of judgment on a point of special pleading, Christy. An obvious stall."

I was still trying to control my anger. "I suppose the motion was never heard," I said. "What did they do? Settle out of court?"

He nodded. "For one hundred ninety dollars, plus all costs."

So the figure was closer to $350. I wondered where a preacher got hold of that kind of money.

"You forget, sir," said Merrill, "that Mr. Avery was com-pletely absolved by the church's Ecclesiastical Council, and restored to his pulpit."

"I forget nothing, Reverend," Quinncannon responded. "Occasionally I ignore something. I believe you and your brother, Joseph, sat on that council?"

"I begin to find this conversation most unpleasant and dis-tressing," Merrill said. "Since Bishop Hedding has seen fit to put you in control of Mr. Avery's defense . . ."

My eyes shot to Quinncannon. So he was the man who was robbing me of my first important case, of my first decent fee since removing to Newport. It was not Merrill, or even Avery, but this Celtic Casca.

"Now, Reverend," the Irishman said, "I seem to recall that on several occasions you have mentioned Mr. Avery's aversion to fornication."

I lost my temper. "If this topic is again to be discussed, gentlemen, and since I am no longer connected with the case, you will have to excuse me."

Quinncannon raised his hand. "If you will remain for five more minutes, Christy, I would take it as a favor."

I stared at him, then flung my arms out at my sides, slapped my palms against my thighs, exhaled noisily, folded my arms and leaned against the door.

The Irishman returned to Merrill. "I am curious, Brother, since fornication is a basic issue at this hearing. Does Mr.

Avery—does your church as a whole, distinguish different degrees of fornication? Is adultery, for example, more serious than promiscuity?"

The minister regarded him coldly. "All fornication is equally abhorrent. The church considers it as Original Sin."

"Well, of course," Quinncannon said. "Nobody credits that quaint fable about an apple." He lifted an eyebrow. "But what disturbs me, Brother, is that Colonel Harvey Harnden and his vigilance committee have come up with so many witnesses to Mr. Avery's alleged proclivity to . . . Original Sin. Avery's been married for years, yet there's that matter in East Cambridge, and two affairs in Lowell, and, of course, that unfortunate business at the Thompson camp-meeting. And yet you persist in asserting Avery's distaste for the . . . act, and, frankly, Brother, I remain confused."

Merrill got to his feet. "Your confusion is your own problem, sir. You are the bishop's choice, not mine. I shall arrange for you to be assisted by another attorney."

Quinncannon said quietly, "No you won't, Brother. I intend to work with Mr. Randolph."

"Out of the question, sir. Brother Avery must not be defended by a liar and fornicator."

"Brother Avery *is* a liar and a fornicator."

"He is *not* a murderer, sir!"

"If true, that is merely the result of a lack of ambition."

"I must remind you, sir, that I speak for the bishop."

"I believe, Brother, that, at the moment, I speak for the bishop. I am associating myself with Squire Randolph."

Merrill glowered at him. "Very well, sir. I shall give you enough rope, as the proverb says. But I must remind you I retain the confidence of the bishop. I do not like your irreverent manner. I do not like your arrogance. I do not like your sarcasm. I do not like you."

"I think, my friend," Quinncannon said evenly, "we understand one another perfectly."

At the door Merrill turned back. "Avery must be exonerated, sir. Take heed. The brethren have formed into a phalanx, and we shall watch closely your conduct of the defense. You, *and* Squire Randolph, would be well advised not to underestimate our power and influence."

145

One corner of the Irishman's mouth tugged up. He said, "'There is a strength in the union even of very sorry men.'"

Merrill looked puzzled. "I do not recognize the text."

"I'm not surprised, Brother," Quinncannon replied. "It was written by a Greek."

🐚 28
Three Letters

"I suppose," I said when Merrill was gone, *"I should* thank you for retaining me on the case as your junior."

Quinncannon caught my tone of resentment and observed me from the corners of his eyes through a cloud of tobacco smoke. "I don't think that will be necessary. You will be handling virtually all of the courtroom work. Whenever a point of law is raised, you will conduct the argument. My role will be limited to two, perhaps three cross-examinations, the summation, and assisting you in plotting the strategy of the defense. For that small service I will receive approximately three times your fee." He leaned back and folded his arms. "Eventually it may occur to you that I am using you rather shamefully."

I could not conceal my astonishment. Already the Avery case was attracting press attention in Boston and Hartford. Soon it would spread to New York and Philadelphia. Never in the history of the United States had a clergyman been accused of murder. This was the sort of case that could catapult an attorney instantly into national prominence—that could, if properly handled, propel even a very young man into the highest legal and political circles.

I stared at Quinncannon's face, trying to read him, and found I could not. Had he forgotten the potential professional significance of the case? I dismissed the notion at once. In my mind I could hear him quietly saying, "I forget nothing. Occasionally I ignore something."

In the end this rumination was compressed into a single, one-word question:

"Why?"

His expression was exasperatingly opaque. "Why what?"

I took out my pipe and began to fill it. "Why are you giving me control of the Avery defense?"

"Christy," he responded with a half-smile, "I am giving you the conduct of the case. With your permission I will retain control."

"All right," I said. "Why are you giving me the conduct of the case?"

"I should have thought it was obvious. However . . . to begin with, you are the local boy, a native, while I am not only an outlander but a foreigner." He paused. "An *Irish* foreigner."

He smiled slightly. "We are dealing at the outset, Christy, with a case that is charged with emotions and laden, on both sides, with bias and long-simmering hatred. The bulk of the evidence is heavily weighted against our client, and our client, himself, is astoundingly unlovable." He raised an eyebrow. "The New Englander has a sense of divine favoritism which rivals that of the Hebrew and almost approaches that of the New Yorker." He waved his hand. "The point is that you were born and raised in this area. You are one of their own. You are personally acquainted with most of the witnesses and you are on excellent terms with Howe and Haile, the presiding magistrates."

A minute passed. Then I said, "Lon, do you believe Avery is guilty?"

"Have you spoken with Wilbur?" he asked, and I nodded. "Who else?"

"Gifford and Cranston."

"Is that all?"

"All so far."

"Well," he said cryptically, "there are others. And there are three unfortunate letters."

"You're convinced," I said, "that the girl was murdered, aren't you?"

"Absolutely," he responded grimly.

"Then, was she killed by Avery?"

He gave me a wry smile. "I have not given that question any thought at all, Christy, and I would advise you not to dwell on it. But, in fairness to you, I will say that, based on what is known at the moment, I cannot imagine who else could have killed her."

He knocked the ashes out of his pipe and got to his feet. "Possibly that disturbs you," he said.

A great many things disturbed me. It seemed evident we were about to attempt to secure the freedom of a murderer. "If the girl was murdered, and we can suggest no alternative suspect, then *what*, Lon, is the basis of our defense?"

He watched me for a moment and then he said simply, "Suicide."

Suicide.

"Lon, we *know* it wasn't suicide."

"*We* may," he said. "The magistrates do not."

"But," I protested, "we are attorneys, officers of the court. Are we not pledged to . . . ?" I groped for the correct phrase. At last I said, "Are we justified in suppressing the truth?"

"The truth?" His eyebrows seemed to form a clove hitch above the bridge of his nose. "What is the truth?"

"The truth," I responded, lowering my voice to a whisper, "is that Sarah Cornell was murdered."

"And all the known evidence points to Avery as the killer?"

"Yes."

"In fact, we have no evidence against anyone else."

"Yes."

"And we know, for a fact, that our client murdered Cornell?"

"Well . . . no," I responded.

Quinncannon leaned back. "There you are, Christy. The law states that Avery is to be considered innocent until proven guilty, but we know that the burden of proof lies with us. Lacking certitude of his guilt, we must not only plead him not guilty, but exert every effort to convince the court of his innocence. Avery is legally entitled to the benefit of any doubt, but we have no reason to expect he will receive that benefit from the prosecution, the justices, or a jury if the case reaches that stage. Surely, as his representatives, *we*, at least, owe him that benefit."

"I can accept that," I said, "but why must we base our defense on the theory of suicide? Why must we argue a patently false position?"

"Hypothetically," he said, "suppose we were certain of the killer's identity—certain it was not Avery—but we could not prove it. What would our options be?"

I thought about it. "I suppose, Lon, if we allowed the prosecution to establish the fact of murder without challenge, the court would assume Avery's guilt and convict."

"Therefore . . . ?"

I nodded slowly. He had made his point. If we knew our client was guiltless and could not establish the guilt of another, then our only option would be to argue that *no* crime had been committed. We, of course, did not know that Avery had *not* killed the girl, but we could not be certain that he *had*. What doubt of his guilt we entertained, no matter how slender, was our debt to him.

Quinncannon withdrew three folded sheets of foolscap from his pocket and placed them on a table.

"Having talked to Dr. Wilbur, you know Miss Cornell first consulted him on October 8 and near the end of that month she told him her condition was the result of an assault on her by Ephraim Avery on August 29 during a Methodist camp-meeting at Thompson, Connecticut. Back in September, by the way, she made the same charge against Avery to her sister and brother-in-law, Lucretia and Grindall Rawson, after Lucretia noticed that Sarah had not had what women call their 'monthly indisposition.'

"Doctor Wilbur urged Miss Cornell to demand support from Avery," the Irishman continued. "She promised to do so. Whether or not she wrote to Avery is unproven. However, on or about November 15 she received this letter. It is dated the 13th and postmarked the 14th from Warren, Rhode Island." He handed me the paper. "That, as these others are, is a copy. All the originals are being held by the authorities. This note was written on yellow paper and addressed to 'Miss Sarah M. Connell Fall River Mass.'"*

I unfolded it:

> *Nov 13th 1832*
> *I have just Received your letter with no small supprise and and will say I will do all you ask only keep your secrets—I wish you to write me as soon as you get this nameing some time and place where I shall see you and then look for answer before I come and will say whether convenient or not and will say the time— I will keep your letter till I see you and wish you to keep mine and have them at the time write soon say nothing to no one*
> *yours in haste*

"Obviously, Lon," I said, "this was written by the father of her child."

"Evidently," he responded, "it was written by a man who believed he was the father of her child."

I conceded the distinction. "But, if he was convinced he *was* the father, then his motive is just as strong."

---

*"Connell" was the actual spelling. All three letters are copied exactly.

"Yes, Christy, but that is not the point."

I was about to ask him what the point was, but another question distracted me. "What was the chronology of these events and communications?" I produced a notebook and pencil. "August 29, Avery has connection with the girl at Thompson."

"According to her statements."

I was writing. "She tells this story to the Rawsons on September . . . ?"

"September 21," he answered, "but there are earlier dates to note. Sarah moved in with the Rawsons on June 2. Sister Lucretia is prepared to swear that menstruation occurred regularly in June, July and August, the last time seven or eight days before the Thompson camp-meeting. The meeting ran from Tuesday, August 27, to Friday the thirtieth. That dates Sarah's last discharge about August 19 or 20."

"And she had none in September?"

He shook his head. "Between September 21 and October 2, Grindall Rawson consulted with his clergyman and his lawyer. The decision was made to ship the girl to Fall River, from where she was to get in touch with Avery."

"Dr. Wilbur found that fact peculiar," I said.

"Do you?"

"Frankly, yes."

"That makes three of us. At all events Sarah was sent packing out of Providence for Fall River on the steamer on October 2. Six days later she consulted Wilbur and, on October 15, he confirmed she was pregnant. On October 21 she brought him the oil of tansy."

I raised my suspicions concerning her story about the drug and how she had obtained it. "Good, good," he murmured. "That possibility had not crossed my mind. My spies tell me Mr. Staples and Colonel Harnden cannot find evidence that Avery purchased the poison, but we have very little time to trace it to the girl . . ." His voice trailed off.

I said, "Sarah brought the oil of tansy to Wilbur on October 21. I don't see how she could have gotten it from Avery before then."

"Why not?"

"Because of the wording of this letter you've shown me. The writer—let's assume it *was* Avery—indicates he has *just* learned of her pregnancy, and it's dated November 13. That's over three weeks after she is known to possess the poison."

"True," he sighed, "but, unfortunately she went to Wilbur

151

with the drug only twenty-four hours after she was seen meeting Avery in Fall River. He preached there the evening of October 20 and was afterward observed with the girl."

"Giving her the bottle?"

"Luckily, no."

Something in his tone led me to ask, "Are these three letters in Avery's hand?"

"Well, Christy, there is some attempt to disguise the writing. I have been allowed by Staples to see the originals and compare them with acknowledged samples of Avery's hand."

"And . . . ?" I saw the answer in his eyes. "Oh, Jesus!"

"At this moment it seems essential," he said, "to prevent the contents of the letters from being read into the record."

I was wondering if we had any case at all. "In this yellow letter, Lon, he asked for her response. Did she write him again?"

Quinncannon straightened up and began to refill his pipe. "The Fall River postmaster, Seth Darling, is prepared to testify that she mailed a letter to Bristol on November 19."

"Addressed to Avery?"

"Darling isn't positive. However, on November 27, a letter was delivered to her at Elijah Cole's rooming house in Fall River where she was then staying. It was on pink paper and came from Providence."

"From Avery?"

He gave me a grim smile and handed me a second paper.

Providence Nov 1831

Dear Sister

i received your letter in due season and should have answered it before now but thought i would wait till this opportunity—as i told you i am willing to help you and do for you as circumstances are i would rather you you would come to this place viz. *Bristol in the stage the 18th of December and stop at the Hotel and stay till 6 in in the evening and then go up directly across the main street to a brick building neare to the stone meeting house where i will meet you and talk with you when you stop at the tavern either inquire for work or go on to the street in pretense of looking for some or something else and i may see you say nothing about me or my family should it storm on the 18 come the 20th if you cannot come and it will be more convenient to meet me at the methodist meeting house in summerset just over the ferry on either of the above eve'g i will meet you there at the same hour*

152

or if you cannot do either i will come to fall river on
one of the above evenings back of the same meeting house
where i once saw you at any houre you say on either of
the above evenings when there will be the least passing
i should think before the mills stop work this i will leave
with you if i come i will come if it does not storm very
hard if it does the first i:ll come the second write soon
and tell me which—when you write direct your letter to
Betsey Hills Bristol *and not as you have to me* remember
this *your last letter i am afraid was broken open were*
your callash and not your plain bonnet you can send
your letter by mail

yours etc B. H.

S.M.C.

let me still enjoin the secret keep the letters in your
boosom burn them up

I put down the paper. "We," I observed, "are in very serious
trouble."

"I concur," Quinncannon said, "but I'd like to hear your
reasoning."

"First tell me, was this letter addressed to Sarah M. *Connell*.
That is, was her name misspelled from *Cornell* as in the yellow
letter?"

"I'm afraid it was, Chris. It was directed 'Miss Sarah M.
Connell Fall River Mass. To be left at Mrs. Cole's.' The same
misspelling appears in all three letters."

"And," I said, "you have compared these exhibits with a
specimen of Avery's acknowledged writing?"

He nodded.

"In which he makes reference to Miss Cornell?"

He nodded.

"And Avery misspells her name there as well?"

Again he nodded. "Without meaning to depress you, little
brother, matters are much worse than you suspect."

"I cannot imagine how," I replied glumly.

"Sure you can," he said quietly. "Try."

I re-inspected the second letter. "For openers this paper reeks
of Methodism. The salutation is 'Sister,' the standard form of
address in their church. There are three references to meeting
houses, one specifically Methodist, and another to a meeting
house in Fall River where he admits he once saw her—a prob-
able allusion to their rendezvous on October 20 when he gave

her the poison. Furthermore he is trying to lure her to Bristol where he obviously lives since he urges her to pretend a search for work and orders her not to mention him or his family or to recognize him if they pass on the street." I glanced up. "How much more do you want?"

"Go on," he said.

"All right. Clearly he is, or thinks he is, responsible for her pregnancy, since he promises to 'help' her and 'do for' her. The letter ties him to her murder in at least two ways. One of the optional arrangements he suggests for their meeting is in Fall River on December 20, which is exactly where and when she was strangled. *And* he instructs her to wear, not her plain bonnet, but the calash into which she changed on the evening of her death. Then he refers to his fear that her earlier letter was broken open." I looked up. "By his wife, I suppose."

"That would be my guess."

"Just tell me, Lon, that there is no Betsey Hills in Bristol, or if she exists, tell me she has no conceivable connection with Avery."

He took out his pipe and answered, "Betsey Hills is Mrs. Avery's niece. She has been living with the Avery family since last spring."

"Damn!" I muttered.

Quinncannon said, "There is another problem with that second letter involving its delivery. It was not sent through the mail, Christy, but hand-delivered to Cole's boarding house on November 27 by John Orswell, the engineer on the *King Philip*, one of the steamers out of Providence. Orswell claims he received it from a tall man outfitted as a preacher."

"Avery?"

"I don't know for certain. The boat is scheduled to stop here tonight shortly after nine on its run from Fall River. Orswell is going to come up from the wharf to see if he can identify Avery. One of us should be there, and I have other appointments."

"I'll be there," I said.

"On December 8," he continued, "Avery was in Fall River again to preach at a Four-Days meeting. That morning he was briefly alone behind the counter of a shop owned by an Iram Smith, in the vicinity of a ream of white paper recently stocked by Smith. Avery left without making any purchase and headed, according to Smith, toward the post office. A few minutes later, by the reckoning of the post master, Seth Darling, a letter was dropped into the outside box. Darling heard it because he had just emptied the box and it fell against the pinewood bottom. As he collected it, from inside the post office, Darling looked out the window and saw a man he thinks was Avery walking away. The letter was on white paper, directed to 'Miss Sarah M. Connell, Fall River, Mass.' The watermark on the letter matches a sheet of Smith's paper found torn in half."

He extended the third letter to me.

"Do you want to read it?"

The truth was I didn't. The evidence against Avery was already overwhelming. I retained no doubt of his guilt. I smiled bitterly, but I read it.

> *Fall River Dec 8*
> *I will be here on the 20 if pleasant at the place named*
> *at 6 oclock if not pleasant the next Monday* eve
> *Say nothing &c*

"So our client actually arranged *in writing* to meet the girl at the place and on the date and at the time he killed her!"

Quinncannon said quietly, "You believe Avery killed her."

I met his eyes. "Yes, Lon. I don't know why it should bother me. *All* my clients are guilty. But, damn it, this is murder." I paused. "Surely *you* think he did it?"

He did not answer for a full minute. Then he said, "I don't know yet, Christy. The evidence against him is awesome but the only significant witness against him is the victim and her declarations are highly suspect. Everything else is circumstantial. Don't misunderstand me, lad. In my view circumstantial evidence is infinitely more reliable than direct testimony. But . . ." he reached for a match ". . . but, you've got to have *all* the circumstances, all the pieces of the puzzle, and your solution must account for each circumstance in a logical pattern. We do not have all the circumstances. Not yet."

He lit his pipe. "On the basis of what we *have* learned, I would say our client is probably guilty, but 'probably' is not a word to be used in a court of law. Besides, we'll know a lot more in an hour."

I guessed his meaning. "We're going to interview Avery."

He nodded and I said, "Lon, do we have *any* chance of winning at this hearing?"

"Is it *that* that's disturbing you? I thought it was only your belief in Avery's guilt." One corner of his mouth tugged up. "Rest easy, Christy," he said. "The prosecution hasn't got a prayer."

155

The Client

The house provided for Ephraim K. Avery by his parish-ioners stood on Church Street midway between the Long Wharf and the meeting house. Cramped, dingy clapboard, sorely in need of paint and repair, the building bore mute witness to the poverty and suffering with which the Methodists professed to believe the road to salvation was paved. The floors were uncarpeted and the wind off Bristol Harbor whistled audibly through the walls and around the window frames. The rooms, at least the entrance hall and the parlor beyond, were cheaply and sparsely furnished. The place was as small and crabbed as the spirits of its inmates.

Avery had been arrested on December 23 on a warrant sworn by John Durfee and Colonel Harnden representing the Fall River Vigilance Committee. However, Justice Howe had not ordered the minister to prison, allowing him to remain with his family under the careless guard of Deputy William Pell. It was Pell who admitted Quinncannon and myself and indicated that the Reverend accused was to be found upstairs "in conference."

A bleak staircase at our right led to a railed landing overlooking the hall. The first door off the landing was closed but the second stood ajar, and from it issued the rumble of several male voices in subdued but heated conversation. The Irishman pushed the door open.

The little room, not much larger than a closet, was Avery's study. A desk table containing a lamp and a Bible fronted the door, a straight chair and narrow window behind it. To the left a bench of unfinished pine served as a shelf for five or six prayer books. To the right was a cot with a ragged blanket flung over it. That cot bothered me. I wondered why a married man felt the need for separate sleeping accommodations.

Ephraim Avery slouched in the chair behind the desk, and four other clergymen were in the room with him. Abraham Merrill occupied the only other chair, as befit his position as the bishop's ambassador. His brother Joseph and Elder Drake stood apart in evident agitation. The fourth, a solid, middle-aged man with large hands and a ruddy complexion, was stationed behind Avery's chair. All except Avery had been talking simultaneously. Suddenly aware of our presence, all were jolted into silence. All, except Avery, shot their eyes toward the door.

Quinncannon entered and stepped aside to admit me. "Gentlemen," he said, "I wish you as good an afternoon as is possible under the circumstances."

Only the fourth minister moved. He came around the desk and extended one large hand to Quinncannon. Though his upper lip was shaven he wore a dark beard encircling his jaws and chin. "I am pleased to see you again, sir," he said in a nasal twang.

"And I you, Reverend Bidwell. Christy, this is Ira Bidwell, Methodist pastor at Fall River. Mr. Bidwell, this is Squire Christopher Randolph, who will lead Mr. Avery's defense at his hearing."

Bidwell's handshake was firm but, before he had done, Avery, without looking up, spoke in a sullen undertone.

"I thought I had made it clear, Brother Abraham, that I would not accede to being represented by a . . ." he was searching for the most offensive word ". . . by a fornicator."

Quinncannon caught the expression of anger on my face. When he turned back to Avery he was smiling, slightly. "On that matter . . . ," he began, and then, "Excuse me, Brother. When I address a gentleman I require the courtesy of his attention."

Slowly the preacher looked up under heavy lids.

"On that issue," the Irishman resumed, "I associate myself only with fornicators. It is a matter of principle. Upon full reflection, Brother, you may find this predilection rather fortunate for yourself."

"Really, sir!" Abraham Merrill was on his feet. "Your attitude is becoming intolerable!"

Quinncannon assumed Merrill's seat. "You will have to excuse us, gentlemen. We have little time and we must discuss the defense with Mr. Avery."

"You wish us to leave the room?" Elder Drake asked in astonishment.

"Out of the question," Joseph Merrill said.

Brother Abraham folded his arms. "I remind you, sir, it is our church that is paying your fees. I insist upon remaining."

Quinncannon withdrew his pipe and pouch. "Now, gentlemen," he said mildly, "on another occasion I will be pleased to discuss with you truly weighty subjects such as the precise dating of the Creation, or..." he glanced at Avery "...the doctrine of Original Sin, or even the question, if it has not yet been satisfactorily settled, of how many angels can dance on the head of a pin. But, in such sordid and worldly matters as alleged rape and murder, you must allow Mr. Randolph and myself to conduct affairs as we see fit."

Abraham Merrill glowered fiercely at the Irishman, but Ira Bidwell placed a hand on his shoulder. "I suggest we retire, brethren. I believe that complete confidentiality is considered necessary between attorney and client. Possibly our continued presence would, to some degree, inhibit..."

Merrill spun around angrily. "Are you implying, Brother Bidwell, that Mr. Avery is harboring guilty secrets?"

Avery's eyes were fixed on Bidwell. Though the latter was at least fifty, he appeared to shrivel before Merrill's superior age and rank like a chastised child. Bidwell felt, rather than saw, the furious glares of Joseph Merrill and Samuel Drake behind his back. Avery's innocence was clearly considered an article of faith. It was as though Bidwell had implied a doubt of the divinity of Christ.

One corner of Quinncannon's thin moustache twisted down. "Brother Abraham," he said, "I have not yet met a man who did not have one or two little things to hide. What Mr. Bidwell may be suggesting is that all four of you will be called as witnesses to Mr. Avery's character. Should you hear anything during our interview this afternoon that might...compromise our client, you would be compelled by your honor and oath to so testify, in which case Mr. Randolph and I could not risk putting you on the stand."

I watched the muscles in Brother Abraham's face somewhat relax as he turned to the Irishman. "I confess, sir, that argument has a trace of merit."

"Brother," Quinncannon responded evenly, "I lack words to express my relief at your confession." He consulted his watch. "You have left me little time to hear Brother Avery's confession. I feel a calm assurance that you will forgive my lack of tact when I ask you, again, to get the hell out of here."

After they had filed out, I closed the door, extracted my notebook, and sat down on the cot. Avery bent forward in his chair, elbows on the desk-top, staring down with his thumbs supporting his chin and his fingertips pressed against his temples.

158

Quinncannon regarded him for a long moment. Then he said, "Now, Brother, we seek a little truth."

Surprisingly Avery began with an apology to me that actually carried a ring of sincerity. "I find I have condemned your moral character, Mr. Randolph, out of mere hearsay and without trial. Such rashness of judgment is totally at odds with the tenets of my church and particularly unforgivable in one of her ministers, especially one who finds himself similarly condemned." He stood and reached out a long, bloodless hand.

I accepted both his hand and his apology.

The clergyman sank back in his chair. "Thank you for your understanding, Mr. Randolph. I am relieved to have that weight lifted from my conscience."

I wondered what other weights he had on his conscience. Then, as the Irishman seemed disposed to let me take the lead in the questioning, I said, "Mr. Avery, why don't you explain the history of your acquaintance with Sarah Maria Cornell?"

Avery shook his head. "A strange, almost haunted young woman, gentlemen. At times she was the most dedicated, the most solemnly devoted member of the congregation. At our Love Feasts she would exhort as if...as if the Holy Spirit were whispering in her ear. No other woman, no unordained *man* was her equal! I have seen her so filled with the spirit of Christ that she had only to raise her arms and lift her voice in prayer, and young men would fall in the dust and grovel in the ecstasy of spiritual rebirth. At such moments Maria was... magnificent!" He paused and a shadow passed over his features. "And yet..."

After a decent interval I prompted, "And yet?"

"And yet," he responded sadly, "she was the greatest of sinners. A liar, a thief, a fornicator." He looked at me quickly, aware of having used the obnoxious word. "I do not speak lightly, Mr. Randolph. She was not merely condemned by a church trial at Lowell, but many times out of her own mouth and in written confessions to me. She even contracted the... the *foul disease*!"

He glanced from Quinncannon's face to mine. "I can prove it, gentlemen, by the statement of Dr. Griggs of Lowell. True, Maria made vile accusations against him but..."

Again Avery drifted off in mid-sentence. I decided to let him ramble. At last he said, "There were so many Marias. She was at once ethereal and profligate; gentle and coarse; warm

159

and loving—and filled with icy hatred. She was a wild sparrow, and a tamed but dangerous falcon. She could, in the same minute—in the same *minute*—plead for merciful forgiveness and threaten terrible revenge. I found her . . ."

"Fascinating," Quinncannon suggested.

"Yes," Avery replied. Then he started as if suddenly discovering one of his psychological sentries asleep. "But only in a professional sense," he asserted. "I wrestled, gentlemen, I wrestled as Jacob for her soul. But, in the end, the demon in her proved victorious."

Abruptly Avery leaned forward, eying each of us intently. "I am not unaware that my brethren and friends have been gathering testimony against Maria's character to present at my hearing. I have protested vigorously that the unfortunate girl should be left in peace, that her memory must be allowed to remain unsullied in the minds of her loved ones."

Quinncannon raised an eyebrow. "Your concern for her reputation appears belated, Brother. You brought charges against her at Lowell and had her excommunicated. You wrote letters to Reverend Dow at Dover and Reverend Storrs at Great Falls denouncing her. You encouraged Abraham Merrill to have her expelled from the camp-meeting at Thompson. You urged Ira Bidwell to throw her out of the church at Fall River. You—"

"Yes, yes, yes, yes," Avery muttered bitterly. "I have no desire to harm the girl further. As God is my witness—!"

"God is not your witness, Reverend," Quinncannon cut in sharply. "We are going to have to make do with Drake and the Merrills." He nodded in my direction.

"Explain your relationship with Miss Cornell, sir," I said. "Keep it simple and factual."

The minister appeared to be struggling for control. For a time he buried his face in his hands. When he lifted his head and squared his shoulders his voice was steady. "I first met Maria when I moved from Saugus to the pulpit at Lowell in July, 1830. She had already been, for some months, a church member in good standing. During July she visited my house seeking work but, Mrs. Avery not being pleased with her appearance, she was refused employment. In August Maria called again, saying she was going to a camp-meeting at Eastham on the Cape, and from there to Killingly, Connecticut, to visit her friends, and requesting a certificate of regular membership in the church. I hesitated, as I had heard her accused of profanity, but gave her the paper conditionally. I told her if

160

I heard a bad report of her conduct at Eastham I would write to the preacher at Killingly not to accept her."

"Had you," I asked, "occasion to warn the Killingly church?"

"No, as she never went there. Instead she returned to Lowell and took work with the Appleton mills. Some weeks later the overseer there complained to me that she bore a very bad character—that she had confessed illicit intercourse with two or more young men. He said he had warned her of his intention to speak to me and she had begged him to allow her first to present her version of the circumstances. She having failed to do so, he felt it was his. . ."

"Duty," Quinncannon said.

Avery nodded. "She came to me two days later and acknowledged unlawful connection with one man, and him only. I told her I had heard of two or more. At first she denied. . ."

I closed my eyes and tried to imagine the scene. Was Sarah Maria the shamed penitent, standing, head bowed, before her spiritual shepherd, mumbling her guilt in bits and pieces as he dragged it from her in harsh, swift cross-questioning? "No, sir, there was only one, sir. I swear!" "There were no more than two, sir. I swear!"

". . . but finally she admitted. . . ."

Or had she confronted him defiantly, her fists on her hips, her voice so loud it could be overheard by his wife. "All right, Ephraim! There were two—there were ten! You fool! Did you ever imagine you were the only . . . !"

"I told her," Avery continued, "there must be a church trial in the usual way, and that it would probably result in her excommunication. I advised her to go to her relations. She inquired if it would not do just as well for her to go to Dover, or elsewhere. I said she could do as she pleased but. . . ."

Again I sought to visualize the moment. Sarah, fearful of returning to her Congregationalist relatives, whimpering: "Might I not as well go to Dover, sir?"

161

Sarah, strident, shouting: "Oh, it will suit you to send me away while you convict me! Should I not go to Dover? Or to hell?" And Avery, furious: "Go wherever you please, you damned little . . . !"

I became aware of Quinncannon's voice. "You arranged for her absence during her trial, Brother?"

"I advised her so, yes, sir. Not only was the charge of a delicate nature, but I considered her crime such that even confession and contrition would not be sufficient to enable her to hold her connection to the church. To preserve the church from reproach, her expulsion was inevitable. I informed her she might, in due time, if she manifested proper humiliation and reformation, obtain a standing first as probationer and then as a member amongst us, but I told her explicitly that, such was her offense, she could not escape excommunication."

Once more I attempted to envision what had really occurred. I tried to picture Sarah, having confessed her crimes, already practicing humiliation and contrition, but the image kept melting into Sarah rampant on a field of scarlet, shrieking epithets and vowing vengeance.

"Compulsive," Avery was saying. "That was the word to describe Maria, Mr. Quinncannon. She loved and hated compulsively. She was compulsively devout and compulsively evil."

The Irishman looked up. "She sinned compulsively and confessed compulsively?"

"Yes," Avery agreed. "Exactly. In many ways she was like a child. She had many moods. She could never control them."

"Did you," I asked, "consider her attractive?"

Avery was alert to the purport of the question. "Not beautiful, Mr. Randolph. She was too . . . seasoned to be beautiful. She was pretty when she took pains, but she could turn ugly in a second."

"When you informed her she would be excommunicated," Quinncannon said, "did you ask for the return of her certificate of membership?"

"I did, but she lied and told me she had lost it on the Cape." Shortly afterward I learned she was in Dover, New Hampshire, and had used my certificate to gain admission to Reverend

162

Dow's church. I felt compelled to write to Dow, especially as new information about Maria had come to me."

"You had heard," the Irishman said, "from Dr. Griggs."

Avery nodded grimly. "Griggs said he felt it his duty to inform me that the girl had applied for his professional assistance for the *foul disease*—that her case was as aggravated as any he had ever known—that she could not sit or stand still, and walked only with difficulty. When he reproved her she replied she was not as bad as he thought; that she was a member in good standing of my church. When he expressed doubt, she produced the certificate. I had no choice but to communicate this information at her trial. She was found guilty of lying and fornication, and expelled."

"Are you aware," Quinncannon asked, "that she charged Griggs with making improper advances to her?"

"I am, sir." Avery managed a weary smile. "Physicians, like ministers, are always vulnerable to such accusations."

The Irishman returned the smile. "Did you then communicate with the girl at Dover?"

"I wrote to her immediately, demanding the return of the certificate, asserting that if the demand was not complied with, I should be forced to publish her in the papers as an imposter, and to denounce her to Brother Dow. She then returned my certificate."

"But," I said, "you had already denounced her to Dow."

"It was my duty to the church, Mr. Randolph."

"I see," I said dryly. "And Maria was kicked out of the Dover church?"

"She next wrote me from Great Falls, New Hampshire," Avery said. "It was a long letter in which she proposed to make a full confession of her crimes. She admitted to unlawful intercourse with several men but denied she was ever afflicted with the venereal complaint. She charged Dr. Griggs with attempting illicit connexion with her. I showed the letter to one of Griggs' students, but did not respond. Then, a week later . . ."

"She wrote again," I guessed.

Avery confirmed it. "She wrote she had heard a sermon from Brother Storrs at Great Falls on the subject of confession and felt constrained to make a fuller acknowledgment of her sins. She now confessed she had been guilty of all the charges lodged against her at Lowell, and that she had suffered from the foul disease, though ignorant of it at the time."

He threw me such a look of helpless pathos that I said, "Was she again lying?"

163

"Not about her sins, Mr. Randolph, but George Storrs has not preached on the topic of confession in seven years."

"Then what, in your opinion, was her purpose in writing you these letters?"

"To force me to write back, I imagine."

"And did you write back?"

"No!" he said firmly. "I heard nothing of her again until early in June, 1831, when she appeared at my house in Lowell on the first Sunday, I believe the sixth. She said she had written to me but I had taken no notice of her letters—that she had come on purpose to ask my forgiveness and wanted it in writing."

"Did you give it in writing?"

"I did, Mr. Randolph, but I stressed that forgiveness from me was nothing—that she must seek it of God."

But he *had* given her the paper. "To whom," I asked, "was this paper addressed?"

"To Brother Storrs."

"Did it not then amount to another certificate of membership, designed to get Maria admitted to the Great Falls church?"

I suppose my implication that she was blackmailing him was clear. "It did not!" he barked. "I merely stated to Storrs that if, in light of all the information he possessed against her character, he should *still* see fit to admit her on probation, we at Lowell would not oppose him. And, when I learned more to her detriment the following day, I wrote at once to Storrs, rescinding my letter of forgiveness and advising him to use his own judgment."

"What did you learn so quickly that led you to rescind your letter?"

Avery's eyes were slits. "The girl had told me another deliberate, willful falsehood!"

Something to do with fornication, I thought, but I did not pursue the issue. Instead I said, "Please explain what happened at the Thompson camp-meeting."

He looked at me in apparent surprise. "Nothing happened at Thompson," he answered.

"How long did the meeting run?" I asked, as if I did not know.

"I believe from Tuesday, August 27, to Friday, August 30. I did not arrive until Tuesday evening and only went to the camp on Wednesday and Thursday. I left early Friday morning."

"Are you aware, Mr. Avery, that Maria was on the camp grounds during that meeting?"

"Not of my own knowledge, sir." Now I knew he was lying.

"On Wednesday morning Reverend Abraham Merrill informed me that she was in attendance and asked me if the brethren should be cautioned against her. I replied that, if she was the same girl I had caused to be expelled at Lowell, they should be warned."

"Were they so warned?"

"I imagine they were, Mr. Randolph, but you would have to ask Brother Merrill. I never saw the girl or spoke with her."

"Not on the evening of Thursday, August 29?"

He met my gaze squarely. *"Not at any time."*

But he *had* seen her and talked to her. I had witnessed their meeting myself. I considered confronting him with his lies and rejected the notion. I was committed to defending him. The less I knew the better I could do my job. As it was, I already knew too much.

"Mr. Avery." Quinncannon's voice reverberated out of the deepening shadows of the darkened afternoon. "I'm certain you are cognizant of the charge made against you by Maria Cornell before her death, the charge made to the Rawsons and repeated to Dr. Wilbur. I ask you now, do you swear you had no connection with the dead girl during the camp-meeting at Thompson?"

Avery eyed him. "I understood I would neither have to take the stand nor swear an oath."

"Your understanding is correct, sir. This is merely for my own information, and that of your God."

"Then, before my God," the minister said, "I so swear."

The Irishman leaned back in his chair and closed his eyes. "Have you been a student of medicine?"

"I have studied physick."

"What is oil of tansy?"

"A drug used to destroy parasites."

"Is it poisonous?"

Avery smiled. "Anything is poisonous in sufficient dosage."

"In the case of oil of tansy, what would be a sufficient dosage?"

"I should imagine anything over four drops would be dangerous."

"Have you ever heard of using oil of tansy to induce abortion?"

"No, Mr. Quinncannon. The notion is quite impossible."

"Then how would you induce abortion?"

Avery seemed startled by the question. "I'm afraid I have no idea."

165

"Don't you?" Quinncannon opened one eye. "Are you at all acquainted with the branch of medicine called obstetrics?"

Avery appeared confused.

"Midwifery," Quinncannon said.

The minister nodded at the familiar term. "Vaguely acquainted," he said.

"Have you ever delivered a child?"

"No, sir."

"Have you ever aborted a child?"

"Certainly not!"

"If you came across a foetus eight inches long and weighing five ounces, how much time would you estimate had elapsed since conception?"

"I would not even attempt a guess."

Quinncannon closed his eye. "In October of 1832, while you were preaching at the Four-Days meeting in Fall River, where and when did you see Maria Cornell?"

"*Very* briefly," Avery answered, "on the evening of the twentieth, outside the door of Edward Mason where I was invited to stay the night. It struck me as an odd coincidence because I had not thought of the girl in months, and that same afternoon Brother Bidwell had raised her name."

Through a billow of tobacco smoke the Irishman said, "Go on."

"Well, earlier in the day, that is October 20, Bidwell had asked me if I knew a Sarah Cornell who was seeking admission to his church. I replied that I knew only a Maria Cornell who had been expelled at Lowell. He described the girl and I said it was very possible they were one and the same, and, if so, that the girl was unfit for church membership, even as a probationer.

"That evening, when I was done preaching, I was returning to Mason's home with Mrs. Mason and other women when someone pulled me by the elbow and expressed the wish to speak to me. I immediately recognized Maria and said I wanted nothing to say to her. She insisted she *must* speak with me and I made excuses and demanded of her what she wanted. She said she had just come to Fall River and had joined a class on trial. If I did not expose her past to Brother Bidwell, she said, she should again attain full membership. I told her it would depend on her behavior whether I exposed her or not. She became agitated."

I could understand her reaction. Though she did not yet know it, Avery had already denounced her to Bidwell.

The minister went on. "'Don't,' says she, 'ruin me here! You have ruined me in Lowell and Dover, but don't ruin me here!' I told her I had not ruined her. She had ruined herself."

"On October 20," I inquired, "did Miss Cornell ask you for money?"

"Of course not."

"Did she then, or at any time by any means, inform you that she was carrying your child?"

"No!"

"Had you any reason to believe she *might* be carrying your child?"

"None whatsoever, Mr. Randolph."

"Did she ever tell you she was pregnant?"

"No, she did not."

"Did she ever threaten you in any manner?"

"No."

"Did she ever, for any reason, attempt to extort money from you?"

"No."

"Did you ever provide her with oil of tansy for any purpose?"

"I wouldn't even know where to find the stuff, Mr. Randolph."

"Did you mail her a letter on yellow paper from Warren, Rhode Island?"

"I never sent Maria a letter through the mail."

"Did you send her a letter on pink paper on November 27, or any other date, through the engineer on the steamboat *King Philip*?"

"I did not."

"Did you ever establish, whether orally or in writing, a meeting with Miss Cornell on December 20?"

"I did not."

"Were you in Fall River on December 8?"

"I was not," Avery asserted, "nor have I ever been in Iram Smith's store, nor have I ever mailed a letter to anyone from the Fall River post office."

I drew a deep breath. "Did you murder Sarah Maria Cornell?"

"Certainly not," Avery snapped. "The whole idea is ludicrous." He fixed a stare at Quinncannon. "Am I to be suspected of this horrible crime even by my own attorneys?"

The Irishman reopened his eye. "Of course you are, Brother. It is our professional responsibility." Quinncannon straightened

167

up in his chair. "Would you say, Brother Avery, that Maria Cornell had reason to hate you?"

Avery regarded him coldly. "No, sir, I would not."

"No?" Quinncannon struck a match and held it over his pipe. "You did 'ruin' her, my friend, at Lowell, at Dover, at Great Falls, at Fall River."

"All of that was her own doing, sir. The result of her rejection of God's grace."

"But, Reverend, does it not strike you that the girl might have wanted revenge against you? You know a note was found in her bandbox, dated and signed the day of her death? 'If I should be missing enquire of the Rev Mr Avery of Bristol. He will know where I am.'" The Irishman watched Avery's face. "Why do you suppose she named you in that note?"

"I don't know." Avery seemed perplexed. "Unless she wanted me to be suspected of her murder."

"But how could she know she would be murdered?"

"She couldn't." Avery suddenly brightened. "But she *could* plan to kill herself."

The Irishman shook his head. "Ah, but then her death would clearly be suicide, Brother."

"Not if she tried to make it look like murder," Avery cried. "Am I on the right path, Mr. Quinncannon?"

"I don't know, Brother. Are you?" He smiled. "How do you imagine she arranged for those three letters to arrive in Fall River?"

"An accomplice?" the clergyman ventured.

"That sounds reasonable," Quinncannon replied. "And the accomplice would also explain her pregnancy, wouldn't he?"

Avery indicated agreement.

"Good," Quinncannon said. "Then all that remains is for you to explain where you were on the evening the girl died."

A correct
MAP
of the Ground described by
the testimony in the Trial of
Rev.d E. K. Avery for the Murder
of Sarah M. Cornell.

References
On alleged Route of Prisoner from
Bristol to Fall River.

N.o 1 Bristol.
2 Pearce's Ferry House
3 Gifford's Ferry Wharf
4 Gifford's Ferry House
5 Hicks' House
6 Abby Earle's Ho.
7 Wm. Anthony's Ho.
8 John Boyd's
9 Isaac Peckham's
10 John Mc Corrie & Elder Drakes.
11 Doct. Man's
12 Charity, or Little Bridge
13 Cranston's Toll House
14 Common Stone Bridge
15 Lawton's Tavern
16 Post Office at Norton's
17 Stack Yard.
18 John Durfee's Ho.
19 The R.I. part of Fall River Village
Route as described in Prisoners
Voluntary Examination.
20 Windmill near Ferry opposite which he left
Road.
21 Met a man Gunning about here
22 Sarah Jones's
23 White Gate
24 Coal Mine & Wharf
25 Met Boy driving Sheep.
26 Asa Freeborn's
27 Union Meet.g Ho.
28 Sister Wilcox's
29 Quaker Hill & Meet.g Ho.
30 O.D. Green's Tav. & Post Office.
31 Wm. E. Cook's.
32 Abner Tallman's.
33 John B. Cook's
34 Butts' Hill

Other Points
35 Pond & Creek.
36 Mount Hope.
37 George Hall's
38 Amy Anthony's
39 Geo. Brownell 2nd
40 Levi Sherman's
41 Oliver Brownell
42 Robert & Dan.l Wilcox

TROY

State Line

BRISTOL

Mt. Hope

Hog I.t

TIVERTON

New Town

P O R T S M O U T H

Clarke's
Hill

Durfee's
Tav.

Vaucluse

N
W E
S

🐚 30

The Alibi

"*I spent December 20, from about two-thirty on, on a* walking tour of the island," Avery began. "I had two reasons for this tour. I had heard that coal there was cheap and thought I would visit the mines and purchase some."

"But the mines are no longer worked," I said.

"True, Mr. Randolph, but I did not learn that until I had almost reached them."

"Go on," I said.

"My second reason was that, shortly after arriving in Bristol, I received a letter from my father, who was stationed here during the Revolution, describing the beautiful scenery around Mount Hope."

I interrupted him again. "Excuse me, sir, but Mount Hope is not on the island."

"I know that, Mr. Randolph. I was about to mention my father's second letter. It would be helpful if you allowed me to get on with my story."

"It would be helpful, sir, if you would restrict yourself to relevancies." Already I suspected his "story" would be difficult to believe, much less to prove. "The second letter?"

"He wrote he had served in Sullivan's expedition to the island and roused my curiosity to see where he had fought that battle."

That had a ring of truth at least. My own father had been with Sullivan. The battle had commenced on the island's west side and culminated in bitter combat near the Quaker meeting house.

"On December 20, as the weather was remarkably pleasant, I left home about two o'clock and walked on to Bristol ferry, about two miles distant. Young Mr. Pearce carried me across and pointed out the direction of the mines.

"I went up the road and got over the wall a little to the north of the windmill, passed over the head of a small stream and some low ground; and when near the mines I met a man carrying a gun. He was dressed in coarse, old-looking clothes, and an old hat, somewhat dented in on the front part of the crown. I asked him if the coal mines were worked and he said they were not. I then asked him if there was coal for sale. He said, 'No.' Concluding that a visit to the mines would be useless, I changed my course from southwesterly to due south."

"Can you describe this man further?" I inquired.

"He was rather short, well set, with the appearance of a rustic. Somewhat past forty. I judged him a local and one who would know if the mines were shut down."

"So you headed south."

"I thought I would call on Asa Freeborn. I came to a gate one side of which was whitewashed, and passed through it between two houses to a lot where sheep and young cattle were being tended by a boy of ten or twelve. I asked if Mr. Freeborn was at home, and the boy said he thought not as he had seen him going away that morning with his wagon."

"Are you aware," Quinncannon said, "that Freeborn was at home?"

"I am now, sir, but at the time I had no reason to doubt the lad. Does something trouble you?"

"Yes, Brother, something does. Billy Pearce states that you said nothing to him about buying coal and, if you had, he would have told you the mines were closed. There is a watchman at the mines who could have testified for you, and Freeborn was at home, but in both instances you allowed yourself to be turned aside by people who, though evidently local residents, cannot now be found." Quinncannon elevated an eyebrow. "Now, Brother, the island is hardly thickly inhabited, and the Methodist search parties hunting for your elusive witnesses have tripled the population. How do you explain their lack of success?"

"I'm sure I cannot, sir."

The Irishman's expression suggested that he was afraid he could. He leaned back into a billow of white smoke, and I said, "Continue, Mr. Avery."

"I then thought I would call on Sister Wilcox and walked south, crossing a stream and keeping down the west side of the island near the shore until I calculated I was nearly opposite her house. It was just after sunset when I lay my course east, but traveling was difficult. The route crossed pastures and fields very rough and uneven, and there were several walls to get over. I had a bad ankle and my discomfort was aggravated by many missteps made in the dark. I came out on the East Road,

I would judge, about six miles from the ferry house, and being uncertain whether Widow Wilcox's house lay to the north or to the south, I decided to forego a visit and return to the ferry. I therefore turned north with the idea that, if I became too fatigued, I could spend the night at William Cook's home some three or four miles above."

"But you didn't stop at Cook's," I said.

"The traveling on the road was much easier," Avery replied. "I found reserved strength."

"And you didn't stop at Sister Wilcox's, or Freeborn's, or the mines."

"I have explained that, Mr. Randolph."

"Then please explain, sir, why you made no effort to visit the Quaker meeting house, which you averred was your original intention."

"Why, I changed my mind and decided to call on Sister Wilcox."

I shook my head. "You might easily have visited both, sir, and with a lot less trouble to yourself. Just south of the stream—where you say you met the boy—a road crosses the island leading southeast. It is called the Middle Road and it crosses the East Road at Quaker Hill where your father fought with Sullivan. From there you could have gone south and easily reached Widow Wilcox's farm in daylight."

Avery smiled. "I fear I am not as familiar with the island as you are, young man."

"Anyone could have directed you, sir. The boy tending sheep. Someone at Freeborn's. But instead you chose to avoid the roads and lay your course through moist lowlands, much of it a virtual swamp, and then over rocky fields and fences and stone walls—and this despite a sore ankle. With this admittedly painful impediment you then hiked over six miles to the ferry in the pitch dark and bitter cold when you could easily have stopped over with Cook, or Samuel Drake, or at Green's Tavern."

"I wished to get home that evening. There was sickness in my family."

"There was, sir, and some will wonder why, given that fact, you left home at all."

Avery's expression grew hard. "Are you saying, young man, that you do not believe me?"

"What I believe is immaterial," I answered. "We must convince two justices tomorrow and, ultimately, probably, a jury."

172

He slumped back in his chair. "I hope I am being wise in entrusting my defense to you."

"I hope you are, sir," I said. "During your whole sojourn that day, did you meet anyone whom you knew?"

He regarded me sourly. "May I continue my story?"

"You may, Reverend, as soon as you answer my question."

"Then the answer is no!" he snapped.

"All right," I said. "You turned north . . . ?"

"I walked up the East Road to the Turnpike and continued toward the ferry house. I passed two persons between Quaker Hill and the toll gate on the Turnpike, but took little notice. I heard the clock at the windmill strike nine as I passed and reached Mr. Gifford's no later than nine-fifteen. It required some time to rouse him and he refused to carry me to Bristol but offered me a bed. Soon after sunrise his son ferried me to Bristol."

Avery lapsed into silence. It was well after sunset and, as neither lamp nor fire had been lit, the three of us sat in a sullen darkness only occasionally relieved by the orange glow of Quinncannon's pipe and my own. The chilly gloom matched my mood. The preacher's alibi was a sieve. My certitude of his guilt was firmly in place, and I could not imagine how we could defend him. I envied William Staples the role of prosecutor. In my mind I could see Avery on the scaffold with the noose around his neck.

"Tell me, Brother," the Irishman said, "have you told any of this to anyone else?"

"Why, naturally, sir. I have spoken of all these matters with my wife . . ."

That, at least, was privileged communication.

". . . and with Elder Drake."

That was not.

"And then I committed it to writing."

"You have made a written statement?" I asked in horror.

"Why, yes, at the urging of the brethren."

"Where is this statement now?"

"I believe Elder Drake has delivered it to Justice Howe," Avery said. "I was advised that, although I did not have to testify at my hearing, it would not look well if I stood entirely mute." His deep voice became suddenly alarmed. "Have I done wrong, gentlemen?"

I was about to tell him but Quinncannon's brogue rumbled out of the shadows. "No, no, Brother. Rest easy. That is your story and we shall have to live with it."

Avery placed his palms on the desk and began to rise. "I don't care for your implication, sir," he said with some heat. "I have told you the truth!"

Quinncannon also got to his feet.

"No, you haven't, Brother. You have told us a little truth and a great many lies. There's no need to be offended unless you are determined to be. Neither Mr. Randolph nor myself have ever heard the truth from a client, or ever expect to. It is an occupational hazard. People only come to an attorney when they are in trouble and a man in trouble never tells the complete truth." He paused. "I would be surprised if you had not encountered the same thing in your own profession."

Silhouetted against the last gray glimmer from the window, Avery's head lowered until his chin seemed to touch his chest. I stood. Then Avery rasped, "At least believe this, Mr. Quinncannon. In the name of my God—on the lives of my children—I swear *I did not murder the girl*!"

Quinncannon put on his hat and opened the door before looking around. "Strangely, Brother," he said quietly, "I believe you."

31

*Mrs. Randolph
Investigates*

"*Christy, I've been dying to tell you! I understand so little* of these things but I'm sure this is important for your case. I mean, it *must* be if Colonel Harnden brought them here in his private carriage and put them up with Widow Bloss."

"Them?" I looked into Amy's excited, beautiful face across the supper table and smiled indulgently.

"The two women who arrived this afternoon. Mrs. Hathaway and her daughter. They're staying in the room next to ours. They're to testify at the hearing tomorrow against Reverend Avery. Of course I tried terribly hard to respect their privacy but, darling..." She put her hand on my wrist and returned my smile. "It really is quite impossible to shut them up."

I leaned back and lit my pipe.

"Don't you want to hear what they told me?" She was about to burst. "Don't tease me, Christy, or I promise you won't get a word out of me."

I tried to keep a straight face but it was hopeless. "By all means," I laughed, "let's have all the dirt."

"Well," she said, "to begin with, the dead girl boarded with Mrs. Hathaway in Fall River after December 1. On the morning of her murder—the ladies are certain it was murder—Miss Cornell said she'd want her supper before six o'clock that night as she was leaving the mill early and had an errand at Joseph Durfee's house. At the mill she asked Lucy Hathaway—that's the daughter, Christy, who worked with Miss Cornell—she asked for directions to *Joseph* Durfee's house, and that's what strikes both ladies as peculiar because..." She lowered her voice. "Because the girl's body was found on *John* Durfee's land in Tiverton, in a completely opposite direction." She paused dramatically. "Doesn't that seem strange to you?"

"Not necessarily. This area is crawling with Durfees. The girl might simply have been confused."

Amy looked doubtful. "At all events, that evening Sarah ate alone and left, Mrs. Hathaway says, between candle light and dark. She said she might return directly but at the latest by nine o'clock. Mrs. Hathaway did not retire until ten and she left the door on the latch for Sarah but, of course, the poor girl never did come back."

She poured another cup of tea and sipped it. "There are other things, small things; they may not matter—But, before she went out Sarah changed into her Sunday cloak and put off her plain bonnet for her calash." She caught my sudden look of interest. "Is that important?"

The second or pink letter carried by the engineer Orswell from Providence had directed Sarah to wear her "callash and not your plain bonnet."

"It might be," I answered. "Did the landlady mention seeing Sarah reading letters on colored paper?"

"She did, Christy! How did you know?"

"My love, you are married to a wizard. I am gifted with spectral sight. The letters were pink, yellow and white, and the girl displayed them conspicuously while being mysterious about their contents."

She clapped her hands. "That's wonderful! That's exactly what both ladies said."

I leaned forward. "Amy, when Sarah left that night, did the landlady say she appeared upset or apprehensive?"

"Quite the opposite, darling. She seemed especially cheerful, which I gather was unusual for her. Mrs. Hathaway says Sarah even appeared—well, the word she used was triumphant. As if she had long been engaged in a struggle of wills and had at last won it. Does that help you?"

I drew in a very deep breath and exhaled noisily. "It forewarns me but it hardly helps my client." A cheerful, triumphant attitude in Sarah not only blasted the notion of suicide—it implied that she believed she had the whip-hand with Avery. The prosecution could well contend that she met him with every expectation of collecting the money he seemed to have promised in his letters, and that Avery, unwilling or unable to meet her demands, had killed her.

"There are others coming tomorrow," Amy said. "Some of the women who prepared the girl for burial. They're to board with Rowena until they've given their testimony. Would it help if I spoke to them, tried to learn what they know?"

I took her hands between mine. "Yes, Amy, it would help me a great deal."

Gently she extracted her hands from mine and then clasped mine in hers. "Then I *can* be of use to you, Christy. Oh, husband, that makes me very happy."

176

32

The Mob

It was near nine o'clock when I rode back to Avery's house. A large crowd of men had already gathered in the street. They milled about in muttering confusion, some of them carrying clubs and guns. I led the Traveler toward the front door and the crowd made way before me. There were a few murmurs of "Evening, Squire," and a few less polite greetings.

Near the door John Durfee hovered in his selectman's suit. He smirked maliciously and tipped his hat. By the lantern above his head I could see that his fingernails were filthy.

Next to Durfee stood a tall gentleman in a gray surtout and wide-brimmed hat. He had high cheekbones and an aquiline nose, and he wore a moustache and a trimmed Van Dyke beard that accented a strong jaw line. As I passed, he ventured a slight bow and touched his hat brim. "Squire Randolph, your servant. I am Colonel Harnden."

"Good evening, Colonel. Would you care to join us inside?"

"Thank you, no, sir. I shall remain where I am. I am expecting a few friends to drop by."

I studied him. He was a vigorous man of no more than thirty-five, well dressed, of obvious breeding and intelligence. He seemed out of place in that motley company. He smiled, showing gleaming, sharp white teeth.

I returned his smile with compressed lips. "As you wish, Colonel." I rapped on the door and was admitted by an extremely nervous Deputy Sheriff Pell.

"Can ye give the password?" Pell wanted to know.

"No, Will."

"Then I can't let you in."

"Will, I am in."

"Well, then someone's made a mistake. How do I know your name, Squire Chris?"

I closed my eyes and cleared my throat. "Will," I said, drawing a flask from my pocket, "have yourself a drink."

177

He took a pull on the flask. "Funny thing, Squire Chris," he said, wiping his mouth. "That was the password."

The hall and the parlor beyond were swarming with Methodists. Fear hung like a haze in the brightly lit rooms. The collective voice of the men outside ebbed and flowed in a rising tide of fury.

I turned to the deputy. "Will, where is Avery?"

He indicated the staircase with a jerk of his head.

"All right," I said. "I expect a man named John Orswell to arrive tonight on the Providence steamboat. I want him passed in at once, Will, whether or not you can drink the password."

He nodded—then suddenly jumped as a rock crashed through a parlor window. The Methodists scurried for cover. Outside, angry shouts could be heard. "Come out, Avery!" "Hypocrite!" "Murderer!"

Pell turned a bloodless face toward me. "They're out there every night since Saturday, Squire Chris."

I ran for the stairs. As I reached the landing, the shrill whistle of the Providence steamer shrieked from the Long Wharf. The pier was only one and a half blocks from Avery's house. Orswell would arrive in minutes. Avery must be prepared to meet him. I turned toward the hall at the moment the steam whistle screamed again. Then an ugly roar went up from the mob outside and another rock crashed through a window.

Below me the Methodists buzzed and swarmed like bees in a shaken hive. Deputy Pell quaked near the street door. His stricken face and glassy stare were eloquent testimony that this duty was more than he'd bargained for when he pinned on the badge. The whistle sounded again, three short blasts, and as it died away another sound, rumbling, rhythmic, ominous, began to rise from the harbor.

I went quickly to the window and scanned the docks. My first impression was that the decks of the steamer were on fire. Flames leaped from every part of the vessel. Then the blaze seemed to move toward the house. It left the ship; it passed along the pier. As it advanced ponderously up Church Street, I saw what it truly was—dozens of fiery, oil-soaked torches, carried by a mob of perhaps fifty men. What had sounded like angry shouts was actually singing.

The tune was "Yankee Doodle Dandy." When they were within a city block I could make out the words:

> Ephraim Avery came to town
> To preach the girls salvation.

Killed a lass and strung her up,
And earned himself damnation.

Ephraim Avery, you will hang
Till your neck is twisted.
Ephraim said he'd rather not,
But the boys insisted.

I called Avery's name and ran for the closest door, throwing it open. Seated on a narrow, unmade cot was a large, doe-eyed woman with graying hair tied into a severe knot behind her head. Her dress was drab and needed mending. Her face was drawn as tightly as her hair and looked just as gray in the half-light of a single candle stub. There was not, about her, the smallest touch of color.

Three little children, two girls and a boy, clung to her skirts. When I flung the door back they gaped at me in voiceless terror and sought to hide themselves in the folds of their mother's garments. The tiniest managed to squirm her way under the woman's knees. The matron spread her arms like wings over her little flock and gazed up at me with exhausted resignation. She was past fear. She was also pregnant.

Though I had seen her before I scarcely recognized the minister's wife. "Remain here," I said. "Don't be afraid. No one will harm you."

I pulled the door shut and went to the next, rapping loudly and pushing it open. Avery sat behind the desk, a lamp and open Bible to one side, some papers before him and a goose quill in his hand. He raised his head slowly.

Outside the mob had surrounded the house. Their chorus was now distinctly audible.

Ephraim Avery, you will hang
Till your neck is twisted. . . .

"I cannot be disturbed now, Mr. Randolph," Avery said. "I must compose my sermon for Sunday service. I thought to preach on the text: 'Yea, though I walk through the valley of the shadow of death. . . .'"

The man appeared calm but on closer inspection I saw that involuntary tremors ran constantly through his body. "Has Mr. Orswell arrived?" he inquired. "I thought I heard the steamer whistle a while ago." He began to rise. "If he is here then I may be interrupted."

He stood unsteadily and buttoned his coat. He spoke in a hollow whisper that I had to strain to hear above the increasingly frenzied chanting from the men outside.

I felt a hand on my shoulder. I spun round and found myself inches from the leathery features and gray, squinting eyes of a man of about forty years. "Squire Randolph? I am the engineer of the steamboat *King Philip*. My name is John Orswell."

He stepped into the room and regarded Avery with curiosity.

"It was my understanding," I said grimly, "that you were to come alone, sir."

"Oh," he replied as the mob again roared, "I am not of that company. The *King Philip* is a common carrier. I assume they paid their passage from Fall River. The matter is entirely Captain Borden's concern. I am here . . ." and he peered intensely at Avery's face ". . . only to see if this is the man who gave me a letter to deliver from Providence to Fall River."

His squint was permanent, the result of over twenty years of stinging salt spray and harsh Atlantic winds. Orswell struck me as a man of nerve, of quiet self-assurance and Yankee shrewdness.

"Well, sir," Avery asked, "do you recognize me?"

"I am not sure I do not, Reverend." The engineer moved forward until only the desk stood between them. "It was a Tuesday, Reverend, November 27, the second day of a Four-Days Methodist meeting. You came aboard about nine o'clock in the morning with a letter to be delivered to Cole's house, a letter on pink paper. I told you I was not allowed, suggested you place it in the letter box, but you insisted. Said it would be a great favor to you, and gave me a ninepence, and I consented."

I said, "Mr. Orswell, consider carefully before you answer. Are you prepared to go before a court and swear this is the same man?"

Orswell hesitated. "To the best of my knowledge and recollection this is the man."

"Then you cannot swear."

Avery said, "It would be a great satisfaction to me and my friends, sir, if you would swear I was, or was not, the man."

"If it can be any satisfaction to you or your friends, I can probably say all I shall ever say. According to the best of my knowledge and belief, you are the man."

The minister's features hardened. "When you claim you saw me, was I wearing glasses?" As Orswell shook his head, Avery

180

snatched up his spectacles and put them on. "Do I now look as I did?" he demanded.

The engineer studied him for a full minute. "Sir," he said, "your glasses do not alter the features of your face."

The noise outside the house had become muted. Somehow I would have preferred the strident chants and shouts. Avery glared at Orswell, then swayed, caught himself against the desk and almost collapsed into his chair. He passed his hand over his eyes.

The seaman turned to leave and I accompanied him out of the room. As we emerged on the landing a great howl suddenly erupted both within and without the house. The Methodists below milled about in panic, squawking, bumping into each other like chickens trapped in an enclosure when they sense the fox is in the neighborhood. Near the foot of the stairs a small band of their braver fellows pressed against some counterforce that was hidden from my view beneath the landing.

In blindingly rapid succession I saw the front door fly open, its frame briefly filled by the wide back of the intrepid Deputy Pell just before he fled into the night. The Methodists flowed out the door like water through a gash cut in a leather bag. The handful of defenders below were driven back until they broke ranks and turned tail, and then, from the rear of the house, the brawling mob broke through from the sink-room and flooded the lower floor. "Avery!" they yelled. "Murderer Avery!" "Come out, Ephraim!" "Show yourself, child-killer!"

I sought Colonel Harnden in the crowd. Surely Harnden could control these madmen. Then I glimpsed his face at the door. His eyes gleamed in the dim glow of the lantern. They riveted on my own and he grinned wolfishly, the sharp edges of his teeth touching his lower lip. Without entering, he yanked the door shut.

For a moment the mob, having stormed the house and occupied it, seemed uncertain of their next move. I slammed Avery's door on him and looked desperately at Orswell. A tired smile creased his weather-beaten face. "It's none of my business, Squire."

He started past me toward the stairs. "Take my advice, youngster," he said, "and let them have the swine. It's not worth getting yourself killed over."

I shook my head.

"As you wish, youngster." He put a pistol into my hand. "You may need that," he said. "I usually keep it loaded. Can't remember if I loaded it today or not." He took a step and turned

181

back. "Maybe there *is* something I can do to help you," he said. Then he went down the stairs through the mob and out the door.

Someone in the back bellowed "Avery!" and quickly the rest took up the chant. "A-ver-y! A-ver-y!" The cry fired them up and they surged toward the staircase, led by Seth Darling, a powerful farmer of fifty who served Fall River as selectman, assistant post master, and sergeant-at-arms of the Vigilance Committee. He was flanked by five or six of the younger and stronger men, including Billy Pearce, and he carried a coil of stout rope. Other men wedged behind them, several toting guns. They began their climb, and I ran to the head of the stairs and raised my pistol, aiming it squarely at Seth Darling's chest.

"Get out of the way, Squire," Darling ordered. "We come here to hang that murderin' bastard and we mean to do it."

"Then you've got to kill me first, Seth, and none of you wants that."

"Come on, Squire Chris!" Billy Pearce shouted. "Ain't nobody looking to hurt *you*!"

"Just put down your piece and ride out," Ben Manchester said. "There's no man in this place goin' to remember you was ever here."

"Can't do it, Ben."

"Damn it!" Billy yelped. "We got nothing against you. Hell, some of us even *like* you. Don't make us kill you." His tone bordered on the plaintive.

I tried to keep the pistol steady. "None of you dares kill me, Billy."

Manchester snarled, "You tryin' to say we ain't got the guts?"

There was an angry rumble punctuated by shouts, and the mob lumbered forward against the backs of their leaders. Manchester took a step up and I shifted the direction of the gun barrel to his head.

"No, Ben, that's not what I mean. I don't question your courage, boys—but how would you survive if I were dead? Billy, who'd get your pa out of jail when he gets lathered up and wallops your ma? Who'd get the law on your neighbor, Seth, when he steals your beef? Iram Smith, who'd sue the peddler when he shortweights you on dry goods? And you, Ben. Who'd get you out of the kind of trouble you had last month with the Widow Lansing?"

Manchester flushed crimson and stepped back. I took a gamble and lowered my pistol. The men fell back in confusion.

I thought I saw my chance. "Go home, boys. You don't need this kind of trouble. If Avery's guilty, the law will hang him."

"The law!" a man growled from near the door. He pushed his way through and mounted the stairs, then wheeled and faced the crowd, holding his arms aloft. It was John Durfee.

"You boys all know me. It was on my land the poor girl was strangled. It's on my land she lies buried tonight. I cut down her poor body from my stack post—I collected her few possessions from her rooming house—I had her laid out in my parlor. I'm the man who swore the warrant against Avery. I'm the man who found the note in her bandbox, the one that said, if she was missing, 'twas *Avery* who'd know why!"

I raised my gun again.

"Colonel Harnden's got witnesses to put Avery in Tiverton the day of the murder," John Durfee announced. "He can prove that Avery fathered her child. He can prove Avery wrote her letters about it and tried to poison her. He can prove Avery set up to meet her the night he killed her!"

"If Harnden's got all that evidence then the law will hang Avery," I shouted.

"I tell you, boys, don't listen to a lawyer's talk about the law," Durfee cried. "How many men in this place been defended by Squire Randolph and got off?"

There was an admiring hum. Several hands went up.

"All right, boys," Durfee said. "How many of you were guilty?"

The hum ceased abruptly. The hands dropped.

"Then how in hell do you know he won't get Avery off?"

And, I thought, how in hell do you answer *that* argument?

Durfee seized the noose from Seth Darling and waved it over his head. "We can make damn well sure Avery pays for that crime, boys! No smooth lawyer's talk. No shyster tricks. We are the *people*! Hell, men, this is a democracy! Are you with me?"

Without waiting for an answer Durfee spun and charged toward me. With a general howl the mob followed him. In seconds I would be engulfed. I recall no thought of Avery, but the image of his wife and children flashed through my mind. My pistol was now pointed at Durfee. I suppose I intended to bring him down. At all events I started to squeeze the trigger.

The heavy pistol kicked up and there was an explosion.

Not a shot. An explosion. I heard it and smelled the gunpowder. Chips of wood and chunks of plaster dropped from

183

the ceiling into the mob. The men on the staircase froze. A billow of smoke belched from the barrel of Orswell's gun.

"Je-sus!" I shouted in amazement. "It works!"

Suddenly the whistle of the *King Philip* shrieked from the harbor. Three long blasts followed by three short and three long again. Orswell had gotten the steam up in the engines. The vessel was preparing to return to Fall River.

"Boys," I said, "the boat's heading out and I figure you'd better be on it. Will Pell's half-way to Newport by now and, come morning, I expect the militia will be here. If they find Avery swinging from a tree a lot of questions are going to be asked. If you all leave now, I don't expect there'll be anyone left here who can remember any of your faces."

The whistle blew again, with more seeming urgency. The men backed off and began to file through the door. John Durfee remained on the stairs, holding the rope. "I'm a plain-spoken man, Squire," he said, "and I'll tell you this. Avery will see the sun rise tomorrow because of you, but he better not see too many more. He murdered that girl and we both know it. I can understand that a man needs to earn a living, and I figure you're looking for a fat fee out of them Methodists for this business. Only thing I'm saying, Squire, is don't extend yourself to earn it." His eyes grew cold. "If Avery gets away, Mr. Randolph, you better go with him, if you want to keep on breathing."

He turned and headed for the door.

"That sounds like a threat, John," I said evenly.

He paused, keeping his back to me. "That's good," he replied. "I was afraid you'd misunderstand me."

BOOK III

The Bristol Hearing

33
John Durfee's Evidence

I had never conducted a case in a crowded courtroom before. Normally the benches behind the rail were empty save for an idler or two, or another defendant awaiting his turn before the magistrate. But the little Bristol courtroom, at ten o'clock on the morning of December 26, 1832, was packed solid with observers, most of them Fall River and Tiverton men who, though generally disciplined and respectful of the court, clearly manifested their support of the prosecution and their simmering hatred of the prisoner and his counsel. Women and children were not permitted attendance, and the female witnesses were sequestered in the First Baptist Church until their testimony was required. The male witnesses were positioned in the first three rows of seats behind the respective tables of the State, to the left, and the defense, to the right. As they entered they presented their summonses to the deputies, who then ushered them to the appropriate section. The process was not unlike the seating of guests at a wedding. I could visualize the deputies asking, "Are you a friend of the victim or the murderer?"

The witnesses in place, the public was then admitted. Those who could not find seats lounged sullenly against the walls. Only the center aisle leading from the rear doors to the swing-gate in the rail was left unpopulated. William Staples, an elderly lawyer of considerable experience and craft with whom I had already locked horns several times during my brief Rhode Island practice, sat at the prosecution table with the lycanthropic Colonel Harnden at his side to assist him in dealing with the evidence gathered by the Vigilance Committee. Quinncannon had permitted this unusual arrangement in return for Staples' agreement to allow Avery to sit behind the rail among the Methodist clergy for the purpose of testing the identifications of the State's eyewitnesses. The Irishman and I occupied the defense table while Justices Howe and Haile perched jointly behind the bench. These conditions obtained throughout the hearing, which lasted thirteen days, concluding on Monday, January 7.

The proceedings commenced with the Court Clerk's reading of Avery's voluntary statement as delivered to Howe by Elder Drake. It was in line with the story told to us by the prisoner the preceding afternoon. Mr. Staples briefly addressed the court, outlining the points he expected to prove, and called to the stand John Durfee, who testified to his finding of the body and its removal to his house. While Coroner Hicks empaneled his jury for the inquest, Durfee, having been informed by the women preparing the corpse that clean clothes would be needed for the interment, had gone to the dead woman's landlady in Fall River for her effects. He had received, from Mrs. Harriet Hathaway, the trunk and a bandbox belonging to Miss Cornell. The trunk was locked but Mrs. Hathaway informed him that the dead woman habitually kept the key in her pocket. Returning to his house, the witness had obtained the key from the women.

"When you had the key in your possession," Mr. Staples asked, "what, if anything, did you do?"

"I opened the trunk and searched it," Durfee replied. "I was particularly looking for letters because Dr. Wilbur had told me—"

"Objection," I said. "Hearsay."

"Sustained," said Justice Howe.

"Do not state your conversation with Dr. Wilbur," Staples instructed his witness. "When you'd opened the trunk, what, if anything, did you find?"

"I found three open letters. They were directed to Miss Cornell, one on yellow paper, one on pink, and the third on a white half-sheet. I read these three."

Staples took up some papers from his table. "I show you now three letters and ask if you can identify them."

Durfee glanced over the multicolored correspondence. "I can, sir. These are the three letters I found in Miss Cornell's trunk."

"Copies," Staples said, "have been provided to Mr. Avery's counsel. I now propose to read these letters into the record, Your Honors . . ." He turned his eyes to me. "Unless there is an objection?"

"Certainly there is an objection," I said without rising. "No evidence has been adduced to connect these letters with the prisoner, or even with the death of Miss Cornell, as Mr. Staples well knows."

188

"Very well," Staples returned quietly. "It is obvious that the defense has reasons to wish these letters suppressed so I will withdraw my motion."

"You will *not* withdraw your motion, sir, until the court has ruled on it!" I was on my feet and angry. "Your Honors, we further object to the prosecutor's gratuitous attempt to characterize the defense's motive in objecting to the reading of documents for which no relevance has been established."

Staples looked about the room with the innocent smile of an aging cherub. It was a favorite trick of his and one which seldom failed, as he was fully aware, to raise my temper. "I have withdrawn my motion," he said calmly. "There is no need for my learned *young* opponent to agitate himself."

The reference to my youth was another well-aimed barb. I took a deep breath, feeling my face reddening. "I ask the court to rule on my objections."

"Both objections are sustained," said Howe, with the air of a patient father settling a dispute between two naughty children.

"Thank you, Your Honor," I said.

"Never mind," said Staples. "The letters will keep. The government can wait."

"I trust," I said, "we are not, this early, being treated to an example of the tactics of snide innuendo with which the prosecution intends to conduct its case."

"Oh!" Staples cried as if mortally wounded from ambush. "Now *I* must object to Mr. Randolph's characterization of the State's tactics."

"Sustained," Howe yawned wearily. "Gentlemen, you are not before a jury. The Bench is unimpressed by histrionics. Shall we get on with it?"

I beat Staples in making apologies to the court and sat down in very bad humor. Quinncannon passed me a note and I unfolded it. It consisted of a single word:

"Relax."

"After the jury had read the letters they were handed back to me," John Durfee said, in response to Staples' next question. "I locked them in the trunk again. The jury, being divided, adjourned, and met again at my house at nine o'clock the next morning. That would be Saturday, December 22. After they had reached a verdict I took the body out and buried it in our family plot on my land."

"Did a clergyman officiate at the burial?" Staples asked.

"Yes, sir."

"Mr. Bidwell, I assume?"

"No, it was Reverend Fowler."

"But . . . ?" Staples appeared astonished. "Wasn't the poor girl a Methodist? And isn't Mr. Fowler a Congregationalist minister?"

Durfee nodded. "Mr. Bidwell refused to perform the ceremony so Fowler prayed over her. After the corpse was buried Mr. Fowler advised another search of the trunk and bandbox. I handed the key to my wife in the presence of my sister. They found a scrap of paper written in pencil mark. I read it and then went to the coroner and told him of the contents."

"As a result what, if anything, did the coroner do?"

"He ordered another jury on Monday, the twenty-fourth. It was the same men as the first jury, excepting two. They met at my house again and Mr. Hicks ordered the body dug up and another examination made by Dr. Wilbur and Dr. Foster Hooper of Fall River. After that the jury found for murder."

Staples smiled and produced another paper. "Mr. Durfee, I show you this document and ask if you recognize it."

"I do, sir. That is the verdict given by the Coroner's Jury on Monday, December 24."

"Your Honors," Staples said, handing the paper to the clerk, "this verdict is offered as State Exhibit A. A copy has been provided to the defense and we propose to read it into the record unless," and he again turned toward me, "there is an objection."

I tensed to object and felt Quinncannon's boot kick mine under the table. "No objection," I said, though I had no inkling of why.

The little clerk read the verdict in a clear treble:

And said jurors upon their oaths as aforesaid further say, that said Sarah M. Cornell came by her death by having a cord or a hemp line drawn around her neck and strangled until she was dead and then hung on a stake in a stack yard belonging to John Durfee, in Tiverton, State of Rhode Island, they also believe, and from strong circumstantial evidence, that Ephraim K. Avery, of Bristol, in the County of Bristol, and State of &c. was principal or accessory in her death. And so the jurors aforesaid, &c. do say that the said Ephraim K. Avery in manner and form aforesaid, of his malice aforethought, the said Sarah M. Cornell did kill and murder or cause to be killed and murdered, against the peace, &c.

RICHARD DURFEE
BAULSTON BRAYTON
ELIHU HICKS, Coroner WILLIAMS DURFEE
DANIEL SHERMAN
WILLIAM BOOMER
ISAAC BRIGHTMAN

When the recital was completed Staples beamed at me in triumph. "Your witness," he announced.

I began to rise but Quinncannon put a restraining hand on my arm.

"Mr. Durfee," the Irishman began, "I have only a very few questions for you. You were the one to discover this unfortunate woman's body, I understand."

"Yes, sir," the farmer responded coldly.

"How much time elapsed between that discovery and the moment you gave the alarm?"

"Not more than a minute. I got down from my wagon and parted her hair to see if she was dead. Then I began to shout. Right afterward my brother and father came running, and you and Squire Randolph rode up over the hill."

"You had determined she was dead?"

"She was clearly dead, Mr. Quinncannon."

"Did you recognize her?"

"I did not."

The Irishman appeared thoughtful. "In the process of examining her, is it possible you might have altered her appearance?"

"No, sir. I just pushed her hair back to look at her face. It fell right back over her eyes."

"You didn't remove her shoes or handkerchief and place them beside her body?"

"I did not!" Durfee was growing purple.

"You didn't, perhaps, fasten some of the clasps on her cloak?"

"No!"

"When you first found the body, who was with you?"

"No one was with me," Durfee growled.

"Is it possible you discovered her comb lying nearby, broke it in two, and threw the pieces away?"

"Why the hell would I do that?"

"I have no idea," Quinncannon said mildly. "Is it possible you did so?"

"NO!" Durfee shouted in anger.

191

"Oh, I think it is *possible*, Mr. Durfee," the Irishman said slowly, keeping his eyes on the justices. "You could not have altered the cord or the body since the cord was frozen and the body was in rigor mortis. But you could have adjusted other physical evidence, even in the space of less than a minute, could you not?"

Staples leaped up. "Objection! That question has been asked and answered several times."

"No!" Durfee snarled. "I want to answer. I did not move anything. I touched nothing but her hair, as I said."

"Very well," Quinncannon said, "but your answer is not responsive, sir. I did not inquire if you *did* disturb the evidence, but only if you *could have*. After all, Mr. Durfee, we have only your word that you gave alarm within a minute of discovery."

"I am under oath," the witness snapped.

"So you are, sir. So you are. I'm gratified that you are keeping that fact in mind."

Staples had remained standing. "Oh, *objection*," he groaned. "Mr. Quinncannon is bullying the witness!"

John Howe leaned forward. "I think, perhaps, I must sustain the objection, Mr. Quinncannon."

"I think, perhaps, you should, Your Honor," the Irishman replied, smiling. To my astonishment Howe returned the smile.

Quinncannon seemed to be circling Durfee, playing with him like a tomcat with a cornered barn rat.

"Now, Mr. Durfee, you obtained the dead woman's trunk and bandbox from her rooming house?"

"I did."

"You procured the key to her trunk, searched it, found, as you say, the letters which you then presented to the coroner's jury after you had read them?"

"I have said so, sir."

"You buried her yourself on your own land, did you?"

"It was the Christian and charitable thing," the witness answered stiffly. "We had then no notion who her people were."

"It was a noble gesture," Quinncannon said without sarcasm. "You then caused your wife and sister to search further for letters and they found one. Remind me, sir, what was that communication?"

The farmer eyed him. "A note in pencil, Mr. Quinncannon. It was found in the bandbox."

"Ah, yes," said the Irishman as if suddenly remembering. "And you passed that note on to Mr. Hicks, who then ordered a new inquest, I believe."

"That's the way it happened."

"I see," Quinncannon said, removing a sheet of paper from our table. "I show you now this document and ask if you can identify it."

Durfee studied it. "That's the first verdict of the coroner's jury, the one they brought in on Saturday morning."

"Defense," said Quinncannon, "offers this paper as Exhibit A and asks that it be read into the record unless," and he smiled at Staples, "the State wishes to object."

Mr. Staples flushed. "We *do* object, most strenuously. This so-called 'verdict' was returned by a jury that was not legally constituted under Rhode Island law. Two of its members were not freeholders."

"If the court please," the Irishman said, "that is close to being precisely my point. Mr. Joseph Cook and Mr. Isaac Negus, who took their oaths as members of the first jury, were later found ineligible to serve, and were replaced by William Boomer and Isaac Brightman. Yet the second verdict, which Mr. Staples has introduced into evidence, is, by its wording, clearly a continuation of the first verdict. In the second verdict the jurors merely *re*affirm their oaths, yet two of their number had never sworn any oath at all and thus had nothing to reaffirm. Therefore, the defense contends that the second verdict has no more legal status than the first. That is, neither verdict has any legal status whatsoever."

"But," Staples sputtered, "you allowed the second verdict to become part of the record."

"We did, Mr. Staples, but only as a written indication of the jury's opinion of the young woman's death as it was formed *after* they had become aware of the pencil note found in the bandbox. We now propose to inform the court of the verdict reached *before* that note was discovered, the verdict reached *on the basis of the physical evidence alone*."

"But that is the State's argument," Staples countered. "The first verdict was founded on incomplete evidence. The jury *was* unaware of that note and its contents." He turned to the bench. "That note is crucial to our case, Your Honors."

Quinncannon scratched a corner of his moustache with the nail of his little finger. "Then why, Mr. Staples, did you fail to introduce the note into evidence?"

"Why, I anticipated you would introduce object to it as you did to the letters."

"That, sir," said the Irishman, "is entirely your problem."

The justices conferred briefly and then Howe said, "The

objection is overruled. The court is inclined to permit more latitude in this hearing than might be allowed in Oyer and Terminer. The verdict of the first jury will be read, subject to the court's later determination of its relevance."

The clerk commenced to read:

State of Rhode Island and Providence Plantations, Newport, ss. An Inquisition taken in Tiverton, in the County of Newport, the 21st day of December, 1832, before Elihu Hicks, coroner of the town of Tiverton, upon the view of the dead body of Sarah M. Cornell here lying dead, upon their oaths do say that the dead Sarah was found dead hung up and confined, with a small cord or rope about her neck, to a stake inside of said stack yard, and the jurors do further say that they believe the said Sarah M. Cornell committed suicide by hanging herself upon a stake in said stack yard and was influenced to commit the crime by the wicked conduct of a married man, which we gather from Dr. Wilbur together with the contents of three letters found in the trunk of the said Sarah M. Cornell, and so the jurors aforesaid &c.

> RICHARD DURFEE, Foreman
> BAULSTON BRAYTON
> JOSEPH COOK
> DANIEL SHERMAN
> WILLIAMS DURFEE
> ISAAC NEGUS

Now Quinncannon returned to John Durfee. "It appears, sir, that the first jury found for suicide and the second for murder. Between the verdict of the first and the convening of the second, are you aware, to your own knowledge, of the discovery of any new, significant evidence aside from the note found in the bandbox and delivered by you to the coroner?"

"I am not," Durfee answered, with an edge on his voice. "The note was plenty good enough to change their minds."

The Irishman addressed the bench. "As the State does not appear disposed to introduce this mysterious note, so crucial that it alone seems to have reversed the inquest verdict and brought the wrath of the United Kingdoms of Fall River and Tiverton down on the head of the prisoner, the defense moves to have it produced, identified by this witness, and read in open court."

194

I gaped at my colleague. He knew the damning content of that paper as well as I did. To me it seemed imperative to our case that we go to the wall to prevent its introduction. I glimpsed Staples whispering feverishly with Harnden. The prosecutor was, if possible, even more confounded than I was. If Quinncannon's purpose was to keep Staples off balance, he was succeeding wonderfully but, I wondered, at what cost to our client. A quick glance at the pews behind me proved that our Methodist brethren acutely shared my concern.

Then Staples stood and said, incredibly, "Objection."

Quinncannon laughed out loud.

"On what grounds, Mr. Staples?" Howe inquired.

"Proper foundation has not been laid, Your Honor."

"In other words, the State did not want to introduce the paper so early in the proceedings." The Irishman relaxed against our table and folded his arms. "Your Honors, as my learned opponent has raised the specter of this infamous note on direct examination, I contend that we have the right to demand its immediate inclusion in the record."

Howe looked at Staples, and the latter shrugged and surrendered the original of Sarah Cornell's note. While Quinncannon went through the formality of having the paper identified by the witness, Staples glared at him. His whole attitude indicated that he knew the Irishman was up to some fox's trick, and he could not imagine what it was.

For the third time that morning the clerk read a piece of evidence aloud:

> If I should be missing enquire of the Rev Mr Avery of Bristol he will know where I am
>
> > Dec 20th
> > S M Cornell

It was a hushed courtroom that strained to hear Quinncannon's soft brogue when he again faced Durfee.

"You have testified that you searched both the trunk and the bandbox prior to the first jury's verdict, the suicide verdict. You have also testified that this note naming Reverend Avery was not found until the following day, a Saturday, after the body was buried, and that it was discovered by your wife and sister in the bandbox." He looked up. "Mr. Durfee, when you searched the bandbox on Friday, why did you fail to find this note?"

The farmer straightened and met his eye. "But I *did* find it."

"Then why did you not immediately bring it to the coroner's attention?"

"Because, on Friday, I did not read it. I merely noticed it had some pencil scrawl but I paid no further attention to it."

Quinncannon shook his head and rubbed his eyes. "Let me get this straight, Mr. Durfee. You, who have confessed to reading every line of every page of unsealed correspondence secreted in the dead girl's baggage—You, who have admitted prowling through her discarded linen and dirty laundry in a seemingly insatiable curiosity over her various communications—*You*, sir, perhaps the most voracious reader of other people's mail in human history, actually came upon a piece of paper, discerned that it contained writing, and neglected to read nineteen words for twenty-four hours?"

"That is correct." Durfee leaned forward and added menacingly, "I don't care for your question, sir."

The Irishman smiled. "I am not excessively thrilled by your answer, sir."

He walked back toward the defense table and said over his shoulder, "After you obtained Miss Cornell's trunk key, Mr. Durfee, when, if ever, was it out of your possession?"

"Aside from the few moments on Saturday when I gave it to my wife, never until Monday, the twenty-fourth, when I turned it over to Hicks."

Quinncannon arrived at his chair and dropped into it. "It really is remarkable, Mr. Durfee. Wherever I look in this strange case I find your footprints there. You discovered the body; you gave the alarm; you obtained the trunk and bandbox; you donated your house for the inquests and medical examinations; you discovered and read the letters and presented them to the juries; you buried the body; you read the dead woman's note and gave it to the coroner; you disinterred the body and then reburied it; you kept the key to her trunk for four days; you are the first witness called for the prosecution. Why, Mr. Durfee, you are ubiquitous! You seem to have done everything except swear out the warrant for Mr. Avery's arrest."

Durfee shifted uneasily in his chair.

One of Quinncannon's eyebrows arched wickedly.

"My God," the Irishman said with mock astonishment. "Don't tell me you did that too."

🐚 34

Mr. Randolph Takes Charge

While John Durfee nearly staggered, glassy-eyed, from the stand, and Staples conferred with Harnden in frenzied confusion, Quinncannon leaned toward me and whispered, "Hold the fort. I've got some people to see."

I nodded, wondering how I could match his skill at cross-examination. The fact was that Quinncannon, while eliciting nothing substantial to connect Durfee with the dead girl, had somehow succeeded in making of the Tiverton farmer a viable alternate suspect.

The Irishman left the room as William Staples said, "The State calls Dr. Thomas Wilbur."

Wilbur first testified to his arrival at the stack yard and initial examination of the body. He had opened her cloak across the abdomen to ascertain if she was fuller than women usually are. He determined that she was.

"Did you have a reason for making such an inspection of the body, Doctor?" Staples wanted to know.

"I did."

"Had the deceased consulted with you professionally in the weeks before her death?"

"She had."

"And what, if any, diagnosis did you make?"

I tensed while Wilbur considered his answer. "Well, Mr. Staples, I concluded, from her symptoms and certain declarations she made to me—"

"Objection to the declarations," I said.

"Sustained," said Howe. "Confine yourself to the symptoms, Doctor. The rest is hearsay."

The witness nodded and explained that he had concluded the girl was pregnant. He rehearsed the dates on which Cornell had visited him, leading up to the night she had brought the oil of tansy.

197

"Did she tell you how she came to possess this poison, Doctor?"

"She did," Wilbur answered grimly.

I got to my feet. "I hope the prosecution does not intend to follow this line of inquiry, Your Honors. Unless Dr. Wilbur knows, of his own knowledge, how Miss Cornell obtained the oil of tansy, any evidence he offers on the subject is hearsay."

Howe smiled. "I'm certain both the witness and Mr. Staples comprehend the meaning of the court's prior ruling, Mr. Randolph."

Staples looked unhappy but he shifted his questions to Wilbur's role at the inquests. The physician's continued annoyance with Coroner Hicks was ill-concealed.

"The examination before the first interment could scarcely be called an examination at all. On the twenty-fourth Mr. Hicks asked for a second examination."

Wilbur described some of the external marks on the corpse. Aside from what he had mentioned to me during our conversation, he noted abrasions and green stains on both knees, the latter apparently caused by "the juice of grass." There were scratches on her legs and on the outer side of the left leg above the ankle; these were sufficient "to start the blood flowing." There was a deep bruise "on her left side, just above the hip." The right side of the abdomen was also "discolored."

During the second examination Wilbur had opened the uterus and extracted a female foetus, which he thought was "about half-grown." Dr. Foster Hooper, who had assisted him, had concurred. The jury had then required an even more thorough examination. He and Hooper had subsequently found her lungs "engorged with black, venous blood, that is, the vessels were distended with dark blood." They found the stomach "healthy." Dr. Wilbur supposed the appearance of the lungs indicated strangulation. Death from a blow on the head would not have caused the same appearance.

Staples said, "Thank you, Doctor," and nodded at me. As he added, "Cross-examine," I became aware that Quinncannon had returned to his chair beside me. I took a sheet of foolscap and wrote: "Do you want him?"

The Irishman wrote back: "Wouldn't touch him with a pitch fork. Go get him."

I smiled and stood.

"Dr. Wilbur, did I understand you to say that the coroner permitted you only the most cursory examination of the body?"

"You did, Mr. Randolph."

198

"Yet you were able to determine, from the condition of the lungs and other factors, that the cause of death was strangulation?"

"That is accurate, sir."

"Based on your examinations, Doctor, can you say with absolute certainty that this strangulation was *not* self-inflicted?"

Wilbur regarded me sadly. "No physician could make such a statement, Mr. Randolph."

"Then you cannot swear that Sarah Cornell did not take her own life."

"Of course not," Wilbur responded.

"Of course not," I echoed. "Now, Doctor, you testified that, when you extracted the foetus, you thought it half-grown. Isn't the normal time of pregnancy nine months?"

"It is," said Wilbur.

"So a half-grown foetus would indicate a pregnancy of four and one-half months?"

"Yes, sir."

"Is it your testimony that Sarah Cornell must have become pregnant sometime between July 20 and August 7?"

"I would say," Wilbur responded, "closer to the latter date. Perhaps the fourth or fifth. It might have been as late as the tenth."

"But no later?"

"No later," the witness said.

I nodded. "Would you agree, Doctor, that all drugs are potentially poisonous?"

Wilbur met my eyes. "I would, Mr. Randolph, if you choose to phrase your question in that manner. It depends on the dosage given."

"But you would say, Doctor, that a little prussic acid is more dangerous than an entire phial of laudanum?"

The witness smiled. "There is no such thing as a *little* prussic acid," he said.

I returned his smile. "Would you say, sir, that there *is* such a thing as a little oil of tansy?"

"Do you mean, is there a less than lethal dose?"

"I mean, is there a less than dangerous dose?"

"Well," the doctor answered, "of course there is, but—"

"No further questions," I cut in and sat down.

Of course, Sarah had told the witness that Avery had recommended three times the dose required to kill her, but that conversation, as Staples and I both knew, was inadmissible as hearsay.

Wilbur looked up plaintively at Howe, who in turn glanced at the prosecutor's table. Mr. Staples kept his eyes on the papers before him. At length Howe said, "The witness is dismissed," and adjourned for the noon meal.

A parade of witnesses marched to the stand during the afternoon but little new information was elicited. Dr. Foster Hooper corroborated Wilbur's testimony concerning the second examination. I had only two questions on cross:

"Did I understand you to say, Doctor, that from your observation of the foetus you believed the dead woman to be 'half gone'?"

"Yes, sir. I meant by that I supposed her term was half over."

"In your opinion, how much time elapsed between conception and death?"

"I should say between 130 and 145 days."

Benjamin Manchester and Thomas Hart described how each had discovered a part of the victim's comb. The comb had been found, broken in two pieces, in the area of the stack yard. It was a curved, tortoise-shell comb such as women use to do up their hair behind. The larger piece, mended with a brass plate and rivets, was noticed by Manchester eighteen to twenty rods northwest of the stack. Hart had spotted the smaller fragment twenty-three rods due north.

Billy Pearce, Peleg Cranston and Jeremiah Gifford told their stories. Pearce and Gifford knew Avery by sight but their testimony brought the defendant no closer to Tiverton on the fatal night than the Bristol ferry. It was Cranston, the keeper of the Stone Bridge, who had to be discredited.

"Mr. Cranston," I began my cross-examination, "prior to December 20, had you ever seen Mr. Avery before?"

"Never, Squire Chris, as I recollect."

"From that day until this morning have you seen Mr. Avery at any time?"

"Nope, I wouldn't say I have."

"How did you travel to court this morning?"

He grinned. "In a fine closed carriage Colonel Harnden sent for me."

"Then," I said, "was it after you had arrived at the court house that Colonel Harnden pointed out Mr. Avery to you?"

"Yes, Squire," Cranston replied in blissful innocence.

Staples groaned involuntarily. The witness shot his eyes

toward him and quickly added, "But I'd of known him anyway."

"Mr. Cranston, are you acquainted with a man named David Davoll?"

"Sure. Davoll lives in Portsmouth and has a blacksmith shop in Tiverton near Lawton's Inn. He's crossed my bridge morning and evening for years."

"On Christmas day after the body was found, did you have a conversation with Mr. Davoll?"

"Might have," was the evasive answer. "Davoll and me talk 'most every day."

"Did you not tell Davoll that you had seen Avery several times before December 20?"

"Couldn't have. Wasn't true."

"Did you not tell Davoll that Avery had *not* crossed your bridge on December 20?"

"No, Squire, I never did!"

"Mr. Cranston, you have testified that you found Avery's tracks in the sand beneath the bridge on the morning of the twenty-first."

The toll-keeper nodded. "He must of crossed back to the Island after I locked the gate at nine o'clock. He had to jump down and walk around the gate."

"Did you, or anyone else to your knowledge, compare Mr. Avery's boots with these tracks you say you saw?"

"Well, no, Squire. When the tide come in it washed 'em out of the sand."

"Is it unusual for people to leave such tracks when they are forced to return after you have locked the gate?"

"Nope. I find 'em there most mornings when I open up."

"So those tracks might have been made by *anyone*."

"I suppose so, Squire, but—"

"Mr. Cranston!" I barked. "On Christmas day did not Davoll tell you that *he* had made those tracks the night before?"

"Not as I recollect."

"Not as you recollect," I echoed slowly and looked up at the justices. "No further questions."

Staples called John Orswell, engineer on the *King Philip*. My first impression of the man at Avery's house had been that he would make a formidable witness and his performance under direct examination did nothing to raise the hope that I had misread him.

201

I undertook his cross-examination carefully. "Mr. Orswell, is there a prohibition against crew members carrying private letters on the steamboat?"

"There is, sir, but the gentleman was most persistent."

"Isn't there a letter box on the steamer?"

"Yes, sir. So I informed the man, but he said to forward it in that manner would only delay it. He indicated there was some urgency about the matter, that he wanted it delivered that afternoon."

"Did he offer to pay you for this service?"

"He did. He offered ninepence and I took it."

I regarded him. "You deliberately violated the rules of your employers for a ninepence?"

Orswell gave me a smile. "I'm afraid so, Mr. Randolph."

I sensed the need to shift my inquiry in a new direction. "This man who gave you the letter—how was he dressed?"

"I have no clear memory of his clothes. He wore a cloak, blue or black, I think, and he had on a hat."

"What color was the hat?"

"I don't know. Some dark color."

"Wide brim or narrow?"

"I don't know, sir."

"What was he wearing under the cloak?"

"I didn't notice."

I leaned against the defense table. "Mr. Orswell, do you consider yourself a particularly observant man?"

"I pay little attention to apparel," he answered, "but I have a good memory for faces."

I phrased my next question with precision. "Do you now, upon your oath, swear that Mr. Avery is the man who gave you that letter?"

"According to the best of my judgment I should say the prisoner is the man."

It was my turn to smile. "That answer is not responsive, sir. I ask you again, will you *swear* an identification of Avery?"

The engineer met my gaze steadily. "To the best of my recollection and judgment—"

"Mr. Orswell," I interrupted sharply. "My question is clear enough. Either you will so swear or you will not. Again I ask you—"

"Objection!" Staples cried. "The witness has answered the question. Mr. Randolph will have to be satisfied with his response."

I directed my attention to the Bench. "With all due respect

to my learned opponent, it is not for him to determine what evasive responses from his witnesses will satisfy me..." I smiled at Staples "... or, for that matter, what will satisfy this court."

I walked back to my chair and then again faced Orswell. "When you received the letter, sir, was it sealed?"

"Yes, sir, with a wax wafer."

"Did the man who handed it to you indicate by whom it was written?"

"He did not."

"Did he indicate any specific knowledge of its contents?"

"No, Mr. Randolph."

I said, "Thank you, Mr. Orswell," and sat down.

Harriet Hathaway, the dead girl's last landlady, gave her testimony essentially as Amy had recited it to me. Then Staples called his final witness for the day.

Lucy Hathaway, Harriet's daughter, was a pretty girl of perhaps twenty-four who had worked with Sarah at the mill and who, at Sarah's request, had "asked Mama" if she could board with them, as she wished a house "more retired" than Cole's. Sarah had been the only boarder. On December 20 at five-fifteen in the afternoon, Sarah had asked for directions to Joseph Durfee's house and left work "not ten minutes later."

Sarah had shown Lucy the three letters (which the witness now identified) and stated they were "from a gentleman in Bristol." Lucy had observed the colors of the paper and the handwriting but had not read them.

On cross-examination Miss Lucy proved to be a gold mine. Quinncannon and I had determined that our best chance, aside from discrediting the prosecution witnesses who claimed to have seen Avery in the vicinity of Tiverton on the twentieth, lay in convincing the justices that Sarah had taken her own life, and that she had, in the weeks before her "suicide," deliberately arranged circumstances to create the appearance of her having been murdered by Avery.

At first the theory had seemed to me so outrageous, and so patently at odds with the facts, that I doubted its wisdom. While I remained uncomfortable over this approach, I had to admit to myself that I had no viable alternative to suggest, especially as I remained convinced of Avery's guilt. Moreover, as the Irishman had gently reminded me in the Bristol Hotel, while I had the conduct of the defense he retained the control. And

I had not forgotten his brilliant cross-examination of John Durfee during which he had managed to imply the possibility of Durfee's guilt without adducing even a wisp of evidence.

Accordingly, my intent in questioning Lucy Hathaway was to establish that Sarah had paraded the yellow, pink and white epistles before her in a manner calculated to be both obvious and mysterious, for the purpose of arousing Lucy's curiosity and implanting the idea that Sarah had a "lover" in Bristol.

When I raised the matter of the letters, however, I reaped a far greater harvest than I, or even the Irishman, could have anticipated.

"Sarah showed me those letters many times, Mr. Randolph. It seemed she was always reading them or fondling them in her lap, just itching to be asked about them. A week or a fortnight prior to the Sabbath before her death I saw her with them and she said, 'Lucy, don't you think it is possible for an innocent girl to be led away by a man that she has confidence in and rather looks up to?' I hesitated and said, 'I don't know.' She then said, 'But what can an innocent girl do, in the hands of a strong man, and he using all kinds of argument?'"

Lucy paused and looked at me for reassurance. "Should I go on, sir?"

"By all means," I said soothingly. "Had she made similar suggestions to you before, Miss Hathaway?"

"Many times, sir. Once Sarah said she had been to many Methodist camp-meetings but would never go again. I asked her the reason. 'Why,' says Sarah, 'because I have seen things transacted there that would condemn them to my mind.' Well, sir, naturally I asked what she meant by that, and she turned away and muttered, 'I can't tell.'"

I was getting a new image of Sarah—Sarah the coy, Sarah the dropper of dark hints of evil things, Sarah the sly seeker of attention. I told myself I understood female psychology and I took a gamble.

"So you again asked her to what transactions she referred, Lucy?"

"Of *course* I did!" Of course she had. "Sarah said, 'Something perfectly *dreadful* happened between a church member and a minister.' She waited a minute and then added, 'And him a married man too.'"

Wonderful Lucy! She had despised Sarah and she was blessed with total recall. I took another gamble.

"Did Sarah ever tell you that her health was bad?"

"Not straight out, sir, but she moped and moaned about so

that one day I asked her if she was well. 'Oh, Lucy,' she says, 'I have not been well since the camp-meeting at Thompson.' I told her she ought to take something. She said she had some pills of Dr. Wilbur." Lucy sucked in her breath and threw me a look of wide-eyed naiveté. "Of course I *never* suspected the *truth* of her condition."

Of course she hadn't.

35

The Knot and the Bonnet

That evening in the taproom of the Bristol Hotel, when the drinks had been served and the late supper ordered, Quinn-cannon produced a length of marlin hemp and double-looped and twisted it rapidly. "This," he said, "is what a clove hitch looks like just before it is tightened." He handed it to me by the ends and pushed the burning candle across the table. "Draw the knot, Christy."

I put the loops over the candle and tightened the knot in the only way possible, by using both hands to yank both ends of the cord simultaneously, horizontally. The twine dug into the wax to the wick. The candle snapped and toppled onto the table, still burning. The Irishman extinguished it with a drop of his whiskey.

"Notice," he said, "that the knot requires the simultaneous action of both hands, pulling in opposite directions. It is impossible to draw it tight with only one hand."

The image of Sarah Maria Cornell's hands, frozen in death, flashed through my mind. The right inside her cloak, the left extended from an elbow pressed to her side, and palm out, fingertips up, as if warding off a blow. The rope around her throat was so tight that death must have been virtually instantaneous. Could she have tightened the clove hitch, even if she knew how to tie one, and had time to withdraw both hands to the positions in which they were found?

I decided she could not and said so, and Quinncannon nodded.

"Then," I said, "you *know* she was murdered by Avery!"

"That she was murdered, yes," he replied. "Dr. Wilbur's testimony alone proves that. But murdered by Avery? Of that we cannot be confident."

Well, damn it, *I* was confident that our client was guilty. I sipped my Scotch and passed a few moments in sullen silence. Something else was bothering me and at last I brought it out.

"Lon, about her bonnet . . ."

His dark eyes focused sharply on mine over the rim of his glass. "What about the bonnet troubles you?"

"Everything," I responded. "First off, she exchanged her usual plain bonnet for her calash before she left her boarding house, and Avery, in the pink letter, specifically instructed her to wear the calash."

His manner became Socratic. "What does that suggest to you?"

"I know it was the white, not the pink letter, which established their final meeting, but why was he so anxious that she wear the calash? A calash differs from a plain bonnet in only one respect. It is pleated like an accordion and can be folded back from the forehead. I can't help thinking her wearing of the calash made it easier for Avery..." I paused and amended, "...for the murderer to put the noose over her head. But that makes no sense because..."

He watched me and waited.

"Because," I resumed, "her bonnet had to be *off* her head at some point. The broken comb proves that. It could not have been removed unless her head was uncovered. And her hair, let down and hanging loose over her face—" Again I stopped in the middle of my argument.

Quinncannon settled back in his chair and puffed on his pipe, content to let me gather my thoughts.

At length I said, "When Sarah met the killer she had her hair done up and secured by the comb. Subsequently she, or he, removed both calash and comb, letting her hair fall free. But—" The idea struck me with an intense clarity. "The calash was replaced on her head *before* she was strangled. It *had* to be, because the ribbon, though untied, was *inside* the cord. The killer *must* have put it on her because she would never have put it on herself without tying the ribbon or while her hair was in her eyes. Don't you see, Lon? It couldn't have been John Durfee who put the ribbons inside the rope because when he found her body the rope was frozen and taut. You pointed that out yourself in court."

A smile slowly creased his face. I realized that everything I had just said had long ago occurred to him. That fact annoyed me but only briefly, for he said, "Christy, you are a man remarkably gifted. I consider myself fortunate to have you as an associate and proud to have you as a friend. You have," he added, in a statement which reminded me of something the Widow Bloss had said at the camp-meeting, "not yet, I think, fully grasped your worth as a lawyer and a man."

To this day I cherish his compliment, but at that moment I did not even acknowledge it. Instead I said, "But what does it all prove, Lon?"

"For one thing, it proves the girl was murdered."

"By Avery," I said. It was a statement, not a question. But Quinncannon shook his head.

"No, little brother," he replied. "That is the reason I am creating the illusion of suicide. The only person in this tangled case who could not have murdered Cornell is Ephraim K. Avery."

I am positive that, at that moment, Quinncannon believed in Avery's innocence. But the minister had taken advantage of the girl at Thompson. I had no more doubt of that than I had that he believed himself the father of her unborn child. Unquestionably she was demanding money from him. Unquestionably he had written the three letters. Unquestionably he had met her on the night she died. He had motive—he had opportunity—he had means. Granted, there were a few loose ends in the physical evidence that had not been fully explained, but to my thinking they were minor points.

It crossed my mind that Quinncannon, being a basically decent man, needed to convince himself of Avery's innocence in order to conduct his defense successfully, especially since the defense was based on a clearly false premise. What had he said? "I forget nothing. Occasionally I ignore something."

I told myself that the Irishman had simply chosen to be blind to the obvious, the overwhelmingly persuasive evidence against Avery. As for me, I knew for a certainty the clergyman was guilty. I justified my participation in his defense on the grounds that my practice was not prosperous, I was newly married and about to become a father, and, to put the matter simply, I needed the fee.

36

Mr. Randolph Reflects

*Abner Davis and Benjamin Manchester had been blast-*ing rocks on Albert Robinson's land, which abutted John Dur-fee's, about four-thirty on the afternoon of December 20. They were thirty or forty rods from the stack yard and perhaps fifteen rods from the stone wall that marked the boundary when they charged the seam with twenty pounds of powder and set the charge. As they ran they saw a tall stranger dressed in dark clothes sitting on the wall and shouted a warning. When they looked up after the explosion they saw the man moving off on foot toward Fall River. Neither made any pretense of being able to identify Avery, but Manchester said the stranger "looked like a minister."

"Ben," I asked, "what does a minister look like?"

"Well, they wear dark clothes."

"Does a doctor wear dark clothes?"

No answer.

"Does a lawyer wear dark clothes?"

A sullen stare.

"Look around this court room, Ben," I said. "Do you see any man wearing *light* clothes?"

Ben Manchester guessed he didn't.

John Durfee was recalled to state he had seen a stranger "a little before sunset" on the twentieth standing sixty to one hundred rods distant from his stack yard. I took the opportunity to ask if, on that night, he had heard any cries from the stack yard. He had not.

Seth Darling had been serving at the Fall River post office in his capacity of assistant post master on November 19, and remembered sending a letter to Bristol. It was "the impression of his mind" that the letter was directed to Avery, though he had no idea who had posted it. The implication was, of course, that it came from Sarah in answer to the yellow letter of November 13, and prompted the pink response of November 27.

Stamps were seldom used in the rural areas of America in

1832. Normally letters arrived with postage due, the amount determined by the town of origin indicated with the date of mailing by the postmark. Envelopes were also unheard of, letters being folded in thirds and sealed with a wafer of melted wax. Mail was called for at the post office and the postage due either paid or charged. Either way the post master kept a record in his book. Mr. Avery, it developed, collected his mail regularly, though he seldom paid the charges in cash on the spot.

It did not, therefore, aid the defense's cause when Darling was followed to the stand by Lemuel Briggs, the Bristol post master, who testified that, according to his records, Avery had received letters from Fall River on November 12, 19 and 30.

Based on the records of Darling and Briggs, Staples now proposed to read the pink letter of November 27 into the record. I fought heroically, but it was hopeless. While the clerk read the damning communication, I reflected grimly that Briggs' three dates fit the pattern of correspondence perfectly:

November 12: Avery receives a letter from Sarah written in Fall River, a letter which Wilbur had urged her to write on October 21, and which, presumably, informs him she is pregnant by him.

November 13: Avery writes the yellow letter which opens: "I have just Received your letter with no small surprise. . . ." The next day he mails it from Warren.

He had asked for an interview and, on November 19, she answered. He received this message the afternoon of the nineteenth and probably wrote his reply that night, but he was afraid to post it and waited until the Four-Days meeting in Providence when he could send it by Orswell. That, I thought, would account for the lack of a specific date on the pink letter in which he pressed her to visit him secretly in Bristol. He had, however, given her the option of other meeting places closer to Fall River, and evidently she had named her own terms in the letter he received from her on November 30.

Thus, on December 8, he had written the white letter, doubtless while in Iram Smith's store, on a half-sheet torn from Smith's stock, in which he agreed to meet her on December 20 at six o'clock "at the place named."

But what place *had* she named? Was it John Durfee's or Joseph Durfee's or one of the meeting houses Avery had suggested, or none of these?

And, if she truly had not accused Avery of fathering her child until November 12, as now appeared, where and from whom had she actually obtained the oil of tansy she'd exhibited to Dr. Wilbur on October 21? Avery would not yet have had a motive to give her the poison. If she'd lied to Wilbur, was there then some validity to Quinncannon's crazy strategy? Was she already planning suicide and endeavoring to frame Avery for her murder?

If so, I reflected, her plans had gone awry, for clearly she *had* been murdered, and unquestionably by Avery. Was that the final irony? Had the minister been caught in the coils of her scheme to implicate him in a crime she never dreamed he would actually commit?

It struck me forcibly that that was *not* the final irony. The final irony was that Avery had killed the girl to prevent her from publishing his paternity of a child he had not—he *could* not—have fathered.

According to the testimony of the State's own doctors, Sarah must have conceived no later than August 10, yet she had not had connection with Avery until August 29.

I wondered what was in Avery's mind—knowing he had murdered her for nothing. For nothing.

Then a fragment of an earlier conversation with Quinncannon flashed through my mind:

"Obviously, Lon," I had said, speaking of the yellow letter, "this was written by the father of her child."

"Evidently," he'd responded, "it was written by a man who believed he was the father of her child."

"But, if he was convinced he *was* the father, then his motive is just as strong."

"Yes, Christy," Quinncannon had answered, "but that is not the point."

I now thought I understood what the point was. *Someone* was the father, and, whatever the preacher thought at the time, it was not Avery. Who, then, could it be? John Durfee? He had certainly made himself conspicuous, as the Irishman had noted, in every phase of the investigation. No other man, with the exception of Colonel Harnden, had demonstrated a greater thirst for Avery's blood.

Or was it Grindall Rawson, Sarah's brother-in-law? She'd been living in his house at the time her pregnancy had commenced. Could he have seduced Sarah, or she him, without his wife's knowledge?

211

Or . . . *did* his wife know?

I became suddenly aware of John Howe's voice calling my name as if from a deep abyss.

"Do you have any questions of this witness, Mr. Randolph?"

Lemuel Briggs was still on the stand. I glanced at Quinn-cannon and he shook his head almost imperceptibly.

"No questions, Your Honor," I said.

"Court stands adjourned until tomorrow at ten," Howe announced, rapping his gavel.

"You look, Christopher," said the Irishman, "like a man who could use a drink."

"At the very least," I replied. I turned around and watched Avery being escorted up the aisle between Deputy Pell and Abraham Merrill. *And*, I thought bitterly, you killed her and the child because you feared it was yours. I closed my eyes and saw Amy's face and imagined the fine, strong boy in her belly—our boy—my son.

And you murdered them for nothing, Reverend, I thought. For nothing.

🏵 37

The Tragedy

I was in the Bristol Hotel taproom with Quinncannon when the note came, hand-carried by the unscrubbed son of one of the Widow Bloss' neighbors. Written in the widow's fussy little script, it contained only three words: "Come at once."

Though the room was warm I felt a sudden, arctic chill. When I was a child my grandmother used to say that meant someone had just walked over your grave.

When the Irishman and I reached the house Rowena Bloss was standing in the parlor. She spoke without waiting for my question. "Your wife is not in danger, Squire. Doctor Wilbur is with her now."

"Thank God!" I cried. "And the child?"

I read the answer in her face.

"She has lost the child," she said simply.

"I knew it!" I said bitterly. I slammed my fist down on the table again and again. "Damn! Damn! Damn!"

Quinncannon seized my shoulders. His eyes burned into my own. "Get control of yourself," he commanded.

All at once I hated him. "Let me go, damn you! My wife needs me."

"So she does, Christy, but not in your current state. Calm yourself."

I broke free of his grasp. "Calm myself," I echoed in a mocking tone. "My child is *dead* and *that* is your sage advice?" Curse the man! Did not *any* human agony move his stony soul? I closed my hand into a fist and struck him in the face. He took the full force of the blow without flinching. Blood trickled from the corner of his mouth.

For one long moment he stood watching me while his lips slowly compressed into a taut smile and his eyes softened with an inexpressible sadness. He began to turn away from me, then abruptly turned back and smashed his own fist against my jaw

213

and I staggered back into a chair and sat, stunned, shaking my head to clear it.

At last I said, "I'm sorry, Lon. I had to hit someone."

"So did I, little brother," he replied. "So did I."

"You can't know," I said. "The anger, the bitterness, the goddamn *frustration*!"

"I know it all, Christy," he answered quietly.

Something in his tone made me search his face. "It's happened to you," I said.

"Twice, lad."

It is odd, the things that go through a man's mind at such a moment. I ached to lay my head in Amy's lap and cry and be comforted, but I knew—I *knew* that it was I who must comfort her.

"You must understand," the Irishman said, "that she feels a guilt greater than her grief."

"She? No, no, Lon, it is *my* doing. All—*all* of it from the beginning has been my fault."

He looked at Rowena Bloss. "Bring a tumbler of whiskey."

She poured it at the sideboard but I shook my head. "I want nothing to drink."

"That's well," he answered, tossing off half the tumbler. "There's not enough here for both of us." He drew a chair near to mine and sat down. "Now, listen to me, Christy!" His voice was almost a growl. "This is *no more your fault than it is your lady's.* Believe that! While you wallow in self-pity you can be of no help to your wife."

I heard what he said but it changed nothing. The blame was clearly mine. It was I who had seduced Amy. It was for my sake she had almost lost her life at Restell's. And surely there was something about me—something *physically* defective— which had caused the child to be horribly flawed and forced Amy to miscarry. In the end I blurted out all of this.

"Bullshit!" exclaimed Quinncannon. He glanced at the widow. "My apologies, madam."

"It is unnecessary, sir," she responded. "I could not have phrased my own reaction more succinctly."

The Irishman stood and looked down at me. "I have a few things to tell you, Christy, most of which you don't want to hear and none of which, in all probability, will you believe, but they need to be said and I wish now that someone had once said them to me. What has happened cannot be blamed on either you or your lady. It was the capricious will of mindless gods. Whether you accept that or not, you must pretend to do

214

so for Amy's sake, for any effort on your part to shoulder the responsibility will only increase her own sense of guilt. Do you understand my meaning?"

I thought I did and said so.

"Then," he said, "go to her."

When I entered the room Dr. Wilbur looked up and closed his bag. He put his hand on my shoulder as he passed out the door. Amy lay on the bed, her eyes on the ceiling, then on the wall, anywhere but on my face. A single tear rolled down her pale cheek.

I wanted to wipe it away. I took out my handkerchief as I crossed the room. Then, all at once, the tear was precious to me. I thrust the handkerchief back in my pocket and held her, rocking her gently, and I felt her body convulse with sobs, and, God! how painful it is to recount this moment even after so many years.

"Oh, Christy," she cried, "forgive me, forgive me. I have murdered your son, your beautiful boy."

"No, darling, no, no." I cradled her in my arms and stupidly muttered the same word over and over. "No, no, no, no."

"I was so foolish," she said. "So *careless*. To have listened to Cousin Charlotte. To have gone to that dreadful woman's hospital. Forgive me," she said again, and then abruptly, "but why should you? How can you?"

I took her face between my hands and said, "Amy! If forgiveness is needed we must forgive each other. But you must understand. Our son is not dead. His soul is still alive. His soul lives in us, in our love for each other. He will be born, Amy. It is only that his birth has been delayed, don't you see?"

There was a long silence. Then, "Christy, do you truly believe that?" spoken in a whisper.

"I do, darling," I said.

"Oh, God!" she cried. She threw her arms about me. "Oh, God, Christy, I do love you so much—so much."

She pressed my head against her bosom and wept, and the tears that I had so long held back filled my own eyes.

The Preacher and the Shop Keeper

Tuesday, January 1, 1833. The new year was launched in a dismal, soaking rainstorm. From the perspective of the defense the atmosphere within the courtroom was quite as miserably murky as the dense fog that rolled in from the harbor and gripped Bristol in a chilling stranglehold.

Reverend Ira M. Bidwell was sworn for the government promptly at ten o'clock. During his testimony he shifted constantly in the chair as though he could not find a comfortable position, and stared apprehensively at Abraham Merrill, who returned his stare with suppressed anger and moody gloom.

Yes, Bidwell told Staples, Ephraim Avery had preached in Fall River on the evening of December 7, 1832, at eight o'clock. Yes, Avery had then spent the night at Bidwell's house and left for Bristol on December 8 on the noon stage. Yes, Bidwell had gone to wait for the stage with Avery. It was a rainy morning so *they had gone into Iram Smith's store* until the stage arrived.

I glanced at Quinncannon and the Irishman shrugged. The prosecution's contention was that Avery had written the white letter to Cornell on December 8 on a sheet torn from part of a ream in Smith's shop. Though the prisoner denied it, Bidwell had just placed him in the shop on the day.

Staples was purring. "Did you observe Mr. Avery writing in Smith's store, Reverend Bidwell?"

"I did not, sir."

"Did you, at any time, see Avery go behind the counter?"

To obtain the paper on which the damning letter was written, the defendant would have had to go behind the counter, but Bidwell responded, "No, sir."

"Mr. Bidwell, did you remain with Avery every moment from the time you entered the shop until the stage arrived?"

The preacher hesitated. "I left Mr. Avery at about the time I would expect the stage to come."

"You left the shop first, sir?"

"Perhaps a few minutes earlier."

"Can you see the depot from Smith's?"

"Well, no, sir, but I assumed the stage was on schedule."

"You *assumed*," Staples repeated. "So you left Avery a few minutes before noon, *alone* in the store. Would you say, sir, that 'a few minutes' was enough time for Avery to write a brief letter on paper taken from a shelf behind the counter?"

"Objected to," I said quickly, "as calling for a conclusion."

Staples withdrew the question. He had scored his point. "Mr. Bidwell, to walk from Smith's shop to the depot, is it necessary to pass the post office?"

The witness sighed. "I'm afraid it is, sir."

Staples turned the inquiry to the subject of Sarah Cornell. Bidwell had first met her in May, 1832, when she came to his house claiming to be a member of the Taunton church and asking to be referred to a boarding house. She displayed a letter from a class leader in Taunton, explaining that she would have a certificate from her minister as soon as he should return. Bidwell took her at her word, directing her to the home of parishioners named Mason. The following Sunday he saw her at his service and she afterward stated she was returning to Taunton, where she worked.

He next encountered her at the camp-meeting in Thompson in late August "in company with a young man" whom she did not introduce. She was now wearing large green glasses, and she said she had left Taunton and was living with relatives in Woodstock, Connecticut. This was on Monday, August 26, and he did not see her there after that, though he understood she had been denounced to the company as a "girl of bad character" by Avery and Abraham Merrill.

He did not meet her again until October 3, when she applied for membership in his own church, reminding him of her letter signed by a Taunton class leader and claiming, but not producing, a certificate. The trusting pastor took her name as a probationer but decided to question Avery concerning her.

His first opportunity to do so was during the Four-Days meeting in Fall River on October 20. Avery then recounted the history of his experiences with the young woman, noting she had mailed three letters to him from Dover in which she had made a "full confession" of all things charged against her at Lowell. The prisoner told Bidwell he had subsequently burned the letters at the frequent urging of his wife, though he now regretted it.

There was little I could do on cross-examination beyond running him through the testimony he had already rehearsed with Quinncannon. Accordingly, after getting Bidwell to state that he thought he "should know Avery's handwriting if I were to see it," I showed him the pink letter already in evidence. The witness saw "no resemblance" to the prisoner's hand. Past that I did not dare to venture and I let Bidwell go.

Iram Smith took the stand, scratching at the stubble of beard on his chin and adjusting the spectacles on his sharp, crooked nose in a gesture born more of nerves than necessity. Yes, he was acquainted with Bidwell and Avery. Yes, they had both been in his shop on the morning of December 8. He understood they were waiting for the stage and he thought Bidwell had left first. Smith also thought he recollected Avery calling for a wax wafer such as is used to seal a letter. He had to leave his store and borrow one from another merchant, a Mrs. Parry. Now that he reflected, he was pretty certain Avery had called for both paper and a wafer, but he refused to state that he had seen the defendant actually writing.

Smith was a shaky witness. I had little trouble getting him to admit that virtually all his testimony had been "recalled" for him by Colonel Harnden. When I dismissed him I even allowed myself a slight sensation of triumph, but Staples had a trump card left in his hand.

"Mr. Smith, I show you this half-sheet of white paper and I ask if you can identify it."

"Yes, sir, it has my initials in one corner. This sheet was found by Colonel Harnden in my presence in a ream that I kept behind my counter."

Staples nodded. "I now show you the so-called white letter of December 8 and ask you to compare it with this blank half-sheet. Do these two correspond in size, water mark, and the edges where torn apart?"

Obviously they did and Smith barely glanced at them before answering, "Yes, sir, they correspond *exactly*."

"I offer these two papers as People's Exhibits B and C," said the prosecutor, "and I now propose to read the letter of December 8 into the record."

"Objection," I said. "The government should first show that the letter was written by the prisoner. If Avery wrote it, it is in his handwriting, and they must show that it is. The correspondence of the two half-sheets is not evidence of the writer's identity. From the evidence it does not appear that someone else *might* not have written the letter. Nor," I added with an eye on Harnden at the prosecution table, "do the circumstances of the astounding discovery of the blank paper absolutely preclude the possibility of a calculated design."

The justices conferred briefly and then Howe said, "Mr. Randolph's objection is sustained. Further proof of the handwriting should be produced."

I began to smile and Howe added, "However . . ." Oh, cursed word "however."

"However, the court has no objection to hearing the letter read pending our determination of its legality as testimony."

Smugly Staples passed the exhibit to the clerk and the goddamned thing was read aloud:

Fall River Dec 8
I will be here on the 20 if pleasant at the place named
at 6 oclock if not pleasant the next Monday eve
Say nothing &c

Aunt Hannah

In the afternoon Staples called three ancient ladies who had laid out Sarah Cornell's body for burial on December 21, the day she was found. Meribah Borden testified that the corpse was very stiff and cold, but whether from frost or rigor mortis she was unsure. The right arm hung down. The left was "drawn up about as high as the neck with the elbow tight against her side and the hand open and turned outwards—that is, with the palm out."

The women had tried to force the arm into a "natural position." but failed, although they applied "hot cloths with hot water, as hot as could be wrung out, to soften the cords, or ligaments." The marks left by the rope were very black, Meribah thought—the face "lightish." The bottom of the abdomen was "very dark," the pudenda "very black clear across, not a white spot to be seen." In this area there were "appearances of violence."

Did Meribah mean that there was evidence of attempts to procure abortion? Meribah did not. "I thought the dead girl very much *abused*."

"Can you think, Mrs. Borden, of a more specific word than 'abused'?"

The rural dowager stiffened. "I can, Mr. Staples. I will leave you to guess at it."

I said I had no questions.

Dorcas Ford had closely examined the deceased's clothing and found "feces stuck to her linen as if mashed on." She had noted "a mark as of a briar across one instep" and scratches and "green stains on her knees such as might be made by the juice of grass." Below the left shoulder blade she'd seen "two small yellowish spots and, round them, some black spots." She also described the bruised appearance of the abdomen but would venture no opinion as to cause. She had placed a yard-square cloth over the private parts on both occasions when the doctors examined the body. "The upper edges," she said, "came above the hips and covered all below."

"Your witness," Staples said.

"No questions," I replied.

"Aunt" Hannah Wrightington, wizened, toothless, well past ninety, had prepared more corpses for the grave than any three undertakers in Boston. Once painfully seated, she rested gnarled, arthritic hands on a gnarled, arthritic cane and peered around the crowded courtroom. Her skin was dry parchment—she drooled slightly—her bird-like head bobbed uncontrollably on a long, scrawny neck—her faded bonnet did not conceal her baldness—but her yellow eyes glistened brightly and she was fully aware of her significance in the solemn proceedings. Her mind was clear and, I thought, it was entirely her own.

"Now, Mrs. Wrightington..." Staples began.

"Everybody calls me Aunt Hannah," she said, in a whiskey baritone that was its own echo.

"All right, Aunt Hannah. I promise you this will not require much time."

"No?" she snapped. "Then why'd you drag me here all the way from Tiverton, young man? I thought my evidence was important!"

"It *is* important," Staples said with some confusion.

"Well, take your time then," she commanded.

Obediently he took his time while the old lady described in detail all the marks on the body to which the earlier witnesses had sworn. She commenced with the face and, after almost an hour, she'd worked her way down to the waist.

"There was a bad bruise on her right side and round to her back, just above the hip bone," Aunt Hannah announced. "It was marks or prints like an open hand, like somebody's fingers pressed hard against her. There was spots like fingers, four of 'em, pushed against her back, and a mark like a thumb on her belly. It looked like someone made a *grab* there."

"Was there a similar appearance on her left side?" Staples asked.

"There was a bruise," she answered, "but not like a hand print. No marks of fingers, just a dark place."

I was afraid Staples would follow up this line of questioning but he was anxious to hurry the witness to another portion of the deceased's anatomy.

"Would you describe what you observed about the area below the abdomen?"

Aunt Hannah looked puzzled for a moment. "You mean the *vulva*?" she almost shouted.

Staples actually blushed. "That is my meaning," he said.

"Well, *say* what you mean, young man! Don't dance around your words. You men are the limit!" She glared about the room. "You talk of a female body as if it were a shrine and most of you are farmers enough to know it's nothing of the kind. God knows the one I saw was no shrine." She paused. "From what I hear it never was."

Staples was attempting to simulate composure. "Please describe the appearance of the . . . the vulva."

"Coal black!" Aunt Hannah exclaimed. "The bruise started just above the cross bone and extended down both legs. That poor child was done rash violence. That's what I said to my husband."

"Your husband?" Staples seemed perplexed. "Excuse me. I understood your husband died thirty years ago."

The old lady eyed him. "That doesn't mean we don't still talk things over," she responded as though the point should have been obvious.

Poor Staples was reeling. He attempted only one final question.

"Mrs. Wrightington . . ."

"Aunt Hannah!"

". . . have you formed an opinion of the cause of the evidence of violence on the . . . the vulva?"

"It was no try at aborting the infant!" she said firmly. "The girl was *violated*!"

"Your witness," the prosecutor said with evident relief. I stood and walked to the witness stand.

"Aunt Hannah, would you tell us how many bodies you have laid out to be buried?"

"Oh, ask the Lord," she answered. "I lost track of 'em."

"Would you say a hundred?"

"I would say more, young man."

"How many of those died of natural causes?"

"Most of 'em, laddie, most of 'em. The yellow fever took them, or the scarlet, or the whooping cough, or childbirth." There were tears in her old eyes. "A lot of youngsters died in the wars, boy, most no older than you."

"How many have you seen," I asked quietly, "who took their own lives?"

"Fifteen," she said. "Maybe twenty. Poor sad creatures like this pitiful child."

"Like Sarah Cornell?" I said quickly.

"Yes," she responded. "Poor lost girl."

"And how many of those you laid out were the victims of murder?"

Her yellow eyes opened wide. "Why, none at all, boy. That is . . ." She hesitated while I held my breath. Then she shook her old head. "No," she said, "none I can remember. None at all."

"Aunt Hannah," I said, "how long have you been a midwife?"

She thought for a full minute and then cackled softly. "I helped deliver my brother when I was nine. I'd almost forgot that. He's been gone so long. Why, it must be more than eighty years I been bringing babies into the world." She smiled toothlessly. "Then there was calves and foals and litters of pups and kittens. I seen a lot of life, boy, and . . ." she sucked in a breath before adding ". . . and a lot of death."

"Aunt Hannah," I asked as gently as I could, for the question would be painful to us both, "have you ever had experience with a foetus that died as a result of either spontaneous or deliberate abortion?"

"I have," she said, in a very thin, quavering voice.

"Drawing on your long years of experience, how old would you say a foetus was if it were eight inches long and weighed five ounces?"

She closed her eyes. I watched her nodding involuntarily, otherwise motionless, for so long that I began to fear she slept. Then she said, "The child, young man—do not use the word foetus—the child would be four and one-half months old."

I said, "Thank you, Aunt Hannah," and retreated to the table.

Grindall Rawson Takes
the Stand

Wednesday, January 2. The skies over the Bristol Court House had cleared during the night. The morning dawned in a flood of sunshine and I sought an omen in the altered weather. Near ten o'clock Quinncannon and I stood outside and watched Colonel Harnden's carriage pull up the drive and the Colonel descend to turn and hand down a woman in her mid-thirties dressed entirely in black with a heavy veil sewn to the brim of her bonnet. As her feet touched the ground she reached up and drew the veil over her face but not before I had caught a glimpse of her pale, frightened features.

No man had ever considered her beautiful. Her eyes were large and hollow and without luster, as if she had been weeping, not just that morning, but for weeks. Her face had the fleeting appearance of a bloodlessness bordering on the ghastly, and the effect was heightened by two spots of bright red which decorated her cheeks, artificially induced, I had no doubt, but whether from custom or vanity I could not tell.

Quinncannon said quietly, "Lucretia Rawson, the dead girl's sister."

She passed up the gravel path within inches of me. Below the dark veil I observed her tightly compressed lips and quivering chin. She seemed to be fighting desperately for control. Behind her marched the Colonel, not exactly smiling but showing his teeth in a manner which suggested less of either the wolf or the serpent than of the hyena.

Then another man stepped down from the coach. He was above average in height and well set up with a broad chest and narrow waist, and outfitted in the leathern Sunday clothes commonly worn by reasonably prosperous artisans. His features were jagged in a manner which, while hardly handsome, might be described as rugged. His skin was swarthy, somewhere between tan and olive, and he was clean-shaven except for a narrow beard that extended from one ear to the other, framing his rectangular face. A great, unkempt shock of black hair partially curled over his brow above dark, narrow eyes.

I turned to Quinncannon. "The brother-in-law?"

The Irishman nodded.

It had been decided that Quinncannon would handle the cross-examination of the Rawsons. Therefore, when Staples called Mrs. Rawson to the stand I relaxed somewhat and contented myself with scribbling a few notes.

Lucretia testified that her sister had come to live with herself and her husband on June 2, 1832, and remained until October 2.

"Do you know," Staples inquired, "any fact respecting her being unwell as females are?"

"A week and one day before the camp-meeting at Thompson she was unwell in that manner, sir. I had the means to know because I did her washing."

"Prior to the camp-meeting, had Maria been regular in this matter?"

"She had."

"And was she similarly unwell in September, after the camp-meeting?"

"No, sir, she was not."

"Before she left your house, Mrs. Rawson, did your sister tell you what she feared might be her situation?"

"Yes, sir," Lucretia said simply.

On cross-examination Quinncannon assumed an air of gentle concern. "Are you all right, Mrs. Rawson? If you wish to rest I can postpone my examination."

"No, thank you, sir," she answered gratefully. "I should rather have it over."

"Very well then, madam. Do you have children?"

She smiled. "Yes, sir, two. James is nearly nine and Ruth is seven."

"By what means were you first made aware that you were pregnant with your children?"

"Why, I failed to be unwell at my regular time."

"As your sister did in September?"

"Yes, sir."

"How long have you been married?"

"Just past twenty-four years, sir."

"In those twenty-four years, Mrs. Rawson, did it ever occur

225

that you thought yourself pregnant only to discover you were not?"

"Oh, yes."

"On these occasions your monthly indisposition was a few days late?"

"Yes," she said, "and we were *so* disappointed."

He smiled. "You and your husband are very much in love, Mrs. Rawson?"

"Very much."

"Has your monthly illness sometimes been as late as a week?"

She answered slowly, "Sometimes."

"Do you remember the date on which your sister confided to you her fear that she was carrying a child?"

"I do. It was September 21."

"All right. Now you testified that, in August, Maria began to be unwell eight days before the camp-meeting. That would be August 19. Was that her normal time?"

"It was, within a day or two."

He raised an eyebrow. "She might be as early as the 17th or as late as the 21st?"

"She might be," the witness conceded.

"In fact, madam, it would not be unusual for a young woman to be as late as a week, would it?"

"Objection," said Staples. "Mrs. Rawson has no knowledge of her sister's history in this matter prior to June. She cannot possibly give evidence as to what would or would not be 'normal' for the deceased."

"Withdraw the question," Quinncannon said. "Mrs. Rawson, when your sister confessed her fears to you on September 21, what was her demeanor?"

"Sir?"

"Was she pleased? Did she seem happy?"

"No, sir. She was very distressed."

"Why, madam, as she was only a little past her time if at all, was Maria so certain that she *was* pregnant?"

"Objection," Staples said.

"Why," the Irishman continued, "would Maria make such a shameful confession when she could not yet be sure she would need to make any confession at all?"

"Objection!" the prosecutor yelped. "Your Honors, Mr. Quinncannon is perfectly aware of the impropriety of these questions. They are purely speculative and call for a conclusion."

"Well, well," Quinncannon said quietly, "perhaps they do

at that. I will withdraw them and release the witness with my appreciation for her cooperation in what is obviously a difficult and unpleasant affair."

Staples glared at him as he returned to our table. Then he said, "The government calls Grindall Rawson."

The man was as calm as his wife had been nervous. He settled into the chair and gave his attention to Staples. He deposed that he lived in Woodstock, Connecticut, with his wife and two children—that he was a weaver and kept his own shop in his house—that his sister-in-law had arrived on June 2 for "a visit," and "after two or three weeks she went to work for me." Maria, he said, had been a Methodist, while he and his wife were Congregationalists. The Rawsons had often asked Maria to live with them prior to June but she had refused. "She gave as a reason that there were no Methodist meeting houses near us."

"Was Maria at the Thompson camp-meeting from August 27 to 30 of last year?" Staples asked.

"Yes, sir."

"On September 21, 1832, did Maria communicate to you her fear of what her situation might be?"

"Yes, sir. She first spoke to my wife and then my wife called me and told Maria she ought to repeat what she had said, and Maria did repeat it in the presence of my wife."

"Did she state the cause of her fears?"

"Objection," I said. "The declarations of the deceased are inadmissible unless they are dying declarations."

"If the court please," Staples argued, "the declarations in question were made in the presence of two witnesses simultaneously, and thus the charges made by the deceased against the prisoner admit of corroboration."

I shook my head and smiled. "Your Honors, this is nothing short of wonderful. My learned colleague contends he should be allowed to place inadmissible declarations on the record solely because he can then call a second witness to *repeat* the same inadmissible declarations." I turned to Staples. "Since the prosecutor has stealthily managed to establish that the deceased made *charges* against the defendant, we will cheerfully acknowledge that she did so, and we are prepared to prove that she made the same accusations against others as well, including a highly respected physician in Lowell. The issue is not whether she made certain statements, but whether those statements were true. She might have made them before more

227

than two witnesses—she might have made them in a public forum before a multitude. That is no evidence of their veracity."

Howe passed a note to Haile and the latter nodded. "Mr. Randolph is sustained," Howe said.

Staples scowled and phrased his last question carefully. "Without being specific as to what Maria stated, and without mentioning any names, will you tell us, Mr. Rawson, did your sister-in-law indicate *why* she entertained the fears she spoke of?"

Rawson looked at him steadily. "She said it was in consequence of what she knew had taken place at camp-meeting."

"Thank you, sir," Staples sighed. "Take the witness."

Quinncannon sifted through the papers before him. When a full minute had passed Grindall Rawson began to shift uneasily in the chair. After two minutes he was positively squirming. The Irishman remained intent on his papers, which, from my seat beside him, I noticed were entirely blank. Then, without standing or even raising his head, he suddenly said:

"Mr. Rawson, what did Maria say to you concerning Mr. Avery's behavior at the camp-meeting?"

I watched Staples' jaw drop to his chest. Behind me I heard a chorus of thunderstruck gasps from the Methodist brethren. I regarded Quinncannon with wounded perplexity. I had, after all, just prevented Staples from introducing that very same testimony and I was still preening.

The witness was also surprised. "Do you wish to know the whole she said?"

At last Quinncannon looked up. "Every single word."

"Maria stated," Rawson began, "that on Thursday, the twenty-ninth, while on the ground, she saw Mr. Avery and he spoke to her. He said, 'I should like to see you and talk with you, Maria.' He then said, 'I will meet you tonight at Elliot's house when the horn blows for preaching.' I understood he was staying at Elliot's house."

"Did she say she kept the appointment?"

"She did, and Avery met her outside and said the house was so full they could have no talk there, and told her to go on ahead and he would overtake her. He did so and they went arm in arm into the woods. He asked her to take her glasses off. They sat down and some conversation followed about Avery having burned the letters."

"These letters, Mr. Rawson. Were these the letters she had written to him from New Hampshire in which she confessed the charges alleged against her at Lowell?"

"Yes, sir."

"Go on," Quinncannon said.

"Well, Mr. Avery said he had not burned her letters but would do so on one condition and settle the difficulty. At that time he took hold of her hands and put one of his into her bosom, or something like it. She said she tried to get away from him but could not. She said he then had intercourse with her, and they returned to the camp. He promised to destroy the letters on his return to Bristol."

"Is that all of it?"

"To the best of my recollection, sir."

"You haven't," Quinncannon said, "omitted even one nasty little detail of Maria's story?"

"No, sir."

"Good." The Irishman leaned back in his chair, stretching his legs under the table, gnawing on the stump of a pencil.

"Did you believe her?"

"Excuse me, sir?"

"Did you believe her story?"

"My wife and I both—"

"Your wife may speak for herself, sir. I ask you again, did you believe Maria's foul little tale of blackmail and violation by a clergyman in the camp-meeting shrubbery?"

"Yes, sir, certainly I believed her."

"What was your opinion of Maria's reliability for truthfulness?"

"I thought her very truthful."

"Did you ever know her to lie?"

"Never!"

"Never?" Quinncannon thought that over, absently scratching a corner of his thin moustache. "Did you ever carry a letter for Maria to Reverend Virgin, the Methodist minister on the Thompson circuit?"

"I believe I did."

"Do you know the content of that letter?"

"I believe she requested a certificate of membership in the church."

"Did she claim she had such a certificate from Reverend Willson at Taunton?"

"I do not remember."

"Come, sir, it is an easy matter to call Reverend Virgin here."

"I suppose Maria may have written something of the sort," Rawson admitted.

229

"Is it now your understanding that Maria had no such certificate from Mr. Willson?"

"I do not know that for a fact, sir!"

"Are you aware that Maria charged a doctor in Lowell with making improper advances toward her?"

"I am."

"Do you believe she told the truth?"

"I do."

Quinncannon's eyes narrowed. "Are you aware, Mr. Rawson, that in both Massachusetts and New Hampshire Maria stated that she was your first and only love—that her sister had tricked you into marriage—but that she, Maria, could have you whenever she chose?"

"That is a lie!" Rawson cried.

"Do you mean that you never loved Maria?"

"Of course not! I love only my wife."

"Then Maria was lying when she made those declarations?"

"Certainly she was!"

"Then, if she lied about *you*, Mr. Rawson, how can we be positive she was not lying about Mr. Avery?"

"Objection!" Staples shouted.

"Withdrawn!" Quinncannon snapped. For the first time in the cross-examination he stood. "During the months Maria lived with you and your wife, did she ever receive male visitors?"

"No, sir."

"To your knowledge, did she ever, I believe the phrase is 'step out' with a man?"

"She did not."

"Is it then your testimony, Mr. Rawson, that between June 2 and August 27 Sarah Maria Cornell had no direct contact with any man at all?"

"It is, sir."

"Except, of course, yourself," Quinncannon added quietly.

Rawson's voice was almost a snarl. "I was Maria's brother-in-law, her landlord and her employer. I was nothing else to her."

"And yet..." The Irishman appeared troubled. "This court has heard the evidence of Dr. Wilbur and Dr. Hooper, and of the most experienced midwife in the state, Hannah Wrightington, that a foetus such as was removed from deceased's womb, a foetus measuring eight inches and weighing five ounces, would be four-and-a-half months old. Now that would mean that the child was conceived in early August, at least three weeks before Maria claimed she was violated by Mr. Avery. And that seems odd because in early August, according to your sworn statement, Mr. Rawson, the only man with whom Maria had any contact was you."

Staples' patience was exhausted. "If Mr. Quinncannon has a question to put to the witness let him put it!"

The Irishman started as if from an interesting dream.

"I beg the court's pardon," he said. "I was merely thinking out loud. A bad habit. I really must break myself of it." He resumed his seat and smiled.

Almost as an afterthought he said, "No further questions."

🌿 41 ———————————————
Sarah Cornell on Trial

*The Methodist fathers had collected a battalion of wit-nesses whom Quinncannon and I organized into three groups: those to prove Avery's good character; those to prove Sarah Cornell's infamy; and those to break down Orswell's evidence by providing the defendant with an alibi for November 19 in Providence so airtight that Avery could not possibly have deliv-ered the "pink letter" to the steamboat's engineer.

Of the prisoner's good works, nobility of mind, purity of spirit and spotlessness of reputation the Merrills, Drake and numerous other brethren waxed poetic and interminably. I let them go on, even at the risk of trying the patience of the court, on the theory that the more time which elapsed in the defense's presentation, the vaguer the aging justices' recollection of Staples' damning evidence would be when they came to consider their verdict.

The Providence "alibi" was methodically established, pri-marily by the same clergy, who seemed not only gifted with total recall of the events of a rather unmemorable day some six weeks before, but appeared to have contrived among them-selves never to have left Mr. Avery unattended for a single moment. However, as Mr. Staples remarked on this matter at length during his summation, I will not dwell on it here.

It was in my efforts to expose the nefarious character of Sarah Maria Cornell that I made what I then considered my most significant contribution to the defendant's cause.

On the afternoon of January 4 I called Miss Mary Ide to the stand. A washed-out, grim little woman of about thirty was escorted up the center aisle by the bailiff and affirmed.

"Miss Ide, please tell the court where you live and work."

"I live in North Providence and work at Lyman's mills, sir."

"Did you ever know Sarah Maria Cornell?"

"Yes, sir. About ten years ago she boarded in my mother's house and was employed at Lyman's. She called herself Maria Snow then, and said she'd been caring for her mother, who was an invalid and had just passed on." The witness added with a snort, "She also claimed she was sixteen years old!"

Her derisive tone said all that was necessary about her opinion of Cornell's veracity but I pressed on.

"Is it now your understanding that Miss Cornell's mother was not dead?"

"*Was* not dead. Is not dead *yet*!" as if the old woman's continued refusal to die was a further affront to the witness. "Maria saved her money and first thing she bought was a black mourning dress. We all felt sorry for her till that young man came and we found out the truth."

"Explain the circumstances, Mary."

"Well, this young fellow came from Providence asking for Maria Cornell and I told him no such person was there. But he saw her and says, 'Why, there she is!' I never heard the young man's name but Maria was very confused and angry. After that we heard something of her conduct in Providence and my mother told her she must leave the house."

"Did you ever personally witness evidence of her misbehavior?"

"I did, Mr. Randolph. Her conversation was not fit to be spoken here and her conduct before young men who came to the house was very bad."

And, I thought, Maria was pretty and vivacious and doubtless tough competition for the plain little daughter of the landlady.

"She told me things one night," Mary continued, "that satisfied me she was unchaste. The next morning I told it to Mother and she said Maria must leave. Maria then went to several families in the village and nobody would take her in because of her conduct."

Obviously Mary and her mother had poisoned the town's mind against Maria. I looked into the witness's green eyes, burning with triumphant envy, and concluded that I could read Mary Ide like the proverbial book. But I was no closer to understanding Maria Cornell and perhaps I never would be.

Staples wisely had no questions of Mary, and I called Samuel N. Richmond, a Providence dealer in dry goods. I approached the natty merchant carefully, anticipating an objection as soon as my opponent realized the thrust of Richmond's testimony.

"Did you ever have occasion to know Sarah Maria Cornell?"

"I did, sir."

"Please state the circumstances."

"It was," the witness said in the rapid delivery we had

233

practiced, "eleven years ago in Providence when she confessed to having stolen a shawl and bonnet worth four dollars from my store."

"Oh!" Staples cried. "Objection! A crime alleged against the victim and supposed to have been committed over a decade ago cannot possibly have a bearing on these proceedings."

I addressed the bench. "I understand the court to have permitted a wider range of inquiry than normal since the nature of this hearing is primarily investigative rather than judgmental. Our purpose, Your Honors, is to look into the state of mind and character of the deceased at the time of her death to determine whether she was capable of suicide and, moreover, whether she was so dissolute as to seek to avenge her imagined grievances against the defendant by attempting to create the illusion that she had died by his hand. To that end we endeavor to trace the erosion of the girl's moral nature from its inception in an affair of shop-lifting until its culmination in her self-destruction."

"Damn it!" Staples yowled. "Excuse me, Your Honors, but there is *no evidence* that the victim killed herself. There is an appropriate time for Mr. Randolph to argue his case—*if* he has a case to argue."

Justice Howe smiled wearily. "The court concurs, Mr. Staples. However, Mr. Randolph's point on the latitude heretofore allowed is well taken. Put simply, sir, you got in your letters and we will permit Mr. Randolph to get in his shop-lifting."

Oh Rhadamanthus! Oh Solomon, oh Solon! By overruling Staples, Justice Howe had effectively terminated the trial of Ephraim Avery and replaced the prisoner with a new defendant, Sarah Maria Cornell. From this point on it was the victim and not her accused killer who was to be judged.

And the strategy had been entirely mine. I had not even broached it to Quinncannon. I caught his approving eye but it was not in his approval that I basked, but in my own self-admiration. I forgot my scruples in defending a guilty murderer. I gave myself the satisfaction of a glance at Staples' downcast face and strutted before the witness stand. If I'd had tail feathers I believe I would have spread them.

"Mr. Richmond, did I understand you to say that Miss Cornell *confessed* this theft to you?"

"Well, she didn't have much choice, sir. She was caught in the act."

"How was the matter resolved?"

"The girl returned the articles and the thing was settled by the interposition of her friends."

234

"Her family intervened and you agreed not to press charges?"

"Well," he responded, "I had the goods back and she *was* very young."

"Take the witness," I said.

"No questions," Staples said.

"Defense," I announced, "calls Charles Hodges."

Hodges settled in the chair and affirmed he was a dealer in dry goods from Providence. I looked toward Howe and said, "If the court please, the testimony of this witness is similar to the last and introduced for the same purpose. If the government has objection it might be well to argue it now."

The master stroke! I made myself the very image of reasonable forthrightness and waited for the inevitable reply from Staples.

"The government has no objection."

I returned to Hodges. "Did you ever have dealings with Maria Cornell, sir, and if so please describe the circumstances."

"I did know her, sir, in 1832 at the shop of John R. Carpenter in Providence, where I clerked. I observed Miss Cornell removing lace goods from the display and stuffing them into her purse. When she left the shop without paying I followed her and confronted her."

"Did she confess the theft?"

"At first she denied it. Her manner was rather strange."

"Did Mr. Carpenter bring charges?"

"He intended to, sir, but I understand the affair was somehow arranged." Of course it had been. It was I who had arranged it.

"What was Miss Cornell's reputation in Providence?"

Hodges regarded me solemnly. "It was that of a thief and a liar, sir."

"Your witness," I said.

"No questions," said Staples.

I said, "Miss Ann Barnes for the prisoner."

Ann Barnes, a lean spinster in her mid-thirties, had worked beside Maria at the Appleton mills in Lowell and gradually become the dead girl's uneasy confidante. "I knew she conducted herself improperly with men, Squire Randolph, from her own confessions to me on the evening before she left Lowell. That was just before she was expelled from Mr. Avery's church."

I relaxed against the defense table. "Kindly repeat what Miss Cornell told you."

"Oh, she said she'd kept company with many, *many* young men—with one in particular many times. I asked how she avoided being discovered at her boarding house. She said she did not do

235

it there. She went down to a village called Belvidere where she had been invited to come and stay nights. Once a young man carried her out in a chaise to a tavern and took her to a chamber where they had wine and—" The witness's face was granite hard. "Maria laughed and said, 'Well, Ann, *you* know!'"

But of course she didn't know. Poor Ann. No young man had ever wanted to take her to a tavern in Belvidere, and Maria knew it. What sort of woman had Maria Cornell been? On the eve of her excommunication from the church which she professed to be her *raison d'être* and her sole link with salvation, Maria had found time to twit her only friend, her homely, unloved only friend, with tales of romantic rendezvous of which Ann Barnes could not even dream.

I said gently, "Miss Barnes, did Maria ever speak of Dr. Graves?"

"Yes, she said he had treated her but whether for the bad disorder or not she did not know. 'But, Ann,' she said, 'this much I know. I have a very bad humor.'"

"Did she ever say that Graves had made improper advances to her?"

"Not at that time, sir. She made that charge only when she returned to Lowell in the summer of 1831 and Graves got the sheriff after her for the debt of ten dollars she owed him for doctoring. Graves and the deputy pursued Maria to my house and she escaped out the rear door to another house. She sent for me to follow her and I did so. She appeared like one out of reason."

"Did she ever discuss Reverend Avery with you?"

Miss Barnes nodded. "After she was expelled from the church she told me she still had Mr. Avery's certificate of membership. 'He asked me to give it up, Ann,' she said, 'and I told him I had lost it on the Cape, but I have got it and can go and join anywhere I like, and Avery may help himself!'"

"When she said this, what was her manner?"

"Resentful."

"All right," I said. "Did Maria ever show you any letter which had passed from her to Mr. Avery?"

"Yes, sir, in summer, 1831, she showed me a copy of a letter she had written him from New Hampshire in answer to his letter demanding the return of his certificate. It was a confession of most of the charges made against her at her trial in Lowell. She said there were three letters—that she had given back his certificate and wanted him to destroy her letters. At that time I advised her to leave town and told her the best place

236

to meet the stage where she wouldn't be recognized. She dressed herself in a disguised habit."

"Miss Barnes, at any time did Maria ever accuse Mr. Avery of behaving dishonorably toward her?"

"No, sir," the lady replied, "she never did."

Again Staples ventured no cross-examination and I called Miss Sarah Honey, a petite factory girl of twenty-three from Great Falls, New Hampshire, who deposed that Maria Cornell had boarded in her mother's house from March 7 to August 7, 1831. "The talk about her was that she was a loose character," said Miss Honey brightly.

"Tell the court what you know of Miss Cornell's movements in June, 1831."

"Oh, yes, sir, well, everyone knew Maria was trying to be a member of Mr. Storrs' Methodist Society. I mean there was no one she didn't tell. Then in early June, about the ninth or tenth I think, she was very upset. She said a minister in Lowell had written lies about her to Mr. Storrs and because of that she was to be kept out of the church."

That fit the known timetable. Avery had written Storrs on June 6.

"That same evening," the witness went on, "Maria was out late and when she came in I asked her where she'd been and, do you know?—she told me she'd gone out to *drown* herself but when she came to the river her courage failed her. Of course, I told her how *shocked* I was but she said she'd been tempted to make away with herself many times before."

"Did Maria shortly after leave Great Falls for a few days?"

"Yes, sir, she went down to Lowell to see this Reverend Avery. I think she said she went to his house to get a letter or something to restore her to the church, but she was furious when she returned. She said Avery was a hard-hearted, unfeeling man who did not treat her with politeness when she visited him. She was very, *very* angry at him."

"Did Maria say anything else about Mr. Avery?"

Miss Honey's brown eyes widened and fairly melted. "Oh, yes, sir! She said she'd get even with Mr. Avery if it was her last act on earth."

Mr. Quinncannon
Sums Up

Saturday, January 5. The defense had just two loose ends to tie up before Quinncannon delivered his summation. The second of these, however, was decidedly less loose than the first.

I put David Davoll on the stand to discredit Peleg Cranston, the keeper of the Stone Bridge. Davoll, who lived in Portsmouth and kept a blacksmith shop in Tiverton, crossed the bridge daily and knew Cranston well. He swore that, after the body was found, Cranston told him that he knew Avery on sight and the prisoner had not crossed his bridge on December 20. The smith also swore that it was he who had left the tracks in the sand that night which indicated a man returning from Tiverton to the Island after the bridge gate was locked—the tracks which the prosecution had strongly suggested were Avery's.

Staples expended much effort in trying to trip up Davoll but the smith stuck stubbornly to his story. It has ever since astounded me that the prosecutor, having spent so much energy attempting to break down the meaningless testimony of Davoll, should have so misjudged the significance of our final witness's evidence that he dismissed him without a single question on cross-examination.

William Hamilton was an unimposing little laborer in a Fall River mill who boarded in one of the houses along the Newport Road in Tiverton, south of John Durfee's farm. On the night Maria Cornell died he had left the mill at the usual closing time, seven-thirty, and walked to Benjamin Hambly's grocery below the state line, not far north of Durfee's stack yard. At Hambly's he'd had his usual bread and cheese and one tumbler of gin and water, and remained to smoke his pipe and listen to the discussion in which he never participated. Eventually he had asked the question that traditionally was his only contribution to the conversation. He had inquired as to the time and the grocer had consulted his watch.

"It wanted seventeen minutes of nine o'clock," William Hamilton said. "I have need to ask, sir, as I have no timepiece of my own, you see."

I nodded sympathetically. "And what did you then do, Mr. Hamilton?"

"Well, sir, as it was rather late I left and walked south." He looked up. "That's the direction of my rooming house, you see."

"I see," I said. "While you were walking, did you hear anything unusual?"

"Why, yes, I did," he answered as if the memory had just taken him completely by surprise. "In the hollow near John Durfee's farm I heard a sound like a loud squall. I thought it might be a cat." He paused and added slyly, "I thought it might be two cats."

There was a slight ripple of laughter in the room and Hamilton beamed.

I said, "Did you change your opinion of the nature of this sound?"

"Oh, yes, sir. It altered and seemed like a human cry. There were three or four shrill cries as of a woman being beaten. Then it stopped for about two minutes. When I next heard it, it sounded like stifled groans. It definitely came from behind Durfee's house, from a southwesterly direction through his orchard. My impression at the time was that it was a woman in distress, so naturally I climbed the hill. But when I got to the crest I stopped and listened and could hear nothing more, so I returned to the road and went home. The truth is, Squire Randolph, I figured Durfee was beating his wife again."

Now the courtroom exploded with laughter. Even Staples glanced up and smiled. I said, "Can you estimate the time of night when you heard these screams and moans?"

"Near as I can figure," Hamilton responded, "it had to be somewhere between eight-forty-five and nine o'clock."

"Were you called to give your evidence before the coroner's jury?"

"The first jury called me, sir. Not the second."

"Your witness," I said.

Staples said absently, "No questions."

* * *

239

Then the Irishman rose to sum up our defense of Ephraim Avery.

"If the court please . . ." Quinncannon leaned casually against the defense table, his arms folded, speaking without notes. "It has been, throughout this hearing, the purpose of the prosecution to complicate and obfuscate the facts surrounding Maria Cornell's death with the intent of demonstrating that a crime of murder was committed by the respondent. They have failed, however, not merely to prove that Mr. Avery murdered Sarah Maria Cornell, but to prove that murder was committed by *any* person against this pathetic and desperate woman. Actually, gentlemen, I debated whether the evidence of suicide was not so obvious that I would be insulting the court's intelligence by offering a summation at all, but concluded it must be done to justify my exorbitant fee to the Methodist brethren."

While the spectators, with the exception of the Merrills, laughed lightly, the Irishman actually sat on the table, one boot resting on the floor, the other dangling in the air. "The physical evidence exhibited at the scene so clearly indicates suicide that I will, for the moment, pass over it. In fact I will, for the sake of argument, temporarily accept the government's contention of murder. But murder by whom, gentlemen? If the prisoner, then it must be proved that the prisoner was in the vicinity of the stack yard on the night of December 20, whereas the prosecution's witnesses cannot place Mr. Avery any closer to Durfee's farm than the Portsmouth side of the Bristol ferry. There is no conlcusive evidence that he passed the Stone Bridge on that day, and certainly none that he recrossed the bridge after dark. The testimony of Peleg Cranston, flimsy even if it were uncontradicted, is directly challenged by that of David Davoll. True, after general suspicion in Fall River fell on Mr. Avery, two or three people suddenly remembered seeing Methodist-minister-types wandering about the area without a care in the world, making no effort at concealment. And the government offers us these witnesses seriously, as if Avery was the only tall man in Rhode Island who dresses in black—as if this was the normal behavior of men contemplating murder."

Quinncannon glanced over his shoulder at Avery. "The respondent has already given a sworn account of his movements on the day in question, but I do not even ask you to believe him. Wherever he was, there is not one sliver of evidence to place him in Tiverton. Any contention that he had the opportunity to murder therefore fails of proof.

"But Mr. Staples will argue that Mr. Avery had motive, and

240

here—I will be perfectly frank with the court—here is where the government has its best hope of obtaining an indictment."

I heard the disturbed grumbling from the Methodists behind me and watched the Irishman swing his legs to the floor and stroll slowly toward the bench.

"The prosecution has assumed that Mr. Avery violated Miss Cornell on the evening of August 29 at the Thompson campmeeting and that, as a direct result, Miss Cornell became pregnant. They will further assert that Miss Cornell informed Mr. Avery by mail of her situation and that, following an exchange of letters, he arranged to rendezvous with her at John Durfee's stack yard at six o'clock on December 20 and did then and there meet her for the purpose of killing her and their unborn child."

Quinncannon turned to face Staples and smiled slightly. "There, now, I believe I have accurately anticipated my learned colleague's position. And I would be the first man in the room to acknowledge its plausibility . . . , if it were in any way plausible." He shifted so as to regain eye contact with the justices. "But, gentlemen, what evidence is adduced to support the government's theory? First, that letters passed between the prisoner and the dead woman. They produce no proof that the girl ever wrote to Reverend Avery on this topic at all. They do, however, introduce two letters purported to be from the defendant to the lady but, here again, where is their proof? The so-called pink letter supposedly sent on November 19 is testified to by John Orswell but his statement is refuted by no less than five witnesses who have accounted for every minute of the prisoner's time in Providence on that day. And as for the white letter dated December 8, with what convoluted tale are we confronted?"

The Irishman began to walk toward Colonel Harnden, who sat at the prosecution table, his lips slightly parted, incisors and canines gleaming.

"Tell me," Quinncannon said evenly, "that a letter denied by a defendant is written in his undoubted hand. Failing that, tell me that it was written before witnesses in such a way that no question can be raised that he is the undoubted author of such a letter written in such a place at such a time. Or, failing that, demonstrate that the letter was written on one half of a full sheet such that each half of the full sheet not only corresponds precisely as to edge and water mark, but that the sheet could have been obtained at only one place and time."

Quinncannon now stood beside the Colonel and addressed

the bench. "Failing *even* that, I would be forced to suggest that the letter might have been written at any place and at any time prior to its postmark. Further, I would argue that the blank half-sheet which corresponds so exactly to the letter might have been brought from outside and so placed within a ream of paper that the merchant who believed he witnessed its discovery might, in fact, have been intentionally deceived. Of course, this would suggest a deliberate attempt to frame the respondent. The defense, while not insisting on this interpretation of the evidence, cannot entirely rule it out."

One corner of his mouth tugged up. "It is on the record that the deceased swore to avenge her grievances against the defendant, whether real or imaginary, if it was her 'last act on earth.' It is also on the record that she admitted to contemplating self-destruction, not once, but an undetermined number of times. Now, it is not required of the defense to prove, or even to present, an alternate theory of an alleged crime, but were we compelled to do so, I would have to ask if the evidence did not strongly imply that Miss Cornell had taken her own life under circumstances so arranged as deliberately to cast suspicion of her murder on Reverend Avery.

"Such a theory would infer, in fact demand, the presumption of an accomplice, since someone other than Miss Cornell would be needed to write and receive the various correspondence. And the most logical suspect would be the man who most vigorously, though unsuccessfully, devoted his energy to tracing those letters to the defendant."

Quinncannon put his hand on Harnden's shoulder and kept it there. "It is also in evidence, from the government's own physicians, that the deceased was pregnant and had been for 16–18 weeks at the time of her death. Yet, by her own reported allegations, she could not have been intimate with the respondent earlier than thirteen weeks before she died. Of course, no valid testimony exists to substantiate her supposed charge against Mr. Avery, but it is clear that *some* man fathered her child. I wonder if it is too far-fetched to speculate that the child's father might not be the same man who contrived, with the dead woman, to implicate Mr. Avery in her fabricated 'murder.'"

The Irishman patted the Colonel's shoulder and walked toward the bench, apparently oblivious to the lethal glare behind him.

Thus was the Colonel added to Quinncannon's list of prospective "fathers" that already included John Durfee and Grindall Rawson. I was ready to believe any villainy of Harvey

242

Harnden but my colleague's intimations seemed so ludicrous that I was astounded to find the justices nodding at him solemnly.

Quinncannon now reviewed the physical evidence exhibited at the scene. "If Maria Cornell *was* murdered, gentlemen, then the facts should point clearly and exclusively to that conclusion, but I submit that they not only fail to do so, but actually point in an entirely opposite direction. Earlier in my summation I indicated a willingness to assume, for the sake of argument, the possibility of murder. I ask you now to assume suicide, an act of deliberate self-destruction committed for the purpose of creating a suspicion of murder against Mr. Avery that would annihilate his reputation, his career and ultimately his life."

Haile and Howe were scribbling notes. The Irishman crossed to the empty jury box and rested against the railing. "Not one of the wounds on the woman's body could not have been self-inflicted." This was clearly untrue but said so quickly that neither the justices nor Staples had time to reflect. "Having bruised herself to create the illusion that she was violated, she removed her calash and comb, breaking the latter in two and throwing the pieces as far as she could. She then drew her hair forward over her face and replaced the bonnet on her head, allowing the tie strings to dangle. She attached one end of the cord—a cord of the type, by the way, commonly used to repair the looms where she worked—and she attached it to the fence post by a slip knot. She commenced screaming and groaning— the sounds William Hamilton heard as he passed along the road near the hour of nine. This, gentlemen, was to reinforce the impression that she had been savagely beaten."

The brogue became intense, urgent. "She drew the cord around her throat in the double loop of a clove hitch. Her right hand was raised up from under her cloak so that the hem draped over the crook of her elbow. With this hand she grasped the nearly taut rope between the two knots, while the left was extended through the gap in the front of the cloak caused by the single open clasp. With this hand she gripped the cord's loose end. Then, simultaneously, she yanked both hands in opposite directions and threw her weight forward! The rope tightened fatally—her right hand released its grip and dropped to her side, the cloak falling over it. The left hand popped open but was prevented from falling by the fastened clasp of the cloak beneath it. And there she swayed on that frigid night, gentlemen, her knees hanging a few inches above the cold ground."

It was great theater. The mobbed courtroom was absolutely silent. The judges seemed mesmerized. It was evident that they believed Quinncannon's theory. At that moment even I believed it, and I knew it was sheer nonsense. I looked behind me at Abraham Merrill. For the first time since the hearing began the wrinkled old face was creased with a smile.

"We know," Quinncannon was saying, "from the testimony of the prosecution's own witness, Jeremiah Gifford, that at about half past nine the respondent was quietly retiring to bed, lighted by his host and unsuspected of crime, on the south side of the Bristol Ferry some eight or more miles distant from the stack yard, having come there on foot with one ankle lately dislocated and sometimes lame in consequence. *And here the statement of William Hamilton becomes crucial, for Hamilton heard the girl screaming at near nine o'clock and there is no imaginable way the defendant could have traveled eight miles on foot, even on sound ankles, in only thirty minutes.*"

This was true, but significant only if what Hamilton heard was actually the girl's dying cries and not one cat or two cats or John Durfee beating his wife or the howling wind off the bay or a pig in heat.

Quinncannon pushed off the railing and strolled toward the bench. "I must now call the court's attention to what I consider the strangest aspect of this affair. A coroner's inquest was held on the day following Maria Cornell's death and the verdict was suicide. This jury heard Dr. Wilbur; they heard William Hamilton; they read the letters found in the trunk; some of them saw the body *before* it was cut down; and they gave a verdict of *suicide*. Yet within three days a second inquest reversed the first and accused Reverend Avery of murder.

"I ask, what new information was possessed by the second jury but unknown to the first that could have caused this radical alteration of judgment? Was the first jury ignorant of Cornell's pregnancy or of her related charge against Avery? No, gentlemen, for Dr. Wilbur had informed them of both. As a matter of fact the first jury was aware of every bit of physical evidence that has been produced here by the prosecution *except one*. I refer to the note in pencil allegedly written by Maria Cornell and found in her bandbox, *and* I remind the court that it was the defense that forced the introduction of this exhibit."

He returned to our table and picked up the note. "And what does this little jotting communicate, gentlemen? It is widely reported and generally assumed to contain an accusation of murder, but it is nothing of the kind. It states merely that, should Maria be 'missing,' Reverend Avery will know her whereabouts. The worst—I repeat, gentlemen—the *worst* interpretation that can be made of this note is that Avery had sent her away to have his child. But we have already proven that the child could not have been his, even if her accusation of violation against him were true, and the defense categorically denies it.

"Is it not infinitely more plausible to conclude that Maria, finding herself in the worst trouble of her troubled life, should again apply for aid to the clergyman to whom she had so often turned, and this even while she plotted the most diabolical vengeance against him? Is it not likely that he, never suspecting her treachery, should again come to her assistance?"

He dropped into his chair in apparent exhaustion but I knew better. He had barely broken a sweat. I sensed an approaching crescendo.

Quinncannon massaged his eyes with the fingers of his right hand. "The ancient Greeks had a phrase, gentlemen," he said softly. "*Philos/aphilos*. It translates to love-in-hate, by which they meant simply that it is possible for one individual to both love and hate another at the same time, as Medea, for example, loved and hated Jason."

I doubted either Haile or Howe had any notion who Medea and Jason were but they inclined their gray heads and looked wise. The Irishman extended his arm and observed his palm as though he could see the justices sitting there.

"I have no wish to attack the memory of this unfortunate young woman," Quinncannon said, "particularly as she can no longer defend herself, but neither can she any longer be subjected to cross-examination and the defense has little choice in view of the fact that her pencil note, *if* she was its author, *is the sole reason why Reverend Avery today stands accused of her death*. What witness has the government produced to charge the respondent with violating the girl at Thompson? What witness charges him with fathering her child? What witness points a shivering finger at this respected pastor and cries, 'Murderer'? Only, gentlemen, *only* Maria Cornell.

"Make no mistake, gentlemen. You have heard from Dr. Wilbur and the Rawsons. You have heard the note, which so influenced the second Inquest jury, read in open court. You have heard Lucy Hathaway relate Maria's subtle hints that she was led astray by a minister at camp-meeting. It may appear that Mr. Avery is being arraigned by a chorus of voices, but

245

there is only one accusing voice behind all this rumble and clatter: the voice of Sarah Maria Cornell."

This speech was delivered in so moderate a tone that the entire assembly jumped when the Irishman suddenly slammed his fist on the table. "DAMNATION! Gentlemen, the respondent stands under the shadow of vile suspicion, arrest, indictment, trial, conviction, execution—*on the unsupported word of a dead woman*!"

He stood and leaned forward on stiffened arms, spreading his hands on the table. "*Philos/aphilos.* Consider the history of this wretched creature. Twice apprehended in petty theft. Addicted to almost every vice; an admitted and convicted liar; a wanton who not only confessed but actually boasted of her depravity on the eve of her excommunication from the church for which she professed so much devotion. An acknowledged would-be suicide. She sought and accepted treatment for venereal disease, then denied her affliction, left town without paying her medical fee and—when her physician sought through legal channels to collect his rightful debt—she insinuated false, foul charges against him, disguised herself, and again fled out of town."

Quinncannon walked around the table and leaned against it, folding his arms. "Consider this lost, deranged woman, gentlemen, and ask yourselves if there was any lie she would not tell, any crime she would not commit, any self-degradation to which she would not willingly sink."

He paused and then said in a much more compassionate tone, "Yet we must not forget, in our condemnation of Maria Cornell, that she was both desperate and seriously disturbed. No man and few women can even guess at the bizarre fantasies of her kindly, handsome minister in which she luxuriated. Ephraim K. Avery was more than her spiritual adviser. He was, perhaps, the father who had abandoned her as a child—the older brother who had years before deserted her and whose companionship she craved. He was, though only in her dreams, the protective, sensitive lover she had hopelessly sought in dozens of hay lofts and coal bins and alleys and taverns.

"She applied for employment in his house in Lowell if only to be near him, to have daily contact with him, but his wife did not like her looks and threw her out, and Maria again tasted the bitterness of rejection. She blamed him and indulged in such open immorality that her employers dismissed her even before Avery brought charges against her. In fact it was the complaints of her employers that forced him to bring her to

246

trial. She had compelled him to turn against her, to 'ruin' her, as she later phrased it, and it gave her a strange sense of power over him, though she had paid dearly for her triumph. She repeated the pattern at Dover, at Great Falls, at Thompson, at Fall River, and finally, fatally, at Tiverton, where she paid the ultimate price. And now she seeks to reach out from her grave and drag him down to hell with her!"

Avery had covered his face with his hands. His shoulders shook convulsively as if he were sobbing. It was my strong impression that his grief was not an act.

"When you consider your verdict," Quinncannon said, "I ask only that you place the *in*direct testimony of the deceased, the only true source of the charges against the defendant, in its proper perspective. Maria Cornell loved Ephraim Avery as violently as she hated him. When she found herself pregnant she fantasized him as the father of her child. She contrived letters, purportedly from him, which she exhibited to her friends, without allowing them to be read, for the purpose of convincing them that her own misconduct, soon to be divulged, derived a great palliation from the high character and strong claim to her confidence of her seducer. Undoubtedly she had the further design of actually swearing her offspring upon him and backing her oath with these specious papers, and to this end she also accused him to the Rawsons and her physician.

"For a time she was able to ignore the real situation in which she stood with the respondent—his exclusion of her from his family, from his church, from the society of his friends. His indifference to her demonstrations of grief—his dissatisfaction with her numerous confessions as signs of repentance or means of readmission to his church—his total want of confidence in her. But when at last the truth of their relationship dawned on her, it destroyed whatever precarious balance of reason and fantasy she had managed to retain. She determined to avenge herself on Mr. Avery if, as she'd once told Sarah Honey, 'if it was her last act on earth.'"

While the courtroom emptied for a very late dinner recess Quinncannon systematically shuffled papers and placed them in a small satchel. I sat on the edge of the table and watched him from the corner of one eye with amusement and admiration. When we were alone I asked, "How much of all that was true?"

"Which part?" without looking up.

"Begin with the reconstruction of the suicide."

"Lies," he said, "all lies."

"What about the idea that Avery didn't write the letters?"

"Avery wrote them." He was filling his pipe.

"And what of that analysis of Cornell's character? Any validity to that?"

He glanced up through billows of white smoke. "A great deal," he answered. "You should read her letters. They're pathetic."

I was remembering the expressions of rapt attention on the faces of the justices and the pale dismay on Staples' features. I felt a grin spread across my own face and choked down a war-whoop. "We've won," I said.

Something in my voice made him smile. "First blood, Christy." The smile faded. "It's not over yet."

I thought he was referring to the hearing. "It's over," I said. I could not understand why he did not share my exuberance. I imagine he sensed what I wanted to hear because shortly he said, "You did one hell of a good job, little brother."

The compliment was given with his usual gruff graciousness, and I tried to reply in kind. "Near the end," I said, "you had Avery in tears."

"Really?" He raised an eyebrow. "Well, I'm glad the bastard had the decency to weep."

BOOK IV

The Final Witness

✿ 43

Avery's Flight

Quinncannon's prediction that the Bristol justices would release Avery proved accurate, but the Fall River vigilantes would not let the matter drop. They obtained another warrant and the wretched clergyman panicked and fled from the state.

"Aside from confessing," I said, "what would you say is the most stupid thing our ecclesiastical client could possibly do?"

I regarded Quinncannon grimly across the table in the sitting room of the suite he had taken in Newport's most fashionable hotel, the Atlantic House. He returned my gaze with a sour smile. "Unfortunately I already know," he said. "The Merrills and Drake put him up to it."

I closed my eyes and massaged my temples. "It's as bad as a confession," I said at last. "Damn it, Lon, where will we find a jury who won't believe that only a guilty man would run from a charge against him?"

He shrugged and reached for his pipe. "We could never find an impartial jury anyway, Christy. Not with all the flap that's been let loose in the press." He sipped his whiskey. "I should warn you I have decided not to ask for a change of venue as you suggested. There is no town in Rhode Island where we can expect to get a fair trial, and, as we will inevitably get an unfair trial, we might as well get it in Newport, where the hotels are comfortable and the restaurants tolerably decent."

He had a habit of bantering when the situation was not at all humorous. I found it annoying. "I suppose the next thing you'll tell me is that we will challenge any prospective juror who does not admit he is already convinced that Avery killed the girl."

"Well, of course, lad. Unless we have a jury of professed believers in the minister's guilt we have no hope of winning the case."

He smiled as if at some private joke.

"You know, Lon, I foresaw the possibility of Avery's bolting after the Bristol hearing. When Avery was released I told Colonel Harnden that, if the Fall River vigilance committee was dissatisfied with the decision at Bristol, we were prepared to give recognizance for Avery's appearance at the March session of the Supreme Court. And Harnden refused. He told me Avery was discharged and there was no reason to detain him, nothing to found a precept on. Then—" I was growing increasingly bitter. "What does Harnden do? He goes back to Fall River and convenes a public meeting to stir the general hatred against Avery again into a boiling frenzy. He obtains another warrant against Avery from that senile old fool, Randall. The Methodists get wind of it, and Avery vanishes—poof!—in a cloud of smoke."

Dragging on his pipe, Quinncannon replied out of another cloud of smoke. "And the intrepid Colonel flies after him in hot pursuit."

"Exactly," I growled, "thus fatally damaging our chances for a successful defense. Hell, we don't even know the whereabouts of our client."

"No," he replied, "we do know where he is. He's hiding out with a family named Mayo in a hamlet in New Hampshire called Rindge to which Harnden will soon trace him." He settled back in his chair. "I hardly think Avery's flight has made our case any more impossible than it already was."

"Meaning it was already lost?"

"Lost?" He looked at me with surprise. "No, little brother, it's won. I thought you saw that."

I wondered if he really believed what he had just said. Even if I had not been certain of the clergyman's guilt I could hardly have shared the Irishman's optimism. "What is our strategy this time, Lon? Do we argue again for suicide?"

He took a while to answer. He remained relaxing in his chair, his hands clasped behind his head, his eyes shut, his lips slowly spreading into an ironic smile.

"No, Christy," he said at last, "this time we admit it was murder. We *insist* it was murder. This time . . ." He opened one eye and fixed it on me. "This time we do everything possible to lose the case. That is the only chance we have to win it."

🏵 44

The Dungeon

Avery had been found in New Hampshire as Quinncan-non anticipated, and dragged back to Newport by Colonel Harn-den in chains and disgrace. The Colonel published a pamphlet in Providence containing a detailed description of the pursuit and capture which, I understand, went through several printings and turned rather a nice profit. Dr. Wilbur also published a number of letters on the case in the newspapers, prior to the trial, in which he revealed every charge the dead girl had made to him against Avery, including the allegation of rape at Thompson and the supposed attempt to murder her by inducing her to take a lethal dose of oil of tansy. The upshot was that every prospective juror in Rhode Island was made aware of damning evidence against our client that would never have been allowed to be heard in court.

Increasingly, I felt our case was hopeless, and my spirits were not raised by the interview I witnessed three days before the trial between Quinncannon and Avery in the Newport gaol.

The minister's cell was in the bowels of the building at the end of a long corridor lined by walls of moist stone, permeated by dampness and stench. We were ushered by Coolidge, the keeper, to a wall of granite, fourteen inches thick, in which was set a small window at eye level and beneath that a steel door through which a dwarf could not pass without stooping. Coolidge threw back the steel plate that covered the window.

"Open the door," Quinncannon commanded.

"Can't do it, sir," the keeeper responded. "I got my orders. Anybody talks to the prisoner's got to do it through the window in my hearing."

The Irishman wasted little time on Coolidge. "We are Mr. Avery's attorneys and our consultation with him is privileged, my friend. You will *not* hear our conversation and I will *not* conduct it through a slit cut in a dungeon wall." The brogue became menacing. "Open the goddamn door!"

The keeper obeyed. We bent down to enter the cell and

253

Coolidge, on Quinncannon's orders, closed the window and remained outside to release us as soon as my colleague should rap with his walking stick.

I was astonished by the ravaged appearance of Avery. His clothes were torn, his hair disheveled, his countenance deathly pale. He stared at us out of listless, glazed eyes and it was a full minute before he showed signs of recognition.

The cell was Spartanly furnished. It contained only a cot, a stool and a slop pail that, to judge from the reek, had not recently been emptied. "They won't give me a mirror," Avery rasped. "They think I'll break it and slash my wrists. They've taken my handkerchief and belt and the laces from my shoes for fear I'd hang myself from the bars." He looked up suddenly and cried, "My God, Quinncannon, get me some soap! I *must* have clean clothes to wear. No man can live like this . . . caged! Breathing in the stink of his own filth."

He sat on the stool, bent forward, his hands clasped between his knees. His shoulders heaved though he was not weeping. His voice escaped his throat like a death rattle. "I did not kill the girl, Quinncannon. I did not. I did *not!*" He looked up at the Irishman. His voice was now a whimper. "I did not kill her. I swear it."

Outside a sudden rainstorm had broken. I could hear it through the small barred window just above ground level near the ceiling of the cell. The storm was evidently violent for water began to seep through the window and puddles formed on the stone floor. The torrent disturbed a large rat that emerged abruptly from beneath the cot and vanished with shrill shrieks into the opposite wall.

Quinncannon lit his pipe.

"Avery," he said, "you had sexual connection with Maria Cornell at the Thompson camp-meeting on August 29, 1832."

It was not a question.

"Before you respond," Quinncannon continued, "you should know that everything you did, from that moment in the Thompson bushes, is known to me and will be brought out at your trial. I want you to be certain you understand this. Avery!"

The Irishman seized the minister by the shoulders and pulled him to his feet. "Hear me, Ephraim. To save you from the gallows I must expose every dirty secret you are hiding. That is your only hope of escaping the noose." He flung Avery onto the cot. "Answer me! You had sexual connection with the girl at Thompson."

254

Avery lay back and covered his face with his hands. At last he whispered, "Yes."

"Louder," Quinncannon said.

Some seconds passed. "Yes," the clergyman repeated.

"Louder!" Quinncannon commanded.

"Yes!" Avery shouted. "Yes, yes, yes! I made love to the girl in the woods at camp-meeting! But it wasn't the way she told it to her sister. I did not—I did *not* rape her—nor did I force her in any way. She—she *knew* that I was . . ." he groped for the word ". . . interested. No, Quinncannon, *fascinated*." The prisoner swung his legs down and sat on the edge of the cot. "She was bewitching, Quinncannon. I do not use the word lightly or figuratively. From the first time I saw her she sensed my . . . my attraction. She manipulated me. She used me to maintain her church membership. And finally, at Thompson . . ."

The minister stood and looked straight into Quinncannon's eyes. I think he'd forgotten that I was present. He squared his shoulders and drew a deep breath.

"I will tell you something," he said to Quinncannon, "that I never thought I would tell to any man. She enticed me. Whatever she told her sister was a lie. I had long before destroyed the letters of confession she wrote to me. I had, you must understand, *no* hold on Maria. But she enticed me. You comprehend, man, she *drove* me to it. And when it was over—" His head dropped and he sank back on the cot. There was a long pause. Then, in a husky whisper, Avery said, "When it was over she laughed."

Avery also began to laugh, not a mirthful sound but a noise of gasping bordering on hysteria. "Don't you see, Quinncannon? The whole charade is comical. What I had waited for . . . dreamed . . . fantasized about—she *laughed* at." He buried his face in his hands. "My *God*, Quinncannon, if I was going to kill her *that* would have been the moment."

Now Avery was sobbing. I watched him closely. I don't believe I have ever felt such contempt for a man. Avery the hypocrite, the wife-beater, the seducer, blackmailer, rapist—*that* Avery was bad enough, God knows—but *this* Avery: this whining, cringing victim, seduced and abandoned! Evil is unpleasant but, when performed with competence and style, it may occasionally excite admiration. Satan is the true hero of *Paradise Lost* and there is a noble quality in the pure, relentless villainy of Iago. But when evil alternately blusters and lurks and slinks, bullies and whimpers—when it manifests itself in bombast and back-stabbing—then it becomes merely despicable.

There are tigers and there are hyenas. If I must confront an enemy I will choose the tiger every time.

She had laughed!

That, don't you understand, was the whole point.

For the first time I saw clearly what Quinncannon had seen from the beginning. Avery was *not* the murderer of Sarah Maria Cornell.

"When did she first tell you she was carrying your child?" the Irishman asked sharply.

"In a letter she wrote me in November from Fall River."

"Not when she spoke to you during the Four-Days meeting at Fall River in October?"

"No, no." The minister kept his head in his hands. "She said nothing of it to me then."

"What did she write in the letter?"

"She said she was pregnant. A physician in Tiverton had confirmed her condition. She said I was the—" Avery fought for control. "She said she had accused me to her relations and the physician but to no one else, and she had no wish to ruin my reputation as I had ruined hers. She demanded that I meet with her at a place and time of her choosing and that I give her . . . that I give her three hundred dollars. She said that was the amount that had been suggested to her."

"And you wrote back to her on yellow paper."

"Yes, immediately. I wanted the matter cleared up as soon as possible. I urged her to retain my letters and return them to me when she received the money. I feared if I did not take action quickly her demands would increase."

"You attempted to disguise your handwriting?"

"Yes."

"And to create the impression through deliberate grammatical errors that the writer was uneducated?"

Avery managed a weary smile. "I'm afraid I was not very clever in the way I went about it."

The corners of Quinncannon's mouth tightened. "Continue describing your communications with the woman."

"She wrote again on November 19, insisting that I come to Fall River," Avery answered, "but I could find no convenient excuse to make the journey. Then, too, I had some difficulty in—"

"Raising the money," the Irishman said.

256

"Yes, sir. It was a large sum and I had to apply to many of the brethren. I explained that . . . that . . ."

"You told the story that one of your children was ill and had to be taken to Boston for treatment." Quinncannon knocked out the ashes of his pipe and grimaced. "Damn it, Avery, don't make me drag the truth out of you. You wrote the pink letter urging her to come to Bristol and paid Orswell to deliver it. It was stupid to let yourself be seen by Orswell. It was stupid to mention the name of Betsey Hills, your wife's niece, in the letter. It was stupid to address the girl as 'sister.' For that matter it was stupid to communicate with her at all, especially in writing. It was stupid to write the note arranging for your December twentieth interview in Iram Smith's store on paper *stolen* from Smith so that the torn edge and watermark could later be matched. It was stupid to meet the girl at all, to pay the blackmail, to accept her word that the baby was yours. It was *unbelievably* stupid to take the girl into the underbrush at the camp-meeting in the first place and render yourself vulnerable to all this grief and humiliation."

Quinncannon leaned back against the wall and folded his arms. "Damnation, Reverend," he said, "if there is anything for which I have a lower tolerance than a client who is stupid and guilty, it's a client who is stupid and innocent."

For a long time the dungeon was silent. The storm outside had subsided but water still dripped from the barred window. The murky puddles on the floor widened. Tiny rivers flowed through the cracks between the flagstones. The dripping sound began to assume a rhythm like the ticking of a clock. It was as though the minutes of Avery's life were slowly being measured and reduced.

The minister remained sitting on the cot, his elbows on his knees, his hands covering his eyes. I noticed that the cot was of the same manufacture as the one I had seen in his study. There, as here, it provided a separate resting place from that of his wife.

At last Avery said, "You *do* think me innocent, Quinncannon?"

"Of murder?" My friend smiled. It was not a pleasant smile. "Yes, I know you did not kill the girl. Which of you suggested that you meet at John Durfee's stack yard?"

"That was Maria's idea."

"Were you able to acquire the full three hundred dollars?"

"Yes, finally."

"And, on December 20, between six and six-thirty, you paid the money to the girl and left her alive?"

"Yes, yes, alive. I gave her the cash and left at once. She *was* alive when I last saw her."

The Irishman nodded grimly. "You should understand, Avery, that as the defendant in a capital trial you are forbidden by law to testify in your own defense, not that we would risk putting you on the stand in any case. You must also understand that it is essential to your welfare and continued reasonably good health that every action to which you have confessed during this interview must be acknowledged in open court."

The clergyman looked up. "Including the . . . the event at camp-meeting?"

"Most particularly the event at camp-meeting."

"No!" Avery cried. "Such an admission would destroy my career."

"So would your execution, Brother," Quinncannon said quietly. "So would your execution."

Mrs. Randolph Analyses
Some Correspondence

"*You must call me Amy, Mr. Quinncannon.*"

The Irishman smiled at us across the table of the Park House Tavern. It was located opposite the Newport Court House, a favorite dining place for lawyers and politicians. We sat at a corner table amid the bustle of the waiters rushing about with heavily laden trays precariously balanced on upturned palms. The din of the diners' conversation was punctuated by the clank of ale tankards and the thump of wooden spoons against pewter plates. My little wife positively beamed. She was, and remains, the only woman I know who is totally comfortable in an atmosphere dominated by men.

"It's so *busy* here," she said. "I imagine terribly important decisions are made here every day."

"Not *terribly* important," Quinncannon returned, still smiling. "That is only the illusion of the men who make them."

She sipped her wine. "You are too modest, sir."

He tossed off his Irish. "You are too generous, dear lady."

"Oh for God's sake," I groaned. "May I introduce myself? My name is Christopher Randolph and I happen to be in possession of a packet of letters which I came to this saloon to discuss with a shameless coquette and a notorious libertine of my acquaintance." I threw the papers on the table. "May I remind you both that in two days we go to trial?"

The letters in question had been written by Maria Cornell between 1819 and the year of her death, all addressed to either her mother or her older sister. Quinncannon had obtained copies and had asked Amy to read them.

"You understand, Mrs. Randolph," he had said, "what I want is a *woman's* point of view. I want your sense of the girl's personality—anything which will help me to comprehend her feelings and motives more clearly."

Amy, of course, was thrilled. Thrilled that she and I were,

in a sense, collaborating in Avery's defense. Thrilled that her opinion was valued by the Irishman. I thought it a gracious gesture on his part. It kept her from brooding over the loss of our child and allowed her to feel useful. I was grateful and I had said so.

He had cast a narrow glance at me. "I'm not much for charitable gestures. We need her insight. I have sometimes noticed, little brother, that a woman's intellectual powers are often less appreciated by her husband than by other men. It is, I suspect, a leading cause of marital discord, for when a man underestimates his woman, that is precisely when she gains the one thing she does *not* want; the whip hand over him."

I recall his words coming vividly into my mind several times as the true events that led up to the murder were revealed during Avery's trial.

But now Amy was saying, "There is a wondrous mystery, Mr. Quinncannon, in the fact that Maria was constantly betraying herself to the Methodists by confessions of guilt and self-accusations of sin of the most outrageous kind, while at the same time she was endeavoring to remain in the church and be in fellowship with its members, and respected by them, striving for that as though her very salvation depended on it."

He watched her and nodded.

"I read the letters over and over, and I thought of what you told me about her. That she was the youngest of three and grew up not even knowing her sister, and how her father abandoned them while she was still a small child. Then her brother, James, ran off to New Orleans before he was nineteen." She paused. "It's particularly sad the way she keeps asking for word of him. She must have worshipped him, being so much younger and without a father. Yet he never wrote her a word, Mr. Quinncannon, and when he visited the others he made no effort to come to her."

The waiter arrived with a fresh round of drinks. We waited while he set them down.

"There are things," Amy said, "*themes* that run through her letters. It's all very strange. There is so much guilt and self-reproach. See here. I have marked this passage. 'Alas my heart is hard and I am as prone to sin as the sparks that fly upward.' She wrote that when she was only eighteen. And here, on her nineteenth birthday she wrote of the sudden death of a young man and said, 'Sometimes I think, *why am I spared*? Perhaps it is to commit more sin, perhaps for some usefulness. God says be ye also ready for ye know not what hour your Lord will come.'"

She put down the paper. "There seems such an irony in that. And there are other references to her sin, her guilt. *Constant* references. Yet, in the same letters she can become impossibly pious."

"Did you notice," Quinncannon asked, "that she was most self-righteous when she was most defensive?"

Amy brightened. "Yes! That's so. And her family kept . . . *accusing* her of things."

He smiled at her. "For example?"

"Oh, there are *dozens* of examples. She wrote her sister from Killingly, Connecticut, in 1822: 'You wrote me that you should not come to Killingly as long as I stayed at this factory. You must remember that your *pride must have a fall*. I am not too proud to get a living in any situation in which it pleases God to place me. Remember that you have expressed a humble hope in God, and never let it be said of you that you were too proud to follow your Savior's steps—who was meek and lowly and went about doing good—suffering the scoffs and indignation of wicked men, and finally spilled his precious blood that you might be saved.'"

She stared at him. "Do you see, Mr. Quinncannon? It is not just that her sister was displeased at her working in a factory. Maria actually *identified* herself with Christ."

"And her sister with the enemies of Christ?"

"Perhaps," she answered. "I hadn't thought of it in quite that way. I had thought of one idea. Do you suppose it might have been that her parents didn't want her?"

The Irishman leaned back in his chair. "What leads you, Amy, to that suspicion?"

"Only that she was so much younger than the other children and that her father disappeared so soon after she was born. And, of course, the way her mother rejected her."

"Rejected her?"

"Oh, yes. Not only her mother, Mr. Quinncannon. Her whole family abandoned her. It began long before she was first accused of shoplifting. That was what set me to wondering, you see, because if they'd rejected Maria only *after* her public disgrace, why then it might be understandable. But her isolation from them happened well before that." She looked at him. "It's all in the letters."

"Tell me," he said.

She drew a deep breath. "Everything Maria did, everything

261

she *was* embarrassed her family. She learned the trade of tailoring but she must have failed at it as she ended working as a weaver in a factory, and they thought that disreputable. She was raised a Congregationalist but became a Methodist and they thought *that* disreputable. They seem to be—" She touched my arm. "Forgive me, Christy, for mentioning her name, but they so remind me of Cousin Charlotte. They're so . . ." She hesitated, trying to decide whether to use the word. Then she exploded with it. ". . . so *damned* respectable!"

"Go on," Quinncannon said.

I watched her with admiration, seeing a side of her I had never seen before—a side that, perhaps, had never been there before. She was astute, concise, analytical—so far from the beautiful little feather-brain I had rescued from the raid on the Masked Ball. I wondered, even at the time, whether there was anything, aside from physical beauty, that attracted a man more to a woman than the exhibition of qualities he considers to belong exclusively to his own sex.

She was looking through the pages. "This one, to her sister. 'Write immediately on receipt of this. I am so far from mother that it will not be convenient for her to write anymore.' And this one, to her mother. 'Perhaps you have forgotten you have a daughter, Maria—but stop, dear mother, I am still your daughter and Lucretia's only sister.' These were *before* her arrest, Mr. Quinncannon, and after it they did not write her for over two years. She learned of the birth of her sister's first child only by accident. Here she wrote, 'I want to see mother, and if any of you want to see me, write and let me know.'"

She raised her head and met his eyes. "But you see, sir, they never bother to *answer* her."

He merely relaxed into a tobacco fog and waited.

"It becomes worse and worse," Amy said. "I've marked the letters for you. In September, 1827, Maria writes the Rawsons and her mother: 'After waiting six months for a letter in vain, I take up my pen to address those who are near and dear to me by ties of nature. . . . Dear Mother, if you have any regard for me do write if it is only two lines.' Still there was no response and . . ."

There was a catch in her voice. "I don't understand how they could be so cruel to her," she said. I put my arm around her. She pushed the letter toward me and I read where she had marked. "'My Dear Mother—Once more I take up my pen to write a few lines to you as nearly a year has again elapsed since I have heard from you. Sometimes I think you have utterly forgotten me."

Abruptly Amy shook her shoulders, sat up straight, and gulped at her wine. "That was the last letter Maria wrote before she went to Lowell in 1829. Did you not tell me that she first met Mr. Avery in Lowell when she joined his church? Did you not say that it was there she got herself in . . . in the trouble that caused him to have her expelled from the Methodists?"

Quinncannon nodded slowly.

"Then, sir, I believe I can show you what drove her to do what she did."

Again she passed a paper to me. "Read it, Christy," she said. "Read it all."

Lowell, Jan. 11th, 1830

To Mrs. Cornell.

My dear Mother—it seems a long time since I have heard from you and I almost begin to think you have forgotten me or you would have written before this. I have written two letters and sent two papers since I have resided in this place, and have not received a line from any of you. I hope you will consider I am a stranger in a strange land, exposed to sickness and death.

I received a letter from you about four months past in which you observed I was a moving planet, but I would tell my dear mother that I do not think I have moved much for two years past. I have not moved so quick that I have outdistanced the mail delivery.

With regard to my views respecting religion, they are the same. I was a great sinner but I found a great Savior. Perhaps my family think it strange that I choose a people different in their views and opinions from that which any of you have embraced. But let me tell you, my dear mother, that the Methodists are my people—with them by the grace of God I was spiritually born—with them I have tried to live and hope to enjoy the bliss of the blest in heaven.

Write so soon as you receive this from your unworthy daughter,

Sally

I finished reading. "There is another letter, Mr. Quinncannon," Amy said, "composed just before her trouble at Lowell."

"I seem to recall it," he responded, "but it would be best, Christy, if you read it aloud."

I took it up.

Lowell, July 4th, 1830

To Mrs. Cornell

I have never received a line from you since last I wrote. I have concluded that you were sick or dead, for it appears to me if you were in the land of the living and possess a parent's feelings you would have written before this. A long time I waited after writing you last year, thinking you would write and let me know if I should be welcome to visit, but at length concluded it was neither your wish nor that of my brother-in-law and dear sister that I should visit.

I am now in receipt of a letter in which you say you should like to have me come to visit this summer. Last summer I made my calculations and should have made the trip if you had written, but this summer I have already prepared to go down on the water to camp meeting where I went last year.

I shall write to Mr. Rawson as soon as I return from the Cape, though I never received a line from him or Lucretia since they were married, but I expect my sister's time is pretty much taken up with her children.

I am your affectionate though absent child,
MARIA CORNELL

"What has happened," Amy said, "is that Maria has grown tired of begging for their love and attention. She's become defiant. As they have refused to forgive her—for her thefts, her factory work, her Methodism—so she now refuses to forgive them. Now that they have at last invited her to visit, she is too busy to go. Instead she will remain with the despised Methodists who are her real friends, her *true* family."

She tried to gather her thoughts. "The pattern is always the same, Mr. Quinncannon. Her people reject her because she has disgraced them. She confesses abjectly and pleads for loving acceptance. They remain cold and she becomes angry. To avenge herself on them she deliberately brings *even more* disgrace on herself and therefore on them.

"At first the disgrace was merely her work and her religion, but later she turned to stealing and immoral behavior—" Her hand tightened its grip on my wrist. "I think many of the stories she told the other girls were untrue, but not all of them. I feel so sorry for her. I don't believe she was *ever* loved by anyone and that caused her to hate herself. She was so self-destructive."

The majority of the diners had finished their meals and departed. The conversational hum of the few remaining stragglers mixed with the ponderous ticking of a massive clock that hung above the hearth. It was ornately carved but it kept the wrong time.

"There is one other thing, sir," Amy said. She still clung tightly to my wrist.

Quinncannon waited.

"The men with whom Maria . . . slept. I doubt that any of them initiated the connexion."

He lifted an eyebrow. "Including Mr. Avery?"

"*Especially* Mr. Avery."

❧ 46 ————————————
The Randolphs at Home

"I had," Amy said, *"a visitor today."* I could hear the smile in her voice.

I lay on my side of the bed, on my back, and stared at a ceiling I could not see. The fire was dead. The lamps had been out for an hour. It was the night before the trial.

I said, "Uh-huh."

The room was cold. We had some weeks before removed from the Widow Bloss' rooming house and moved into the quarters at the rear of my office. I preferred the privacy but it was hard on Amy. She had enjoyed the bustle and the company of the other boarders. Now, in Newport, she had little communication excepting with tradesmen. Preparation for the trial kept me away much of the time. Many evenings, and this had been one, I came home to find her already retired.

"Christy," she said, "you're not going to close your eyes all night, are you?"

I said, "Probably not."

She rolled over on her side and rested her arm on my chest. "Is it that you think your whole career depends on this case?"

"It is, darling, that my whole career is sliding into the sewer because of this case. I spent half the day trying to teach a Fall River factory girl named Jenny O'Hara how to tie a clove hitch so that, when we call her to testify that she and Maria Cornell were required to use that knot in mending their looms, she'll be able to demonstrate it for the jury!"

I sat up, fumbled for a match, and lit the lamp. "Jesus Christ, Amy, is *this* what the law is? Fake evidence! Perjured testimony! Watch closely, ladies and gentlemen. At no time do my hands leave my wrists. Lift the correct shell and find the little pea. Damn! It's cold in here."

I went to the fireplace and slammed logs onto the irons. "You begin, mind you, with the best of intentions and the purest of motives." I was hacking away with an ax for kindling. "Then you make a compromise. Just a tiny one, you understand. Just

266

because you haven't had a client in a month and the rent is due. Then the landlord starts dropping in more often than the clients, and right behind him is the grocer and the butcher and the blacksmith and the tinker and the tailor and the tapster—What the hell is that?"

"Brandy," she said, handing me the tumbler.

I gulped at it and swallowed hard. "And before you know it the only decent, honest, respectable, god-fearing people you know are the ones you owe money to!" The fire began to crackle. "God *damn* it, Amy! I started out to save the world and now I think I may be the man who shoves it over the brink."

I flopped back on the bed and stared at the flaming tongues licking up the sides of the logs. Amy asked, "Have you said it all?"

"Probably not."

I closed my eyes and listened to the fire and waited for her to put her arms around me. She didn't do it. When she next spoke I realized that her voice came from the furthest corner of the room.

"You haven't asked me," she said.

"Asked you what?"

"Who my caller was today."

I didn't give a damn. I desperately wanted her to hold me. "All right, who was your caller today?"

"Catherine Avery."

I opened my eyes. "What the devil did she want?"

Amy smiled. "Actually she was looking for you. She wanted you to know how grateful she was to you for defending her husband."

I shook my head. "The best thing that could happen to that woman would be her husband dangling from the end of a rope."

"Oh?" she said in that annoying way that implied disagreement without open challenge.

"My God, darling, the man abuses her, bullies her, degrades her, cheats on her. He isn't worth the price of the cord to hang him."

"Christy," she said softly, "she loves him."

"Then she's a damn fool."

"Perhaps, but my heart went out to her." She sat beside me on the bed and took my hand in hers. "I feel so very sad for Mrs. Avery, and for Maria. Though we never met, reading her letters makes me feel I knew her. And sad, too, for Mr. Avery.

They seem to have been swept up in a tragedy none of them could control."

"That," I said, "is a woman's notion. They could have controlled it. They were too damn weak to even try."

"That," she responded, "is a man's notion."

She leaned over suddenly and kissed me. "Christy, Christy, don't doubt yourself. Don't doubt your work. You told me you knew Mr. Avery was innocent. I don't know much about such things, but doesn't that mean you must do all in your power to save him?"

She placed my hands on her breasts and encircled her arms around my waist and pressed her lips against mine and slowly I lay back on the bed and she lay on my chest.

At last I gazed up at her and smiled. "I do believe, Amy, darling, that you are attempting to seduce me."

She smiled back at me. "If I succeed, Christy, darling, that will make us even."

🐚 47

Mr. Quinncannon and Mr. Randolph Confer

The transcript of the Avery trial, compiled by Mr. Benjamin F. Hallett, has recently been published, and the older reader will remember the newspaper accounts, widely circulated at the time, both of the testimony and of the trial's startling and violent conclusion. It may also be recalled that the press was united in its certainty of the minister's guilt, and in its ridicule of what was at first considered the inept conduct of the defense.

As the evidence adduced by the government at the trial did not differ materially or significantly from that presented at the Bristol hearing, I do not propose to try the reader's patience with its repetition. Rather I would explain the circumstances, until now unknown, that lay behind the defense's strategy, and those that led up to the trial's remarkable climax.

The court met first, it will be remembered, on Monday, May 6, 1833, in Newport, before Judge Eddy, Chief Justice, assisted by Judges Brayton and Moore. The government was represented by Albert C. Greene, Attorney General, assisted by William Staples and State Senator Dutee J. Pearce. It required several days to select a jury, principally because it was virtually impossible to find a talesman who had not already decided that Avery was guilty. All prospective jurors excused for cause were challenged by Justice Eddy, not by Quinncannon. When the third long day ended without a full jury being empaneled I asked the Irishman why.

"Because it doesn't make a damn bit of difference whether the jury is prejudiced against Avery or not," he replied. "If this case has to go to the jury at all Avery is as good as hanged. I *want* a prejudiced jury, just in the unlikely event we must go to appeal."

He lit his pipe. "I'm not being fair with you, Christy. There are things I plan to do—tactics I'm going to use—which will

269

be perceived as . . . incompetent. Perhaps disreputable. The problem is that the evidence is so dramatically—so over-whelmingly against us." He looked at me. "I think you know that Avery is incapable of murder."

"Yes," I said, "I know."

He leaned back in his chair and cradled his head in the clasp of his hands behind it and shut his eyes. It was a long time before he spoke, but when he did his words came quickly.

"The problem, Christy, is that I know who killed the girl and I'm not sure I can prove it, and therefore, whatever I may have said to you earlier, I'm not confident we can save Avery from the scaffold, but the one thing that's clear to me is that our only hope lies in letting the prosecution put their entire case before the jury, without contradiction or challenge or, with few exceptions, even cross-examination, because it is the evidence of their witnesses that will save our client, but, Christy—"

We were seated at the table in the salon of his hotel suite, in the captain's chairs that were not part of the usual furnishings but that he had requested of the management. He leaned forward with his elbows on the table and said, "This could get rough. The newspapers are already attacking us. If my strategy misfires they will be unmerciful."

I had never heard him acknowledge even the vaguest possibility that he might be in error, that he might fail. To me he was the personification of self-confidence. I thought of him facing the mob at the time of the great hoax. I recalled him sitting calmly in the midst of Madame Restell's hired thugs.

"You have your career ahead of you, Christy," Quinnncannon said. "You have political aspirations. You're a newly married man. Now listen to me carefully, lad. The case upon which we are currently engaged is unpopular and may be hopeless. Even if we win and Avery goes free, it could all blow up in your face. The best advice I can give you is to get out of this mess while you can." He waited before adding, "I'll see to it you lose no money by doing so."

I puffed on my own pipe and felt my lips form a smile around its stem and then I said, "You Irish son of a bitch!"

He observed me under a raised eyebrow.

I was both touched by his concern for me and annoyed that he thought I would consider abandoning him during Avery's trial. I was moved, too, by his fears over my vulnerability and his confession of his own.

"Do you happen to recall," I asked, "what you told me after

270

we rode into the mob together when all of New York turned out to see Manhattan sawed off and repositioned?"

The Irishman smiled. "There are reasons why you may prefer not to associate yourself too closely with this case or with me and my conduct of it."

"Goddamn it, Mr. Quinncannon!" I exploded. "Stop looking out for my best interests! Stop assuming you are the appropriate judge of what my best interests are! Kindly cease interfering with my God-given right to make my own mistakes even if the worst of them is to involve myself with a Celt of dubious character in the convoluted defense of an obnoxious and sinister gentleman for the most vicious of crimes."

He gave me a steady gaze. "You're taking a serious risk, little brother."

"With you, big brother, I'll take it."

He kept his eyes on mine and then suddenly he nodded and, "All right, Christy," he said, "I'll tell you who murdered Maria Cornell."

271

🐚 48 ───────────────

The Prosecution

The attorney general, Albert Greene, was a venerable and formidable opponent, an imposing man in his fifties with a great shock of white hair, a booming, basso voice, and the flair of a stage actor. He was then at the peak of his career. He had more than three decades of courtroom experience and, perhaps worst of all for our cause, he was a close, personal friend of the chief judge, Nathaniel Eddy. Moreover, he and his co-counsel had prepared their case with industry and precision.

By contrast Quinncannon, as he had once pointed out to me, was a foreigner, an Irishman, and despite his polished manners and aristocratic bearing, it was inevitable that the deep bias of the Yankees on the bench and in the jurybox against his countrymen would prejudice our presentation. Then, too, there was the antagonism of the press and the ugly pretrial publicity to deal with, as well as the general public antipathy toward the Methodists. As the damaging evidence against Avery mounted, day after day, and Quinncannon made no effort to prevent it from reaching the ears of the jury or even to cross-examine the government's witnesses, I became, not withstanding my respect for my friend, downright panicky.

John Durfee, Aunt Hannah Wrightington, Harvey Harnden, Peleg Cranston, Jeremiah Gifford—witness after witness gave testimony for the prosecution and left the stand without being asked a single question by Quinncannon. When Greene called Lucretia Rawson to establish that the victim had accused Avery of forcing her at Thompson, the Irishman waved his hand.

"The defense has no wish to prolong these proceedings unnecessarily," he said with a yawn. "We will stipulate that the defendant had sexual intercourse with Maria Cornell on August 29 at the camp-meeting in Thompson."

There was a stunned silence in the chamber, followed by a collective gasp from the pews occupied by the Methodist faithful. Even Greene seemed astounded. "You admit Mr. Avery raped the girl?"

"We do not admit to rape. We admit to intercourse. I trust the distinction is clear."

The attorney general smiled. "The distinction is duly noted, Mr. Quinncannon. An admission of intercourse is sufficient to prove my case."

Quinncannon returned the smile. "And to prove mine, Mr. Greene."

I stared at him. I knew his theory of the crime. I knew, or thought I knew, how his mind worked. Yet, for the life of me, I could not understand his strategy.

Grindall Rawson followed his wife to the stand and repeated his testimony at Bristol almost verbatim. When Greene turned to our table the Irishman did not bother to look up from his notes. "No questions at this time," he said, in a tone that implied a state of total boredom. It was the same tone and the same words with which he had declined to cross-examine Durfee and Harnden and all of Greene's witnesses, but this time Judge Eddy felt compelled to comment.

"It is the duty of this court, Mr. Quinncannon, to protect the interests of the defendant by assuring that he receives a competent defense. During this trial several persons have given harmful evidence against the prisoner and the court must note for the record, and with some alarm, your failure to attempt to refute any of this testimony."

Quinncannon glanced up. "I stand rebuked, Your Honor. I shall endeavor in future to comport myself more professionally."

But he didn't. Or at least he didn't appear to do so. He did not question the Fall River and Bristol post masters called by Greene to lay a foundation for introducing the yellow and pink letters, nor did he challenge Orswell's claim that Avery had hired him to deliver the pink letter to Maria, and he failed to cross-examine Iram Smith and Reverend Bidwell when Greene used them to prove that Avery had been in Smith's store on December 8 and torn off part of a sheet of paper on which he'd written the white letter.

When Greene then proposed to read the three letters into the record there was no objection. "On the contrary," Quinncannon said, "defense will stipulate that all three were, in fact, written by Mr. Avery to Maria Cornell."

Judge Eddy scowled. "Mr. Quinncannon, have you read these letters? Are you aware of their contents?"

"Fully aware, Your Honor."

"And you still are satisfied to acknowledge your client's authorship and to allow the jury to hear them?"

"'Satisfied' is not the word I would choose, Your Honor."

"And what word would you prefer, sir?"

"Adamant," Quinncannon replied.

Eddy's eyes narrowed. "Do you realize that these papers may be used to establish both motive and opportunity?"

The Irishman smiled. "Motive has already been established," he answered easily, "and as to opportunity, we will stipulate now that Mr. Avery was in Tiverton on the evening of December 20 and that he met Miss Cornell at or near John Durfee's stack yard at or about six p.m."

The Methodist brethren went white. Greene could not suppress the grin which widened across his face. Eddy looked down at the letters and shook his head. Then he gaveled for order.

"Your excellent reputation preceded you to this court and this trial, sir," he said gravely. "That is the only reason I am allowing you to continue as defense counsel. You practice, sir, a very unorthodox style of law, and I must again warn you that you are currently on very thin ice. In the court's opinion you are flirting with disbarment."

Again he looked at the damning letters. Then he gave a sigh and said, "The clerk will read these documents into the record."

✤ 49
Doctor Wilbur Testifies

*The attorney general evidently considered Richard Wil-bur his star witness, for the physician's evidence was the grand finale of the government's case. The old man's testimony did not differ materially from his statements at Bristol nor, for that matter, from the opinions he had expressed to me immediately after the murder. I recall vividly my conviction at the time that Wilbur had, figuratively speaking, hammered the last nail in Avery's coffin.

Several times I thought Quinncannon should have objected to Greene's questions but he never did. Instead he leaned back in his chair, arms folded, legs stretched out under our table, eyes closed as if he were asleep. It struck me abruptly. That was the same attitude he had assumed when I had first seen him at the trial of the "skin-stables" swindler, Deodat Peck.

At the conclusion of his examination of Wilbur, Greene turned and said smugly, "I expect my learned colleague has no questions for this witness."

A pause. One Irish eye opened beneath a raised eyebrow. "Oh," in a thick brogue, "your learned colleague might have one or two questions, Mr. Greene."

And suddenly, for the first time in the trial, Quinncannon was on his feet, surcharged with energy, all pretense of ennui gone, stalking the witness. Every man on the jury, every man on the bench, every man in the courtroom was instantly alert, leaning forward in his chair. I alone leaned back and relaxed, feeling the tension drain out of me and mentally mixing a metaphor. So, I thought, the Irish fox *has* been playing possum.

"Now, Doctor," he began, "in a case as complex as this it is essential to clarify the chronology of the events if we are to reconstruct what occurred."

Wilbur eyed him.

"Miss Cornell first consulted you on October 8?"

"She did."

"At that time did you diagnose her condition?"

"No, sir. I suspected her pregnancy but waited to confirm it."

"And did you confirm it?"

"I did."

"When did you inform her of your findings?"

"At her second visit to my office."

"That would be on the evening of October 15."

"Yes, sir."

"And at that time she told you that the father was Reverend Avery?"

"Well," Wilbur answered, "I had to force the truth out of her."

"The truth?" The tone of the brogue was ironic. "But you *did* manage to wrench this 'truth' from her, Doctor?"

"I was most insistent," the witness replied.

"On what date did you next see her?"

"On October 21, after the factory closed."

"Is that when she showed you the oil of tansy?"

"It is."

"Please repeat for the jury your earlier testimony, Doctor. Where did Miss Cornell say she had obtained this substance?"

"She said she had it of Reverend Avery the previous evening and that he told her it would abort the baby, and that he had prescribed the dosage."

"And the dosage allegedly prescribed. Had she taken it, would it have killed her?"

"It was," Wilbur responded, "at least four times a lethal dose."

"But she did not consume any of this poison."

"Fortunately, sir, she consulted me before doing so."

"Yes," Quinncannon said. "That was fortunate, no doubt." He faced the jury. "It is already on the record, Doctor, that Miss Cornell was seen in Fall River by several witnesses in agitated conversation with Mr. Avery on the evening of October 20. She brought the poison to you the following night. Did she tell you when and where she received it from Mr. Avery?"

"She said he had given it to her in Fall River the previous evening," the physician answered.

The Irishman nodded. He rested against the defense table and ran his thumbnail along his lower lip.

"Dr. Wilbur, I have no desire to try the court's patience, but I wish to be clear on your reasons for believing the girl was murdered while lying on her back as opposed to hanging herself in the position in which she was found."

276

Wilbur assumed the attitude of a patient professor lecturing an inquisitive but slow-witted student. "There are four major reasons for that conclusion, sir. First, at the moment of anoxia—" He glanced at the jury. "—of strangulation, gentlemen. At that moment feces are inevitably excreted. In this case the feces were found mashed and frozen against the victim's back. Now, the fact that she died out of doors, at night, and in cold weather would explain their frozen condition but—" He looked about the court apologetically. "If I seem to be indelicate I ask your pardon, gentlemen, but upon excretion the feces would be warm. Had she hanged herself in the manner suggested by her position when discovered, the feces would have dropped to the ground. Naturally, given the weather conditions, they would eventually have frozen, but not *against* her back unless she was lying on her back when she died."

Quinncannon asked, "Does not that circumstance suggest that Miss Cornell remained for some time on her back after death before her body was moved?"

"Oh, yes, but there are many other reasons for that assumption."

My friend held up his hand. "All in due course, Doctor. What are your other arguments against suicide?"

"The presence of livor for one thing," the witness said, "and of course the paleness of the face and lack of marks in the hay under her feet, which would have indicated a death struggle."

"Had Maria hanged herself, would such marks have existed?"

"In my opinion they would, Mr. Quinncannon."

The Irishman strolled toward the jurybox. "Kindly explain livor, Doctor."

Wilbur addressed the jury. "Livor is the settling of blood in the body after death, the result of gravitational pull or force. It produces a splotchy appearance on the skin and generally requires six to twelve hours to complete."

"These marks aid in determining whether a body has been moved after death?"

"Yes, sir."

"Were such marks present in the body of Maria Cornell, and if so, where were they found?"

"They were present, sir, in the skin of the lower back."

"And what does that circumstance suggest, Doctor?"

"Livor mortis occurs after death only in the most dependent portions of the body, Mr. Quinncannon. Had the woman hanged herself we would have found livor in her lower extremities,

277

her legs, you understand. That we discovered it, instead, in her back, indicates that she was killed while lying down."

"I see," the Irishman said, with the air of someone learning an interesting fact for the first time. He began to pace slowly before the jurybox. "You mentioned the paleness of her face, Doctor. What is the significance of that?"

The witness's tone remained patiently professorial. "If she had hanged herself in the position in which she was discovered, that is, with her head hanging forward, the face would be a purplish black."

Quinncannon nodded. "I'm curious about the bruises that cannot be explained by livor. I refer to those on her sides at the waist and those in the pelvic region, Doctor."

"I can only surmise, sir."

"Feel free to surmise," my friend said.

"I fear my testimony must again be somewhat indelicate."

Quinncannon relaxed against the bar and frowned. "There is nothing so indelicate as murder, Doctor."

Wilbur watched him for a few moments. "Very well, sir. One of the marks on her sides was clearly made by a human hand, a large hand, doubtless that of a man. My presumption is that the other bruise was inflicted in the same manner and therefore that the man who made those marks gripped her tightly while . . ." He hesitated. ". . . while astride her."

"While violating her?" Quinncannon asked.

Wilbur shot an angry glance at Avery. "While *raping* her," he answered coldly.

The Irishman took his time with his next question. "Would you not agree, Doctor, that, assuming those bruises were inflicted during coitus, their presence may merely indicate excessive passion without in any way proving rape?"

The witness thought that over. "Yes," he said with obvious reluctance, "I would have to agree."

"Have you ever known rape to produce bruising in the pelvic area?"

"I have."

"In your opinion, would that explain the marks on that part of the body?"

"No, sir. The discoloration was too dark and extensive. I should say the girl was savagely beaten before her death with a blunt instrument, a cane or stick of some sort."

"*Before* her death, you say?"

"Yes, because after death the heart action ceases and blood is no longer pumped through the body. Therefore, within a minute or two at the outside, no degree of pressure will produce a bruising of the skin. In my view the killer would not have had sufficient time to create the marks I observed on the dead woman's body unless she was beaten while still alive."

"All right." Quinncannon scratched pensively at a corner of his thin moustache. "Something else puzzles me, Doctor. When Maria's corpse was found her facial muscles were relaxed. If she had been so horribly abused and then strangled, wouldn't you expect to see an expression of fear or pain on her face?"

The physician smiled. His attitude was becoming patronizing. "That is a phenomenon which seldom occurs except in Gothic novels, sir. Its absence in this case is no more surprising than the discovery of an indentation on her cheek where it rested against the stackpole from which she was hung. You see, Mr. Quinncannon, the muscles of the face are so thin, so pliable, that any expression of the features at the time of death will probably disappear within a few minutes. The weakness of these muscles would also account for the indentation of the cheek. Since much of the girl's weight was supported by the pole, the pressure of that weight would overcome counter-resistance by the facial muscles, even when rigor was present."

Quinncannon considered that. "Was rigor still present when you first examined the body on the morning after the murder?"

"It certainly was."

"Please describe rigor mortis for the jury, Doctor."

Wilbur cleared his throat. "Rigor is a progressive stiffening of the muscles as a result of coagulation of the muscle protein that usually commences four to six hours after death. Since cold retards the process, I would say, in this case, closer to six hours."

"Now, Miss Cornell was found with her legs bent back under her body and only her toes touching the ground. You have argued, Dr. Wilbur, that other physical evidence proves she died while lying on her back. What would you say was the position of her legs at the moment of her murder?"

"Obviously, sir, her knees were up with her feet resting flat on the ground."

The Irishman gave a half smile. "And what was the position of her arms and hands under rigor?"

The old man brightened. "I had almost forgotten that. The right hand hung down where it had fallen and lain on the ground, but the left arm, or the lower part of it, was extended through an opening in her cloak. The left elbow was close to

279

her side but the hand was up, palm out, fingers uplifted, as if warding off a blow. That circumstance fits my theory exactly."

"And what is your theory exactly?"

"You may regret asking that question, sir."

Quinncannon smiled. "I'll take my chances, sir."

"Then," the witness replied, "the position of the left arm from the elbow to the wrist might be explained by the action of the cloak in preventing its gravitational descent, even if the girl had hung herself, but in that event the hand and fingers would have fallen. That they did not is proof that she died while on her back." Wilbur leaned forward in the chair. "You see, Mr. Quinncannon, the cord around her neck was so tight that it must have killed her almost instantly. At that moment her left arm and hand were in the position in which we later observed them, after they were made rigid by rigor. Obviously the palm and fingers were bent backwards at the wrist with the tips of the fingers lower than the heel of the hand. Therefore, I must conclude Miss Cornell could not possibly have died by suicide."

Quinncannon raised an eyebrow. "Do all these circumstances suggest any other conclusions to you, Doctor?"

"They suggest," Wilbur responded, "murder."

"Oh, well, of course it was murder," the Irishman said easily. "I was alluding to something even more obvious but, never mind, sir. We will solve this mystery, with the aid of your expertise, soon enough."

The physician shifted his weight. He seemed uncomfortable, but perhaps that was only due to the length of time he had spent on the stand.

"Is it not true," Quinncannon asked, "that rigor mortis first begins in the muscles around the head and the neck and spreads downward through the body?"

"That is so."

"Now, you testified that there were grass stains on the knees of the victim. Will you speculate as to their origin?"

"I believe the girl was killed outside the stack yard and her body dragged to where it was found. During that process the stains to which you refer were acquired."

My friend nodded. "Kindly remind the jury, Doctor. When you examined the foetus which you discovered in Maria's womb after her death, what was your estimate of the time of gestation?"

"Four and one-half months before death, sir."

"All right." The Irishman suddenly spun around toward the rear of the room. "Mr. Russell, would you come forward?"

A lanky man in the clothes of a farmer stood and began to limp down the aisle. I stared at him, wondering who the devil he was and what connection he had with our case. Before he had reached the swing-gate, Quinncannon had positioned himself next to the jury box and signaled Russell to stop.

"Dr. Wilbur," Quinncannon said, "this gentleman is Edward Russell of Portsmouth. He is suffering from a sprained ankle very similar to the injury that afflicted Reverend Avery on the day of Maria Cornell's murder. A week ago I hired Mr. Russell to walk, in the dark, from John Durfee's stack yard to Gifford's ferry house. The distance is more than eight—closer to nine miles. Mr. Gifford, a prosecution witness, has testified that Reverend Avery arrived at his house between nine-fifteen and nine-thirty on the murder night. Mr. Russell is prepared to testify that the same journey over the shortest route possible would require at least three hours. That means that Reverend Avery must have left the stack yard *no later* than six-thirty."

"Oh, I must object, Your Honor." Greene, the attorney general, was on his feet. "I have been patient, heaven knows, but Mr. Quinncannon appears to be rehearsing his summation. If he wishes to put Mr. Russell on the stand this is not the proper time, and if he wishes to ask the witness a question, why then, let him ask it."

"Objection sustained," said Judge Eddy, emphasizing his decision with a rap of his gavel. "I must confess, Mr. Quinncannon, that I fail to see the object of your discourse."

"Do you?" The Irishman smiled. Then he turned to the witness. "Doctor Wilbur, in your opinion, did Mr. Avery have sufficient time to murder Miss Cornell and still reach Gifford's by nine-thirty?"

"Certainly, sir."

Abruptly Quinncannon turned to the prosecution table. "Do you wish redirect?"

Greene rose. "One or two questions," he said. He knew, mind you, Greene *knew* he had won the case. For that matter, so did I. As Quinncannon settled comfortably in his chair I groaned inwardly. I could not believe he had been so stupid as to ask that last question and leave the memory of Wilbur's damning answer fresh on the minds of the jury. I glanced at Avery. He was as white as a ghost.

"I would remind the jury," Greene said, "that it is in evidence that the accused wrote the so-called 'white letter' establishing a meeting with the victim at six o'clock on December 20, the night she was killed, and that, according to her landlady in unchallenged testimony, Miss Cornell returned to her rooming house just after five-thirty, ate a light supper, and went out again before six o'clock, in apparent good spirits, saying she might be back shortly but certainly no later than nine. The defense has admitted that the defendant arranged a rendezvous for six that evening with the victim, and that he had sexual connection with her at Thompson."

"Mr. Greene," Quinncannon said quietly, "who is rehearsing his summation now?"

"If that is an objection," Judge Eddy sighed wearily, "I will sustain it. Kindly put a question to the witness, Mr. Prosecutor."

"Dr. Wilbur," Greene began, "is it possible that the child Miss Cornell was bearing could have been fathered by Mr. Avery on August 29 at the camp-meeting?"

Wilbur shook his head. "Quite impossible, sir. She had already been pregnant for several weeks."

"But, Doctor, is it not accurate to say that Mr. Avery would have had *no way of knowing that he was not the father*?"

The physician started to respond but Judge Eddy interrupted him. "One moment! Mr. Quinncannon, that question clearly calls for a conclusion. Have you no objection to make?"

"None at all, Your Honor." The Irishman smiled. "In fact we will stipulate that Mr. Avery *did* believe the accusation made against him by Miss Cornell."

The judge was scowling. "Counsel will approach the bench." In a furious whisper, out of hearing of the jury, Eddy addressed Quinncannon. "If your intention, sir, is deliberately to force a mistrial, I warn you I will not allow it. No decision of this court has ever been reversed and that record will not be spoiled by your incompetence, be it genuine or calculated. Perhaps you did not take my previous threat of disbarment with sufficient seriousness."

Quinncannon's eyes narrowed. "If the court will permit me to recall three government witnesses, and will grant me some latitude in my cross-examination, I will demonstrate the innocence of my client and produce the murderer."

Eddy looked at Greene. "Any objection, Albert?"

"No objection," the prosecutor said with a smirk. "I am a firm believer in giving a man enough rope."

The justice closed his eyes and rubbed them with his fingers. Then he said, "Very well, Mr. Quinncannon, but look to it you do not use that rope to hang yourself, and your client into the bargain."

When we had returned to the table the Irishman put a reassuring hand on Avery's shoulder and then spoke to me in a low voice. "Have you your pistol about you, Christy, as I requested?"

Greene said, "Your Honor, the state rests."

"I have the gun," I said, "but I still don't understand why you asked me to bring it."

"There is excellent reason to expect that an attempt will, within the next hour, be made to murder me," Quinncannon answered.

I gaped at him while he rose and said, "The defense recalls John Durfee to the stand."

✤ 50

The Final Witness

Judge Eddy reminded Durfee he was still under oath and the farmer slid into the witness chair. Quinncannon consulted some notes.

"Just a few questions, Mr. Durfee, on the appearance of Miss Cornell's body when you discovered her. You testified that the knot at her throat was a clove hitch, while the knot at the pole from which she was suspended was a slip knot."

"I have said so." Durfee's manner was sullen.

"Her bonnet was on her head with the ribbons untied but hanging down?"

"That's right."

"The ribbons were inside the cords around her throat?"

"Yes."

"Her face was pale—not discolored?"

"That's how it looked to me when I pushed back her hair."

"Her hair was down over her face?"

"It was very long and thick and dark," the witness said.

Quinncannon was gnawing on his pencil. "What I don't quite understand, Mr. Durfee, is how this set of circumstances could have occurred. We have heard testimony that her comb was found in two pieces at some distance from the stack yard. That, and the fact that her hair was loose and her bonnet ribbons untied—doesn't all this suggest that her comb and bonnet were off when she was killed?"

"Objected to as calling for a conclusion," Greene said.

"Overruled," the judge said. "The court has agreed to permit the defense some degree of latitude and will allow the question, subject to a subsequent motion to strike it from the record. The witness will answer."

"Yes," Durfee replied. "It looks like somebody took off her calash and comb before he killed her."

"But if that is true—" Quinncannon seemed perplexed. "How is it that the ribbons were found *inside* the cord?"

For the first time the witness avoided the Irishman's gaze.

284

"I would guess that the killer put her bonnet back on her head before he strangled her."

My friend nodded thoughtfully. "Now that makes sense, but then why was her hair down over her face?"

"I don't follow you."

"Oh, it's simple enough," Quinncannon said. "You've heard Dr. Wilbur testify that the girl must have been murdered while she lay on her back, and then moved and strung up to your stackpole to simulate suicide. Obviously she was either killed while her bonnet was on or while it was off. Since she died while on her back, how do you imagine her hair fell forward over her face?"

Durfee considered the question carefully. "I should say that when the killer hung her, her body sagged forward and the force of that motion threw her hair over her face."

"Then the killer did not replace her bonnet until *after* he had tightened the cord around her neck and suspended her corpse from the pole?"

"It would seem so," the farmer answered.

"But, then, Mr. Durfee, how do you explain the presence of the bonnet ribbons *inside* the cord?"

The witness held fire for a minute. Then he gave a helpless shrug. "I can't explain it," he said.

Quinncannon smiled. "I have no more questions of this witness." He paused before adding, in an almost menacing tone, "For now."

"No redirect," Greene said.

"The defense recalls Grindall Rawson," said the Irishman.

Our second witness strode to the stand and took his seat with a confident air. Quinncannon sat on the defense table, arms folded, one boot resting on the floor, the other dangling.

"Mr. Rawson, are you aware that, following your marriage to her sister, Maria Cornell boasted to certain young women with whom she worked or boarded that you really loved *her*, that she could take you from your wife whenever she wished?"

"I have heard such testimony given."

"Any truth to it?"

"None whatsoever, sir. I never even met Maria until she came to visit us last summer."

"That was on the second day of June, 1832?"

"I believe so."

"And on June 16 you employed Maria?"

"I did, sir, at my wife's request. The girl had a troubled

history and my wife thought it best that she make her home with us."

"Your wife felt a sisterly affection for Maria?"

"She did—yes, sir. And a sisterly concern. They were very close."

"Were they?" Quinncannon's back was to me but from the tone of his voice I knew he had raised an eyebrow. "Did you share your wife's affection and concern?"

"Naturally, sir, I felt toward Maria as an older brother would feel."

"Protective?"

"Yes," Rawson said. "That is the way I would describe it."

"Much of Maria's troubled history involved her promiscuous behavior with young men, did it not?"

"Unfortunately it did," the witness answered.

"Did your protective attitude toward her include limiting her opportunities to repeat such indiscretions?"

"My wife and I were most careful to control Maria's relationships with men, if that's what you mean."

"But not careful enough."

"Sir?"

"She managed to get pregnant anyway, didn't she, Mr. Rawson?" Quinncannon walked toward the jury box. "Maria must have been exceedingly resourceful," he added to no one particular. "Do you consider yourself a religious man?" he asked abruptly.

"I am a member of the Congregational church."

"That is not exactly responsive to my question, sir, but let it pass. What was your opinion of Maria's affiliation with the Methodists?"

"Quite frankly," Rawson replied, "I was unhappy about it, as was my wife. We felt it was an unhealthy atmosphere for the girl. We had heard many stories of the outrageous..." He searched for the word. "...comportment that went on at their 'love feasts,' as they term their camp-meetings. We feared Maria was far too susceptible to such temptations."

"All right," Quinncannon said. "Explain again the events that occurred on the evening of September 21 of last year."

"My wife awakened me about nine-thirty," Rawson said, "to tell me Maria had made a confession to her that she wished repeated in my presence. Maria then admitted that she was carrying a child."

"Did she name the father?"

"She said it was Reverend Avery. That he had forced her

286

at the camp-meeting in August in return for his promise to destroy certain embarrassing letters she had written to him."

"Did you believe Maria's story?"

"At the time we had no reason to doubt it, sir. The girl was so abject and distraught."

"What was your reaction to her confession?"

"To be honest, I was furious. Mrs. Rawson and I had taken infinite pains to protect the girl from just such a disgrace. I had at first forbidden her to attend the camp but she wheedled and cajoled and begged me into distraction. When at last I consented it was only on condition that she swear a solemn oath to me never to leave the company of her own sex, nor to permit any man to approach her or address her except in a crowd. She promised me faithfully to honor my wishes but—"

"But promises meant little to Maria," Quinncannon suggested.

"They meant *nothing!*" the witness growled.

Quinncannon tapped a pencil absently against the edge of the defense table. "You have said that you and your wife used great care to prevent communication between Maria and any man from the time of her arrival on June 2 to her departure for Thompson on August 27. To speak candidly, I find that difficult to believe."

"Nevertheless, sir, it is true."

"Did you not have two other apprentices who lived with you?"

"Boys!" Rawson scoffed. "Mere children, one fourteen, the other twelve. They slept in the shop and entered the house only for meals."

"Did no young men ever call on her?"

"There were one or two. John Payne and young Browning, but they were only allowed to visit her in the parlor and always either my wife or I was present. We knew our Christian duty toward the girl."

"Did you accompany her to her Sabbath meetings as well?"

"There are no Methodist societies in our neighborhood, sir. Maria attended services with us at the Congregationalist church. I insisted on that as a condition of her remaining with us."

"I see." Quinncannon came around the table and sat down. "Now, you say that, on September 21, you believed Avery to be the child's father. Did your wife also believe it?"

"She did, sir, at the time."

"Do you now believe that Avery was responsible for Maria's pregnancy?"

"No, sir. I've been in court when the doctors testified and I've come to learn that Maria was too far gone when she died to have conceived at the camp-meeting. But of course we could not know that in September."

"Is it your impression that, when Maria first accused Avery, she thought she was telling the truth?"

"Such was my impression," the witness answered.

"You acted on the assumption that Avery was the father?"

"Yes, sir."

"And what action did you take?"

"I consulted with my pastor, who advised me to speak to a lawyer. He suggested we contact Mr. Avery, inform him of Maria's situation, and demand a sum of three hundred dollars on threat of publishing his name."

"Did you communicate with Avery?"

"We did."

"No, sir," Quinncannon said. "Did you, personally, contact Avery?"

"Well, no," Rawson answered. "It was Maria who wrote to him."

"Was it on the advice of your attorney that this be left to Maria?"

"No, sir. My wife and I thought it best."

"Was it on the advice of your attorney that Maria leave your protection and remove alone to Fall River in spite of her delicate condition?"

"No. Again Mrs. Rawson and I thought it for the best."

"Did Maria at any time consult a local physician before going to Fall River?"

"My wife and I—"

Quinncannon cut in savagely. "You thought that would be for the best, too, did you? You drove the girl out of your home, deprived her of the comfort and care of her own people, placed her in the hands of an unknown doctor, forced her to have her baby among strangers, required her to negotiate alone with a man you believed had brutally raped her—and all this you thought in Maria's best interests?" He leaned forward, elbows on the table, long fingers massaging his temples. "Could it be, Mr. Rawson, that you were just a tiny bit afraid of the scandal?"

"Certainly not!" the witness snapped back.

"It did not disturb you that Maria's situation would soon become obvious to the neighbors? That your family would be the object of gossip in the general store and foul jokes in the tavern and whispers in the Congregationalist cloakroom?"

288

"It did not bother me in the least, sir!"

"But," the Irishman said slyly, "it *did* bother your wife."

Rawson did not respond at once. "My wife," he at length admitted, "was somewhat agitated by the prospect. She had urged me not to apprentice Maria. She feared the girl would disgrace us. I opposed her with a stubborn will. I thought keeping Maria with us would be..."

"For the best?" Quinncannon ventured.

"Yes. For a time I thought I had made the right decision, but the girl was incorrigible. The very instant she went back to her Methodist friends she returned to her sins like a dog to its own vomit! I realized then that, in spite of all her protestations of reform, she would never be anything but a *filthy little slut*!"

"Then it was your wife who insisted Maria leave your home?"

"With my full support," Rawson said bitterly. "Maria had brazenly betrayed the trust I'd reposed in her. At her *first* opportunity, mind you, Mr. Quinncannon. I saw what a fool I'd been. The girl was unfit for decent society. I did not want her under the same roof as my children to foul their pure, unformed minds."

The Irishman stood, stretched and strolled toward the jury. "I'm puzzled by Maria's actions after she left your home, Mr. Rawson. Did she discuss with you what she would do when she reached Fall River?"

The witness shook his head. "I knew only that she would seek factory employment and board, if possible, with a respectable widow in a small house, away from the other girls. I understood she intended to consult a local doctor and then make her arrangements with Avery. I had no wish to know even that much, sir. I washed my hands of her."

"Her timing seems peculiar," my friend observed. "She reached Fall River on October 2 but did not contact Dr. Wilbur until the eighth, six days later. It was another week before she revisited Wilbur, only to have him confirm a condition of which she had long been aware. Then she spoke to Avery on the twentieth during the Four-Days meeting in Fall River but failed to mention her pregnancy to him."

Rawson interrupted. "There, sir, I think you mistake."

"Do I?" Quinncannon's manner seemed almost apologetic. "Kindly explain, sir."

"I recollect Dr. Wilbur stating that Maria brought him the oil of tansy on the twenty-first and said Avery had given it to her the night before. She must therefore have confronted him on the twentieth."

"Well, that makes some sense," the Irishman conceded, "but if so, how did Avery obtain the poison so quickly? Do you suppose he just happened to be carrying it with him in the event some girl or other should surprise him with such a charge?"

"Then obviously Maria had accused him before the twentieth."

"Possibly, but then why was Avery so astounded at her pregnancy when she wrote to him concerning it in November?"

"I'm not aware that he was, as you say, 'astounded.'"

Quinncannon smiled with one corner of his mouth. "Consider, Rawson, that the Bristol postal records indicate a letter arrived for Avery on November 12 postmarked Fall River. The next day Avery wrote the yellow letter to Maria. You'll recall he began: 'I have *just* received your letter with *no small surprise* and will say I will do all you ask only keep your secrets.' Sounds as though the twelfth was the first he knew either of her condition or that he was suspected of causing it, doesn't it?"

"I can imagine another explanation, sir. Perhaps he worded the note deliberately to suggest he had no prior knowledge."

"To what purpose?" Quinncannon inquired mildly. "His letter was intended for her eyes only, and surely she knew when she had informed him."

Rawson shrugged. "I have no opinion."

"Now, here's another odd circumstance. Maria delayed almost a full month after Wilbur diagnosed her pregnancy before communicating with Avery. Why, Mr. Rawson? She'd accused Avery to Wilbur on October 15. Why not seize the opportunity to confront him face to face five days later?"

"Has it occurred to you, sir, that she met him in a public place before several witnesses? It's unlikely she would raise such a sensitive matter in the hearing of strangers."

"Well," Quinncannon said, "she accosted Avery publicly. In fact she apparently wanted as many witnesses as possible to the little scene she staged. But most of their conversation took place in private, out of earshot. She had ample time to tell him of the child, yet she waited twenty-two days before writing him of her threats and demands. 'I will do all you ask,' he wrote back, 'only keep your secrets.' Her delay is inexplicable...unless she needed the time to confer with a confederate."

Albert Greene leaped up. "I trust, Your Honor, Mr. Quinncannon is not preparing to suggest the girl planned her own death in a manner designed to get Avery hung for her murder."

"I am not yet ruling out the possibility," the Irishman said.

"That defense may have persuaded two doddering old fools in Bristol," Greene said sharply, "but it will not humbug a Newport jury nor save a killer from a Newport rope!"

Quinncannon addressed the bench with a patient sigh. "Mr. Greene appears exercised. If a brief recess would allow him to calm himself, the defense would not object."

"Damnation! I am *not* exercised!"

"Take your seat, Mr. Attorney General," Judge Eddy said.

"Damn it, Nate—!"

"Albert!" the judge thundered. "Sit down and shut up!"

Quinncannon had positioned himself next to the witness stand. "May I continue, Your Honor?"

Eddy waved his hand.

"Mr. Rawson, how many children do you have?"

"Two."

"You were married some years before they were born?"

"Yes, sir. We were disappointed many times."

"Disappointed in what way?"

"On several occasions my wife failed to have her monthly indisposition. Each time our hopes were raised and each time she was ill as women are in the second month. We began to fear our union would never be blessed."

"All right. You have stated that on September 21 your wife believed that Avery had fathered Maria's child. Is that still your testimony?"

"It is the truth, sir. I see no reason to change it."

"Don't you?" Quinncannon faced the witness squarely. "Mr. Rawson, it is on the record that Maria must have conceived during the first part of August. The girl's menstruation normally began on the nineteenth or twentieth of the month. I submit to you that she failed to menstruate in August and that your wife, who washed her clothing, knew it. I submit to you that Maria also failed to have her period in September—that your wife then was certain of the girl's condition—that she confronted Maria on September 21—that she knew for a fact her sister had become pregnant *before* the camp-meeting and that Avery could not be responsible."

Rawson's hands started to shake. He gripped the arms of his chair tightly. The blood drained from his face. He gasped for air like a man being strangled.

"Will you answer me, Rawson, or must I call your wife to the stand?"

"No! No!" Rawson cried. "Leave her alone. We've put her through enough hell!" He turned furious eyes on the Irishman. "All right, damn you, she knew—we both knew!"

"All three of you knew on September 21 that Avery was not the father."

"Yes," the witness kept repeating. "Yes, yes."

"And the three of you plotted to blackmail Avery!"

"Blackmail!" Rawson shouted. "Who speaks of blackmail?"

"What would you call it, Rawson? You knew Avery was innocent and you schemed to extort three hundred dollars from him on a false charge. If that isn't blackmail, it will do until blackmail comes along."

"Maria," Rawson sputtered, "Maria may have had such a plan. My wife and I knew nothing of it."

"Stop it!" Quinncannon commanded. "Don't perjure yourself any more than you already have. You went to your minister and your lawyer knowing Avery's innocence and you represented him as the father. You were advised that three hundred dollars was the sum to demand and you sent Maria to demand and collect it. You were involved in the whole dirty business up to your hairline from the very beginning."

"No," Rawson muttered. "It's not true."

"Where," Quinncannon barked, "did Maria get the oil of tansy?"

"From Avery. She had it of Avery."

"You're lying, Rawson. She got the poison from you. I expect a search of the records of your physician and apothecary will turn up an old prescript for the drug.

"Maria knew Avery would be in Fall River for the Four-Days meeting. She approached him publicly, making certain they were seen together, to create the illusion that he'd had an opportunity to give her the poison. Twenty-four hours later she brought the drug to Wilbur and convinced that good-hearted, gullible gentleman that her lover was trying to kill her."

Rawson hunched forward, his face in his hands, while Quinncannon returned to our table and relaxed in his chair. I had seen him like this before. It was something akin to watching a slow fuse. You kept waiting for the explosion.

"Now the hook was baited, Rawson. The trap was set. Poor, luckless, respectable Avery. How could he know Maria was lying? On November 11 she writes accusing him and demanding he 'do for' her. On the thirteenth he mails the yellow letter and she replies on the eighteenth, insisting on a meeting. On the twenty-seventh he sends the pink letter by Orswell, asking her to come to Bristol, but on the twenty-ninth she refuses, naming instead Durfee's stack yard for the rendezvous, and on December 8 he posts the white letter setting six p.m. on the twentieth as the time."

The Irishman closed his eyes. "Poor, helpless Maria. So crafty and so utterly alone. Leaving her boarding house that cold night in such high spirits, her mind whirling with thoughts of reward and revenge. She may return at once, she tells the landlady, but no later than nine o'clock. And she is never going to return at all."

The courtroom was silent. Quinncannon stood and walked almost casually toward the witness. "You have admitted that you and your wife knew Avery had not fathered the child. Did you know who the guilty man was?"

"No!" The denial exploded out of Rawson. "That is, we could not imagine. We had been so careful to watch her."

"In all those weeks the girl had never been alone with a man?"

"Never. She met them only in Mrs. Rawson's presence or my own."

"Or your own," Quinncannon echoed quietly.

Rawson slowly raised his eyes.

"She was a fascinating creature, wasn't she, Rawson? A pretty girl—a girl of many moods. Vivacious, teasing, bright with laughter—then suddenly downcast, even tragic. A spitfire, yet so battered, so vulnerable. You'd never known the likes of Maria before, had you?"

Rawson stared straight ahead, glassy-eyed, as if entranced. "No," he answered, drawing out the word. "There was no one like Maria." He turned toward the Irishman. "Oh, she could be cruel, sir. Believe me, she could be unspeakably cruel, but she could be gentle, so very gentle. I never knew from one moment to the next . . ."

"You found her exciting?"

"She brought life into the house, Mr. Quinncannon. I felt— I felt emotions I had forgotten, emotions I'd never experienced. Intense emotions. They caused me pain—most of them—but I was alive. Do you understand me, sir? I was grateful even for the pain. I actually welcomed the pain, because I *felt* it. I felt *something*."

"Did you love her?"

"I never thought of it that way. This is a hard country, Mr.

Quinncannon, and it yields a hard life, rigorous, demanding. We are the children of an angry God. Here a man does not marry for love. He marries a strong woman who will keep his house and bear him children and carry her share of the load God has placed on his back. Our lives are useful to God's good purpose but they are . . . *numbing. Deadening.* Maria made me realize that. I think that was the cruelest thing she did."

"Did you make love to Maria, Grindall?"

Rawson shot a sharp look at the Irishman but his will to resist was gone. He surrendered the admission with profound relief. "Many times. Too many times."

"Your wife knew this?"

"Yes."

"Your wife knew also that you were the father of Maria's child?"

"I have caused," Rawson said, "that good woman so much suffering—so much humiliation." His eyes darkened and his voice took on a flinty edge. "For nothing! For a shallow, selfish, nasty little slut! I wish to God I had never laid eyes on her!"

Quinncannon watched him for a moment before saying, "I have no further questions."

"No redirect," Greene said.

"The witness is remanded to the custody of the sheriff," the judge said, "until it can be determined whether he has engaged in activities that might warrant criminal prosecution."

Quinncannon said, "The defense calls, as our final witness, Lucretia Rawson."

❧ 51

The Confession

The final witness, heavily veiled, was led down the aisle by the bailiff. She sank into the chair. Only her mouth and chin were visible and her taut lips glistened, not from the rouge that respectable New England ladies never wore, but from beads of sweat. It was the custom to sequester female witnesses; therefore, Lucretia was unaware of the testimony which was already on the record.

Quinncannon positioned himself directly before her. "Mrs. Rawson, how many years older were you than Maria?"

"I was fifteen when she was born."

"How old was she when you left your mother's home?"

"Three or four."

"Maria had no clear memory of you from her childhood?"

"No, sir."

"Maria first wrote to you when she was eighteen, did she not, seeking an invitation to your home so you could be reunited?"

"Yes."

"And over the years she wrote several more times in the same vein?"

"She wrote from time to time."

"Did you respond?"

"On occasion."

"Did you invite her to visit you?"

"Not at first."

"Not, in fact, for ten years," he said. "Why, after so long, did you suddenly decide to take her in?"

"My husband and I felt it was our duty."

"Your DUTY!" Quinncannon roared. "You turned cold backs to your sister for ten years and then all at once discovered you had a *duty* to her?"

He approached the jury, shaking his head. "When you did respond to her letters, did you address her in terms of loving endearment and affection?"

She heard the sarcastic tone in his voice and bristled. "You may care for the word as you please, sir, but I wrote to her out of a sense of duty—my duty as a sister and a Christian. I advised her on proper deportment as beseems a young woman. I urged her to self-improvement."

"As a matter of fact you chastised and lectured her on her religious beliefs, her manner of getting her living, her nomadic ways. When she was caught in a theft you refused to communicate with her for two years." He turned to face her. "Whose idea was it that Maria be apprenticed to your husband?"

"Mr. Rawson thought it best for her character," she answered.

"Did he find her attractive?"

She stiffened. "He was fond of her as a brother should be."

"Come, Mrs. Rawson, she was bright and spirited. She was fifteen years younger than you. She was a pretty girl, wasn't she?"

"I suppose some men thought her so."

For a long moment he studied her. "Mrs. Rawson, kindly lift your veil."

She seemed startled. "Must I?" The tone was plaintive.

"Yes, madam, you must."

She lifted it slowly. "I'm afraid I'm not at my best. I'm in mourning, you must understand."

Her eyes were puffy and ringed with black—her cheeks drawn and sallow. I watched the jury watching her. "You may lower it again," Quinncannon said.

He walked to the table and leaned against it. "Explain what occurred on September 21 after you confronted Maria and your husband with their treachery."

No reply.

"He has already admitted he was the father, Lucretia."

She had begun to weep softly. "From the moment Maria came she played the coquette. He was infatuated with her. When she had just arrived she put her arms around me and laughed and said, 'Now that I am at last with you, dear sister, I shall never leave you again. I shall make you love me so much that you will never wish me to go.'

"I saw at once her plan. She enticed him wickedly, sir. After only two weeks—*two weeks*—he had apprenticed her. I begged him not to—I begged him to send her away—but the foolish man was blind. He called her a harmless child.

"I suspected them, of course. He was so jealous of her that he drove away all the young men who came to court her. It was never him she wanted. She never loved him—she *couldn't*

296

love anyone. She wanted his child as a hold over us, so we could never rid ourselves of her. They did it—" She was sobbing uncontrollably now— "They did it in our, in *my* bed."

"Do you wish a recess to compose yourself, madam?" he asked gently.

"No, no, it must be said now. I must tell it all now. That night, when I accused her, she asked how I could be certain and I said, 'Because I wash your laundry,' and then she laughed and said, 'It is all true, Lucretia, and it is Grindall's baby. From now on, dear sister, I shall be mistress in this house and you shall be the laundress.'"

Quinncannon's mouth tightened at the corners. "Tell me what you know of the plot to blackmail Avery."

"They planned it that very night. Maria said he had seduced her at the camp but he meant nothing to her. She said they could convince him it was his child and entrap him into writing incriminating letters that she would keep as a means to control him. She went to Fall River and saw the doctor there for fear our local doctor would suspect the truth."

"Who suggested the oil of tansy?"

"My husband. It had been prescribed for a bad stomach. Maria thought it a wonderful touch."

"Whose notion was the pencil note?"

"Grindall was afraid Mr. Avery might try to murder her. He said if Avery knew of the note it would prevent him."

"Go on."

"On December 20 we went to Fall River and lodged in a small country inn, a place where we wouldn't be recognized. We waited for Maria but she never came."

"What do you imagine happened to her, Lucretia?"

She looked up. "Obviously Mr. Avery murdered her in spite of their precautions and arranged to make it appear she took her own life. Perhaps he did not believe the note existed."

"But he knew of the letters. He knew she still had them. Would they not deter him as effectively as the note?"

"I cannot explain it," she said simply.

"Mrs. Rawson, it is proven that the walk from Durfee's to the ferry house took three hours. Avery debarked at Gifford's at two-thirty and traveled to Tiverton, where he was observed loitering about until six. Then he was seen walking north toward Durfee's. He returned to Gifford's between nine-fifteen and nine-thirty. Thus he was no longer at the stack yard after six-thirty. The medical evidence, particularly the livor and rigor, proves Maria died on her back and was not moved for at least

297

six hours—that is, until *at least* twelve-thirty a.m. He could not possibly have arranged the body as it was found."

He paused. "Why, madam, did you delay so long after the murder before hanging your sister to the stackpole?"

"But," she cried in alarm, "I didn't!"

"You did, madam," he said firmly. "The arrangement has all the markings of a woman's hand. The skirts smoothed neatly back under the legs. The precision of the placement of her shoes and handkerchief. The replacement of the bonnet on her head. It is as if she were laid out for burial, and that is woman's work. The grass stains on her knees show she was dragged to the stack. A man as powerful as Avery, even with a bad ankle, would have carried her. Maria was a small woman. But another woman, older and not strong such as yourself, could not have lifted her entirely off the ground."

There was a long silence. When she answered, her voice was remarkably controlled and calm. "She took everything from me. She repaid my kindness with perfidy and laughed in my face. She was evil and, be it sin or no, I hated her. Yes, Mr. Quinncannon, I murdered Maria."

The confession was made in so matter-of-fact a manner it seemed anticlimactic. The courtroom observers were stunned. Grindall Rawson, seated between two marshals, shouted, "No, Lucretia! Be silent! Speak nothing!" I watched Quinncannon and marveled. It was all happening exactly as he had predicted.

"Why," he asked, "did you wait so long to move her body?"

"It required some time to determine what to do. I am not in the habit of planning such things, sir."

"You delayed for over six hours, remaining beside your victim near a well-traveled road and a populous farm house in a frigid wind on a bitter cold night?" He smiled sadly. "Mrs. Rawson, you are a woman of courage and clear mind with an infinite capacity for loyalty and love, but you are a hopelessly incompetent liar."

The lady squared her shoulders and, in an eloquent gesture of pride and defiance, she raised her veil. "Mr. Quinncannon, you are a very clever man no doubt, as lawyers go, but you are quite wrong. I did kill my sister without regret. I am prepared to swear to it."

He took up his cane and walked toward her. "Then tell me, by what manner of knot did you fasten the cord to the stackpole?"

"A slip knot."

He withdrew a cord from his pocket and extended it and the cane. "Kindly tie one on this stick, madam."

She did so and he slid it off and undid it. "What sort of knot did you use to strangle her?"

"A clove hitch, sir."

He tossed her the cord and snapped, "Tie one!"

But she could not.

"You can't protect him anymore, Lucretia," he said gently. "We both know your husband murdered the girl."

Quinncannon had resumed his seat. Behind us there was an angry cry and then a chorus of shouts and the sounds of scuffling boots and chairs overturned. I caught Grindall Rawson's livid face out of the corner of my eye as he reached the swing-gate and hurled himself over the bar, lunging madly at Quinncannon, a ten-inch blade in his upheld hand, and I gripped my pistol and fired. The bullet ripped through Rawson's right shoulder, spinning him around as he dropped the knife, and suddenly a dozen hands had flung him to the floor and held him face down until he ceased to struggle and commenced to moan.

Through it all the Irishman had not so much as stirred. He sat in the eye of that hurricane like a chessmaster pensively planning the next six moves.

"Damn you, Lon!" I bellowed. "You might have been killed!"

"I have infinite faith in you, little brother," he returned calmly. He faced the witness. "Explain what occurred on the night of December 20, madam."

She looked down at the prostrate body of her husband and touched her handkerchief to her eyes. "I love that fool so much. I've lost him twice." Again she was crying. "He went to meet Maria that night. He said he wasn't going to let Avery see him. He said he was going to protect *her*, in the event Avery tried to harm her. When he returned he said, 'Lucretia, we're free of her.' He tossed the money on the bed. There was three hundred dollars. He was excited. I said, 'My God, Grindall, what have you done?' and he said, 'I've killed the bitch.'

"He told me there was no cause for worry, nothing to connect him to her death, but when he went to the bed I sat awake for hours. I was so frightened, so horribly frightened." She broke down, covering her face with gloved hands.

Quinncannon said, "Suppose I tell the story and spare Mrs. Rawson further anguish. After Avery paid the money and left, Maria began to tease Rawson, and taunt him too, I think. She removed her bonnet and comb and let down her hair and laughed at him. He intended to kill her all along—he had brought the rope for that purpose—but he couldn't resist the temptation to kill her at the moment of sexual climax. Maria had seduced and betrayed him, and that would crown his vengeance. He withdrew the cord from his coat. The knot was already loosely tied. He looped it suddenly around her throat and yanked it tight with all his strength, then quickly loosened it, leaving it in place. Maria was semi-conscious. With his staff he beat her savagely across the belly. It was a horrible revenge he took on both the girl and the child she had tricked him into fathering. Then he seized the ends of the rope again and finished her. He picked up her comb and, as if it were the last living part of her, he snapped it in two and threw away the pieces."

Quinncannon stood and rested against the bar. "That is how Mrs. Rawson found her. In her misguided effort to cover her husband's crime, she dragged the corpse to the stack, tied a slip knot in the cord's longer end, and managed to prop the body up and slip the loop over the pole. When the body slumped forward the hair fell over the face. Mrs. Rawson put the bonnet on her head—then realized that the ribbons must be inside the rope or it would be evident it had been placed there after death by a hand other than the dead girl's. She pushed Maria back against the pole and with the rope no longer taut, she loosened the noose and pulled the ribbons inside it. When the corpse slumped again it fell against the pole, creating the indentation found in the cheek."

He addressed the witness. "That's what happened, Mrs. Rawson, isn't it?" He waited, then repeated, "Isn't it?"

The poor woman nodded silently.

When the chamber had emptied, Quinncannon and I sat alone at the defense table smoking our pipes. We had not spoken for almost half an hour when he remarked, "There is one final irony to this tragic affair, Christy. I didn't raise it in court today because it would have been too cruel. It's best Lucretia Rawson never learns it."

"What are you talking about?"

"Rawson committed the perfect murder," he answered. "He would have gotten away clean but for his wife's meddling. Maria imagined she was in complete control of the scheme, and all the while Rawson was making her the unwitting accomplice in her own murder, a murder he intended to blame on Avery.

"He convinced her to keep Avery's letters, and even to write

300

the pencil note naming Avery and actually dated the day Rawson planned to kill her. They made certain that Avery would be seen wandering all over the area. By suggesting alternate dates for the meeting they forced Avery to name the murder date in his last letter, thus establishing opportunity. By convincing Avery of his paternity and forcing him to communicate with her in writing, they established motive. It was so simple it was brilliant—the perfect frame."

I said, "No wonder Rawson was so excited when he returned that night. He had pulled it off without a hitch."

"Yes, Christy, and the beauty of it was that Maria cooperated fully in the plotting of her own death, and she never knew it. I think the scheme began to form in his mind the evening he learned of her liaison with the clergyman. His wife testified to his violent jealousy. Rawson would be avenged on Maria *and* Avery, and three hundred dollars richer into the bargain.

"But his wife moved the body while Avery slumbered at Gifford's, acquiring a perfect alibi. That blew Rawson's classic little murder plot straight to hell."

Epilogue

Grindall Rawson was convicted of the murder of Sarah Maria Cornell. At six a.m. on February 17, 1834, in the yard of the grim state prison near Providence, he was hung before a festive crowd. I declined an invitation to attend.

One week after her husband's execution Lucretia Rawson committed suicide by hanging herself from a ceiling beam in her kitchen. Her children were rescued from the orphanage by Rowena Bloss, who is raising them as her own.

Colonel Harvey Harnden published a broadside recounting his pursuit and capture of Avery that went through thirty-one printings and left him, financially, tolerably comfortable.

Dr. Wilbur's pamphlet on the medical evidence and his interviews with Maria were also reprinted several times but, as the physician had neglected to secure a copyright, all profits were retained by the publisher.

Just before he sailed out of Boston bound for Dublin, Quinn-cannon sent me a letter he had received from Joseph Merrill. "In spite of what may at the time have appeared evidence to the contrary," the letter ran, "the bishop and I never lost faith in your ability to carry the recent, regrettable affair to a satisfactory conclusion. Please be assured that our prayers are always with you, distinguished sir, and that you have our eternal gratitude."

At the bottom of the page was a single line in the Irishman's hand:

Gratitude is what a man gives you when he doesn't want to be bothered to return the favor.

Q

The Methodist brethren conducted a hearing that exonerated Avery of all wrongdoing, and the clergyman was permitted to resume his Bristol pulpit. His congregation, however, refused to attend his services, and it was not long before Avery was preaching to an empty church. The brothers Merrill, having officially set their house in order for the record, now went about driving Avery, not simply out of Rhode Island, but clean out of the Methodist Society. At last the harried minister gathered his family and headed west to be swallowed up in the oblivion of the frontier.

On December 20, 1833, Amy gave birth to our first child, a fine, healthy, beautiful son.

It was more than a year after the trial before I saw the Irishman again. I had resumed my practice in New York and he had just returned from Dublin by clipper ship. We met at Niblo's Garden, and when our drinks were served he offered a toast.

"To you, Christy, and your beautiful wife, and to your newborn son."

"To friendship," I said, "and to my little son, Lonnie."

His glass froze half-way to his lips and he shot me a sharp look. "And have you named the lad for me then?" He put the glass down on the table and a smile slowly creased his face.

I also smiled. "Amy and I both felt—"

Quinncannon raised his hand. "I have never been so honored, little brother."

"Nor I, big brother."

We drank and then Quinncannon reached for his pipe and said, "Aside from increasing the population, what the hell have you been up to?"

About the Author

Raymond Paul lives in New Jersey and teaches at Montclair State College. His other novels include THE THOMAS STREET HORROR.